face

face

Joma West

TOR
DOT
COM

A Tom Doherty Associates Book
New York

FACE

Edited by Lee Harris

A Tordotcom Book
Published by Tom Doherty Associates
120 Broadway
New York, NY 10271

www.tor.com

Tor® is a registered trademark of Macmillan Publishing Group, LLC.

Library of Congress Cataloging-in-Publication Data

Names: West, Joma, 1986- author.
Title: Face / Joma West.
Description: First edition. | New York : Tom Doherty Associates, 2022.
Identifiers: LCCN 2022008293 (print) | LCCN 2022008294 (ebook) |
    ISBN 9781250810298 (hardcover) | ISBN 9781250810304 (ebook)
Subjects: LCGFT: Science fiction. | Novels.
Classification: LCC PR6123.E84 F33 2022 (print) | LCC PR6123.E84
    (ebook) | DDC 823'.92—dc23
LC record available at https://lccn.loc.gov/2022008293
LC ebook record available at https://lccn.loc.gov/2022008294

Our books may be purchased in bulk for promotional, educational,
or business use. Please contact your local bookseller or the Macmillan
Corporate and Premium Sales Department at 1-800-221-7945, extension
5442, or by email at MacmillanSpecialMarkets@macmillan.com.

First Edition: 2022

Printed in the United States of America

0 9 8 7 6 5 4 3 2 1

For Ba,
who read it the most and kept on pushing me
even when I grumbled.

And for Baj,
who made me believe I could write it
and all the others.

face

(Menial 63700578–Jake)

When he wasn't working, Menial 63700578 went by the name of Jake. Jake wanted to get his hands on Madeleine Burroughs. He wanted to run his fingers through her thick chestnut hair and possibly, maybe, perhaps, get close enough to her so he could draw in her scent. And not the wafting scent of her perfume that trailed behind her everywhere she walked—he wanted to smell the deep earthy scent of her natural skin. Fresh on her. Instead of the way he usually smelt it on the crumpled clothes she left for him to pick up off her bedroom floor. Jake wanted to get his hands on Madeleine Burroughs, have her look him in the face and whisper 'Jake'.

Sometimes he imagined being pressed up against Madeleine in a close embrace, skin to skin, tight enough that even in his imagination he could not tell where her skin ended and his began, all was just smooth, pale and soft.

Of course, he didn't talk about this. He hardly allowed himself to think about it. But on the odd occasion, when it was all too much, he would go on the In and find the confessor.

Before Jake had met the confessor, he didn't understand what the thought of Madeleine Burroughs did to him. He didn't have the words to describe his thoughts and feelings about her. The confessor had given him words.

He remembered his first confession. His chosen face floated in the cloud, a passive expression pasted to it, giving no sign of how clueless he was. All he knew was that his thoughts were wrong and overwhelming and he couldn't understand what was happening in his head.

He was afraid that first time; scared that he was part of a scam, that his private thoughts were not private at all and that soon everyone would know how damaged he was. The confessor was patient with him.

'I don't know your name. I don't know where you're from, what level of the hierarchy you're on, what you look like. This face you're using for this conversation is all that I know about you. There's no way for anything that you say to be tracked back to you personally.'

Jake still didn't speak.

'It's okay,' the confessor said. 'You don't need to speak. But remember, this is about letting go of the feelings that affect your day-to-day existence. Confession is a way to unburden yourself. It's a service, not a trap.'

Jake let the confessor talk for a while. He didn't say a word; he just breathed into his comline and waited. He didn't know what he was waiting for but he knew when the waiting was over.

'I look at her,' he said, when he was ready.

'Who?' asked the confessor.

'I . . .'

'It's okay. You don't need to use names if it's difficult for you. You could make up a name if that's easier?'

'No. No, she's just . . . her. The woman.'

'The woman.'

'Yes.'

'And you look at this woman.'

'Yes.'

'You know there is nothing wrong with looking at people?'

'No, I . . . I *look* at her.' Jake didn't know how else to say it.

'I'm not sure I understand what you mean.'

'She . . . when I look at her I have . . . feelings.'

'Can you describe these feelings?'

'I don't . . . I don't have words.'

'Can you tell me what happens when you have these feelings?'

That was difficult. It wasn't complicated; it was just hard to say it out loud. He did, though. Eventually.

'I touch myself.'

'Where?' asked the confessor.

'I touch my . . . penis? Is that the word for it?' Jake knew the question gave away that he was a menial. Only a menial would struggle this much with words. It wasn't necessary for them to learn any vocabulary beyond what they needed in training. But he thought 'penis' was the right word. He had come across it on the In. It seemed right.

'What you use to urinate?'

'Yes! Yes. My penis.'

'So, when you look at this woman you touch your penis?' asked the confessor.

'Not when I look at her. But after. When I'm alone. My penis changes and I touch it.'

'How do you touch it?'

Jake explained what he did and that was the day he learned the word 'masturbation'. The confessor told him a lot.

The confessor wasn't one person. It wasn't even lots of people. It was just someone. Some face, generic and simple and totally focussed on one thing: the person confessing. Jake sometimes wondered if the confessor was just a computer programme. But then the confessor's responses to him—to everything he shared—were so personal and empathetic. He didn't think a machine could fake that kind of humanity. It didn't really matter either way to him. He was just glad that he could talk. It felt like he had dirt crusted just under his skin, and talking about it—about Madeleine Burroughs—pulled it out.

'Hello, Jake,' the confessor would say, because after a while Jake had begun to use the name he had given himself instead of Menial 63700578. He felt he had to because his name—Jake—was an important part of his fantasy. He had to hear her say it.

'Hello, Jake,' the confessor would say. The confessor's profile would float before Jake's eyes and the confessor's voice would sound in his ears, close, like a whisper.

'Hello, Jake. How are you today?' That was a difficult question to answer. Jake was never sure of the truth; he always hesitated, but the confessor would wait.

'Hello, Jake. How are you today?' Silence. And then he would speak.

'Fine,' Jake would say.

'Fine? Is that why you're here?'

'Where's here?' Jake had a feeling he might be smart. He would often answer a question with a question, turning something simple into something complex. He liked to think this was a sign that he could play that game called Face.

'Jake, you're deflecting. I don't think it's healthy for you to waste your own time.'

'Time. Such a strange concept,' Jake would say, because he was smart. People didn't think menials were clever but in Jake's case he was sure they were wrong. He was underestimated; they all thought his kind was shit. No, it was worse than that. They didn't think about them at all. Menials were nothing.

'Time is a strange concept. But we all experience it linearly, so let's focus on your confession, shall we? It won't be long before you have to clock back in to work.'

'I have ten minutes.'

'Good. Let's not waste them. What would you like to confess?'

'The same thing I always confess.'

'I need to hear the words, Jake. You have to let them out before you can feel better.'

'You *know* what I've been thinking.'

'I can't read minds, Jake.'

'I've *told* you!'

'Tell me again, Jake.'

'Why do you do that? Use my name so much?'

'It's important to you, Jake. That's why I use it. You're deflecting again. I know this is difficult, but it really is better for you to let it all out.'

'Do you have a confessor?'

'This isn't about me, Jake.'

'But do you? Do you need to talk to someone else? About the things we all say—the thoughts we put in your head? You must imagine it all. It would be hard not to. When I talk to you, do you see me with my hands pressed to her face? Can you picture me as I bury my face in her hair? Do you hear her whisper my name?' She was still just 'the woman'; Jake couldn't say her name out loud.

'Is this what you've come here to confess, Jake?'

'Do you enjoy listening to us? All us freaks and perverts. I bet there are loads of us just talking talking talking about flesh on flesh. Do you ever imagine the smell of it? I do. Sometimes, when I touch her in my head, I don't just use my hands. I press my cheek to hers, lean my forehead against hers, sometimes I get so close our eyelashes entangle. And then I bend my head, put my nose to the nape of her neck, and pull her in, really smell her. And the thought of it is so vivid I can almost feel . . .' but he didn't know what it would feel like. He couldn't.

'Is this what you've been imagining?'

'Is this what you imagine? When you listen to us? What do I look like to you? Do you think about me? Do you think about my body when I tell you what I do to myself?'

'Jake, this is a safe place. We leave aggression in the Out.'

This was a normal confession. Jake found it difficult but whenever he was done talking he felt . . . satisfied. Yes, that was the word. Ten minutes would disappear and he would get up, go back out into Madeleine Burroughs's pristine apartment and do what he was told to do.

Saving Face

To Stud was everyone's port of call when they decided to choose their first child. Well. It was the first port of call for anyone who was anyone. So when Eduardo and Tonia decided it was time to grow their family they downloaded the book. Eduardo opened it up on his slate and Tonia leaned in as close as she dared to read over his shoulder.

> Having a child is a wonderful thing. It is a symbol of the evolution of your relationship with your loved one/s. It is the single most important step you will ever take in this relationship. As such, it must be treated with respect. One does not simply buy a baby off the rack.
>
> There are countless social implications to be navigated when deciding how to have a child, but it has long been undisputed that going to stud is the best course for any self-respecting prospective parents.

'I'm sure it wasn't like this for my parents,' she said.

Eduardo sighed and Tonia wondered what the sigh meant. Was he tired? Was he having second thoughts about a child? Was he sighing simply because he didn't know what to say? Did he just need to sigh?

Tonia studied his face hoping to discover that he was having second thoughts. She was having second thoughts. She didn't know how she had let it get this far but now she felt she couldn't say anything unless she knew he would agree with her.

Eduardo smiled. Tonia straightened up and looked away from him. She didn't want to engage with that smile of his. She'd gotten used to the embarrassing sensations his smile always caused in her body—the light flutter in her stomach, the involuntary return smile, occasionally an excruciating moistening in her underwear—but she tried to limit the damage. When they were alone she could look away freely, without a care, safe from other people's observations and extrapolations and inevitable conclusions about her. Eduardo never seemed to notice but she wasn't foolish enough to presume that meant he didn't notice. He used that smile on her to great effect. That was how she had let things get this far. That was how he had got her to say 'yes, of course we should acquire a child'.

'I don't think any of this shit is going to help us,' he said, gesturing to his slate. 'We need to make an appointment with a baby doctor.'

Tonia kept her face as still and quiet as she could—he couldn't see her disappointment.

'Have you any doctors in mind?' she asked. Eduardo gave a dry chuckle.

'Plenty, but we can't afford any of them.'

'You want Dr Wójcik, don't you?' Tonia divined.

'Of course. Who wouldn't?'

'I suppose you've let slip to Schuyler about this whole baby business?'

Eduardo smiled at her appreciatively.

'You know me too well,' he said.

'Do you think he'll actually help us?'

Eduardo shrugged.

'Probably not, but I thought I may as well prod. We have a bit of time. Let's see what happens.'

It was Tonia's turn to sigh.

'You think I'm risking too much?' Eduardo asked her.

'No, no, I've seen you in action. Schuyler is good at seeing through things but I trust you to not have laid things on thick. It's just . . . exhausting. The hoops that have to be jumped through.'

'If we weren't jumping through these hoops we'd be jumping through some others,' Eduardo said, standing up and walking to the bar that divided the living room from the kitchen. 'Drink?' he asked.

'Please,' Tonia said, and she leaned back into her armchair and closed her eyes. She definitely needed a goddamn drink.

Madeleine was throwing a party and the thought of it filled Tonia with dread. She wondered if it was Schuyler's idea. Was this party because of Eduardo? Tonia shook the thought from her head. She was growing arrogant; of course this party wouldn't be about them.

Besides, Madeleine threw parties all the time. It was practically all she did.

Tonia couldn't refuse the invitation. She sent their RSVP, prompt and polite, and she and Eduardo talked about the event: who would be there, what entertainments Madeleine would procure, what fashions the attendees would be sporting. They worried over what they would wear. They let Madeleine's party eclipse all other thoughts. They did not talk about a child.

The day arrived and a menial answered the door before they even touched the buzzer. They pressed their coats onto the menial and stepped away from it, taking in the room as subtly as possible, trying to keep their eyes still, their expressions quiet, their joint face inscrutable and all the while trying to appear as though they were not trying at all.

'ToDdie' Schuyler said from across the room, and he opened his arms in an expansive gesture that said: *These people are special.*

Schuyler. The man everyone wanted to know, be, be loved by. And he was calling them special. It was a favour Tonia knew they would never be able to repay. She felt all attention on them for a moment, and it was both excruciating and wonderful.

'Ooh! Ooh, you're here!' Madeleine squealed as she entered the room, and she swooped down upon them and kissed the air dangerously close to their skin. 'How *marvellous* that you're here!'

Tonia smiled, small and gracious. When she looked up she caught sight of Schuyler over Madeleine's shoulder. He rolled his eyes, almost imperceptibly, and then he winked at her. It took her aback.

'Finally,' Madeleine said, 'someone *interesting* has arrived.' She laughed a tinkling laugh and spun on her heel. 'Schuy! Drinks! Where *are* you?'

Schuyler held up his hands in apology and left the room. Madeleine turned on them once more.

'It's just *perfect* that you're here. I was *so* glad when I got your confirmation. I've invited someone that I just *know* you'll be *thrilled* to meet. Of course, she's not here yet . . . only second tier so far; you're the first tops to arrive!'

And there it was. The put-down. The judgement. Madeleine had put them in their place before the party had even really begun.

'Where are the girls?' Tonia asked.

'Oh you know,' said Madeleine, waving a hand. 'They'll be on the In.'

'They have more virtual existences than I care to count,' said Schuyler, appearing at Madeleine's shoulder. Madeleine laughed.

'Hon, there is *no* such thing as *too* many faces,' she said, turning to him. 'Where *are* the drinks?'

'I've ordered,' he said as a menial walked up bearing a tray of frosted glasses. The buzzer went and Madeleine spun around.

'What are you doing?' she asked the menial with the tray. 'Why isn't anyone by the door? I told you earlier that I don't want to hear that buzzer go tonight.'

The menial didn't reply, just bowed and went to answer the door. Madeleine smiled at Tonia and Eduardo.

'It's *amazing* how they still seem to slip up every so often. You'd have thought, being trained from such a young age . . . Oh well.' She shrugged.

She really looked like she wasn't bothered at all, but Tonia was sure she was seething inside.

'I'd better go greet the new arrivals!' said Madeleine, and she was gone.

'So. Have you made any decisions regarding this child, yet?' Schuyler asked, skipping all small talk in the way only a really important person could. Eduardo took it in stride.

'We're still gathering data. But I think we're close to making a decision about what we want.'

'Good. And I think Madeleine has a surprise for you on the child front, too.'

'That sounds ominous,' Tonia said, and she immediately regretted it. Schuyler looked at her. The curve of his smile was dangerous. Eduardo was very still. Tonia forced a smile of her own.

'Can I refresh your drink?' Schuyler asked her and, without waiting for her answer, he took her glass. He took her glass: put his hand out, reached for it and closed his fingers over both it and her hand. The moment was stunning and Tonia froze.

Skin on skin. His fingers were cool and soft. He pressed the back of her hand with just so much pressure that . . . it felt like it was intentional. He was touching her hand. He was holding her fucking hand. Wasn't he? Or was this in her head?

She looked at him expecting to see a reflection of her own shock there but his expression was cool. It had to be in her head. And yet . . . she stumbled back, pulling her hand away, and in the rush of the movement the glass slipped between them and shattered on the floor. All bubbles of conversation dissipated. Almost everyone turned to look. Tonia kept as still as possible. Eduardo quickly stepped in to fill the vacuum.

'I'm sorry, honey. You said you weren't feeling well and I still insisted that we come.' He looked at Schuyler. 'I just felt it was bad form not to come after we had confirmed our attendance.'

A menial materialised before them and began to clean up the shards of glass and ice.

'You're very thoughtful,' Schuyler said, loud enough for the room to hear. And then he turned to Tonia. 'I would hate for you to leave now that you're here. Perhaps a drink of water?' Tonia nodded, grateful, and Schuyler walked away.

'What's going on?' Eduardo asked her, and the fact that he needed to ask meant that he hadn't seen. He didn't know Schuyler had touched her, he hadn't noticed the contact. If there had even been any.

The skin on Tonia's fingers felt like it was burning. That touch was so real, it had to be real, she could still feel the smoothness of Schuyler's skin, the slight stickiness of a palm that had been moisturised, looked after, nourished. A palm that felt cool and yet hot as a brand. Her stomach felt like it was swimming and her mouth filled with salinic spit—the telltale precursor of vomit.

'Tonia? What's wrong?' Eduardo's voice broke through her queasiness.

'Nothing,' she said, swallowing the spit down, willing her insides to stop writhing.

'It's definitely something,' Eduardo mumbled, but he didn't push it any further than that. Tonia took a deep breath. *It wasn't real—it didn't happen—I'm just stressed.* She said those words over and over again in her head. Breathe in. Breathe out. Repeat.

She breathed her way back to composure.

Time stuttered forwards and Tonia found herself stiff, attached a bare inch from Eduardo's side, negotiating a series of precarious conversations, almost all of which were about children. It seemed like Schuyler hadn't been shy about telling people their news. And every time Tonia looked up she felt as if Schuyler was there. *It wasn't real—it didn't happen—I'm just stressed*, she repeated, but it was as though that moment of contact had linked them. He was always there, always looking. And she wanted to look back, to study him, to dissect his face, to work out what he was really thinking. He had touched her. The thought was sickening.

Then came Madeleine's surprise. It was less a gift for Tonia and Eduardo than it was a demonstration of Madeleine's importance. Her facevalue. She had invited Dr Vidya Wójcik to the party. Tonia looked at Eduardo and she could tell by the tightness around his eyes that he was furious. He had wanted to be put in touch with Dr Wójcik, he had not wanted her publicly presented to them like a gift. Madeleine might as well have just told the whole party that Tonia and Eduardo's future child was only going to be a success because she, Madeleine, had made it possible. For the first time that day Eduardo was at a loss for words. Tonia was just grateful to focus on something that got her out of her thoughts.

'It's such a pleasure to meet you,' she said, gliding over Eduardo's discomfort with an ease she hadn't known she possessed. She saw Dr Wójcik appraise her favourably.

'The feeling is mutual. SchAddie have told me so much about you.' She turned to Schuyler. 'You weren't exaggerating,' she said. 'They have a perfect aesthetic. Really. You're a stunning couple,' she told them. 'And I understand you're thinking about committing to a child?'

'You're very gracious,' Eduardo said. 'We try our best, but our aesthetic is far from perfect.'

'Our hosts have a monopoly on perfection!' Tonia added, and she smiled prettily at Madeleine. Madeleine kept her face quiet.

'You're too modest,' Schuyler said. And was he looking at Tonia with emphasis? Was she imagining it? *It wasn't real—it didn't happen—I'm just stressed.*

'I'm glad you came, Vidya,' Schuyler continued. 'We should leave you to talk, but do come find us later. It's been too long, we're due a catch-up.' Schuyler steered Madeleine away, a hand hovering close to her shoulder, but of course he never touched her. The doctor, Tonia and Eduardo watched them as they all calculated their next words. The doctor spoke first.

'It's fairly unsubtle as far as faceplay goes,' she said. She was talking about Madeleine and her game of one-upmanship. 'Don't worry, I'm not trying to trick you. I don't indulge in it myself,' Dr Wójcik told them. That was impossible to believe. 'It's an important aspect of my work; I have to build trust with my clients and I take that very seriously. The best way to develop trust is through honesty. I take confidentiality seriously, too. Anything you say to me is in the strictest confidence, even at a social gathering.'

Tonia resisted looking at Eduardo.

'Clients?' he said. 'Isn't that a bit premature?'

Dr Wójcik smiled.

Tonia felt nervous as they walked into Dr Wójcik's office. She didn't let it show. She just focussed on the doctor, who was, naturally, beautiful. You couldn't attain her level and be anything less.

'Your parents did beautiful work with you,' Tonia said, before they had even sat down. Her mouth was running away with her, giving away what her face had not. Dr Wójcik smiled.

'My parents popularised the current trend of contrasts. Starting with me.'

'I've read about them,' said Tonia.

'What have you read?' Dr Wójcik asked. She didn't seem particularly curious about an answer, however, and Tonia hesitated.

'Well, everyone wants a Wójcik baby,' Eduardo jumped in. 'They practically invented the boutique baby shop. The way the In tells it, your mothers had a preternatural ability to create the most perfect children. An ability they developed in you . . .' he added.

'Schuyler Burroughs was one of theirs, wasn't he?' Tonia asked, and as the words came out she wished she could swallow them back up, erase the thought, forget Schuyler Burroughs existed. *It wasn't real—it didn't happen—I'm just stressed.*

'Yes, his baby blueprint came out of this very office,' Dr Wójcik said. She was smiling. Her voice was coloured with amusement also. 'And of course, after him, there was a rash of other baby shops copying his look. So many beautiful, dark-eyed, black children everywhere . . .' Dr Wojcik's voice trailed away, but her smile remained. Then she gathered herself together. 'So. Let's get to it. Why are you two here?'

Tonia tried not to look at Eduardo, tried not to let her confusion show. What did she mean, why? Wasn't it obvious?

'Everyone wants a Wójcik baby,' Eduardo said again.

'Why not go to the Hú centre?'

Eduardo laughed. Dr Wójcik didn't.

'You aren't serious?' he asked.

'It's an option. Why aren't you thinking about it?'

'Well . . . I mean they're fine. Didn't your parents use them, Tonia?'

Tonia nodded.

'But they aren't fine for you?'

'They wouldn't add anything to us. We're already a Hú sort of couple, it wouldn't help us move up.'

'So you're concerned with your face?'

Eduardo looked at Tonia as if he was looking for reassurance. She kept her face impassive.

'Aren't we all?' Eduardo asked. Dr Wójcik smiled.

'Yes. We are.' She shifted from her amused prodding into a businesslike tone. 'This is all about face. I'm here to help you choose the kind of child that will make you look the best that you possibly can. We're going to decide what you need in a child to look like the perfect family. And to make that happen I have only one thing to ask you: Do not indulge in faceplay in this office. I don't have time for it. If you are both direct and honest with me then I can help you bring the perfect child into this world quicker than you could imagine. Are we clear?' They nodded. She smiled, yet again.

'Well then, let's get started! What have you considered so far?'

'It's . . .' Eduardo hesitated.

'Go on.'

He shook his head.

'It's confusing,' Tonia jumped in. Just saying the words made her heart race. Admitting to feeling confused to anyone other than Eduardo was terrifying. And when she thought about it, she couldn't even remember telling him something like that. Dr Wójcik gave her an encouraging nod, which made her want to stand up and leave the room. She looked at Eduardo. He was rigid in his seat, trying and failing to cover up his extreme discomfort.

'The sooner you talk to me the sooner we can get through this,'

Dr Wójcik told them. 'I know this is uncomfortable for you, but every-thing you say in this room will stay here.'

'There's a lot to consider,' Eduardo said. 'We weren't sure where to start. We discussed the sorts of traits we were interested in but that just threw up a whole new set of questions . . . there's so much to weigh.'

'Okay. What do you know about the history of stud?'

'Well, its rise is fairly recent. My parents went to stud but before that insem and beaker babies were the preferred methods of procre-ation,' Eduardo said.

'Yes. Exactly. It used to be normal for people to use their own genes to create their child and sometimes they would even carry the child to term themselves. That thankfully began to die out and stud farming has, for the most part, replaced it.

'When the practice first started, people made fairly conservative choices. Couples wanted little versions of themselves, so they would choose a sire and dam that looked like them. At first, it seemed to work well but then we began to see a rise in cases of infantile hostile detachment syndrome and paranoid personality disorder. There was a direct correlation between these conditions and couples who had chosen children to look like them. In marriages of triads, and larger groups, however, instances of these psychological issues were close to nil. Following studies on these conditions, my parents hypothesised that if couples chose children that contrasted with their image there would be a greater likelihood of the child and parents bonding as the child grew up. And along came me.'

'So you were part of their experiment?' Tonia asked. She couldn't decide if the question was rude or not, but she knew she had to ask it.

'I was. They were very clear about what they wanted: a child to fol-low in their footsteps. They had to judge prospective donors on their mental acuity, skills and their personal interests. And then they had to choose what aesthetic they favoured. And they had a sense of hu-mour. An Indian doctor; they thought that was just hilarious. It used to be a stereotype, you know? All Indians grow up to be doctors. And since they were both white they liked the idea of this brown-skinned, black-haired baby to contrast with them.'

'They chose you because it was funny?'

'In part. Like I said earlier, this all boils down to face. My parents were prominent scientists who were changing the world. When you reach that level of celebrity—'

'—You can get away with just about anything,' Eduardo finished.

'Exactly. They could choose the way their kid looked based on a pretty shit joke. You two, on the other hand, can't.'

'What can we do?'

'That's the question. I think aesthetics are a good place to start. They'll help us narrow your options. Your current aesthetic as a unit is charming. You clearly chose each other carefully. You reflect each other, like brother and sister, which is great because it means your child will be set against one look. It also means that we can choose subtle contrasts.'

'What do you have in mind?' Eduardo asked.

'With your skin tone and eye colour you have several options. Olive-skinned people tend to go for darker children but since you're both already fairly dark, I would personally go the other way. And with your green eyes . . . a paler, dark-eyed child would make an impact. Is that an aesthetic you feel comfortable with?'

'What do you think?' Eduardo asked Tonia.

She shrugged.

'Do you want to go darker?' asked Dr Wojcik.

Tonia closed her eyes and tried to conjure up the image of a child. *Her* child. It was useless.

'I can't see it,' she told them.

'Easily remedied,' said the doctor, and she slid her fingers across the slate on her desk. The wall on her right glowed white as she cast the image from her slate to its screen, and a baby filled its centre. 'This is the template baby. We can play with the aesthetics, aging it to show you how it would mature. And when you have an idea of what you want to end up with, we can run the programme alongside the catalogue and find matches that would yield an approximate result. So . . .' She tapped the slate, and a colour wheel appeared. She selected a dark brown and coloured the baby's skin. 'This is as dark as you could go. Any darker and you would verge on vulgarity. A child of this colour would have dark hair. So if we age it . . .' She drew her finger across the age scale, and the baby became a toddler. 'This is what it would look like at age four.'

Tonia and Eduardo studied the child. It was a boy. His skin was a rich, coffee-coloured brown and his hair was thick and black and fell around his face in waves. His eyes were dark.

'Could we give him green eyes?' Eduardo asked.

'Certainly,' said the doctor, adjusting the boy's eyes. 'But I wouldn't recommend it.'

'I like it,' said Tonia.

'They're too much like yours. It could have a profound psychological impact on you.'

'She's right,' said Eduardo, staring up at the boy's face. 'There's something uncanny about it. Can you change it back?'

The eyes went brown but the green eyes lingered in Tonia's thoughts.

'A girl,' Tonia said.

The boy became a girl.

'And the green eyes again, please.'

There she was.

'Can you make her skin paler?' Tonia asked. 'Paler. Paler. Stop. One shade darker.'

'Tonia,' said Eduardo, and he put out his hand almost as if he was offering it to her.

'There she is,' said Tonia. 'It's me.'

'You can't have that,' Dr Wójcik said, looking at Tonia. Tonia smiled.

'No, of course not. Make her paler, please.'

Dr Wójcik obliged.

'Could we age it so we see what it looks like into adulthood?' Eduardo asked.

'Certainly.'

Toddler became teenager became adult.

'What do you think?' Dr Wójcik asked.

'She's pretty,' Eduardo said.

'You don't sound convinced . . .'

Eduardo shook his head.

'No, she really is pretty. But even with that paler skin she looks a lot like Tonia. Doesn't she?' He turned to look at Tonia. Tonia was enchanted.

'She really is like me, isn't she?!' she said.

'I think you're right,' Dr Wójcik said. 'Here.' She made adjustments and the woman's eyes darkened. She made her lighter still, and changed her hair—darker, curlier, thicker.

'Age her down, please?' Eduardo asked. 'I just want to make sure she looks pretty in all the age phases we'll be responsible for her in.'

The doctor de-aged the image. As it regressed back into baby form both Eduardo and Dr Wójcik turned to look at Tonia. Tonia looked at the baby. She felt sick.

Tonia had met Eduardo the usual way—on the In. She hadn't really been thinking about coupling, but a friend had suggested that it would be the easiest way for her to boost her static profile. She had done as well as she could on her own; she was a moderate draw but she had to face facts—she was not blessed with charisma.

Tonia had filled out details on the Insite, put her best face forward, and waited for offers. She had never been very proactive. Offers came—fewer than she had expected or hoped for—and they weren't especially enticing: People who thought they were better looking, funnier, smarter and more important than they were. People who thought she was dumber than she was. People who thought they could use her or play with her, and some who thought they could hurt her. She met a few of them, out of interest, out of boredom, and every one was a disappointment.

She was on the verge of removing her face from the Insite when Eduardo appeared. When she saw him she saw herself. But where she was content to remain passive, he was active. He filled the criteria she lacked, and he saw her value where many couldn't. Being valued was a wonderful feeling.

They met in the Out, at a café. Eduardo picked the place. It was beautiful, full of chipped mosaic tables and green hanging plants. Wherever you sat you felt sheltered, hidden. It was cool and calm. And he was sitting waiting for her, looking so much more beautiful than she had expected.

Tonia had tried to find the café again, just before all the talk about children had begun. Of course it didn't exist in that state anymore. The café, like everything else, had changed its face. Tonia wished she could go back, though—to that time, to that interior, to that moment when she first saw Eduardo. No. She wished she could go back further. Everything had changed with Eduardo. She hadn't wanted anything so much until she met him. And that was the one thing she hated him for.

They were informed that the dam was pregnant. Tonia had imagined the moment ever since she and Eduardo had agreed on which people to use to make their baby. She had prepared herself to greet the news with joy; she had practiced it. But when the news came she didn't smile. She couldn't bring herself to clap or laugh with delight. She didn't move.

'Did you hear that?' Eduardo asked. 'We're going to have a baby.'

Tonia looked at him, tried to smile again, but it didn't come.

'Tonia?'

She nodded, tried for that smile one more time, and it flickered and faded.

'Are you okay?' he asked her. He reached out to her, his hand open, close to her elbow, and, for a moment, she willed him to move that extra millimetre, for his fingers to brush her skin. Closer. Closer. Closer. But his hand was still, open, and then closed and retracted. The touch never came. And Tonia felt relief. She smiled.

'We're going to have a baby,' she said.

Eduardo nodded.

'Are you sure you're okay?' he asked.

'Yes. No. I don't know.'

'You're not sure about this?'

She shrugged.

'You know that having a child will help improve our social standing. We've climbed as high as we can without one.' It was the beginning of a speech she had heard before.

'I know,' she said. 'But I . . . it's just . . .'

'What?'

But she couldn't say any more than that. They sat in silence for a while. Tonia made a list of guesses in her head: *He wants to talk about names. He wants to plan her birthday. He wants to start looking for nannies.*

'Maybe we should talk to Vidya,' he said. That wasn't going to be one of her guesses. Tonia frowned.

'Where did that come from?'

'It's just something I've been thinking about. I mean, we've been finding it difficult. Concluding this business. And I think neither of us has quite adjusted to the thought of having an actual, real-life child in our lives. And it's part of her job to help us with those kinds of adjustments. So maybe we should talk to her.'

Tonia shivered.

'I know it's not a natural thing to do,' Eduardo said. 'It's difficult.'

Tonia waited for him to say more. He didn't. She shrugged.

'I'll think about it,' she said as she stood up. She walked over to her bedroom. When she reached the door she hesitated.

'Eddie?'

'Yeah?'

'I'll be ready, Eddie. When the time comes.'

'I know you will,' he said. She knew he was lying. He knew she knew he was lying. They let the pretence stand between them.

ToDdie: We are thrilled to announce that we're pregnant. Due date is
    November 23rd.

Schuyler phoned. Tonia felt that flutter in her stomach that was usually reserved for Eduardo. She felt angry. She felt like she could hurt someone and she wanted it to be Schuyler. She wanted to ignore him. But a ringing phone must be answered, so she took a deep breath and patched in.

'Hello?'

'Great news, Tonia. How are you feeling?'

'Good!' she said. 'Really good!' There was a pause as they each waited for the other to speak. 'I'm surprised to hear from you,' she said. 'Usually you call Eddie.'

'We've already spoken. He seems excited.'

'Yes. Yes he is. We both are. We're thrilled.' There was another pause. Tonia found herself focussing on each of his breaths. She remembered the feel of his fingers against her hand. She shuddered. 'And you? How are you?'

'We're well. Maddie was just saying that she was thinking about throwing you a baby shower. How d'you feel about that?'

'A baby shower?'

'A baby shower.'

'That's awfully kind of her. Please let her know how grateful I am.'

'Yes, of course.' Another pause. 'Are you busy?'

'Now?'

'Yes.'

'Why?'

Schuyler laughed. It was one of those careless laughs that Tonia had always wished came naturally to her. It was like he was simultaneously interested and uninterested in whatever she said, and when he said goodbye he managed to sound both warm and distant. And she sat there and thought about him, his voice, his fingers . . .

'Tonia?' She jumped at the sound of her name. Eduardo frowned at her. 'You okay?' He looked concerned. His voice was soft, and there was something about the way he was standing—a kind of strength— that called to her. She closed her eyes and imagined herself crossing the distance between them and pressing against him. She could almost feel his heart beat next to hers. She shuddered and, standing, stumbled over to the bathroom.

'Hon, what's wrong?' Eduardo asked.

Tonia made it to the toilet just in time. She vomited into the bowl. Her stomach writhed as she choked out bile. And then she was just retching air; her throat burned and her belly heaved. She wiped her mouth with the back of her hand and sat down on the cold tiles. Eduardo was standing at the door, watching her. Waiting.

'I'm fine,' she told him. 'It's just nerves.'

'Have you talked to . . .' He looked away, not able to meet her eye.

'The shrink,' Tonia finished for him. She had been seeing a psychiatrist, once a week, for a month now. It had been Dr Wójcik's suggestion. Eduardo still couldn't get used to the idea. He worried that even saying the words out loud might make the fact public. And what would they do if people knew she was seeing a head doctor? They would lose so much face. Even a perfect baby wouldn't be able to make up for the ground they would lose amongst their friends and followers. Tonia smiled.

'She tells me that this kind of anxiety is perfectly natural. Apparently I should embrace it. It's part of my journey as I evolve into a suitable mother.'

Eduardo cracked a smile.

'Does my lack of anxiety mean I'm going to be an unfit father, then?'

Tonia laughed and got to her feet. She felt weak and unsteady and as she walked over to the sink she stumbled. Eduardo rushed forwards, hands out, ready to catch her. She didn't fall. They stood there, staring at each other, neither of them sure of what to make of what had just happened. They knew he would have caught her. She wished he had caught her. The look on his face said he felt differently.

Eduardo rushed out of the room. Tonia sagged against the sink. Her stomach stirred ominously. She swallowed. Her mouth tasted of rust and acid. An alert throbbed at the corner of her eye and she groaned. She looked into the mirror, organised a smile, and then she picked up the message. Madeleine. Baby shower. Life.

'Here's to the new parents to be!' Schuyler said, waving a drink in the air. Several glasses joined his and the delicate tinkle of crystal made Tonia want to cry.

She closed her eyes and smiled her widest smile. The baby shower had turned into a party such as only Madeleine could throw. Tonia wasn't even sure she knew most of the people present. But everyone cheered for her and Eduardo. She opened her eyes and looked for him. His smile was tight and self-contained. His jaw was hard and she wished she could put her hand to it, to smooth that hardness away. This was all wrong. But it was too late.

She looked across at Schuyler. He smiled at her and winked. What did that mean? Her eyes fixed on his hand, his fingers gripping a glass stem, long strong fingers, and she had to fight the wave of queasiness that threatened her. She wanted to grab Eduardo and get out. But of course she didn't want to grab him. Not literally. Did she?

'Eddie!' she called out, bright as an advert. 'Could you make me one of your trademark cocktails?'

Madeleine laughed.

'To not being pregnant!' she toasted. 'May we all drink *deep* and enjoy!'

Eduardo's smile stayed fixed, rigid, and he obliged. He went into the kitchen and Schuyler followed. Curious, Tonia followed too, but she stopped at the door and listened. She heard ice chink. She heard a bottle open.

'How are you?' Schuyler asked.

'Over the moon,' Eduardo said. His voice was full of warmth. Tonia softened at the sound of it. Maybe he really was happy. Maybe this wasn't a disaster.

Schuyler made a noise in his throat. Tonia wished Eduardo would ask him what that meant. But of course, he didn't. He couldn't.

'How's Tonia?'

'Tonia?'

'This is a big decision. You're over the moon; so, how's Tonia?'

'Good. But then, we've already said that, haven't we?'

Schuyler laughed that same careless laugh. Tonia was glad Eduardo hadn't asked him what he was getting at. She felt that they should already know. He wanted something. But she couldn't tell what.

'When are we going to play Go?' Schuyler asked.

This time Eduardo laughed.

'You're relentless about this. You know it's no fun for me when you always win.'

'I'll go easy on you, then,' said Schuyler.

'Yes. That will be totally satisfying.'

They laughed together.

'Sarcasm doesn't suit you, Eddie.'

They moved, their footsteps clear on the kitchen tiles, and Tonia walked away before they came out.

When she got home she was glad to take off her shoes and sit down. She flexed her feet, heard the bones in them crack, and then she slumped down in an armchair. Eduardo stood at the edge of the living room and looked at her.

'What?' she asked.

'You're beautiful.'

Tonia couldn't remember the last time he had told her that. She started to cry. Big, full-bodied sobs. She bent forwards, put her head to her knees and wailed. When she looked up Eduardo was gone.

It squalled and squirmed—a writhing bloody mess. Its face was scrunched up and wrinkled and its tiny hands were clenched tight.

There was no happiness here. *Stop touching me*, each cry seemed to say; *stop touching me!* The nurse cleaned it and slid it into the thin plastic papoose that would act as its protection for now.

There she was: their baby girl. Thinking it didn't make it feel any more real.

'There she is. Our baby girl,' said Eduardo. But hearing it didn't make it feel any more real and he didn't sound interested at all. They weren't interested at all.

The nurse handed the baby to Eduardo. He took it dutifully and looked it in the face but Tonia knew he wasn't interested at all. He bent down towards the little thing and whispered something in its fuzzy red ear. Tonia couldn't hear what he said. Then he straightened up and offered her the baby. She had practiced for this moment, had tried holding dummy babies, learned how to make her body soft and inviting, to act like it was natural to hold a living creature. All the practice in the world wasn't enough. She shook her head, refused the child, but she looked at its face. It was little, and it was ugly. It would be that way for a while, she guessed.

'Is it happy?' she asked Eduardo.

'No. She's not,' he said, and his face said even more. He was disappointed. With the baby? With her? She couldn't tell. He didn't seem ill at ease holding the thing. Did that mean it was Tonia he wasn't happy with? He walked out of the room and Tonia followed.

'Where are you going?' she asked.

'I'm taking her home.'

'We have to register it. There's paperwork. There's . . . things. To be done.'

'I'll do them.'

'Now?'

'Now. As I go. Go home, Tonia. I'll do it all.' And just like that, Eduardo was gone. Down another corridor, down another set of stairs, down, up, away, gone, disappeared, absent. He and it. So Tonia went home.

Their flat was full of absence when she got there, and she didn't know what to do with herself, so she patched into the In, and there they all were: her friends, crowding the network and clamouring for attention. They had their best faces on, and they were wishing her congratulations. Tonia kept her distance, maintained superiority, and prayed for Eduardo to come home soon. Now she was on the In, she couldn't get out. Everyone had seen her. She was trapped. She wanted to pull her face off, but everyone was talking at her: You must be so proud! and How does it feel? and What does she look like? and question after question after question, until finally the door hushed open and she made her goodbyes and turned to look.

The pit of her stomach fell through her feet. Eduardo held the baby so gently.

'Hello,' Tonia said.

'Shh,' Eduardo shushed her. He didn't look up. He kept his eyes on the baby. His hard jaw had softened, his flint eyes were water, and he smiled. Tonia reached out to him, a pleading gesture, but he didn't see it.

A woman walked into the flat and past Eduardo. Efficiency wafted in her wake. She nodded at Tonia and found her own way to the kitchen.

'Who—'

'—Dry nurse.'

Tonia nodded. The baby woke up. It wriggled in Eduardo's arms and began to whimper, building up steam before it began to wail. Tonia watched Eduardo's face. Far from being alarmed, he smiled, rocked it gently and murmured words to it that Tonia couldn't hear. He took it into the kitchen. She followed them and watched as he handed the baby to the dry nurse, who began to feed it with the formula she had just prepared. Eduardo watched it feed.

'She's called Shea,' he said, not taking his eyes from it. 'It's official.'

Tonia wasn't sure what to say but she was saved the trouble as Eduardo glazed over, taking a call.

'Hello? Schuy! Beautiful. So beautiful, I don't think I've ever seen anything like her. She's perfect. Oh, hang on a sec, she's just feeding. Here . . . there! Shea. Our choice.'

He spoke so warmly it was disconcerting. Tonia had never heard him talk to Schuyler that unguardedly. And then the gates slammed shut and his voice cooled.

'She's quite tired right now. But we were talking about having you and Maddie over for dinner sometime, so you can see Shea. Maybe in a week or two when we've settled into a rhythm. Oh. Yes, of course, hang on, I'll focus back. There.'

Tonia watched as he watched the baby feed. She could tell that he was relaying the moment to Schuyler too. They were both there, watching this little thing, sucking greedily on a rubber nipple. And they were silent.

Eduardo took parental leave. This was unusual and met with general surprise. Tonia worried about it; she felt like it was affecting their facevalue. When she mentioned it to Eduardo, he snapped.

'If you don't care, you have face enough to handle it.'

This wasn't true but she could see his point. He felt that they were just about important enough to get away with eccentric behaviour, and she knew she couldn't say anything to change his mind.

Eduardo wrapped his life around the baby. The baby cried. He comforted. And Tonia had no idea what to do.

It was a couple of weeks before they invited anyone to see the baby. Dr Wójcik, Schuyler and Madeleine were the first to visit. Tonia picked her clothes for the occasion with special care. She brushed her hair straight until it fell like water, glossy and black, with that sheen of green she had always been so proud of. Her skin was clear and fresh and when she looked in the mirror she was sure she appeared to be everything she ought to be. But of course, no one looked at her when they came in. All eyes were on the baby.

'This is Shea,' Eduardo said proudly. He held the baby close and, if it wasn't for the plastic papoose that kept her shielded from him, he would have appeared horrifying—touching her skin to skin.

Madeleine cooed but didn't really look at it, and Dr Wójcik smiled and said nothing. Schuyler stepped close, though, staring at it intently.

'You're right. She's perfect,' he said. He looked over at Tonia. The way his eyes held hers made her pulse quicken. He looked at her as intently as he had the baby.

'I thought . . .' he said. 'I didn't know . . .' but he never said what he thought or what he didn't know and all Tonia understood was that he was speaking to her only. He smiled at her, not a real smile, and then he turned back to Shea.

'She's yours,' he said, to Eduardo.

Eduardo smiled at him and Tonia could see how soft his face was. He was utterly relaxed. And for a moment she was almost sure she saw

Schuyler reach out and touch Eduardo's arm. She was almost sure she saw Eduardo smile at that. She was sure she wanted to run away.

Instead, she smiled and spoke and charmed and when the night was over her face ached. She stretched her cheeks with a yawn and then sighed in relief.

'Eddie,' she said. He was standing by the window looking out into the world. The baby was asleep. They were alone.

'Eddie?'

'Yeah?'

'How are you?'

Eduardo turned around and smiled at her.

'Perfect,' he said, and his face told her that was true. Tonia burst into tears. Eduardo left the room.

(Menial 63700578—Jake)

Jake watched Madeleine as she sat at the dining room table, patched into the In. She sat straight, her arms flat against the tabletop, her eyes closed. Under the lids those eyes flickered as she watched the action of the In unfold. Every so often, a smile would cross her face, a whisper of a giggle would escape her lips and sometimes she would sigh. Each sound, each expression, enthralled him. He mentally traced every inch of her. She was wearing a soft, diaphanous shift, over a skintight bodysuit. The clothes created a combination of hard and soft lines, making her look both strong and gentle. The sheer fabric and the tight suit left little to the imagination. Jake watched her, undressed her, tasted the salt of her skin, and just as things were about to go too far for his imagination Schuyler came into the room, Reyna close behind him.

'Maddie,' he said. Madeleine shook, then blinked up at him.

'I was just taking care of a few loose ends,' she said. Her voice was caramel. Jake looked at her perfect still face, and then retreated to get the family's dinner.

They were all silent as he pushed in the trolley. He served and left.

He sat at the kitchen table and watched the monitor that displayed the dining room. He watched Madeleine eat. She cut her food into small pieces. She took a bite and laid fork and knife down on either side of her plate. She chewed. He watched her mouth. She smiled. He watched her mouth. She spoke. He watched her mouth. That perfect mouth. She opened it to take another bite. He watched.

It took him by surprise when she stood up. He hadn't been paying enough attention. Something had happened. She stood and left the room. Where was she going? He stood up. But following her wasn't part of his job. He watched the others as they sat and ate and talked as if nothing was wrong. He didn't know what they were talking about. There was no audio. Naomi said something, stood up and left. Reyna's plate was clear. Schuyler was finished. It was time for the next course. Jake placed the plates on his trolley and took it in.

Whenever Jake was asked to do something by Schuyler Burroughs, he had a brief moment when he thought about smashing Schuyler's face in. This wasn't something he ever talked about. Not even to his confessor. It thrilled him to imagine his skin, taut across his knuckles, pressing hard against the soft flesh of Schuyler's cheek. But Jake would smile, and then do what he had been told to.

Recently, he had noticed Schuyler looking at him. It was an unusual sensation—having eyes on him. He wasn't meant to be seen. At first, he thought he was imagining it, but then their eyes began to meet. Schuyler would contemplate the menial, openly, and Jake found himself almost eager to be scrutinised. He liked being seen. But at the same time, he worried that Schuyler would see more than he was willing to show. He would read his face, guess at his thoughts, know that not so deep down Jake wanted to hurt him. And hold his partner. And the fear of being found out made his desires feel dirtier. He was sick.

'I'm sick,' Jake told his confessor. 'I'm really sick. Do you get this a lot? Do other beakers say the same kinds of things to you? There are other people like me, aren't there?'

'I can't talk about other confessions, Jake.'

'I'm not asking about the confessions! I just want to know, do other people feel like this?'

'I can't talk about other confessions, Jake.'

'I'm not asking about the confessions! Am I a freak?'

'You are not a freak, Jake.'

'How can you tell?'

'I know. Trust me. I know.'

'Why should I trust you?'

'You've already trusted me with your confessions, Jake. Have I let you down somehow?'

'No.'

'Then trust me. I can tell when I'm talking to a freak. You are not a freak.'

That line wasn't a machine's line. There was definitely a human behind the confessor. Who? What kind of person?

'Who are you?' Jake asked, not for the first time.

'I'm your confessor.'

'But who *are* you? How did you start doing this?'

'You're not here to hear my story, Jake. I'm here to hear yours.'

'It would help me. To know more about you.'

'I want to help.'

'How does confessing help?'

'Confessing has always helped people. People used to confess to a priest, or to a god, or they would confess to a crime. Confession allows people to unburden themselves. And without the weight of their secrets they were free to move. To move on. It's harder now to confess to a real person, to a real face, because that affects how people see us. So confessing in the safety of the In is a logical choice. People are afraid to show their true faces but they can't hide their feelings and thoughts forever. They have to let them out. Confessing helps us move.'

'Do you confess?'

'Sometimes.'

'What do you confess to?'

'This isn't about my confession. You aren't here to hear my confession. I am here to hear yours.'

'Don't you trust me?'

'I . . .'

Jake smiled.

'Jake. This is a service that's been designed to help people. It's a safe space for you to say whatever you want to say. The time you spend here is *your* time. It's my job to listen to you. Nothing more. You can trust me, but you are my client. I'm not yours. This only works one way.'

'But trust doesn't work like that.'

'You've never had a problem with this before.'

'I have a problem now.'

'I'm sorry, Jake. I don't want to make things difficult for you. I only want to help you.'

'You could help me by telling me more about yourself.'

'I'm afraid I can't do that, Jake. Why don't we take a moment to think, and then you can tell me what's really bothering you?'

Jake took a moment to think. And then he patched out and looked around his bare room—the space the Burroughses had given him to live in. He had nothing to say to the confessor. Nothing new. And confessing didn't seem all that important right now. There was more going on. More that he didn't understand. He wished his brain worked faster, that his thoughts came quicker and made more sense. He was sure his slowness was part of his beaker heritage. If he had been born in stud . . . but then if he had been born in stud he wouldn't be a menial. He'd be on the ladder. A rung closer to Madeleine Burroughs. A rung closer to her looking him in the face. . . . Jake was getting hard. He looked at the time. They wouldn't need him for a few more minutes.

Vidya

Faceless

Vidya wasn't especially surprised by the invitation to SchAddie's latest soiree, but she hadn't been expecting it. SchAddie were the kind of couple that would entertain her every so often but Madeleine didn't have the confidence to court Vidya for regular appearances at her events. This was why Schuyler was the one who did the inviting in the end.

The call was brief. A few traded niceties, a few nods to their long association, and then—because he didn't believe in beating around the bush—Schuyler got to the point of the matter:

'We have some friends that are thinking about including a child in their unit.'

She read between the lines:

'They can't afford me, can they.'

'No.'

'Would you be footing the bill?'

'Of course not.'

'So you're asking me for a pretty big favour then.'

'Come to the party and meet the couple. They have a lot of potential. Their aesthetic is stunning. I promise they'd be worth your while. In fact, I may as well send you a few of their handles so you can do some research fir—'

'It's okay, I'll come and see them.'

Vidya liked surprises.

'Madeleine will be thrilled.'

'I bet she will,' said Vidya. They traded goodbyes and disconnected.

Vidya was one of those rare stud creatures that kept close contact with the parents that raised her. Most people, when they were established in their own right and capable of supporting themselves, preferred to distance themselves from the parents that had had them for their own gain. There was no love lost when child left parent.

It was not affection, but rather professional courtesy, that kept Vidya tied to her parents. After all, they were the first to compile a stud catalogue, and they were incredibly high up the ladder. So Vidya went to see them every six weeks or so, to trade any useful information they might have gathered. She caught a train and made her way to the ridiculous house the Drs Wójcik had recently taken over.

The house was another one of their jokes, gaudy and tasteless. As Vidya walked in, she didn't suppress a shudder at its ugliness.

'That's my girl!' Ida Wójcik said as she walked up to meet Vidya. They leaned towards each other and kissed the air in greeting. 'The thing I love the most about you is your consistent demonstration of real feelings.'

'One of the many things I don't love about you is your consistent repetition of old sentiments.'

Ida laughed, but Vidya knew she was neither amused nor unamused. Ida was the most artificial person she had ever met. Vidya took a moment to disable the In connection in her eyes—her mothers insisted on full privacy, of course—but she left her recording function on.

'O!' Ida called up the sweeping staircase.

'Ja, ja!' a voice called down.

'Shall we?' Ida asked, and she herded Vidya into a large, decadent room that was all gilt and mirrors and pale damask.

'Sit,' she commanded, and she took up residence on a sofa that looked horribly uncomfortable.

'You look good,' Vidya said. She was being polite, but it was also true. Ida was in her late eighties and yet she looked barely a day over fifty. She was sharp in her cream silk blouse and dusky gold suit, tailored tight to her body. Somehow, she both complemented and contrasted with their florid surroundings. She was a magnificent creature.

'So. The news,' Ida began. 'Brace yourself and listen—there's been an offer. To couple with you.'

'Ida—'

Ida held a hand up and shook her head.

'I know you've never had the interest or the need, but this is different. This could be big.'

Ida never said the word 'big' lightly.

'Go on,' Vidya said, and her mother smiled.

'Her name is Ducha Wanjiku.'

'Wanjiku . . . that means nothing to me. Why would I—'

'She comes from a family of menial farmers.'

Vidya had nothing to say to that. Ida filled the quiet with bluster:

'Where *is* O?' she muttered as she rang a ludicrous brass bell that had been sitting on a coffee table. A menial walked in.

'Fetch Otilie,' she told it, and she busied herself with straightening up her jacket as she waited for Vidya to reach some kind of conclusion to her thoughts.

'Darlings!' Otilie said, floating into the room on chiffon, perfume and alcohol. Where Ida was sharp and collected, Otilie was soft and messy. She was no less beautiful, however, and, for all their faults, her mothers seemed to adore each other. Yet another rare thing about the Wójcik family. 'Has Ida told you the news?' Otilie asked, and she glided around the room, taking her time to choose a place to sit.

'Yes.'

'And?'

'Why?'

'Why the interest? Diversification of business interests. Ducha wants to learn more about the designer baby stuff,' Otilie said, waving a hand dismissively.

'The designer baby stuff?' Vidya said, smiling.

'The designer baby stuff,' Otilie said, waving her hand again before bursting into peals of laughter.

'Can you give me a little more?' Vidya asked Ida.

'Actually no. Ducha didn't say very much. It was a pretty terse interaction.'

'How do you know her family are in the menial business?'

'Please! We've been in this profession for over sixty years. I think it's safe to say that we've probably forgotten a good deal more than you've learned.'

'Don't exaggerate, Ida. It's ugly,' Otilie said.

'You get my point, though,' Ida said.

'I get your point,' Vidya agreed.

'So, what do you think? Will you meet her?'

'Why did she approach you? Why not come to me directly?'

Ida and Otilie traded a look.

'We've known the Wanjikus for a long time. An established connection. A *private* connection. And they are a very private family.'

'Okay, but—'

'I don't think we can answer any more questions. Either you meet her or you don't. Either she'll give you answers or she won't.'

'Your choice,' Otilie said, leaning forwards to grab the bell. 'And I think . . . champagne suits this room very nicely. Drinks should always match the drapes, don't you think?'

The door opened as though automatic, and Vidya caught sight of a menial hovering behind it. No host to greet her; an indication of just the kind of level this party was entertaining. A quick glance around the room and Vidya knew this was not her kind of crowd. Then she saw Madeleine.

Madeleine's beauty was a little on the obvious side for Vidya's taste, but she had to admit the woman had excellent style. If she could only keep her mouth shut she would pass for classy.

'Vidya!' Madeleine said, and Vidya suppressed her irritation at the mangled pronunciation of her name. 'How wonderful to *see* you!'

Madeleine swooped towards her and for a moment it looked like she would launch herself into a show of intimacy, kissing the air at Vidya's cheeks, but she stopped just short. Vidya smiled at her, graciously.

'And it's wonderful to see you too. I was really pleased that Schuyler thought to offer an invitation.'

'I'm *just* thrilled you could drop in!'

'Well, I had a little time to kill, and Schuyler promised an interesting prospective project,' Vidya told her, looking around for Schuyler, but also hoping she might see the couple he had spoken of; she was sure she would recognize them.

'Yes, well, come with *me*. I'll show you around and take you over to Schuy and ToDdie.'

Madeleine steered Vidya through the crowd, showing her off, making sure no one missed the famous doctor. Vidya smiled and endured the display until finally Madeleine brought her before Schuyler and the couple she had been looking for.

'And here, may I present the *pro*spective parents! This is Tonia and Eduardo,' Madeleine gushed, so very pleased with herself. Schuyler somehow managed to keep his face expressionless but Vidya was sure he felt embarrassed. At least she hoped he did. Certainly, Eduardo was trying his hardest not to do or say anything demonstrative, but the woman Tonia showed some poise when she stepped forward and said:

'It's a pleasure to meet you.'

Her smooth delivery was impressive given her social standing and Vidya regarded her openly.

'The feeling is mutual. SchAddie have told me so much about you,' she lied, and turning to Schuyler she said: 'You weren't exaggerating. They have a perfect aesthetic.' She appraised Tonia again. 'Really. You're a stunning couple.' Another lie. They were pretty, but not so extraordinary as to pique her interest. She wasn't sure why Schuyler had brought her here, unless it was purely to serve Madeleine's ego.

'You're very gracious,' Eduardo said. 'We try our best, but our aesthetic is far from perfect.'

'Our hosts have a monopoly on perfection!' Tonia added, and she smiled prettily at Madeleine. Vidya enjoyed the little jab.

'You're too modest,' Schuyler said, overindulgent to his low-level friends. 'I'm glad you came,' he said to Vidya. 'We'll leave you to talk, but come and find me later. We're due a catch-up.' Schuyler steered Madeleine away and Vidya and the couple waited until they were far enough away before turning to talk to one another.

'It's fairly unsubtle as far as faceplay goes,' she said. When the couple said nothing she continued:

'Don't worry. I'm not trying to trick you. I don't indulge in it myself.' This time she wasn't lying. Stretching the truth a little but not lying.

'It's an important aspect of my work; I have to build trust with my clients and I take that very seriously. The best way to develop trust is through honesty. I take confidentiality seriously, too. Anything you say to me is in the strictest confidence, even at a social gathering.'

'Clients? Isn't that a bit premature?' said Eduardo. Vidya resisted the urge to laugh at him. The thought of anyone turning down her services was laughable, but she had to wonder why she was offering her services to them at all. The fact that the couple seemed to be wondering the same thing made her more inclined to like them. She picked up a cocktail from a passing tray and started going over dates for an appointment.

Vidya would have made time for Schuyler if the party had been a bit more highbrow. He was an interesting man, and she would have liked to discuss his thoughts on his daughters' prospects. But the party was not more highbrow and she felt like a zoo animal—everyone trying to get a good look at her or get her attention. She didn't bother to say goodbye, and it was only when she was on the train home that she felt she could breathe freely. And then she received a message:

IO: Dearest, come over next week. We're making borscht ;)
       xoxoxoxoxoxoxoxoxoxoxoxoxoxo

She knew that meant the meeting was set. And suddenly she couldn't breathe so freely anymore.

Vidya wasn't surprised when Schuyler called. She enabled the vid so she could read him properly and he smiled at her, a picture of beauty.

'You ran out so fast we never got a chance to talk,' he said.

'I don't appreciate being put on display like that,' Vidya told him, and he had the decency to look regretful. He didn't blame Madeleine but his reply, 'I thought you didn't engage in faceplay,' outmanoeuvred her, and Vidya laughed.

'So, what is it about this couple?' she asked.

'You saw them. You must have noticed the potential?'

'You keep bringing up this potential. I saw a pretty pair. What makes them different from any of the other pretty pairs?'

Schuyler sighed and leaned back in his chair.

'I don't know,' he said. 'They just . . . took my fancy.'

So it was a project. Like his daughters.

'How are the girls?' Vidya asked. Of course, she followed them—she followed all of the children she created—but she wanted to hear how he was finding them.

'Reyna is . . . amazing. She just seems to be going from strength to strength. She decided she wanted to brand out, so she's spinning faces, always In.'

Vidya nodded.

'And Naomi?' she asked.

Schuyler gave her a ghost of a smile.

'Changeless. Stubborn. Dull.'

Schuyler was a clever man but when it came to his daughters he never seemed to have much clarity.

'Are you sure about that?' Vidya asked him.

'Yes.'

'I don't think I bred her to be dull.'

'Oh, I don't mean she's stupid,' Schuyler hurried to assure her. 'I just find her whole angry teenager act . . . boring.'

'I see,' said Vidya. She left her words hanging to embarrass him.

'She's Madeleine's project,' he said. 'I was never very interested in her.'

'Hmmm.'

'I didn't mean to insult you.'

'You didn't. I'm just not sure we see her the same way.'

'Have you spent much time with her?' Schuyler asked, moving quickly from defensive to offensive.

Vidya smiled.

'Of course not. Have you?'

Schuyler laughed, having no clear route out of that question.

'And what about you?' he asked. 'Have you thought about designing a child for yourself?'

'Now, why would I need to do that?'

'To show us all how it should be done.'

'I couldn't care less what I show anyone, Schuyler. You know that. And isn't that what you keep trying for yourself? To show everyone how little you care?'

'What makes you say that?'

'Well, isn't it?'

Schuyler smiled. 'Yes, Vidya.'

There was nowhere for their conversation to go after that—both of them aware they wouldn't hide much, neither of them willing to show much.

'I'm sure this ToDdie couple will prove fertile ground,' Vidya told him.

'Thank you,' Schuyler said before hanging up.

There hadn't been anyone on her roster for a while, so, despite her misgivings about their 'potential', this ToDdie couple were actually a welcome break from a stream of nothing.

Her secretary ushered them in and Vidya was pleased to see them looking cool and collected. It was all face, of course, and that would have to be the first thing to go, but she was happy to know she would be working with people who could keep their shit together when it was necessary.

'Your parents did beautiful work with you,' Tonia said as she sat down, and the rush and tumble of her words undid the good work Vidya had been admiring.

'My parents popularised the trend of contrasts,' she said. This was not true, but everyone believed it and Vidya propagated the lie to keep Ida and Otilie happy. The truth was that contrasts had been growing in popularity organically. Ida had spotted the trend and jumped on it: she wrote a paper, presented lectures, and, since Vidya was already on the way, it wasn't long before she was presented to Ida's willing audiences also.

'*Look at our beautiful daughter. She's going to be a doctor, of course,*' they would laugh.

'Yes, I've read about them,' Tonia said.

'What have you read?' she asked, though in truth she didn't really care. She had heard it all before. Tonia read her and hesitated to answer.

'Well, everyone wants a Wójcik baby,' Eduardo jumped in. Vidya liked that. They worked as a team. He continued: 'They practically invented the boutique baby shop. The way the In tells it, your mothers had a preternatural ability to create the most perfect children. An ability they developed in you . . .'

'Schuyler Burroughs was one of theirs, wasn't he?' Tonia asked.

'Yes, his baby blueprint came out of this very office. And of course, after him, there was a rash of other baby shops copying his look. So many beautiful, dark-eyed, black children everywhere . . .' It should have diluted his allure, but everyone was always so fascinated by that man. He had an indefinable quality that kept his look, his face, every aspect that made him Schuyler Burroughs perfectly unattainable to the masses. Her mothers had done good work there, she had to give it to them. Vidya refocussed:

'So. Let's get to it. Why are you two here?' she asked. She noticed both of them stiffen a little, making a great effort to control their faces, no doubt.

'Everyone wants a Wójcik baby,' Eduardo said again.

'Why not go to the Hú centre?' Vidya asked.

Eduardo laughed. People always seemed to laugh at that one.

'You aren't serious?' he asked.

'It's an option. Why aren't you thinking about it?'

'Well . . . I mean they're fine. Didn't your parents use them, Tonia?'

Tonia nodded.

'But they aren't fine for you?'

'They wouldn't add anything to us. We're already a Hú sort of couple, it wouldn't help us move up.'

Good. Honesty. Awareness. ToDdie knew who they were and what they needed to do to be better.

'So you're concerned with your face?' Vidya said, following the usual script.

'Aren't we all?' Eduardo asked, and that was honest too. Vidya smiled.

'Yes. We are. This is all about face. I'm here to help you choose the kind of child that will make you look the best that you possibly can. We're going to decide what you need in a child to look like the perfect family. And to make that happen I have only one thing to ask you: Do not indulge in faceplay in this office. I don't have time for it. If you are both direct and honest with me then I can help you bring the perfect child into this world quicker than you could imagine. Are we clear?' They nodded. Vidya smiled. Getting rid of faceplay was a good rule. It cut through a lot of bullshit. Things moved so much more quickly when people were talking without calculating what their words might do. It was Otilie's rule, but making the work easier had never been her particular goal. Otilie was only ever interested in knowing people; knowing them with such depth that should she ever need them they would be beholden to her.

'Well then, let's get started!' Vidya said, all brightness and light.

It didn't take long for her to work out that Tonia was far from brightness and light.

When the couple left, Vidya called Ida.

'This is a welcome surprise,' Ida trilled.

'I'm worried about a client,' Vidya said, and Ida changed from effusive to businesslike.

'What's the issue?'

'I'll give you a review,' Vidya told her, and she selected the recording of her meeting with ToDdie and streamed it to Ida. She fast-forwarded the frames until she reached the template baby:

'Could we give him green eyes?' Eduardo asked.

'Certainly,' said Vidya, adjusting the boy's eyes. 'But I wouldn't recommend it.'

'I like it,' said Tonia.

'They're too much like yours. It could have a profound psychological impact on you.'

'She's right. There's something uncanny about it. Can you change it back?' said Eduardo.

'A girl,' Tonia said.

Vidya changed the sex.

'And the green eyes again, please. Can you make her skin paler? Paler. Paler. Stop. One shade darker.'

'Tonia,' said Eduardo.

'There she is,' said Tonia. 'It's me.'

'You can't have that,' Vidya told her.

'No, of course not. Make her paler please.'

Vidya cut the feed there.

'What do you think?' she asked Ida. Ida sighed.

'Not the kind of person I'd be recommending motherhood to. She's emotionally unstable.'

'My thoughts too. The guy, Eduardo, seems ready, though. Do you think he could redress the balance?'

'Possibly. I'm not sure I'd take my chances on that, though. Why are you interested in this couple? I don't recognise them.'

'They aren't particularly important. Schuyler Burroughs is interested in them.'

'Oh really? Do you know why?'

'A pet project. I think he's going through some sort of midlife crisis. Or Madeleine has finally driven him a bit mad.'

Ida sighed again.

'He's been rather a disappointment to me. His parents aren't that bothered, Janine still seems to be proud of him. I think she rather enjoys the fact that he married down.'

'Yes well, there's marrying down and then there's marrying down,' Vidya said, and Ida laughed.

'You turned out better than we had hoped,' she said.

'I wish I could say the same for you two,' Vidya replied, and Ida laughed again—a real cackle.

'So, what do you recommend I do about this couple?' Vidya asked, getting back to the matter at hand.

'Indulge Schuyler. He may know what he's doing. But make sure you keep a close eye on them. We don't want any breakdowns tainting our reputation. We only provide perfection.'

'Thank you. I'll see you next week,' Vidya said, and she ended the call.

Ida and Otilie moved out of their grotesque palace in record time. Almost as soon as they declared themselves bored of their surroundings, the packing had begun. Vidya only got the notification a few hours before she was meant to visit them—they had been surprisingly quiet about the move on their profiles.

She made her way to the centre of the city and their new penthouse flat. It was so tasteful it was unsettling, and when Vidya stepped into the cool, monochrome confines of their new 'home' she understood the choice. Sitting before her, more statue than woman, was (she presumed) Ducha Wanjiku. Ducha was the most beautiful person she had ever seen. She was beautiful in a way that frightened Vidya. There was an unreal quality to her, as though she wasn't quite human. Ducha was dark. Her skin was oil, her eyes were shards of jet. She was dressed in a tight black suit and wore black patent-leather heels. Her hair was shorn tight to her head. She wore no jewellery. It was as though she had styled herself to be an absence of light. And she sat on a white armchair in a white room and watched Vidya as she stood in front of her, back to the front door, wondering if she wanted to walk forwards or run backwards.

'Darling,' said Otilie, rising from a chair on Ducha's left. Vidya walked into the room. 'Ducha, this is our daughter, Vidya.'

Ducha gave Vidya a nod, but said nothing.

'Right, well. We'll leave you two to talk,' said Ida, standing up from Ducha's right. The Drs Wójcik exited the room swiftly and Vidya was left to stand before Ducha and wonder that she had never seen her before.

'Won't you sit?' Ducha asked. Vidya obliged her, taking the seat Otilie had vacated. The white of the room forced Vidya's eye to seek the darkness in its centre. Ducha smiled at her.

'Your mothers prepared the place well,' she said, acknowledging Vidya's preoccupation with the aesthetics before her. 'I have something of a penchant for white. It's a silly eccentricity, but then life is long and we all have to have our little quirks to get us through the days, don't you think?'

Vidya understood that Ducha was talking to her, understood the words themselves, but couldn't quite comprehend that she was being spoken to, at least not immediately. Then she remembered herself.

'Yes. I suppose most people do.'

'I trust you've disabled your In connection?'

Vidya nodded.

'And you are not recording this meeting.'

Vidya understood that was an instruction and not a request. She closed her eyes and swept them left under her eyelids to switch off her recording function. She opened her eyes to Ducha's sharp gaze.

'Your mothers tell me you have a knack for honesty, and an ability to keep secrets.'

'It's part of my job.'

'But it isn't just your job. You enjoy honesty, they say.'

'It's less work than playing face.'

'But keeping secrets is hard.'

'It depends who you're keeping them from. I find it doesn't present much of a challenge. There's no one really worth sharing them with.'

'What about your mothers?'

'I consult with them. The business is theirs, after all. It means letting them in on a few things every so often, but it hardly matters in the grand scheme of things.'

'Hardly matters?' Ducha raised an eyebrow.

'No one knows I share information with Ida and Otilie.'

'So you keep your secret sharing secret at least.'

'Why don't we get down to why you care about this aspect of my work.'

Ducha smiled.

'I'm sure your mothers have told you I'm interested in coupling?'

'Why? And why me?'

'Is it really very strange? People couple all the time.'

'For hierarchical gain in the public eye. I have never seen you before which means you aren't on any platform. You're a ghost. Coupling is about as necessary to you as shoes for a fish.'

'Yes, I see you don't like playing. That's good. I like to be direct also. And in all honesty I don't want to couple at all. I'm looking for a business relationship.'

Ducha clasped her hands together and leaned forwards, studying Vidya's face.

'This is where your ability to keep secrets comes in. Regardless of how our business concludes today, once I leave this place you must forget me. You cannot speak about this meeting to anyone. I'm no one. I always have been and I intend to remain no one for the rest of my days. If it appears like you might jeopardise my anonymity then you, and your mothers, will be dealt with in an . . . efficient manner.'

'Efficient?'

'Not everything has to be spelled out, does it?'

Vidya tried to smile, but it wouldn't come.

'Why don't we get down to business?' she asked.

'Yes. Well. As I assume you know by now, I come from a family of menial farmers. We've been in the business since Hayashi began the programme. She needed funding and the Wanjikus provided. We've been there through all its bumps in the road and now we have a perfect product.'

This time Vidya did smile.

'You disagree.'

'Well, I hardly think they can be considered perfect. I hear stories all the time; substandard work, menials zoning out, wandering off, attempting to communicate with owners . . .'

'Employers,' Ducha corrected her.

'I thought you wanted me to be honest?'

Ducha seemed amused.

'You described our perfect product.'

'How? I know what it takes to make a baby and I *know* they can be made better. You could make a perfect workforce easily, one without any faults at all. It would help if you castrated them in the first place, and—'

'I think you've rather missed the point,' Ducha told her. 'I am running a business. If our product didn't run down, if it was "perfect",' she said, 'well then, what use would we be really? The turnover would decline, we'd have to start selling to a lower class of customer and the exclusivity of menials would be lost. Menials aren't the most efficient helpers. They aren't the best idea. They work because they are the only idea we offer and we are the only people in a position to offer anything at all. We keep them flawed because it suits our agenda.'

'So, what do you want with me?'

Ducha leaned back into her chair and stretched out her legs. She studied Vidya.

'What?' Vidya asked her.

'Nothing. It's just that I rarely get an opportunity to talk to someone outside of our farms. I never get an opportunity to have a conversation outside of the family. I'd like you to tell me a bit about yourself. Aside from your job, what do you do?'

'Enjoy life.'

'How?'

'That's quite a question.'

'What do you enjoy doing?'

'I like to learn. A lot of people live for their faces. Their time on the In is spent on their platforms, maintaining and building. I've never needed that, so I use the In differently. I learn.'

'What are you learning?'

'Anything that takes my fancy. I'm learning Portuguese and taking classes in architecture these days. They challenge different parts of the mind, so I find I'm sufficiently stimulated.'

'Stimulation is important?'

'You don't think so?'

'I spend most of my time working. I find that distracting enough.'

'And what does your work entail exactly? All you've told me is that you farm menials.'

'I am in charge of the growing side of things. Do you learn for learning's sake or have you an aim in mind?'

'Does it matter?'

'No, I'm just curious.'

'You're avoiding the matter at hand. Why did you ask for this meeting if you weren't ready to have it?'

'I am ready. I just don't know if you are the person I really want to be having this meeting with. I'm asking questions to help me decide.'

'You want to know if I'm a suitable match for you?'

'In part.'

'Well then. I'll tell you what I think you should know. I am what my mothers made me. I'm naturally curious, I'm very clever, and I'm the best birthing doctor I've ever come across. People think that arranging stud matches is pure science but it's more than that. You need to be able to read people, get a feel for them, see their scope and the possibilities unfolding before them. You have to understand what people are capable of achieving, understand what they want to achieve and where their ambition ends. Beyond that you have to have a clear understanding of the way the world is moving, the way fashions are changing, the thirst and hunger on the In. You have to know the influencers and be an influencer but you can't ever let your input be seen. You are striving to be a conduit for someone else's vision but if their vision is wrong you have to correct it without them knowing. Being a birthing doctor means knowing more than just science. You have to have as broad a mind as you can. And so I learn. I look to other areas and disciplines. I take a lateral approach to my work. I look for the esoteric as well as the obvious. I try to know as much as I can about it all. I learn for learning's sake, but it also has an aim. My mothers made me to be the best. I want to be the best. I work for it. With that in mind, I don't have time for faces. And being this good means I don't need them either. I am accepted and adored without needing to be anything other than what I am. So. Am I the person you want to be meeting with?'

Ducha laughed. The pink of her mouth was almost a shock to Vidya and for a moment she felt a flutter in the pit of her stomach. A phantom feeling.

'Let's eat,' Ducha said and, as if they had never left the room, Ida and Otilie stood before them and led them to the room next door.

The dining room was white but the dining set—glasses, spoons and all—was black. Very theatrical.

'Please, sit,' Ida instructed them. Ducha took the head of the table and Vidya sat on her left. Ida and Otilie took places on Ducha's right and smiled at their 'daughter'.

A menial came into the room and filled their wineglasses. Vidya thought about how red wine in black glass looked like death. She laughed internally, at herself. She was becoming maudlin.

A moment later, a different menial came in with dinner. The borscht was bloodred against the black bowls and the white room.

'This graphic design is a little tacky, don't you think?' Vidya asked before spooning some soup into her mouth. Ducha smiled and Ida frowned playfully.

'Oh come on! It would be a crime not play off our guest's beauty as much as possible. Let's just enjoy the aesthetics.' Otilie slurred a little. Ducha raised a glass in her direction.

'Is this all we're eating or do we have other red foods to enjoy?' Vidya asked.

'Let's just get everything out on the table. We've had you watched since your birth,' Ducha said, and she really looked at Vidya then, eyeball to eyeball, gauging her completely.

Vidya put down her spoon.

'Could you start from the beginning, please?' she asked.

'Yes. I suppose that makes the most sense. Everyone talks in circles these days. It's sometimes hard to remember how to run a conversation start to finish, with all the information and none of the guessing.'

Vidya said nothing to that, so Ducha continued.

'Like I said earlier—the Wanjiku family has been invested in the menial programme almost since its inception. We started with only a small share but we expanded quickly. Now there are a lot of dealerships out there, a lot of farms, but every one of them has Wanjiku backing. We *are* the menial programme. Every specimen is ours. We've reached the limit of our expansion in terms of menials. However, there has been a push for us to expand into other areas. We've always had a close relationship with certain boutique baby developers and your mothers are no exception. I do believe some of our money has gone into developing your enterprise, has it not?' Ducha said, looking at Ida and Otilie. Ida nodded. 'Out of all the baby shops, yours is the best. That said, my people haven't always felt totally comfortable with it. Our involvement with you has never been . . . solid. We've been keeping our options open, watching the baby shops develop, working out how we might want to use them. With that in mind, you, Vidya, have been watched since your birth.'

Vidya nodded.

'Right. And?'

Ducha smiled, a little tightly.

'And so far, I've found you to be the most promising partner. Your mothers did excellent work with both your design and their nurture of you. If anything, you've exceeded our expectations.'

'You're still obfuscating.'

'Yes, well this is where everything gets more difficult to explain.'

'What do you want?'

'Control of your shop.'

'Why? You control the menial output, so why do you need more?'

'Are you asking because you don't know the answer, or because you want to make me say it?'

Vidya liked that. She liked Ducha. She couldn't remember the last time she had liked someone—perhaps she had never liked anyone, or perhaps she had gotten rid of the memory to make room for more important things. It felt good, though. To like someone. And the question Ducha asked helped her make that final leap into the motives behind this coupling.

'You want to become monitors.'

There was an element of danger in saying those words. Vidya knew she shouldn't have spoken them out loud—even secure walls can sometimes hear—but she needed to say it, to see everyone's faces, to know that her understanding was correct. Ida and Otilie were stiff. Ducha was a statue.

'I have a new couple I'm working with,' Vidya said, and her voice felt loud in the stillness of the room. 'If you come to the shop tomorrow I can show you why I'm the best at what I do.'

The first and only order of the day was to finalise a match for ToDdie's child. Vidya set her parameters and let the computer do the rest of the work.

'Is that the Liemann Mann programme?' Ducha asked, as she watched the computer work. Vidya nodded.

'An elegant design. And . . . results in less than a minute,' she said, smiling at her screen. She brought the results out of screen mode and into her AR settings, floating the information up into the air so they could both see it clearly as she navigated to the prospective dam and sifted through her details first:

Name: Bambi Gallo
DoB: 30/06/20__
Conception: Stud 胡 centre.
    Dam: <u>Adriana Williams</u>
    Sire: <u>Aristotle Agato</u>
    Parent: <u>Charly Chalmers</u>

'The Hú centre? You use their progeny?' Ducha asked.

'Sometimes. Not often and I try and use one-offs . . .' Vidya tapped on Adriana Williams and looked at her conception status:

Conception: Stud 胡 centre.
    Dam: <u>Therese Therese</u>
    Sire: <u>William Brown</u>

Vidya tapped Therese.

Conception: BB VANKO

'There—see that,' she pointed out to Ducha. 'I knew Adriana didn't feel right. Beaker baby from the Vanko centre. Definitely undesirable. Not good enough for any of my clients—even the unimportant ones.'

'So, what do you do at this point?'

'Well, I ran the details through Liemann's programme to get a wide view. I'll run them through a few more times and narrow the options. Usually I end up with stock that comes from this shop, the St Clair shop or the Shahs. And then I run those options through some extrapolation programmes to see possible trajectories for off-spring.'

'Why don't you just go straight to those shops for stock in the first place?'

'I like to keep the pool as wide as possible in the first instance—it gives me greater scope for unique creations. And there are hidden gems out there. I wouldn't trust someone that didn't approach their work with an open mind. One of the reasons I'm so good is because I put the work in; I believe I juggle more possible combinations than any other baby doctor.'

'Everyone in the boutique baby shop field believes they're the best, you know.'

'They may believe it, but I'm the only one that's actually right.'

'What makes you so sure?'

'My results. Here. Let me take you through a list of people from my shop.'

When Ducha left, Vidya began to work in earnest. Come day's end she had narrowed her options somewhat—a fairly impressive list of predominantly Mediterranean-styled breeds—but there was still a long way to go; there was only so much she could do in a day. She left her office and went to stretch out in her gym. On the train ride home she completed some of her Portuguese exercises. When she got into her flat she felt both stiff and mentally blank. Thinking back, she realised that she had lost focus several hours ago. Everything in her head was about Ducha. All she wanted to do was to talk about her with someone.

Vidya laughed at herself. Talk to someone? That meant only one thing. It was time to get out the old journal.

Vidya's parents were very clear with her right from the start. They gave her a list of rules, which they taped above her cot. Of course, it took until she was in a proper bed to be able to understand them and by then they had been stuck to her bedroom door:

- Don't talk to people in confidence—not even your mothers.
- Don't keep an online journal.
- Don't talk to a confessor.
- Don't join forums.
- Don't commit anything to the In.

These were rules to live by and they served her well, but there were some things you just had to talk about. Vidya decided to keep a journal at the tender age of six. It was secret, as journals should be. Even then she was prudent, making sure her eyes weren't recording as she wrote. She started out in English but soon thought of changing languages periodically. It wasn't long before she simply wrote in a code of her own. By this point journalling was more of an intellectual exercise than a necessity, and after a while she tired of it. But there are always some things you just have to talk about. . . .

Vidya retrieved her journal. The last entry had been two years ago; an issue with the mothers. She stretched the spine of the book back and laid it out flat on her writing desk.

'Like a patient etherised upon a table,' she muttered.

Two blank pages gleamed up at her. So she sat down, turned off the recording function in her eyes, took out her pen, and began to write a scrawl of ink and drips and drops, a black mess of thought. As she wrote she began to feel good again.

Ducha doesn't operate in the same world as the rest of us. I want to ask her more, to find out how she was raised, what her child-hood was like. What does living a life unseen do to a person? I feel it could only have been a good thing. And yet she's not careless. She keeps much hidden, as if she were under eyes. But then even she can't escape the monitors. Stupid to think otherwise, my mind is sluggish today.

  Something about her agitates me. I can't put my finger on what it is. Her face crops up in my thoughts at the oddest of moments. She surprises me. It puts me in mind of that boy . . . What was he? Who, rather? I think I wrote about him all those years ago. I must have been about twelve. I remember he was very unimpor-tant. And that he was very beautiful. Is that all it is? I'm being swayed by a pretty face? Pretty? Insulting, I suppose. Ducha doesn't belong to words. Listen to me! I need to exorcise this, whatever it is. But I have a feeling that Ducha and I are going to continue down this path. Her plan . . . is it hers? Or is she simply a tool? I need to meet her people. To do that, I have to commit to this . . . Is it crazy? To take on the monitors?

I think part of me has never really believed in them. Not that I didn't think they existed, the evidence is, well, evident. But the idea of them being ordinary creatures. One of us. Someone you might pass in a queue, or see on a train. And what are they really achieving? What do they want? On a surface level, I understand but . . . why bother? The thought of it all exhausts me. But if I go on with Ducha, that's what I'm agreeing to. Do they really exist?

She certainly knows more than me, about the way this world of ours works. I believe her. I think I believe in her too. There's something there. I feel like if she wanted to she could achieve anything. From an academic perspective it would be fascinating to observe.

When she smiles I find it hard to breathe. It's like she freezes all functions. Will the muddling pass? If it doesn't, I'll be useless.

But to know more! She is opening a door into a room I never dared think about. There is so much more I could learn—things that I could never access from this side of that door. The question is—will I lose my wits on the way through? I'm taking this metaphor too far. Another sign of my limited functionality right now.

This is a gamble. Intellectual curiosity is driving me to her, but I worry about my state of mind. Perhaps making a decision will make a difference—that has certainly been the case in the past.

IO are thirsty for this. I wonder what they think they will gain. I wonder . . . They seem less put together these days. O has been in decline for quite some time, but I? I'm not sure if she's seeing clearly anymore either. Is it age?

What I need is to talk to Ducha. Properly. Without boundaries. An impossible thing. Not without choosing first. Seeing her today, how alive to the work she seemed. A match—I think—if ever I'd wanted one. She's made for this. She has the same desire to know things that I do. Made like me. Made by IO. Really, we could be sisters. That beautiful creature was made like me. The thought is . . . unsettling? Exciting? Like I said, she agitates me. Agitating is the best word for her. If we do this, there is no turning back. Will we be agitators? I like the sound of that. I feel I have been passive for too long. Receptive in all things. It is time to do something with all I have inside me. Something more. We all make our grooves and run through them. It's time to change. Isn't it? It is.

The bell rang, and Vidya felt it was strangely on cue, as if whoever it was knew that she had reached the end of her writing. She put the journal away, switched her recording function back on and went to see who it was.

As Vidya approached the door, she was alarmed to see it already opening.

'Hey! What the—'

A man stepped inside and held a hand up, and there was something about the way he stood, the way he gestured to her, that made her stop.

'Vidya Wójcik, I need you to come with me.'

'Who are you?'

The man smiled.

'Please, come with me,' he said, and he held her door open and waited for her to acquiesce. Perhaps it was his absolute certainty that she would that made her do it, but as she found herself outside and stepping into a waiting car, Vidya felt that everything was wrong. This was not who she was. She was not the acquiescing type. She tried to open the car door and jump out, to go back into her home, but by now the door was locked and the car began to move. She closed her eyes, looking for an AR connection to the In, but the car was a dark zone.

Alone in the back, she had no one to ask about what was going on.

'What's going on?' she asked herself out loud, as if maybe making it a conversation would help her work it out on her own. 'What's going on?'

There was no answer.

'What's going on?' she asked again, once the car stopped and she was outside, in the custody of the man who had ushered her out of her home. He did not answer her. Vidya knew there was no reason to ask again. She made another attempt to connect to the In, though she was not surprised to find a void where her AR facilities would be.

She saw she was in a covered car park. There was nothing that disclosed location. She was guided towards a set of doors and found herself in a bright building, all artificial lights and cream interiors. Clinical but not blinding. A lift hushed open and her guide indicated she should enter. She did.

'When you reach your floor, follow the lights, please,' the man said from outside the lift.

'Wait, how do I—' It was too late. The doors hushed closed and Vidya felt the lift go up. There were no floors as far as she could see, but she felt she was climbing high. The door hushed open again. Lights shone in the walls at ankle height, marking out a path that led her to her right. At the end of the passage, she turned left and followed the lights to the door at the end of the corridor. The door opened silently as she approached. She stepped in. The room was cream and chrome and there were a table and two chairs. The ceiling glowed with a soft light—clean and bright. There was nothing else.

Vidya sat. She checked the time in the top right corner of her eyeline—2253. A minute passed. Then another. Five minutes passed. As the sixth minute passed into the seventh the door opened and someone walked in.

'Dr Wójcik.' The person sat down in the chair opposite her. They were so beautiful, so perfect in their androgyny that, in spite of herself, she asked:

'What baby shop did *you* come from?'

The person smiled openly, and this genuine show of amusement on their face sent a thrill through Vidya. It was disarming.

'I'm afraid you're going to leave here with most of your questions unanswered, Dr Wójcik.'

'Where is here?' Vidya asked. The smile before her grew a little. 'Who are you?'

'I'm what you might call a monitor. I believe you have a rough idea about us and what we do; it's actually far less than you think, I imagine. You'd be surprised by how many people do our job for us.

But we are in charge of keeping an eye on things. Making sure things run smoothly.'

'And why am I here?'

'For a chat!' The smile was now just shy of a grin.

'About . . .'

'I understand you've spent some time with Ducha Wanjiku, recently.' It wasn't a question.

'Yes.'

'You're thinking about coupling with her.'

'It's been discussed.'

'You've shown no interest in coupling before. Why the sudden interest?'

Vidya didn't like this. She didn't like not having time to think, needing to answer, to keep things pleasant.

'It's not that I haven't had an interest in coupling before, I've just been disinclined to take the offers I've had.'

'So why this offer?'

'Our families have a history.'

'I think we all know that has no bearing on this decision.'

'Do all of us know that?' Vidya asked, pointedly looking around the empty room.

There was a full grin before her now.

'The Wanjikus are a very important family. It's a good choice for you.'

'Why is this of any concern for the monitors?'

'You needn't be coy. You know why we're interested.'

And she knew the monitor was right. There was no need to hide anything. They knew everything already.

'What do you want from me?'

'As I said—the Wanjikus are a very important family. We would like them to continue being an important family. We would like them to keep doing exactly what they have been doing since they became a very important family. We would like them to enjoy their position in our society. We would like you to enjoy your position in society. Ducha Wanjiku is a good choice for you.'

Vidya nodded.

'Excellent.' The monitor stood up.

'Hold on.'

'Yes?'

'How did you know? I mean . . . I was so careful. It wasn't me, was it?'

Another smile—a kind one.

'You could take all the care in the world, but how private do you think private is?' The monitor's voice was soft, as if saying the news gently would make the news itself gentle.

'But I even turned off the recording function.'

'Did you?'

There was nothing to say to that. Vidya stood up and exited the room. The monitor walked her back to the lift. As they reached it the doors hushed open and Vidya walked in.

'There will be someone to meet you downstairs,' the monitor told her.

'Wait.' Vidya held her hand over the lift door. 'I have one more question.'

'Yes?'

'What baby shop *are* you from?'

The monitor grinned and, without a trace of distaste, they reached forwards and took Vidya's hand. They eased it away from the lift door so that it could close.

'I'm not from any baby shop,' they said.

The doors hushed closed.

Vidya was afraid to think. She knew reading thoughts was impossible but, on the other hand, was it? Did she really know anything about what some people were capable of?

'I turned the recording function off,' she said out loud to her empty flat. 'I—' and Vidya looked at her hand then. The hand the monitor had so cavalierly moved for her. Vidya could remember the cool skin on hers, a little dry and papery, but skin all the same. Skin to skin. But of course, why would they care?

'You're above all things, aren't you?' Vidya said. 'You can do anything you like.' She looked around the flat. 'And me? Even if I live honest, I live designed, don't I? Don't worry. I understand what I'm supposed to do.'

She flexed her hand and studied the skin on the back of it. It was unchanged. Of course it was unchanged. Her hand was unchanged but now her life was entirely different.

A message alert pulsed in her eyeline. Ducha. She knew she had to look at it but it was the last thing she wanted to do now.

Ducha: Call I0.

Vidya grunted. If anything, she wanted to talk to her mothers even less than she wanted to talk to Ducha.

She tapped in the contacts and connected with Ida.

'Darling! Where are you?' Ida asked.

'At home.'

'At home? Why?'

'Because I live here, and I'm tired, and I want to stay at home.'

'But we need you. *Now.*' Ida cut the connection. That was how it worked with her. So Vidya got up, got ready and left.

Ida and Otilie were still living in their white space. Its clean bright surfaces made Vidya flinch as she stepped inside.

'Hello?'

'Finally!' Otilie slurred, and she poked her head out of a room to Vidya's right. 'Come in. Let's get this show on the road.'

Vidya followed her into a living room—this one different from the one they had used the last time she had come. The room was all red and there, in the middle of it, sat Ducha, cross-legged on a cushion on the floor. Ida sat beside her.

'Vidya,' Ducha said, smiling with all her teeth. She gestured to a cushion beside her.

'Is this your place or my mothers'?' Vidya asked. Ducha permitted herself a small chuckle.

'Well, if this goes the way I hope it will, then what's mine is yours and what's yours is mine,' she said, addressing them all. Ida was smiling pointedly at Vidya. 'So. This brings me to the point. What is your decision about our partnership?'

'Yes,' Vidya muttered. Best to get it over with. There was no way out of it. 'My decision is yes. Yes to everything.'

'Are you sure?' Ducha asked, and the trace of concern in her voice made Vidya look up at her. Seeing that beautiful hopeful face made her sad. She nodded.

'I'm sure.' After all, it was all she could do.

'Excellent!' said Ida, clapping her hands together.

A loud pop came from the corner of the room and there was Otilie, pouring out champagne, spilling as much as she served.

'It doesn't match the decor but on an occasion like this . . . perfect,' she said as she handed Vidya a glass and grinned at her. 'Our little girl has always been so smart!' Vidya couldn't tell if Otilie was being sarcastic or not. What did she know? But then she was just a lush, really. What could she know? She might have been great once, but Ida was the only thing that kept her going. Vidya wondered if that was love. But, of course, it didn't matter.

'Perfect,' Vidya said as she clinked glasses with the others. 'Just perfect.'

After the decision had been made, and the knowledge of how things would proceed from now on had settled, Vidya was more focussed on her work than ever. And the one thing on her roster was ToDdie's baby.

It took her three days to find both a dam and a sire that she was happy with. Once that was taken care of it was a simple matter of insemination.

When Vidya finished the job, she looked at the dam, lying there, legs spread. No matter how many times she did this, she always marvelled at how any woman could offer their stud services. It was fine for men, they had the easy job, but these women were not only giving up nine months for some unknowns—they were participating in some of the most intimate physical contact you could have. How were there any women in this line of work at all?

Vidya knew that many different reasons drove women to farm themselves out. Most of those were financial. But now she wondered if there wasn't more to it than that. Perhaps the monitors had something to do with it. Perhaps the monitors had everything to do with it.

'Am I done here?' the dam asked.

'Yes, of course. Get cleaned up and we'll show you to your room. This is your second child, isn't it?'

The woman nodded.

'Good. You know the drill then.'

Tonia did not seem happy when Vidya delivered the news of the pregnancy to them. Eduardo did his best to cover for her, but it came as no surprise when he contacted Vidya later and said he was worried about his partner.

'I don't know if she's ready for this. I don't even know if I am.'

'You will be. You have nine months to get ready.'

'How can you be sure?'

'I've been doing this for a pretty long time,' Vidya said with a smile. She decided she liked Eduardo. He seemed to have a natural talent for honesty.

'And Tonia?'

'She could be ready. Easily. But she'll probably need a little help to get there.'

'What can I do?'

'I'm not sure you can do much. I think she should see a specialist.'

'What?'

'I encounter this kind of thing a lot, so naturally we retain a psychiatrist on staff. It's all very normal. It may seem frightening at first, but it could do a world of good.'

'I . . . I don't know about that. I don't think that's right for us.'

Vidya opened her hands, a kind of peacekeeping gesture.

'Just think it over. Talk it over. If you decide you want to try it, I'll book you in. If you don't want to do it then there are always confession booths on the In.'

'Which do you think is better?'

'Confessors aren't professionals. They don't offer advice, and most of them wouldn't understand the situation on a specialised level. They're just there to listen.'

'I'll talk to Tonia,' Eduardo said.

'How was work?' Ducha asked, when Vidya got home.

'Fine,' said Vidya.

Of course everything would always be fine as they wandered through the lives chosen for them, controlled by an invisible hand. It would always be fine. Vidya sighed and sat down. She thought perhaps she could study. Nothing to lose and nothing to gain.

The call from Schuyler was a surprise this time. Vidya hadn't thought about him in quite some time, having wrapped up her work with ToDdie, and what with all the time she was spending with Ducha.

'How have you been?' she asked him. He looked tense.

'Fair to middling,' he replied.

'And what can I do for you today? I assume you're calling for another favour.'

Schuyler affected a hurt look.

'You wound me,' he said. 'Can't I just call for conversation?'

'Well, I suppose there's a first time for everything,' Vidya said. 'But let's not pretend.'

Schuyler nodded.

'I had a weird chat with Naomi just now. She's . . . getting worked up about something. To be honest, I wasn't sure how to handle it and it's something that probably shouldn't get out. I thought of you. You expressed some interest in her and I thought perhaps you might talk to her.'

'Could you give me a bit more than that?'

Schuyler gave her a somewhat smug smile.

'I seem to remember that you like surprises. I think if you give her a call you might be surprised.'

Vidya wasn't sure she could be surprised by anything anymore but the prospect was intriguing. She smiled back at him and nodded.

'I have some time on my hands. I'll call her.'

She cut her connection with Schuyler. Naomi. Last time she had checked on her the girl was doing surprisingly well with what superficially seemed like quite an unimaginative face. Vidya noticed the little tweaks and nuances Naomi had affected that had given her face a boost. Smart little changes to acts that could have come off cliché. It had impressed her. Naomi had taken a less-is-more approach instead of trying to impress with numerous different identities, and Vidya liked that. It was the kind of approach that dovetailed with her own. Schuyler had said she was 'getting worked up about something' . . .

Vidya got herself a drink and settled down on her best chair. She wanted to be comfortable. She scrolled through her patch, found Naomi's ID and gave her a vid call.

Naomi picked up quickly. She had control of her expression, her eyes narrowed in what could be considered suspicion—or maybe just fatigue—and she'd set her jaw, somewhat aggressively. It was beautiful on her and Vidya took a moment to appreciate the aesthetics she had helped conjure into being—the perfectly blended brown skin (as if she really was half Schuyler and half Madeleine), the tawny natural hair that Naomi had allowed to grow into a cloud around her head, and those hard honey-brown eyes that were staring at her just a shade shy of angrily.

'Schuyler said you wanted to talk to me,' Vidya told her, and she dropped her head back a little into the soft cushions behind her, matching Naomi's aggression with a show of nonchalance. 'He said I might be surprised.'

Naomi's expression faltered and for a second she just looked scared. The vulnerability was so charming, Vidya didn't want to lose it. She laughed, catching Naomi's attention.

'Don't worry about face. It slows things down,' she said. 'What d'you need?'

Vidya could see her mind working as she weighed up the situation. It was an expression she was used to. Her clients made it every time she challenged their face. It was delightful to see how quickly the moment passed as Naomi took a leap of faith and said:

'I started a project awhile ago, looking at menials.'

Schuyler had been right. Vidya was surprised.

'They confess, you know?' Naomi told her. 'I run a confessional and menials will come in and confess to all kinds of things I'd never have thought them capable of thinking about.'

So this was what she was getting worked up about. Vidya didn't think she'd ever have guessed. She never spent time thinking about menials at all, at least not beyond their flaws. Confessions? The thought was surprisingly exciting.

'Really? Like what?' she prompted Naomi.

'There's been quite a range but one thing that comes up a lot is a need for physical self-gratification. I was wondering about that for a while. Many of them bring up the fact that they masturbate and that it's something they aren't supposed to do and I've come to the conclusion that it's less about the physical feelings than the sense of taking some kind of ownership over themselves. I mean every aspect of their lives is controlled. Of course this is armchair psychology and really the more I learn . . .'

'The more you realise you don't know,' Vidya finished for her.

'Exactly!' Naomi smiled. She looked so relieved to be understood. She was so wasted in her family, SchAddie had no idea.

'You know, I tried talking to Schuyler about you once,' Vidya said, wondering if she could bait Naomi into a different conversation. 'You're much more interesting than he thinks you are.'

For an instant Naomi looked like she was going to follow the new thread being offered to her but then Vidya saw that slight shake of the head.

'Do you know anything about menial training?' she asked. Fair enough. Vidya would follow her instead.

'It's never really been my field of interest. I prefer making perfect people instead of imperfect ones.' Vidya wasn't sure where she hoped Naomi would go next.

'But are they really imperfect?'

'Of course they are.'

'How are you so certain?'

Vidya pressed farther back into her chair, really sinking in. She thought about all the things she could say. Wondered what she should say. Wondered what she was supposed to say. . . . She imagined what would happen depending on which words she said next. She looked at Naomi. She was so alive to the questions she was asking. So curious and interested. So beautifully unselfconscious. And Vidya didn't know what to do.

Well. She rarely indulged in faceplay, so what was the point in doing it now? She decided not to think too much and go with her gut.

'You won't have heard about this because it's all happening behind closed doors, but I'm about to couple.'

Naomi was surprised and she started to flounder trying to think of what to say. Not interested in the platitudes she might dredge up, Vidya cut her off with a wave of a hand, bringing Naomi's focus back to her.

'I'm not actually allowed to talk about it, so I'll keep certain things vague, but the person I'm attaching myself to is in the menial-farming business. And, naturally, we've talked about menials. How they're developed. The science behind it. It isn't a million miles away from my own work though the menial programme lacks a certain refinement.'

Vidya knew she had said more than she should have, but she had hoped perhaps her words would draw Naomi onto safer ground. Baby making. Things Vidya really knew about.

'Could you get me into a training facility?' Naomi asked, skewering that hope.

'No.'

'And you can't tell me anything about your prospective partner. Why?'

'Because it maintains the proper order of things.'

'Can you at least tell me what you know about menials?'

'What are you trying to find out?'

Naomi started talking and Vidya was surprised by her thoughtfulness. Her focus on something totally other and beyond herself. She seemed to really care about the subclass and the way she spoke about them, raw and unplanned, made Vidya want to agree with her. But everything Naomi was saying and asking—about personhood, about fair treatment, about hierarchy—went against the natural order. Vidya wanted to laugh. If Naomi had had this conversation with her eight months ago, she might have found an ally in Vidya.

'Why do we make them, keep them, force them to be the way they are?' Naomi asked her.

Vidya sighed. She knew she couldn't give Naomi any good answers. Her eyes strayed to her hand and she remembered the monitor's touch. She wondered whether, if Naomi knew how things really were, she would care about menials.

'I can only tell you what I think,' she told Naomi.

'So, tell me what you think.'

'I think that ever since the very beginning, we have been afraid of ourselves and of each other and of the whole world. And we've been fighting that fear by trying to take control of everything around us. It manifests in all sorts of ways but the most relentless and insidious part of all this is the way we constantly try and control other people. On the most innocuous level we do it with our faces. Manipulating what people think of us by showing them what we want them to see and making it as difficult as possible for them to see through the masks. And on the most damaging level we've done it by actively subjugating people to our will and forcing them to do our bidding. The high that comes from that must be even better than training an animal to do tricks. You take a thinking feeling human being and you strip them of their personhood and make them yours. That's an ultimate sort of power. And our world is built on hierarchy. You can't enjoy your power if you don't have anyone to overpower. History is littered with cultures of oppression. People deciding that others were beneath them for arbitrary reasons, and then forcing those "others" to work for them in the harshest and most degrading ways. But we've evolved now. We don't have to choose a people to make "other". We simply make people. If anything, the menial system is more humane.'

For a moment, Vidya had her. Naomi was ready to agree, perhaps ready to drop the topic. But then Vidya saw that slight shake of the head again.

'How is it more humane?'

'Well, the menials are built for purpose. You said it yourself— they're simple, stupid. And biologically they're imperfect; they begin to degrade quite early.'

'But surely building them that way is inhumane?'

'Is it inhumane if they aren't aware of it?'

'But they are aware of it. On some level, they understand what they are and where they stand.'

'How can you be sure about that?'

It was a cheating question and Naomi knew it, wouldn't let Vidya get away with it, was determined to present the other side as clearly as she could. The argument was getting deeper than Vidya wanted it to. She attempted to wave away Naomi's frustration with her.

'I'm not really trying to argue with you on the humanity of it all. I don't really like the whole menial culture myself. I'm just trying to put it into some historical perspective.'

'Well, that's all very well, but just because you might think the menial system is more humane than previous systems doesn't make it right.'

'No,' Vidya conceded. 'It doesn't.'

'So?'

'So what?' Vidya willed Naomi to drop the subject.

'What can we do about it? It isn't right. It shouldn't be this way. It isn't—'

'Fair?' Vidya cut her off. She wanted to end this conversation now, but she felt she owed Naomi a good ending. One that didn't leave her totally lost.

'Naomi, nothing has ever been fair. You should just be glad you're at the level you're at where, as long as you maintain your facevalue, you can pretty much lie back and coast through life.'

'But what's the point in that?' Naomi asked. 'Why can't I do something? Why can't I try and make things fair?'

'You *can* try and make things fair. You can try and do anything and everything you want to. You're a rich, intelligent, resourceful young woman and you can try and put all of those things to use. I just don't want you to get your hopes up. Because you aren't the first person to wake up and start thinking all these things. The world is a very old place and it's seen its fair share of revolutionaries. But at the end of the day . . . well, look around.'

She almost had her now. She was struggling under the weight of Vidya's argument.

'But . . .' Naomi attempted.

'But?'

'But it doesn't have to be someone like me. It could be someone like you.'

Fuck.

'You could change things,' Naomi said. 'Your partner is a bloody menial farmer. You could influence them.'

Vidya shook her head.

'Why not?' Naomi asked her. Why not indeed? What could Vidya tell her? That she was trapped? That although her life was infinitely more comfortable, she was about as free as a menial at the end of the day?

'You don't know what you're asking me because you don't really understand the magnitude of it all,' she said.

'What am I missing?'

'Oh Naomi,' Vidya sighed. 'I'm sorry. I'm sorry to disappoint you. I don't think I can take this conversation any further. I'm under certain . . . obligations . . .'

Vidya heard the door of her flat open and her stomach dropped with dread. For a moment she was sure the monitors had come back.

'Vidya?' Ducha called from the entrance hall, and Vidya almost laughed with relief. She turned back to her vid.

'It's getting late. But, Naomi?' Even as she opened her mouth to say her next words she was warning herself to stop. The words kept coming, though:

'I know I told you not to get your hopes up, but if you want to do more you should.' What the fuck was she saying? She knew she should stop there, but she didn't want to. When she looked at Naomi she felt hopeful.

'Don't let anyone stop you,' she said. 'Schuyler never really understood what I gave him when I made you, but you're a remarkable girl. You should follow your instincts. I'm sorry, but that's all I have time for. Are you okay?'

Naomi nodded.

'Maybe we'll talk again someday,' Vidya said. She smiled at her and cut the call.

'What are you doing?' Ducha asked, walking into Vidya's bedroom.

'I was just finishing up a call.'

'Anyone interesting?'

'Not really,' Vidya lied. She didn't want to get into it. But . . . 'Ducha?'

'Yes?'

'Do you think maybe I could learn a bit more about the menial programme?'

Ducha was surprised.

'I thought you found the work lacking sophistication,' she said.

Vidya smiled at her.

'It is. But perhaps . . . well, maybe I could offer some tweaks here and there. After all, you're learning about the boutique side of breeding.'

Ducha gave her a flat look.

'You know how I feel about the menial formula.'

Vidya raised her hands.

'I promise I'm not going to try to change your system.' She was sure she couldn't even if she tried.

(Menial 63700578—Jake)

Madeleine had been organising the party for months. It was important that she pull out all the stops and yet the whole affair had to feel casual and almost spontaneous. Jake enjoyed watching her work. She was remarkable.

A lot of second-rate people arrived first. That's how Madeleine had described them. Jake had listened as she to'd and fro'd over who to invite.

'Second-*rate* people? But then the extra numbers *will* give us *just* the right dy*nam*ics for when the top-tiers arrive!' she had said, her beautiful voice resonating around the flat.

The first tops to arrive at the party were Schuyler's friends, Tonia and Eduardo, although calling them tops was 'a stretch', Madeleine had said. Jake let them in and took their coats. They made a valiant effort not to look at him but he caught Tonia's eye as she handed him her coat. And handing him the coat was very different from just discarding it, or flinging it in Jake's direction. She handed it to him, almost as if they were on the same level. Shocking behaviour.

He hung up their garments with habitual care.

'You,' Jake heard, and he turned to find Schuyler right behind him. That familiar urge to do something violent came over him. He clamped his jaw and bowed his head, surprised at how difficult it was to master himself.

'Drinks. Four,' Schuyler said. And then he stood there. It was as though he were waiting for something. Jake nodded, kept his eyes down, willed Schuyler to walk away. When he did, Jake went to the kitchen to retrieve some cocktails. Fielding drinks wasn't his job today. The Burroughses had brought in extra menials to cater the party and Jake was meant to stay at the door. But Jake didn't care that he was meant to stay at the door. He was getting Madeleine a drink. That was much more important.

Jake was walking the drinks up to the four tops when the door buzzer rang. Madeleine spun around and looked him right in the eye. It was the first time she had ever really looked at him and it was all he could do to keep his tray steady. He couldn't avert his eyes. He was committing every detail of hers to his memory. They were dark brown and heavily lashed: big, liquid, almond shaped, enticing.

'What are you doing? Why isn't anyone by the door? I told you earlier that I don't want to hear that buzzer go tonight.' Her voice broke through his swimming thoughts and he bowed and retreated. As he walked away he heard her say:

'It's *amazing* how they still seem to slip up every so often.'

He almost smiled as he thought about slipping his arms around her.

Jake didn't leave the door for the rest of the party.

Raised voices weren't a common occurrence in the Burroughs household. All four members avoided extended periods of contact with one another and when such periods were unavoidable they were all very good at keeping their cool. Both Reyna and Naomi took beta blockers on a daily basis. This was considered cheating, but there was no reason for anyone to know they were doing it. Besides, most people did it. Even Madeleine. The only person Jake had never seen using was Schuyler. There was something superhuman about Schuyler's ease in every situation. There was something smug. Jake wasn't sure he had more than one volume to his voice. Until he heard raised voices.

'I don't know what you're so upset about!' Madeleine said. Even in anger her voice was caramel.

'Oh, don't pretend naiveté,' Schuyler said; his voice was still low but there was a gruffness to it that made it seem louder.

'I was *being* helpful.'

'You were trivialising them to make yourself more important. When are you going to realise that at our level, *that doesn't work!*'

'I don't understand why you care so much!'

'Your face is my face!' said Schuyler. 'I can't have you reducing me to some simple little . . .'

'What? Say it! What am I reducing you to?'

'The way you grasp for advantage, it's like you've never even seen the top. You're cheap, Maddie. I knew that when I met you but you just get cheaper as the years go by.'

If Madeleine spoke, Jake couldn't hear it. He left his room, walked out onto the landing and looked down into the dining room below.

Madeleine was sitting at the head of the table. Her hands were clasped in front of her, the grip tight. She looked down at them and Jake couldn't see the expression on her face. Schuyler stood, looking at her. His own face was relaxed into raw 'Schuyler'—a clear expression of disappointment and disgust. It was the first time Jake had ever seen someone show their 'true' face. Schuyler was magnetic and repulsive, and Jake couldn't look away.

'You're not stupid,' Schuyler said. 'You must have known how I felt. I haven't been hiding from you, I—'

'God, I know! You've done anything *but* hide!' Madeleine's voice dragged at Jake's focus. He saw she was looking up now, looking at Schuyler. Her face was set, stiff, the control visible. She was straining to keep it straight and that was a shock for Jake.

'Enjoying the entertainment?' a voice asked, making Jake jump. It took all he had not to blush at being startled and he turned to look at Naomi. She eyed him and he eyed her back.

'I could have you fired for looking at me, you know?' she told him. He nodded. 'Can you speak?' He nodded again. 'Well?' He looked at her, blankly. 'Are you enjoying the entertainment?' she asked.

Jake looked down into the dining room again. Madeleine and Schuyler had their eyes fixed on each other. They weren't saying anything. It was as though by appearing beside him Naomi had triggered a pause button. But then Madeleine sagged where she sat. She turned back to the table, to her clasped hands, and she sighed.

'I don't know what you want,' she said. She spoke quietly but her words still carried up to them.

'She's an idiot,' Naomi said.

'No,' said Jake, his voice clear. Not loud, but clear.

'No?' said Naomi, perhaps a little surprised, but it was always hard to tell with her.

Jake didn't say anything else. He just watched Madeleine as she stared at her hands and struggled to keep her expression set.

Tam

Face

It hadn't taken long for Tam to realise that he did not belong where he was. He was only six when he asked his parents about his lineage and they were more or less unhelpful. It wasn't that they didn't understand what he was asking them—they just didn't understand that he was smart enough to understand everything they could tell him.

Taolin and Tegan had an irritating habit of talking down to him, as if his age and his IQ were the same. By rights they should have had a beaker baby—that was basically all they could afford—but they had won a lottery on the In. They could go to stud, free of charge. Tam found this out when he hacked into their In feeds, aged seven. The stud they had won into was the Vanko baby shop and, after some research, Tam realised that Taolin and Tegan had won not one lottery, but two. The Vanko shop had a shady reputation; there was no telling what kind of kid you would get out of them. But Tam was a beautiful specimen. One in a million. He did not belong where he was. And that left him with only one option. He had to climb up.

Taolin and Tegan did the best they could with what they had, but they were a far cry from the role models Tam longed for. So he spent his time on the In, learning about hierarchy, studying people on each rung of the ladder in the hopes of being able to distil the one basic necessity that could raise him up to a station in which he belonged. And then he found Schuyler Burroughs.

There was a man to model himself on! It was one of Tam's more embarrassing secrets that between the ages of eight and eleven he played pretend. The pretend was always the same. Schuyler Burroughs would spot Tam on the street and recognise himself in the boy. It would hit him so hard he wouldn't be able to turn aside or ignore him. He would have to know who Tam was, and in so doing he would realise that this boy—this child of unknown genetic material— was actually his. He would take Tam under his wing and teach him everything he knew about being perfect. This was Tam's great pretend. And for a while he really did believe that perhaps, secretly, he might actually share blood with Schuyler.

Nonsense, of course. They had the same rich black skin but Tam's face was less fine featured, and he had what he considered a hideous cleft in his chin. There was no way they shared blood. There was no way Schuyler's genetic material would be available to an enterprise like Vanko's anyhow.

The pretend was far-fetched but Tam knew that if he wanted to get ahead he would have to be more like Schuyler Burroughs in every respect. So he followed him. It wasn't always easy—Schuyler's In footprint was small and that was part of his appeal. And there was lesson one for Tam. Be unavailable. Of course, being unavailable meant little when no one knew you existed but he had to start as he meant to go on. So he kept his profiles secure, he kept the bare minimum of information on each platform he used (and he used few) and he insisted on going to physical school. The best way to learn the true art of face was to be out there, face-to-face with humanity.

This was Tam's true beginning.

Physical school was a challenge. One Tam enjoyed. How do you make an impact when you are trying to show you don't want to make an impact? How do you make people want you without announcing yourself as there, present, rich, interesting?

It was an intricate puzzle and Tam felt as though he had to make most of the pieces himself. But there was Schuyler Burroughs to emulate. Tam pored over any video footage he could get of the man. He read his body over and over again until he knew exactly how to hold himself, how to walk and how to stand. He spent hours in front of the mirror practicing smiles, one for every occasion. He recorded himself talking and played himself over and over again, working out where his modulation was off, trying to redesign his voice. He worked out, took care of his skin, hydrated, shopped carefully, made sure he was as beautiful as he could possibly be.

He bided his time. Patience was key. And it worked. Slowly slowly slowly, he began to feel eyes on him. He heard questions asked, peer to peer, no one quite brave enough to ask him—the unknown entity—

anything directly. Stories started to grow around him. He confirmed and denied nothing. He just kept going about his business the way he always had. He was mystery, style and power. At least at PS 323. And for a moment that was enough. But just for a moment.

The Burroughs family had a beautiful aesthetic. Of course. Schuyler and Madeleine were complementary contrasts; Schuyler was strong and dark—black skin, black hair, deep dark eyes—and Madeleine was a willowy woman with milky white skin and auburn hair. They were both graceful. Linking their looks together were their two 'daughters'. The younger girl, Naomi, looked like she really could have been theirs, with her brown skin and her hair curling into a natural afro, but she wasn't built like Madeleine or Schuyler; she was small and wiry. In the photos Tam had seen of her, she always looked dissatisfied. Reyna, also small, was quite different. She had clearly come from Far Eastern stock, and she always looked like a mystery.

When Tam started following Madeleine Burroughs he was disappointed. She was beautiful but vapid. She had none of Schuyler's class. Tam could only assume that his hero had married her as a joke. He wasn't sure he got the punch line and that was another reason why he had to work harder and climb higher. There was only so much he could learn from Schuyler at a distance. He longed to get closer to him but, boroughs away from anything fashionable, Tam knew it was virtually impossible. He clung to that word 'virtually'.

He tried to deep-dive into Schuyler's In presence but there were blocks everywhere—he was well protected. There was no hope of finding a way to the man directly, there was no dirt he could dig up, no information he could mine. So he started to investigate him from a lateral perspective.

Naomi was high tier simply because of the circumstance of her birth. She was static, making no attempt to develop her presence or define herself out with the family. She came across as a nothing type of person. Nothing about her piqued the interest. Nothing about her sang. But Reyna was perfect. She was everything Tam could be if he had the right kind of help. If Tam could get a line on her . . . Of course, as soon as he thought the thought he got to work. It was a long game, but worth it.

Planning his way into Reyna's world was remarkably simple. After all, she was everywhere. She had profiles every which way he looked, and once he collated them properly and read between the lines, he started to get a pretty clear picture of who the real girl was.

Tam saw her as a shark. She didn't make friends, she hardly made connections, and she spun profiles as though her life depended on it—keep swimming or sink. Her In presence hardly coincided with any of her family. She was making an effort to stay isolated. The closest thing she had to an ally was a girl called Genevieve. Genevieve was as beautiful and brutal as Reyna herself, and the alliance seemed prudent—support each other or eat each other. If Reyna were to couple with anyone, Tam was certain it would be Genevieve. They even looked like a perfect pair with their almost-matching, delicate Asian features. But Reyna was on the record as being anti-partnering. And if Reyna wasn't looking for a partner, that meant no one would be stupid enough to proposition her.

Sometimes being a little bit stupid could pay dividends. Coupling. That was Tam's endgame. It would get him into her home and put him right there next to Schuyler. Right where he was born to be. So, Tam had to get himself on her radar.

After going through everyone she knew, from schoolmates to sponsors, to people who shared the same daily commute as her, Tam started to narrow down the list of those who could get him into her presence. Focusing on the lower-level top-tier flavours of the day gave him a decent portfolio to work through. Then it was just down to excellent research. And that gave him Howard.

Howard Møller was a high-level not-quite-nobody. Not the shining specimen his parents had hoped for in their design of him, he made do. He was blandly handsome and just about smart enough to get by at physical school. His parents were important enough that it would take a lot to push Howard down the ladder. They were important enough that people wanted to be friends with him. They were important enough that Reyna would sometimes give him the time of day.

Being middling seemed to suit Howard very well. He had an invite to every event that was worth a damn, but no one took any notice if he slummed it—and slum it he did. He seemed to love hitting every club night going and the seedier the pub the more likely he was to be there. He thrived when surrounded by lower-class climbers. He loved the high regard they gave him. He loved being adored without having to put any effort in. In the underworld he was a king.

It was simple to make his acquaintance. Howard's schedule was easy to access—like a lot of people, he chose to keep it badly hidden so a decent amount of his followers would know where he was at all times. So, after double-checking his whereabouts, and triple-checking the intel he had gathered, Tam donned a second-skin suit and made his way to Ballaban's Speakeasy.

Howard was sitting at the back of the pub, surrounded by social climbers hoping to impress him, all of them talking at once but all of them plugged into ports in their chairs and intermittently glazing over to participate on the In through VR.

Tam sat at the bar, ordered a drink and plugged into a port himself. He scrolled over Howard's profile walls, saw that he was active and decided to jump right in with a message.

> O'Shanter: You look bored. I can entertain you.
> HowieMo: Don't know you, do doubt you.
> O'Shanter: Nothing to lose by giving me a go.

Howard didn't start a reply for what was almost a worrying amount of time. Tam kept his eyes on the mirror behind the bar, watching Howard's actions and reactions without needing to turn around.

> HowieMo: What do you have in mind?
> O'Shanter: You'll have to join me to find out.

Tam saw Howard smile and shake his head with the obvious intention of dismissing him.

> O'Shanter: One drink. Or maybe I'll just go and have a drink with
>   Kalimba Baku.

Howard stiffened. The change in his demeanour was loud enough that even his low friends seemed to notice. There was a chorus of 'are you okay?'s and then he was smiling and shaking his head and saying 'I'm perfect!'

HowieMo: Where are you?
O'Shanter: At the bar.

Howard looked up and Tam turned just enough to get his attention before looking back at the mirror. He saw Howard appraising him and this was where he felt confident. He knew Howard was well disposed to pretty guys. Howard came over and took the stool next to him. Tam didn't look over but he unplugged and made sure Howard saw him unplug.

'What are you drinking?' Tam asked.

'Limonata.'

Tam ordered. They waited. It was important for Tam that Howard speak first. It was good for Tam that Howard had never had much waiting power.

'How do you know Kalimba?' Howard asked.

'I wouldn't record this exchange if I were you,' Tam said.

Howard sighed. He clearly wasn't good under pressure. He turned off his recording function and took a sip of his drink.

'How do you know Kalimba?'

'Not through the same link as you.'

'So it's blackmail.'

Tam shrugged. It was better not to say anything.

'What do you want?' Howard asked.

'An in.'

'Why me? There are plenty of other well-connected people out there.'

'Doesn't that question demonstrate precisely why you?'

It took a moment for Howard to unpick that.

'Fuck,' he said. Tam smiled.

'Don't worry. We're both going to do well out of this.'

Despite all the money at Howard's disposal, he had never paid for serious protection. He'd gone with a mid-range package, no muss no fuss, and his In was laughably easy to hack into. Tam thought, with a fetish like his, he should've been more careful. But then again Howard was born high tier. He hadn't climbed his way up there. There was a complacency that came with that kind of privilege. So it hadn't taken long for Tam to uncover all the interactions Howard had had with a person called Kalimba Baku.

Kalimba was a lot more careful to keep their profiles locked up, but eventually Tam broke through all the firewalls. What he found was a wealth of secrets. It was a gift that would keep on giving. He kept his focus, though, downloading Howard's files only—a small trespass that would probably go unnoticed.

Kalimba had kept their entire conversation history on file. They had also filmed Howard on various occasions, Tam assumed without his knowledge. It was clear Kalimba knew what they were doing. Tam only needed a small portion of this file to get what he needed. He didn't even need to make contact with Kalimba themself. And Howard never even asked for proof. It seemed enough for him that Tam knew. He actually seemed relieved about it. He never once seemed to think about just denying Tam's assertions. He never once tried to test the boundaries of what he could get away with with Tam. He just fell in line.

'What do you need?' he asked. And that was it.

The next big event was Jessop's party. Tam had little interest in the kind of image Jessop had created for itself—branding was not his mission—but he knew Reyna was very much invested in following a path similar to Jessop's. She wanted to be everywhere. That meant she would definitely be attending the do. It was an exclusive event, so just being there would speak volumes for Tam. He knew people would know he had something on Howard, but he was banking on them being more impressed with him than repulsed by him.

Tam prepared meticulously for the party. He researched every possible attendee. He found his outfit—expensive but he designed an agreeable payment plan for it. He practiced his gestures, his smiles, his conversational tics. He role-played his meeting with Reyna time and again, preparing for all scenarios he could imagine. He was ready for everything.

Tam prepped Howard too. Reyna was all about individual branding; she was so staunch on the matter that he reckoned coupling never crossed her mind. He needed her to be thinking about it when she met him, though, even if it was in the most lateral of ways. She needed to have the word—at the very least—floating around her head. The easiest way was to drop it on her, clear and out of the blue.

When Tam told Howard to ask her about coupling directly, Howard balked.

'*Everyone* knows where she stands on coupling. It would be suicidal to ask her about it. I may as well give up my whole life.'

'Don't be so dramatic.'

'This isn't drama! I'm dead serious.'

'Reyna doesn't care enough about you to report your exchange to her masses. She would rather not be seen associating with people like you beyond societal niceties. I can guarantee she'll listen to what you have to say, think you've lost the plot, and that will be that. It won't go further.'

'How can you guarantee something like that?'

'She doesn't need you, Howard. What's the point in destroying you? It would go against her image.'

A few more assurances later, Howard promised he would do as Tam asked.

Tam resisted the urge to get Howard to stream his interaction with Reyna directly to him. He knew Howard probably wouldn't be able to handle the pressure of knowing Tam was listening to everything he said, seeing through his eyes. But when Howard called to report his mission accomplished Tam asked to view the memory.

Howard had delivered a perfect blend of being bold and awkward simultaneously, Tam could hear it in his voice. And although Reyna's face didn't give much away, he was sure the strangeness of Howard's behaviour would have stuck with her. She would be thinking about coupling for a while yet. He was sure. He was sure. He was sure.

The suit Tam had ordered was cut just like the last one he had seen Schuyler Burroughs wear, but he had added his own personal flair to it. It was sequined. All black. So when Tam stood in front of the mirror admiring himself, he saw how he glistened. He was a dark and shining thing. He smiled the smile he had been practicing the most and, happy with the outcome, he turned away. It was time to go.

Tam went to Howard's place.

'You're overdressed,' he said, as Howard opened the door. The boy looked ridiculous in a white suit with puffed shoulders, a yellow shirt with spilling lace cuffs and a pink cravat. He'd clearly been spending too much time slumming it.

'Where's your wardrobe? I'll pick something out for you,' Tam told him.

Howard led the way without a word. He was clearly too nervous to object to anything Tam said.

Tam found an elegant white suit and handed it to Howard. He thought the contrast between them would be striking; they would seem a couple themselves. When Reyna saw them she would think that word again. He was sure.

And then they were moving, on the train, walking past the queue and walking through the door. If Tam had even the slightest bit of romance about him, he might have felt like Cinderella, but he was all focus and ambition and when he stepped over the threshold and saw the people beyond he felt as though he had come to the right place. He belonged.

There was Jessop in the corner, a throng of its entourage surrounding it, and he recognised them all—they were somebodies. There was Mitchell. There was Bian_Cat. There was Peter, Mopsy and Cotton-tail—the triad people loved to follow and loved to make fun of. Everywhere he glanced there was someone he recognised, someone he followed, someone he had hacked and dug the dirt on, someone he was waiting to deploy on his Go board. He never did more than glance but he filed them all away, he remembered what each of them wore, who they were talking to, what their body language said. He walked and worked the room, trying both to draw notice and also to shrug it away—he was walking a fine line—and then Reyna came in and Tam's stomach contracted with nerves.

'She's here,' Howard whispered from his side.

'I have eyes,' Tam told him.

'Now what?'

'Give her a second to do her thing.'

Reyna barely moved from the door. People swarmed around her, everyone kowtowing, paying respect, compliments, dues owed. And then Genevieve was through the door and the pair of them began a silent dance.

It surprised Tam, how beautiful it was to watch Reyna and Genevieve together. He had only seen them on the In and there they seemed more like rivals than friends. But here, in the Out, they were softer with each other. They flowed around each other, preempted each other, and when they looked at each other Tam felt he saw genuine respect and admiration in their expressions.

Genevieve distracted whilst Reyna set up an old-school camera—a BroccoliForest prop, Tam was sure of it. If anyone other than Tam had noticed her doing it, they didn't let on. And then Genevieve and Reyna were posing, moving with purpose, their expressions perfect. Reyna looked absolutely perfect.

Was she wearing pink? Tam was sure she never wore pink but this dress looked so . . . right. It was only a shade warmer than the tone of her skin, sheer, dramatic, it left her bare. Bare and beautiful. He realised she looked a lot like Hayashi Haruka. Was that by chance? Had Schuyler Burroughs somehow designed her that way? Or had she made herself up to look that way?

Reyna had been present for almost half an hour before Tam decided it was time to meet her. He was sure she wouldn't be staying much longer than that and he wanted to be one of the last things she saw here.

'Introduce me,' he told Howard. Howard, to his credit, seemed dry-faced and steady on his feet. He nodded and walked Tam over to Reyna Burroughs.

'Reyna! I'd like to introduce you to Tam,' Howard said.

Reyna looked past her AR displays as Tam stepped forwards and he wasn't sure if it was real but he thought he caught a flash of revulsion on her face. That wasn't something he had prepared for. But then she was smiling.

'Hello,' she said, and the word was unfettered, just a simple greeting.

'Nice to meet you,' he said, and he smiled—the smile he had practiced over and over again, just for this moment. And yes, he was sure he saw it now—a tightening around her eyes. Her smile lost some of its elasticity, she was hardening. This was not a scenario he had thought of. He was unprepared. He kept his expression cool, watched her openly, and he waited. She had to say something. She had to talk first. Waiting for her to speak was the only way he could control this conversation. She met him in the middle, silence for silence, keeping her smile up. And then, when enough time had passed with neither of them giving an inch of ground to the other, she refocussed her attention on her AR system, turned and walked away.

Tam permitted himself a soft sigh, as tension left his body.

'What just happened?' Howard asked him.

'I met Reyna Burroughs,' Tam said.

'But . . . I would hardly call that a meeting.'

Tam chuckled.

'It was definitely a meeting,' he said. It was not the meeting he had expected, and it had not gone as he had hoped, but it was definitely quite a meeting. She had reacted to him. It was strong. He was sure he was under her skin now.

'I thought . . .' Howard was just smart enough not to say what he thought out loud. 'What now?' he asked instead.

'Now? Now, you'll have to arrange another meeting.'

'When?'

'Give it a moment,' Tam said, trying not to get irritated with him. 'She needs time to think about all of this. Just . . . keep an eye on her. Let me know what she's up to. I'll keep tabs on her too, and the time will present itself. It always does.'

Howard didn't look so sure about that.

'I'm going to head home now,' Tam told him.

'Really? But we've barely been here.'

'I've been here just long enough.'

'But I've barely spoken to anyone.'

'So? Go speak to people. I don't need you to come home with me, you've done your job for now.'

The surprise on Howard's face was almost endearing. Then he smiled and stepped away, and Tam made a quiet exit.

Considering how long he had been watching her on the In—how long and how calculatingly—how long and how emotionlessly—how long and how scientifically—the fact that he found her beautiful in person was a surprise he couldn't quite get over. Of course he had always known she was beautiful. Beauty was a given. But in person, it was a beauty that affected him. He had reacted to her more honestly than he had expected to.

He played back everything he had seen at Jessop's. He projected it onto his white bedroom wall so he could really get up close and see it life-size. No. He was less affected by her than he was by seeing her with Genevieve. They were such a natural couple that he thought it was almost a shame they weren't one.

Tam shook his head. Weird thought. But then . . . he stepped close to the wall and watched them as they posed together and then bent their heads towards each other, speaking in a hush. They were so very beautiful.

The moment proceeded, Genevieve slipped through the room with Reyna trailing behind her, both of them with their AR functions engaged, demonstrating their power and distance, so beautiful . . . then Tam remembered himself.

Howard's call came much quicker than Tam had anticipated.

'She wanted to know what you had on me.'

'Naturally.'

'She said she could help me.'

'Of course she did.'

'I told her it was better to meet you.'

'Good.'

'I told her she could meet you at GraceNotes this weekend.'

'Really?' Howard's proactive approach was surprising. 'How did you sell that? *Did* you sell it?'

'I think I did. I suggested BroccoliForest might enjoy the scene.'

'She never takes her out.'

'I know. I pushed it a little.'

'Did she look like she was thinking about it?'

'I don't know if she looked like she was thinking about it but she said out loud that she would think about it, so maybe that counts.' Howard's delivery was beautifully deadpan.

Tam laughed.

'Wow. Okay. Can you show me a replay?'

'Of course.'

He only watched it once. And then he started prepping for Grace-Notes.

GraceNotes was crowded. Tam had dressed in a beautifully tailored, silver rubber suit. He kept his makeup minimal—he wanted to stand out from the crowd through lack of ostentation. He was relying on his own personal gravity to hold the eye of anyone who looked at him.

Howard was already installed in his favourite part of the club and, although Tam had expected it, he marvelled at how early Howard had got there. His thoughtlessness might have been attractive if there were more intelligence behind his eyes, but Howard was simply simple. It was quite sweet really. Tam smiled at him—a rare real smile—and he took up a space of his own, close to Howard's group, associated, but not a subject. He watched as more people flooded in, so many of them enjoying the momentary frisson of padded limbs brushing by one another in a simulation of physical contact. Everyone was cushioned and quilted and rubber-clad. The real thrill seekers wore membranous plastic in an effort to appear as naked as possible. Music made the floor throb and those who came for that fake contact leapt into thrashing dances, throwing their bodies into sharp, thrusting shapes as though they were weapons, set to penetrate the unwitting.

The air was thick with powder and perfume as people forced their bodies to stay dry and unreactive, but underneath it all there was the heavy scent of sweat and Tam could just imagine how excited Howard was getting at what Kalimba Baku would have for him in the back room when the club was closed.

More people crushed in and Tam forced his face to stay cool, but as he watched his stomach filled and he wanted to be sick. He found them all so disgusting. He understood why people came to places like this; they were a mixture of fetishists and climbers—the climbers all dressed up and desperate to have the high-and-mighty fetishists notice them. They were fools if they thought any progress they made here would be permanent, though. You just had to look at Howard to know that. Every one of these places Howard went to he had an entourage of hangers-on. He permitted them access insofar as it made him look good, but you could see he wasn't interested in anything but himself. He didn't keep it a secret. His disdain was carved into his expression; no one meant anything to him and Tam doubted he knew any of his flock's names. They were fools.

It was a club full of fools.

And then BroccoliForest floated into the room. He smiled at her and waited to see what her next move would be. She didn't fuck about, she walked right up to him with a smile, and all he could do was nod and look away, because he hadn't expected her to be so direct. Tam willed her to speak. She didn't. He knew he should wait her out but, much to his surprise, he felt nervous now and suddenly his mouth was moving and words were coming out and he was cursing himself out inside as he said:

'Even BroccoliForest is a cut above a place like this, no?'

'Everyone wants to see pictures of animals at the zoo,' Reyna said, and Tam felt his body loosen with relief that she had responded.

'So it's a work event for you.'

'Hopefully.'

'Take a picture of me,' Tam offered, and this time when he spoke he looked her in the eye, because he was serious, and she had come to this shithole to see him, and whatever might come from the night he would have her remember him not just from a photo but from the look he gave her, eye-to-eye her equal. Reyna brought her vintage camera to her eye, took a moment to frame him, and then snapped. There. He had let himself be caught. And now he wanted to run.

'I think that's enough of this,' he said, and he made for the exit.

'What?' Reyna asked as he moved past her, and Tam could have laughed then because he knew he had her now. He wasn't behaving by the rules and if there was one thing he could tell from 'Reserved' Reyna it was that she liked to be in control of everything. She had to follow him now. She had already given way to him by coming out to GraceNotes, so if she didn't follow through he would always be that person beyond her.

Tam walked out of the club but he waited for her by the doors and of course she came. Her composure was good, but stiff enough for him to notice.

'Come on,' she said to him, making a point of taking control. He didn't think he would have done that if he had been in her shoes—

she was trying too hard now. It made her less alluring and Tam wondered at her making him nervous earlier. He followed her.

She had walked him to the train station. Under the white lights her makeup looked heavy and she looked tired. BroccoliForest looked very different from the Reyna he had seen at Jessop's. She had led him to the platform for the train that would take him back to his borough. They had waited for the train in silence, both of them resisting the urge to switch on their AR systems, making sure the other one knew they were standing in the here and now, not engaged in the In. When the train arrived and its doors shushed open she spoke:

'Let's meet tomorrow. I'll send you details.'

She had turned then and walked away, not too fast, not too slow and not looking back.

The café was in her neck of the woods. Tam arrived late but even so she wasn't there. He would have preferred to have her waiting for him but it wasn't the worst thing that could have happened. He chose a table in the middle of the room so that neither her arrival nor her departure would be easy for her. He ordered a coffee and waited, staying on the Out so he would spot her when she arrived.

She was plain Reyna when she arrived—trying so hard to be unnoticed. But she was noticeable, of course she was, her parents had made sure she would be beautiful. Even with the act she put on (and she could act, he had to give her that), and the dull clothes, and clean face, she was strikingly beautiful. She didn't look so similar to Ms Hayashi now. Tam tried to think of a point of comparison but all that came to mind was a maiko, innocent and not yet polished to perfection.

She came and joined him and did not question the spot he had chosen for their meeting. He hadn't expected her to. She sat down and looked at him. He looked back. His coffee went cold as they kept the scrutiny up. Eventually she spoke:

'What do I get from you?'

He could tell from the tone of her voice what she was talking about. She was jumping right into the heart of the matter. He had to admit it was pretty cool, being spoken to with such commanding directness.

'The same kinds of things you'd get from most relationships. Some added bonuses.'

'I've never had any interest in coupling. And if I did . . . Genevieve is the most natural choice.'

Part of him didn't want to argue with her about that. Part of him wanted to see them together for real. But he had to argue about it.

'Coupling with someone who brings nothing unique to the table? She's your virtual twin; coupling with her would be safe, dull, forgettable. The gains are nonexistent,' he told her. Not true. Not if they were smart about it. But close to true. In any hands that were not absolutely perfect it was absolutely true.

'And matching with a second-rate nobody does what? What bonus do I get?' she asked him. She was trying to provoke him into some kind of reaction but the clumsiness of it was laughable. It melted any kind of regret he might have had about getting between her and Genevieve.

'Well, I'm not a nobody,' he told her. 'And I thought you were good at this game. Can you really not see the angles?'

'I see you using me as a step up the ladder.' She was being so simple it almost alarmed him. Was she doing it on purpose? If it was an act, what was her endgame?

'You're not wrong,' he said, buying time to think about what she was up to. 'But do you think I would have gone to all this trouble to meet you if I didn't think I had something to offer? *Think*.'

'I'm not that good at this game,' Reyna said. Tam made sure she couldn't see he was stunned by the statement. Had she meant to say that out loud?

'What?' That was all he could think to say.

She looked at him, trying to understand what he was thinking, but he didn't let her in.

'I get it,' she said. 'But why me? There are plenty of strong candidates for coupling up.'

And those words laid his questions to rest. She wasn't as good at this game as she made it seem. It just proved that being top tier afforded you so much more leniency than if you were born anywhere else on the ladder. Look at Howard. Look at Reyna Burroughs. She wasn't perfect at all. And for a second Tam felt angry because if he had had their advantages he could imagine who he would already be. Instead, here he was, pleading his way up. It made him angry and sad and—for the smallest moment—hopeless.

'It's because of my father, isn't it?' Reyna said, finally catching on. 'Yes.'

Reyna sighed as though being a Burroughs was a burden, and Tam had to suppress an impulse to kick her.

'Okay,' she said. It was an okay to everything. Tam smiled at her.

It was a start. Now came the fine details. Tam had his plan all mapped out already. He didn't bother to discuss it with Reyna. After their last meeting he wasn't sure he wanted much of her input just yet. Instead he sent her a message detailing their every move in the lead-up to announcing their coupling. She responded not with a message but with a package containing a jacket she had worn a day before.

He carefully curated an outfit to go with the jacket, found a setting and took a photo of himself in as close to the style of Broccoli-Forest as he could. He sent the picture to Reyna. She edited it and posted it as per his instructions. She did not message him but sent a package with a shirt that had the word 'Reserved' embroidered on its back.

Responding in kind, Tam had Howard take a photo of him in the shirt instead of trying to get Reyna involved. He sent the picture to her and she sent the picture out into the world. The response was immense.

Tam allowed time to build up suspense and speculation before photographing himself at Reyna's favourite café, in her favourite booth, drinking her favourite drink. He sent the image to Reyna. He sent her her shirt back. She sent him a picture. He posted and tagged.

Who is he?
What is he?
His level?
Have they coupled?
Is this for real?

The comments had a strange effect on him. He was nervous. But he was excited too, here, on the cusp of everything he had been hoping for. He sent Reyna a message:

Time to do something together.

Reyna replied:

I know a good place to meet. Will send you details. Sending you an outfit.

Even though she had disappointed him in some respects, Tam couldn't fault her aesthetic. When it came to the look, she really was perfect. The clothes were perfect. The location was perfect. The pose—her call—perfect.

They met at an abandoned gym that had, amazingly, not been re-purposed. Tam had never imagined that a place this old and strange existed in the city. People used to come and sweat in places like this.

'How did you find out about this place?' he asked Reyna.

'Just found it exploring. Good setting for shoots.'

He didn't ask her any more. It was clear she didn't want to share and he didn't have the energy or the patience to artfully pry. He let her direct him, waited for her to take the shot of the two of them to-gether, and then let her leave him there.

While he waited for her to get a good distance between them (they couldn't risk being seen together before this photo dropped) he wan-dered around the gym. The air in the place was thick and stale. Dust was heavy on everything, turning all things into the same shade of grey. Row upon row of familiar and unfamiliar equipment filled the space. Tam tried to imagine every machine in use, row upon row of people straining, sweating, smelling, and the thought made him shudder. He hurried out and made his way home to a hot shower, and he tried to wash the thought of so many people being so disarmed from his mind.

An alert blinked in his eyeline just as he emerged from the water. He accessed the notification and saw the photo. They were so beau-tiful next to each other and for a moment the sight of her surprised him yet again. He downloaded the image and then posted it under his O'Shanter handle. By now, all of Reyna's followers followed him. It was seen and shared in seconds. Comments flooded in.

A few hours later, the most important comment was posted.

Reyna: Match made in heaven

There was no turning back now.

Tam exploded up the ladder—at least in digital terms. He was still a mystery. Everyone was talking about him but the conversations were limited to the same old questions: Who is he? Where's he from? Who are his parents? What's his breeding? Is he a Wójcik? He must be a Wójcik! Where has he been this whole time? Why didn't I know about him? Who is he? Who is he?

Old, tired questions. But they kept asking them. Because, what else were they going to do? And with his followers growing exponentially Tam felt he had to do something more, begin to act, begin to be seen. He messaged Reyna:

Tam: Can I come over tonight?
Reyna: Why?

Why? Wasn't that obvious? Tam typed a flippant response.

Tam: Why not?
Reyna is typing . . .
Reyna is typing . . .

Christ she was slow! How could she be this slow!?

Reyna: Not an answer

Not a particularly inspired response. Clearly she wasn't sure how to handle him.

Tam: That's a no?
Reyna: No

Tam: No, that's not a no?
Reyna: I'll let you know
Tam: Good enough

And it was good enough. It was basically yes. Tam got ready and waited for her to invite him over.

His nerves began to build as he stepped off the train. It was only hitting him now that he was about to step into Schuyler Burroughs's home. He could be about to meet the man himself. Tam had to stop and take a few meditative breaths to calm down. He didn't want to resort to a beta blocker, so he took his time and waited for his heart rate to slow down before he moved. Then he walked slowly.

Reyna buzzed him into their building and he took the lift up to the Burroughses' floor. She answered the door herself. She didn't say anything, merely waved him in and then walked upstairs. Tam followed, trying to take as much in about the apartment as he could without seeming interested.

The place was tasteful, all chrome and glass and white and silver. If anything he found it a little bland, and that was another surprise. He hadn't expected to be anything but impressed by everything Schuyler Burroughs had had a hand in (family excluded), but this place wore its sterility a little too brazenly. It lacked a unique imprint.

Reyna's bedroom was an extension of everything else—plain, perfect and impersonal. Tam walked around it, absorbed it, and then made a beeline for the wardrobe, because he was beginning to think that Reyna's clothes were the most beautiful thing about her. He felt her watching him as he flipped through her outfits.

'What?' Reyna asked out loud, and Tam could tell from her tone that she wasn't talking to him. He stayed where he was but tuned in to her conversation.

'Why?' Reyna asked.

A moment passed and then she laughed.

'I only asked why!' she said, her voice sugary innocent. It was ugly. He might have to try to train her out of things like that. He turned to her and raised an eyebrow—his way of telling her he wasn't sure about her performance. She gave him a deadpan look in return and spoke to whoever was on the end of her line:

'How else am I going to stay sharp?'

Tam turned back to Reyna's clothes to hide the amusement on his face.

'Whatever you want to talk about, I'm not the person to talk to,' Reyna said, and her voice made Tam turn back to her. Reyna waved a hand impatiently, warding off any questions, so Tam decided to launch his own conversation.

'I got a Miyake package yesterday,' he said. He went and sat down at her desk. 'I think we should plan a public outing soon.'

Reyna lay down on her bed and it got Tam's hackles up. She was so dismissive of everything. It wasn't charming or artful, it was just lazy and rude.

'There's an event this weekend, at the Lupercalia,' Tam continued, determined that she would hear him. 'It would be a good opportunity.'

She didn't even bother to use words, just mumbled a sound of acknowledgement.

'We should coordinate,' Tam said as lightly as he could, given how impatient he was feeling.

'Let's go out now,' Reyna said, and Tam was surprised, yet again.

'What?'

'I need to stretch my legs,' she said. 'And besides, we blindsided everyone with our In campaign. Now they're expecting a big outing. We don't want to be one of those couples that give people what they expect.'

Tam barely had to think about it. It made perfect sense. He was surprised he hadn't thought of it himself. Reyna sat up and when she looked at him he thought he saw a smile somewhere on her face.

'What should we wear?' she asked him.

Although Reyna was small, Tam found enough variety and stretch in her clothes to fit into a suitable outfit. They settled on an inversion— her in black and him in cream. They did their makeup side by side, thickly lining their eyes in colours swatched to each other's skin tone.

They contoured their faces so their bone structures matched. Reyna slicked her hair down and tied it in a small bun at the nape of her neck so it echoed Tam's close crop. Tam realised he was enjoying himself as he critiqued their look in the mirror. A quick glance at Reyna told him that she was not. He resisted the urge to sigh.

'Shall we?' he asked her.

She opened the door and then froze. Tam moved up behind her and saw him standing there. Schuyler Burroughs. Beautiful, powerful, unfathomable Schuyler Burroughs. He was shorter than Tam had expected.

'Reyna,' Schuyler said, and then he smiled at Tam. It was the smile Tam had perfected himself. 'You have a guest.'

Reyna stepped out of Tam's way, so he could come through the door.

'This is Tam. Tam, Schuyler.' Her voice was bone-dry boredom.

'You could muster some enthusiasm,' Schuyler said, and he pitched his voice in stark contrast to hers.

Tam bowed in deference to him.

'It's a pleasure to meet you, Tam. Why are you here?' Schuyler asked.

'That's a fairly indelicate question,' Reyna said, and she had the audacity to sound disapproving. Of Schuyler Burroughs! Tam watched Schuyler's face. His expression was as bland as milk. Perfect response! Tam could barely contain himself.

'It's an honour,' he said. 'To meet Schuyler Burroughs . . .' Fuck. He was gushing. It was disgusting that he was gushing. Tam took a beat and then said: 'I'm here for Reyna.'

'And why might Reyna need you?' It was a fair question. Tam swallowed.

'Schuyler,' Reyna said, and she sounded just on the verge of being stupid.

'It's not my place to speak for her,' Tam said in an effort to regain any lost ground. He wondered if he had had any ground to begin with. What had Schuyler thought when he had seen him?

'Later,' Reyna said, walking past Schuyler and heading for the stairs.

'It was nice to meet you,' Tam said. He kept his voice neutral and followed after Reyna. He imagined Schuyler watching them walk away and so he walked the walk he had practiced, the Schuyler walk, all confidence and carelessness. It was only when he got out of the flat that he could breathe again, though.

He let Reyna lead the way and they hopped on a train. Tam barely paid attention to where they were heading. He had just met Schuyler Burroughs. A dream had come true. He was finally in contact. He felt taut with nerves. He felt full of energy. He felt confused—unsure of himself now. He needed time and space to think. He needed to figure out his next steps. Instead he was following Reyna into a cocktail bar that was all flashing lights and the smell of artificial fruits.

In amongst the neon rainbow the two of them looked divine— heavenly creatures if ever there were such things. Heads turned as they wandered past. They looked fucking good. Tam tried to focus on that; on his face and hers. On them. It worked. And when they were done and he was on his way home he felt an enormous sense of satisfaction. He looked at his In feed. Hundreds of images of them had been uploaded in the last couple of hours as every person who saw them had scrambled to show their story of Reyna and Tam, Out and about. Their images were starting to get tagged—Tayna, Treyna, Reytam, Ram. People liked and loved and commented away. Tam watched the traffic and allowed himself to smile. He was almost somebody now.

It wasn't a terrible idea for her to stop going to school. Tam imagined there was very little she could gain from the institution now. But it surprised him. It seemed a left-field decision for someone who was turning into a brand. Reyna hadn't even announced her decision to stop going; Tam heard about it through Howard. Since she hadn't told him directly, he decided it was better not to ask her about it. He mused on it for a moment and then shifted the direction of his thoughts. There were more pressing matters to focus on.

He and Reyna were seen as a high-stakes couple now. They were as close to being a single unit as one could be without marrying, so they had to work together to keep their game up. He messaged her informing her that he was coming over. Her reply was prompt and perfunctory. A menial showed him to her room when he got there. Schuyler was nowhere to be seen.

Reyna didn't get up from where she was plugged in, didn't raise her head or say hello, as Tam entered her room. She said 'Tayna' and Tam jumped into the subject easily.

'It sounds awful,' he said.

'Better than Reytam,' she said, and he had to agree.

'Where's your father?' he asked her.

'Why?' she said, and there were a thousand things in that 'why'; a challenge, dismissal, judgement, hurt, anger, fear, disgust . . . He wanted to dive into that word and discover everything he could. He wanted to know who Schuyler Burroughs really was. But what he saw on Reyna's face was barely suppressed pain and he didn't want to force her.

'I won't ask. We'll just focus on Treyna,' he told her.

She looked grateful.

'Plug in,' she said. VR. He supposed it was a more secure way of doing things. He shrugged to himself and plugged in.

It was always the same. She seemed to be calcifying into her plug. Every time he came over, she was there in the same position, typing, swiping, coding, encoding, writing, rewriting, living on the In. He couldn't coax her into using AR, so he would join her, join his feed to hers, and together they would work on their face. They were enjoying high traffic, but they were beginning to have to recut and recycle material. Tam didn't like it. It was inelegant.

He couldn't stand spending too much time with her either. She didn't say anything. She was a mannequin, posed in a corner of a room. Whenever he opened her bedroom door he felt the odd sensation that he was looking at a museum diorama of a perfect girl's life. Only there was no life in it. In fact the whole Burroughs household was lifeless. Tam would hear Madeleine's false laugh pierce the air at regular intervals as though she was programmed to do the same thing over and over again every day. He had never actually met her, but once he had walked past her where she sat at the dining room table, frozen, plugged in, a plastic smile on her face. He had never seen or heard Naomi. He asked Reyna about her sister once and Reyna had just shrugged. That was all the conversation he could get out of her. And the person he wanted to see the most was nowhere. When he had tried asking Reyna about him again, thinking perhaps she might be ready to talk now, she didn't even shrug. She didn't look at him. She didn't move at all.

Tam tried the In to find out more. Schuyler's posts were few and far between. They had always been that way. Tam had always found that intriguing but now he found himself bored by it. What was it about Schuyler Burroughs that everyone loved? What did he love about him? He couldn't quite remember anymore.

Tam met up with Howard one afternoon. They could have just spoken on the In but, after all those hours spent holed up with Reyna, Tam was longing to be Out. He asked him:

'What do you think of Treyna?'

Howard, artless as he was, couldn't hide a smirk.

'Boring,' he said.

Tam nodded.

'What do you think of Schuyler Burroughs?'

Howard thought about that for a bit.

'To be honest, I don't think about him much. He's cool. Very handsome.' Howard shrugged. 'I'd like to be like him.'

'Why?'

'Well, everyone wants a piece of him, don't they? He's rich, he comes from a great background, he has great style.'

'Have you ever met him?' Tam asked.

'Nope. You? You must have, right?'

'Once.'

'What was he like?'

'Charming. We didn't talk for long but he was definitely charming. I wonder, though . . .' Tam caught himself before he said any more.

'What?' Howard asked.

Tam smiled. He wondered if he really had been charming at all or if Schuyler simply was whatever people projected on to him. Tam had so wanted him to be charming. He was so sure of his brilliance. But the more time he spent with Reyna the less sure he was about Schuyler. After all, Schuyler had chosen everything about his daughter. That said something about him.

'Nothing,' he said.

'Why are you asking about him?' Howard asked.

'I'm just doing a little research.'

'For Treyna?'

Tam just smiled at Howard.

'Would you like another drink?' he asked him.

When Tam and Howard parted ways, Tam felt at a loose end. He didn't want to go back home. What he wanted was to know what he was doing. And the question that kept floating to the fore of his mind was 'Is Treyna over?'

Getting Howard's opinion hadn't really helped. It had just confirmed his suspicions. What he needed was a different perspective. After all, he had sunk so much time and effort into starting this relationship with Reyna. To let it all go . . . the thought hurt.

He decided to go for a walk, hoping that the exercise might stimulate his thoughts. He followed one of the coloured lines marked on the pavement, and kept a distance from the few people around him. As he walked he reviewed everything he and Reyna had done as a couple. He thought about Reyna. She had changed in the time he had known her. Was that because of him? It was hard to say. Ever since the beginning she had resisted giving him very much of herself at all. He had found it frustrating but he had respected it. Now he felt maybe that was what was holding them back. But it was more than that. What was wrong with her?

He looked up and realised he was close to the neighbourhood where they had done their first shoot together. The old gym. Strange that his body had brought him here. He was about to turn away and head back the way he had come when he spotted a familiar figure coming out of the gym. Genevieve. She saw him and stopped. There was a moment of hesitation before she took control of herself and walked up to him.

He waited for her to speak. She took her time, took him in, smiled and said:

'Hello.'

Tam nodded. He didn't want to offer her any more than that but at the same time he didn't want the moment to end so he held her gaze and smiled back. They stood in silence, measuring each other, and Tam found it invigorating to have her eyes on him, to have her thinking about him but giving nothing away. It was the same thrill he had had when he first met Reyna.

'Why did you come here?' Genevieve finally asked him. He shrugged.

'I didn't know I was coming here until I arrived,' he said. 'What about you?'

'Photo shoot.'

'Can I see?'

'Sure, at the same time everyone else sees the shots.'

Tam nodded appreciatively.

'Where's Reyna?' Genevieve asked him.

'Probably where she should be,' Tam answered.

Genevieve gave him another look he couldn't read. A small hard stare as if she was trying to get inside his head and read his thoughts. And then she stepped aside and made to walk away from him.

'Wait,' he said before she got away.

She looked at him questioningly, and suddenly Tam felt like she was the one controlling the rhythm of the interaction. He was asking for favours. But he knew what he wanted to do now and knowing that was such a sweet relief he couldn't help himself.

'I'd like to talk with you. Could we go somewhere?'

She seemed to measure him again. Then that hard stare came back. And then a nod. A gesture asking him to follow. And she walked off, not looking back to see if he was coming after her.

They walked like that for what felt like a long time to Tam. He hadn't checked the time when they had started so had no idea if it was his eagerness to talk that was making the walk seem so long and slow, or if they really were going on something of a trek. Finally Genevieve stopped at a small outdoor café. She picked a table and sprawled down on a seat with an elegant carelessness. Tam sat down opposite her.

He knew that she would wait for him to talk, maybe even start sifting through her feed as she did, and he didn't want to give her the space. She was controlling enough of the conversation as it was. So he jumped straight in.

'Reyna's changed.'

Genevieve raised an eyebrow but didn't show any inclination to comment.

'Perhaps I pushed her too hard but this coupling isn't working well for her.'

Genevieve laughed.

'There was a reason why she never wanted to couple before you came on the scene,' Genevieve told him. He read between those lines. Both Reyna and Genevieve had known she wasn't able to handle a dual identity.

'She played the game well,' Tam conceded.

'She reached her limits and stayed hard pressed against them.'

'People thought you two would couple,' Tam said.

'People think whatever they're going to think.'

'I thought you two looked like a great couple.'

Genevieve snorted. Then she looked at him, waiting for whatever it was he really wanted to say to her.

'We've probably reached the end of our road,' Tam said, picking his words carefully. 'Of course I don't want to damage Reyna's face, so if we split it will have to be handled very conscientiously.' He watched Genevieve's expression, trying hard to parse out her thoughts. She didn't give anything away.

'If Reyna emerges from this moment with me, what will you do?' Tam asked her.

'What has her emerging got to do with me?' she countered.

'Well, you two were once close. And I think people would be happy to see your brands working off each other again.'

'People are stupid.'

Tam laughed, an artfully articulated bark of a laugh.

'You want to know what I think about her,' Genevieve said. 'You want to know what I think so that you know whether or not to keep at this or to bail out and try and save your face as much as possible on your own.' She was right, of course. 'But you can't actually ask me, so I'll do you a favour. And you'll remember I've done you a favour.' She waited for him to make a decision. Tam nodded in agreement. 'I think Reyna is damaged. I don't think she'll ever be the same. People aren't interested in her anymore. They might be polite and invite her to an event here and there but the glamour is gone.'

Tam nodded. He had thought as much. He looked at Genevieve, a pointed look that asked her if she might say more.

'My thoughts on you?' she asked him with a surprisingly sardonic smile that perhaps told him more than words would. 'You are just wrapping yourself in a bow and handing yourself over to me, don't you think?' she asked him. That stung.

'I don't think what you think of me is any great mystery, Gen. I was actually thinking more along the lines of building a working relationship here.'

She laughed.

'After what happened to Reyna?'

'Reyna is doing that to herself.'

Genevieve nodded.

'Fair point. So what, are you thinking we would be the next big couple?'

'God no, I've barely had a chance to consider you! I wouldn't couple until I had done some due diligence.' Tam enjoyed saying that. Genevieve gracefully accepted the insult with a smile. 'What I was thinking was more akin to how you and Reyna used to play off each other. But much less frequently. Just the odd . . . flirtation.'

'Mutual recognition and respect.'

'Exactly.'

Genevieve looked thoughtful.

'I would be interested. But it depends on how well you extricate yourself from this . . . couple thing.'

And that was what he had been looking for. A clear sign of what his next step should be. He nodded.

'Let's talk sometime,' he said, and he stood up and left. He didn't look back.

Tam went to the Burroughs house. He rang the buzzer and waited for the door to open. He waited. And waited.

Madeleine opened the door. She looked so awful that Tam didn't even wonder why it was her and not the menial answering the door, he was just transfixed by her. Her skin was drained of all colour, and her face was drawn. She had scraped her auburn hair, dark with grease, back into a tight ponytail, and she wore nothing but a simple cotton dressing gown. She was a wisp of a person. She smiled at him.

'*You* must be Tam,' she said, putting some force into her voice. 'How *love*ly to finally meet you. Forgive my appearance. It's maintenance day, don't you *know*,' and she laughed, that same laugh he had been hearing for weeks.

'The pleasure's all mine,' Tam said, polite as ever.

Madeleine nodded. Then whatever strength she had seemed to leave her.

'I think Reyna might be upstairs,' she said, and she floated away from him and into the living room.

Tam took a moment to look around downstairs. Apart from Madeleine, there was no one there. He went upstairs. He walked along the hallway and past Reyna's room. He stopped at a door. He wanted to push it open, to see if there was anyone else around. Instead he put his ear to it and listened. Silence. He crept around the rest of the upstairs, never bringing himself to open any of the closed doors, but listening hard for signs of life. There were none. The place was empty and sterile.

Finally, Tam pushed open Reyna's door. There she sat, as always. Despite her looking nothing like Madeleine there was something uncannily similar about the two of them now. They seemed spent, like they had given the last of themselves away.

'Hi,' Tam said.

Reyna made a noise.

'What are you doing?' he asked.

Reyna shrugged.

'Have you checked our stats recently?' he asked. He wanted to make sure she looked at where they stood and understood why he was doing what he was doing. It felt like the only fair way to go about it.

Reyna shrugged again. He knew she would, so the anger that shot through him was unexpected. He took a moment to compose himself. Then he plugged in and shared his screen so she couldn't ignore him anymore.

'Look,' he said, and Reyna looked.

'What am I looking for?' she asked, and he had to suppress his anger again.

'We're not moving,' he said, evenly.

'It happens,' she said. Flippant.

'Not to great players,' he said, holding on to that monotone.

Reyna shrugged. Again.

'Reyna!' He put as much force in his voice as he dared, just to make sure she would pay attention to the important parts of this conversation.

She finally looked at him. She seemed so glazed over, heavy and unthinking that it surprised him. She was such a different person than the beautiful diaphanous creature he had met at Jessop's. It couldn't have just been the pressure of their coupling that had done this to her. There had to be something more to it! Tam couldn't help wanting to know what. Perhaps it was a secret that would give him some kind of leverage over the family?

'What's wrong with you?' he asked.

Reyna laughed.

'Nothing's wrong with me,' she said.

'There's something wrong with you. You and Madeleine . . . like copies of each other.' He shuddered at the thought of that. The thought of Reyna being the same as Madeleine—a kind of beautiful trap. 'You used to be good at face,' he told her.

'I *am* good at face!' Reyna said.

He looked at her and he could tell she knew she was lying. He could tell she knew this was the end. And her last move would be to keep quiet. Whatever was happening here, she wouldn't be the one to tell him.

'I'll make some moves, begin a breakup process. I don't want you to bring me down,' he said.

Reyna nodded.

'Goodbye,' he said.

'Tam.'

What? What could she possibly say now?

'Yes?'

'You'll do well, regardless,' she said.

He didn't know how to take that. It was both condescending and encouraging. He looked at her sitting there in front of all her screens. She was small and unimportant. He supposed she had always been that way. Realising it hurt. He felt stupid. He had never felt stupid before.

'I know,' he said. That was all he could say.

As Tam left the room he was surprised to see Schuyler Burroughs out on the landing. He was looking down into the dining room, but when Tam came out he looked up at him.

'Tam,' he said with a nod and a smile. And then he shifted his attention back to the dining room.

Tam walked over to the railing and looked down too. He saw Madeleine sitting at the dining table, plugged in, her expression blank in her drawn face.

'Kind of a sorry sight, no?' Schuyler said.

Tam looked at him, surprised by the candour. Schuyler didn't meet his gaze, but continued to watch Madeleine, and a sneer of disgust came over his face. It was ugly and alarming in its honesty. Tam watched him carefully. His posture seemed different than he remembered—he looked a little sunken, as if he couldn't handle the weight of being himself anymore. He seemed small and powerless, just like his daughter.

This was the man Tam had wanted to become. He had worked so hard to get into his vicinity, to see if there was anything he could learn from him, and yet Reyna had never let him anywhere near Schuyler. The mystery and allure of the man had grown. But now Tam could see him plain as you like and he was disappointed.

As he walked away from their home, Tam thought about the Burroughses again. How disappointing they had all been. Still. He had got something from them. He was higher than he had been. It was a start. And unlike Schuyler Burroughs he would not make a stupid mistake like Madeleine. He would play the game. He would become much more than any of them had ever thought to be.

(Menial 63700578–Jake)

'I need to talk.'

'I'm here to listen, Jake,' said the confessor.

'No. I need to talk. I want to talk. I want to talk to someone.'

'We're talking right now, Jake.'

'On the In.'

'You want to communicate on the Out?'

'Yes! How many different ways do I have to say it?'

'You want to talk to me?' The confessor sounded surprised. Definitely not a machine.

'No. Of course not. I want to talk to *her*.'

'. . . The woman?'

'Yes. Her. The woman. The one I talk about. The only person I ever talk about.'

'Jake, calm down.'

'I am calm!' He was calm.

'I don't think you are, Jake.'

'I . . .' Jake began, but there was nothing to say. This whole exercise seemed futile. 'I want to talk to her. On the Out. In the world. Using my mouth. I want to look her in the face and talk to her. I want her to look back at me.'

'This is an important confession, Jake.'

'It's not a confession.'

'Of course it is, Jake. Menials can't do whatever they want. Your wants are irrelevant. So it's important for you to express them in a safe environment. To confess them.'

'What'll happen if I do what I want?'

'You know what will happen, Jake.'

'Yeah. But only if someone reports me.'

'What are you suggesting, Jake? Higher-tiers will always report unusual activities amongst lower classes and menials. The only way you can . . . What are you suggesting, Jake?' He wasn't imagining it. That last question was pitched. The confessor was afraid. Why?

It took Jake awhile to realise what it was. The implication he had made. There was only one way to be sure a person kept quiet. There was only one way . . .

'Jake? Jake, what are you suggesting?' The confessor's voice shook. Hearing the tremor gave Jake a thrill. He didn't say anything. He waited, wanting to see what the confessor would say next.

'Jake?' The confessor just said his name.

They both waited.

'Jake, what are you going to do?' The question was a big one. Jake smiled. The face he was using on the In didn't.

'What *am* I going to do?'

'Jake, I have to let you know that if I suspect you are going to be a danger to anyone I have a duty to report you. Your confessions will become public property.'

'What if I'm a danger to myself?'

'Jake.'

Jake didn't say anything and another silence bloomed.

'It doesn't matter what happens to me, does it?' he finally said.

'Jake.' This time the confessor's voice was soft. Almost sad. But Jake thought he must be imagining that. Wishful thinking.

'Have you ever met another Jake?' he asked.

'What's the relevance of the question?'

Jake shrugged, though he knew the confessor couldn't see the real him.

'It's just the way you say the name sometimes. Sometimes you sound . . .'

'What?'

'It's nothing,' Jake said. Because he realised it really was nothing. The confessor was no one. They meant nothing to each other.

'Jake, I think we need to talk through your feelings right now. This sudden impulse to make a connection, to turn your fantasy, or at least part of it, into something real—this is dangerous ground. We need to find a way to defuse it, Jake.'

'You're scared.'

'No.' The word was emphatic. It reminded Jake of himself, standing on the landing, looking down at Madeleine. He'd said 'no' with such certainty.

'No?'

Jake knew Schuyler was watching him as he gathered up the dirty dishes and placed them on his trolley. He did his best to look unconcerned.

'Are you afraid of us?' Schuyler said, and Jake knew he was talking to him. It wouldn't do to assume, though. He had to wait for a more direct address.

'Menial.' There it was. Jake stopped what he was doing and turned to Schuyler, but he didn't look at him. 'Are you afraid of us?'

'No.'

'Why don't you look at us?'

'That's the rule.'

'Whose rule? When you belong to a household you follow the household's rules. I've never told you not to look at us.'

'It's part of our training. Are you unhappy with me?'

Schuyler laughed.

'You misunderstand. I'm curious. After all, everything I do is influenced by what I read on the faces around me. How can you function if you don't study faces?'

'It's not a necessary skill. Menials remain static.'

'Of course, yes. But you're people. You're made from the same stuff I am. It follows that you, like everyone else, have a desire to better your situation. Climb the ladder.'

It was an amazing thing to hear: that they were made from the same stuff. It was something no stud-born aristocrat would say. And yet Schuyler had said it. And he had said it as calmly as saying water was wet. Jake held his nerve and made the obvious reply.

'Menials aren't on the ladder.'

'Everyone is on the ladder,' Schuyler told him.

'As you say.'

'Is that part of your training? To agree with me?'

'I was trained to keep the running of a household smooth. I was trained to provide for those I work for—to give them everything they might want or need, if it is within my power to do so.'

'So, if I were to tell you that I want you to speak with me honestly—to share your thoughts and opinions—what would you say to that?'

'I have no thoughts and opinions. I am trained to serve.'

Schuyler laughed again.

'I'm sure that isn't true.'

Jake had no reply to this. He stood and waited for something else.

'If I told you to speak honestly, you wouldn't, would you?' Schuyler said. Jake couldn't speak. 'You have secrets. But you aren't smart enough to hide that you have them.'

Jake could tell Schuyler wasn't trying to insult him. He was stating facts as he found them, but they stung nonetheless. He felt his heart beat a little harder and his mouth go dry. He could feel his fists clenching, his fingernails digging deep into his palms. He focussed on these little things: the small movements that he hoped went unnoticed. He focussed on them and hoped his face was quiet through it all. And yet despite that, his skin was hot. It was probably flushed. Irrefutable evidence of the humiliation he felt. And he couldn't help himself. He looked up. He looked right at Schuyler. And Schuyler smiled.

'There you are,' Schuyler said, and he stood up and walked over to Jake. He looked him in the eye and Jake found himself thinking how warm Schuyler's eyes were. How different they were from Madeleine's.

Schuyler stood a little too close to him, just within that invisible circle of personal space, and yet he didn't touch him. He just stood there. Close, oppressive, intimidating. And Jake held his nerve. He looked at him.

'They say you menials are different,' Schuyler said. Jake felt his breath on his face. 'But you look just like us. The only difference . . .' Schuyler grinned. 'You have no control of your faces. Not when it matters.'

Schuyler looked away and stepped back, and Jake felt free to move. Schuyler walked across the room. Jake watched him for a moment before returning to the dishes he had been tidying away. He finished clearing the table and pushed the trolley to the kitchen door but before he went in Schuyler spoke again.

'It's special, you know? Being free with your expressions. It's . . . it's just being free.'

Jake stood in the doorway and thought about that. He wasn't sure what Schuyler meant. He wanted to ask, but of course he didn't.

Naomi

Menial 63700578

Naomi was reading the assigned textbook from Morton's psych class. *Psychology: The Science of Mind and Behaviour*, 98th edition. It was interesting, but it didn't tell her much more than she already knew. It just gave fancier names to everything. She was meant to be preparing a project; a study in Individual Differences. She had to pick a case study and find a real-life equivalent. The project felt dull and uninspired. She could already see the results, and everyone's project would be the same. It would be easier just to make it all up and put together the presentation ahead of time.

As she came out of the In, she heard the murmur of speech. Schuyler was talking to Reyna in the hallway outside. It was dinnertime. An alert flashed up at the bottom right-hand corner of Naomi's vision:

Madeleine: Dinner

Naomi shut down her AR function. She sat still for a moment, gathered herself, pasted a sarcastic smile on her face and went downstairs.

'Where's Naomi?' she heard Schuyler say.

'I called her a minute ago,' Madeleine told him.

'Present and correct,' Naomi announced herself.

'Sit down,' Schuyler said.

As they sat at the table the menial came in pushing a trolley. It moved with care, placing plates before them. Naomi watched it work.

'What are you having today?' Schuyler asked everyone.

'Isn't it obvious?' Naomi asked back. The words came out mechanically, their pitch was automatic.

'Well, if it isn't the teenage cliché,' Reyna muttered and, despite herself, Naomi found that the words stung. It surprised her. She had heard them before and it usually never mattered. She did her best with what she had.

'Oh sorry. Do I disappoint you, Miss Original?' she asked Reyna.

'Disappointment requires prior expectations and I've never expected anything from you,' Reyna said, smiling sweetly.

'Now girls, I expect a *higher* form of face from you. You're both capable of more than this,' Madeleine said.

'Ah, so *you're* the disappointed one,' Naomi said, grinning at their mother. It was a relief to turn her face on Madeleine, always the easiest one to wrangle within the 'family'.

Madeleine didn't dignify the jab with a response—Naomi didn't expect her to—and they all began to pick at their food in silence. As soon as the first course was over, the menial emerged from the kitchen. Naomi watched it as it walked around the table. What was it thinking as it sat alone and watched this 'family' eat together? Its face was gormless; slack jawed, like it was doped. Naomi wondered if that was the default menial 'face'. She hadn't really looked at them before. It was proper to treat them as invisible. And then the idea occurred, as naturally as an exhalation. Menials. They could be her project.

'Tonia and Eduardo have decided to choose a baby,' Schuyler said, breaking through her thoughts.

'I *know*, I think it's *wonderful!*' Madeleine said, her voice setting Naomi's teeth on edge. The gushing, passive-aggressive positivity was nauseating. To all of them. Naomi grunted.

'You think it's a bad idea?' Schuyler asked her.

'It's a minefield,' Naomi told him. 'And they're green.'

'They're also static right now,' Reyna said. 'Having a child is the only way for them to move up the social hierarchy.'

'If they get it right,' Naomi said. 'It's a gamble and they could slide either way.'

'If we give them a helping hand we can make sure they slide up,' Schuyler said.

'And what do we get in return? Favours shouldn't be freely given. Honestly, I don't really understand why you bothered making "friends" with them in the first place. They don't add to your cachet at all.'

Schuyler smiled at her. Naomi didn't like it. It was one of his

inscrutable smiles and she had learned a long time ago that inscrutability was belittling.

'Well, that's the *best* thing you've said in *ages*, Naomi,' Madeleine
said, and if Naomi could have winced with impunity she would have.

'Just because you can't see the benefit outright, doesn't mean it
isn't there,' said Reyna. 'You're only looking three steps ahead, little
sister. Try looking ten.'

Those words were Naomi's cue. She fixed Reyna with a dark look:
the appropriate hate-filled face that she knew Reyna wouldn't take
seriously. It had to be done, though. Her face had to be maintained.
And it wasn't hard to dredge up the look. She had had enough practice and Reyna was sufficiently annoying.

'The further ahead you look, the less definite the consequences.
By making your moves based on a distant future you are gambling
with our status instead of theirs,' Naomi argued.

'Have you considered the couple fully, though? They have very
favourable chances for success, especially *with* our influence. And of
course, by "our" I mean Schuyler's influence.'

Schuyler sighed and said:

'I wish you would call me Dad.'

Naomi snorted.

'Please. "Dad" sounds so low level,' Reyna told him. 'It's practically
menial.'

'"Father" then. Or "Pater",' he laughed. 'Just stop using my name
as if I were merely an acquaintance.'

'You *are* merely an acquaintance,' Reyna said.

'This is what I get after having raised you all your life. I hope you
never choose to have children,' he said.

Naomi looked at Reyna, curious about her response. Reyna
shrugged.

'Well, that will depend on whether or not it's beneficial to my status in the future. You know that. I do think there are unjustifiable
risks involved in choosing children, however. Fashions are changing
so quickly that I think human life is just too long to bother investing
in it. You choose your child and by the time it's born and finally grows
into the looks and mind you chose for it, it's already out-of-date. You
have to be mind readers to get it right. And even then, there's no pre-

dicting the public's appetites. If there was a way to have interchange-able children, all at the different stages of life, then there would be some merit in the whole enterprise. We could change them the same way we change our faces—choose the most appropriate one for the day we're going to have.'

'For once, I agree with my sister,' Naomi said.

'Such *smart* girls,' Madeleine said, and she raised her glass to Schuyler. 'We chose *such* smart girls.'

The disgusted look Schuyler gave Madeleine was surprising. Vir-ulent and uncharacteristic; Naomi found it necessary to take a deep breath and count to eight in response. It helped her keep up the ap-pearance of being unmoved. She looked at Madeleine and wasn't surprised to see her face crumbling. Madeleine stood up.

'I have to use the amenities,' she said. Wise choice. They watched her walk away.

'Father?' Reyna said, once Madeleine was out of earshot.

'Have you considered yourselves?' Schuyler said so abruptly that for a moment Naomi was confused as to what he was talking about. 'You're here because I chose you,' he continued. 'You speak so cava-lierly about interchangeable children and the pros and cons of choos-ing lives. What of yourselves? What would have become of you if I had thought about children the way you are now?'

Naomi looked at Reyna.

'I doubt I would have been born,' Reyna told him. She spoke steadily, her face carefully presenting cool reason and lack of emotion.

'How does that make you feel?' Schuyler asked her.

'That's a redundant question. I am and so I can't possibly say how I might feel about having not been.'

'That's weak, Reyna. You know that's not what I was asking. What about you, Naomi?' Schuyler asked.

Naomi shrugged and affected a bored drawl as she said:

'This conversation is too full of hypotheticals for my taste. I would rather be on the In right now.'

'We haven't finished dinner,' Schuyler said.

'I have no appetite.' Naomi stood up and slipped up the stairs be-fore Schuyler could argue with her.

The true answer to his question was that Naomi wished he *had* thought about children the way she did. A second child was an unnecessary affectation. Naomi, when she realised this, was surprised Schuyler had allowed for her to happen. She was disappointed in him. If she had been given the choice she would have preferred not to have been born. And not just because she was an unnecessary second child. Life just seemed so pointless. And on top of that, it was such hard work.

Naomi had the skills. She was quite good at faceplay and she knew she would do well in life. Not as well as Reyna, though; Reyna was the expert, a closed book. And it didn't even matter that sometimes she used beta blockers; the point was that she had no personality. This made her almost perfect. Naomi, on the other hand, was afflicted with personality—but she had learned how to use it.

Naomi played the 'teenage cliché' with absolute precision. She had chosen the face when she was nine and spun it into a popular attraction. She had garnered a surprising following for her simple recordings of pure insolence. She was admired. Where Reyna juggled faces with the dexterity of an eight-armed goddess, Naomi had learned that she could make less count for more. It didn't mean she enjoyed it, though.

Naomi had been informed, at age seven, that she was going to start school. Physical school. Reyna had been enrolled for two years prior, and had flourished. It was time for Naomi to follow in her footsteps. Naomi was not happy. At seven, she hadn't yet learned how to control herself. She cried. Then she begged. She begged through her tears and her snot and her sobs. Madeleine threw a box of tissues at her and told her to grow up. Schuyler . . . Naomi couldn't remember what Schuyler had done, only that he hadn't helped her, and the very next day the household menial was taking her and Reyna to physical school.

Reyna—perfect Reyna—abandoned her at the gates and Naomi realised she would have to swim alone. This was her first proper lesson.

Naomi was reasonably clever. It didn't take her long to figure out the purpose of physical school: It was a crucible. The only way to come out of it was to master faceplay. And it didn't take her long to get the hang of that.

Still. Her face was beginning to wear on her. She couldn't drop it—it had too many fans—and she didn't want to develop it either. The whole thing was just so boring.

When she got back to her room, Naomi picked up where she'd left off in *Psychology: The Science of Mind and Behaviour*, 98th edition, and she thought about her project. Menials. That might not be boring. That might actually be very interesting.

'Hey, Naomi.'
  'Hi, Naomi!'
  'Hey, NayNay!'
Naomi scowled at them all as she walked down the hallway to her first class, but her heart wasn't really in it. And as Madeleine had pointed out to her the other day, if she kept this up she was going to age really fast.

The day, like every day, was a difficult array of forced interactions with people she didn't care about. By the time she ended up in psych she was already exhausted. Morton asked them about their project plans. To maintain her face, Naomi pretended she didn't have a plan nor did she intend to make one. She was irritated about the time and energy that maintenance wasted. She had to wait for all her classmates to leave before she felt remotely safe enough to approach Morton and, even then, hanging around, talking to a teacher, trying to do something she was interested in, felt really wrong to her.

'Yes?' Morton asked her.

It took Naomi a minute to realise she was holding the pendant of her necklace tight in her hand. Her beta blockers. She tried to let go in a casual sort of way and she focussed on keeping her expression dead, but her mouth was dry, and she wanted to swallow. She could feel a squirming in her guts, her heart beating hard, and even though she had thought about it beforehand, she found that the words she was looking for had escaped her.

'Well?' Morton asked. He sounded bored and his attention was clearly on something in his AR sight line.

'Menials,' Naomi said. She spoke in a monotone, which was a relief.

Morton leaned back against his desk and really looked at Naomi then. It took a lot of her nerve to keep her face straight.

'What about them?' he asked.

'Thought they'd make a good subject,' she said with a shrug.

'For your project?'

'No, for conversation,' she said with unquestionable sarcasm. Being sarcastic was too easy but at least it gave her a place to hide. Morton sighed.

'What were you thinking about doing with them?'

'Thought I could pick one to study. Then try to find a case-study equivalent. I mean, menials are basically normal people. Only they aren't. I'm . . . I'm sort of interested to see if the way they're born and brought up makes their basic psychology different from ours.' It was difficult for her to say all of that and still sound uninterested. She thought she'd done an okay job.

She looked at Morton. He wasn't smiling. Only he looked like he was somehow.

'You ever hear of confession booths?' he asked her.

'Course.'

'You ever use one?'

Naomi gave him a flat *are you an idiot* look and Morton laughed.

'You'd be surprised by how many people do use them.'

'What's this got to do with menials?' Naomi asked.

'Like I said: You'd be surprised by how many people use confession booths.'

Naomi couldn't help frowning.

'Menials confess?' she asked. Morton nodded. 'To what?'

'Oh, to all sorts. It's not just menials. A *lot* of people confess.'

'Really?'

'Really.'

Naomi thought about this.

'I still don't understand what it's got to do with anything.'

'Well, you raise an interesting question. How different are menials from us?' Morton asked. 'We're the same species and yet they're born differently, raised differently, educated differently. They don't live on the ladder but they're free to observe the rest of us that do. How does this affect them? Does it alter their psychology? Or do they have the same wants and needs as everyone else? There's a lot to explore here. The question is how to get at the information. You could observe a menial. You must have one at home?' Naomi nodded. 'But observation won't get you very far. You could try talking to it. But I doubt that would get you very far either. Menials are trained not to question, not to talk, not to behave in any way that isn't serving. No menial worth its salt would talk openly to you. And that's what you need if you want to understand their psychology.

'So. This brings me to confession booths. What do you know about them?'

'They're spaces on the In where people can go to talk about things they can't allow themselves to bring up on the Out. Or on the In, even. Stuff they can't talk about in front of people that know them. They're basically private spaces.'

'Right. And each confession booth is run by the "confessor". I think when the whole thing started the confessor was just a machine, but machines have a limited ability to respond to different situations. There were some complaints and a new system was put into place. The 'confessor' is now all sorts of people. Anyone can run their own booth, as long as they adhere to the protocols.'

'What are the protocols?'

'Well, a confession booth is a safe space. As a confessor you have to listen without judgement, offer advice where you can and make the confessee feel as comfortable as possible—which means they have your total assurance that you will keep their confessions private. Confessees are largely anonymous and they usually use template faces as their avatars. There's no way of knowing who they are, where they're from, or where they are in the hierarchy. Only there is. If you're any good at reading people, you'll know. People give things away all the time. They can't help it. So naturally, I know that several of my confessees are menials.'

'You're a confessor?'

Morton nodded.

'And as a confessor, I get a pretty good insight into people.'

'So, are you suggesting I make my own booth?' Naomi asked.

'No, that would take too long. What I suggest—and this is only if you're absolutely serious about this—is that you take over my booth. I have menials you can study.'

Naomi looked at him, tried to read his face. He didn't give much away.

'Are you serious?' she asked.

'If you are.'

Naomi stayed on after school. She headed to Morton's classroom.

'So?' she asked as she came in. It was an aggressive, interrogatory 'so'.

Morton pulled out a chair for her and gestured for her to sit. She did.

'Right. In order to transfer my booth to you we have to patch into each other,' he said, sitting opposite her and plugging into a port. Naomi nodded. A direct link like this, using ports instead of clouds, was much more secure. Naomi took a moment to switch off her AR In feeds before she plugged into the port next to his. She closed her eyes and searched her patch for him. In a moment they were connected to each other's surface desktop.

'I'm going to plug into the In now and you can see exactly what I'm doing.'

She watched as Morton connected to the In. Then she was flooded with his In feed: white space at first and then a dozen messages (he'd censored them into a vague blur) rising and fading from the bottom right corner of her eye. His eye. His eyes were hers. He ignored the messages and picked an icon out of the many that hovered, only partially in view, at the top of his vision. The icon showed two doors, side by side, connected by a roof. His focus stayed on the image until it expanded outwards, flooding their vision with a field of night blue. Dotted across this field were small, burning stars.

'The stars are the people that come to this booth to confess. A star shines brighter when someone is entering the booth,' Morton told her.

'Do I have to keep checking on the booth to see if someone's there, or will I get a notification?'

'The confessions will join your regular message stream. You'll get one and then, if you want to see the person you're talking to, you can move into the booth, or you can just treat it like you would a normal message and deal with it in text. You can only access the booth when you're plugged into a port, so you can't interact with it as you go. It's a way of ensuring user privacy.'

'The people I see in the booth aren't the real article, though,' Naomi said.

'Are people ever?' Morton asked.

'What if someone wants to confess when I'm in the middle of something?'

'That's where the booth settings come in handy. I've programmed a specific set of responses tailored for each of my confessees. If they want to talk when I'm busy I set it on auto and they get tailor-made machine responses until I'm ready to plug into a port and take over. It's all ready for you to use. Simple enough?'

'Yeah.'

'Good. Well, I'll transfer it to you now, then.'

Morton waited for Naomi to re-enable her In feed.

'Where do you want it?' he asked her.

Naomi opened up her feed next to his. She indicated the top tool-bar and Morton, having closed the booth, slid it from his feed to hers.

Naomi closed the patch and blinked. Then she looked at Morton.

'I'm interested to see what you do with this,' he said to her.

'That everything?' she asked him.

Morton smiled and nodded.

'Good luck,' he said, sounding so bright and hopeful.

Naomi didn't bother answering.

Days passed and no confessions came. Naomi found herself checking the confession booth over and over again, willing one of the stars to flare up, wishing something would happen. She studied the saved interactions between Morton and the confessees; they were her property now. She learned about each person who used the booth; what they were afraid of, what they worried about, who they were.

And then three confessions hit her simultaneously. She checked the names:

LucidLucinda
Karaxxx32
Janusz_Parrott

She activated auto settings, and then clicked on LucidLucinda.

'Hello,' she said as the face of a beautiful woman filled her screen. 'Do you have anything to confess today?'

'It's happening again,' LucidLucinda said. 'I want to kill her. I can't help myself. I think about it all the time. I went into her room last night, while she was asleep, and I watched her. I don't know how long for. And all I was thinking about was wrapping my fingers around her throat. And in my imagination, I wasn't even wearing gloves. It didn't even occur to me how awful that was until later. I mean, I could have thought about poisoning her, shooting her, stabbing her with a kitchen knife . . . any of those things would have been fine. Right?'

'Right,' Naomi said.

'But strangling her? With my bare hands?' The woman's image shuddered. Naomi guessed this was a carefully programmed move-ment—a way to signal to the confessor that she knew her thoughts were wrong.

'But it excited me, you know? I was . . . it was amazing. It was like having a double dose of Happiness. I only left her room when it looked like she was waking up. And then this morning, at breakfast, she smiled at me. And I don't know if it's my imagination but she seemed more affectionate than usual. It was weird. Like maybe, on some level, she knows? Do you think that's possible?'

Naomi shook her avatar's head.

'It's easy to feel like we have glass heads. That everyone can see our thoughts. But you have to remember that even the lowest players hide their true face.'

'She knows me better than anyone. She can read me.'

'That doesn't mean she knows your innermost thoughts.'

'But what if she does know? What should I do?'

'You're worrying about something you have no way of knowing about.'

'But I should do something, right? I can't go on like this?'

'Remember, I'm only here to listen. I can't guide you. What you do outside of this booth is up to you.'

'But you have to have some thoughts about it! Come on, you have to have an idea? I . . . what if I . . . act?'

'Do you feel like you're going to act?'

LucidLucinda was quiet. Then:

'No.'

'How do you feel, now that you've talked about it?' Naomi asked her.

'Empty.'

'Empty is good. Empty is a fresh day with a fresh face.'

'Yes.'

LucidLucinda left the booth. Naomi turned to Karaxxx32's star but it was now dim. Janusz_Parrott was still active. Naomi clicked on him—

'But it's now happened on forty-five separate occasions this week. I'm keeping a record. I'm starting to worry that this is going to affect my position in the company.'

Naomi did a quick review. Janusz_Parrott was worried he was allowing his boss too much facevalue. He had started laughing at her jokes.

'And there's a certain look she gets, whenever I come into a room. I'm worried she's thinking about demoting me.'

The man was an idiot. If his boss was letting that much slip, it would be a simple matter to take her job.

'What are you doing to combat your instinctive reactions to her?' Naomi asked.

'I'm on beta blockers.'

'How many do you take a day?'

'I was up to six hundred milligrams but my work started suffering. I've had to reduce. The worst thing is that I think everyone knows I take them. It's lowered my facevalue even more.'

'Have you tried not using any medication?'

'I couldn't do that! I'd be a mess.'

'What do you think you should do?' Naomi asked him.

'What do *you* think I should do?' Janusz_Parrott asked in return.

'I'm not here to give you advice—I'm here to listen and facilitate your thought process. Confession is intended to bring you some relief. Does sharing your worries help you relax?'

Janusz_Parrott sighed heavily. It didn't seem like a carefully programmed response, but a real one. Naomi wagered that his avatar was probably quite similar to his real face—it wasn't especially attractive: average in most ways, a reflection of a totally ordinary man. Or perhaps this was a consummate player? Perhaps everything Janusz_Parrott had just related was fabricated; designed for some other purpose than what it seemed.

Naomi shook her head. The thought was a fruitless one.

'It does,' Janusz_Parrott said. 'Talking to you . . . I feel like I know you. It's soothing to hear your voice.'

Naomi was using the same voice Morton had used—the voice of a woman, perhaps middle-aged, deep and slow, each word carefully enunciated.

'Could you talk to me some more?' Janusz_Parrott asked.

'What would you like me to say?'

'Anything. Could you tell me a story?'

'It's not my function to tell stories, I'm afraid.'

'I just want to hear your voice,' Janusz_Parrott told her, a desperate edge creeping into his own. 'Please!'

'I can count for you,' Naomi told him. She counted to a hundred and twenty-seven before Janusz_Parrott disappeared.

It was over a week before a user who identified as a menial entered the booth to make a confession. Naomi was in class when it happened. Not wanting to miss the opportunity to interact with a menial properly, she stood up and left. No one tried to stop her. She went to the nearest plug-in station and entered the booth in her avatar.

'Hello,' Naomi said.

'Hi,' the menial replied. Its avatar was flashy; too perfect, too manicured, too unnatural. All the details were addressed, right down to its bejewelled fingernails. Only someone clueless would have made an avatar like that. People like that were known as Red Ferraris. They were as good as faceless.

'What would you like to confess?'

'I . . . I did it again.'

Naomi reviewed the menial's file. Its primary confession was about masturbation.

'What did you do again?' Naomi asked. Morton had noted that this menial responded best if made to say the words.

'I masturbated,' it whispered.

'Okay. What did you think about this time?' Naomi asked.

'I was thinking about a dress.'

'What kind of dress?'

'I saw it on a pop-up ad the other day. Dior. A sleeveless, peplum dress. The skirt was cut above the knee and it was dark green, but the top was pale. The ad put me in it and I could feel it. It was close-fitting but the material stretched.'

'Did you think about yourself in the dress, or was it the dress on its own?'

'I was in the dress.'

'What shoes were you wearing?'

'I didn't think about that. I didn't think about anything but the dress. I was thinking about the dress, I . . .'

The avatar shuddered and blinked and Naomi had the disconcerting realisation that the menial was getting aroused by the conversation. The arousal wasn't the disconcerting part. It was the fact that Naomi could see it, there was no barricade in the way, the menial had no ability to hide its face, even in avatar form.

'How long did the masturbation last?' Naomi asked it.

'I don't know. Awhile. I was late getting lunch.'

'Why do you think this is something to confess?'

'You know why,' the menial said.

'Tell me again.'

'Well, it's not for us.'

'Explain.'

'Why? I've told you before. You know this.'

'But it'll help you to articulate it.'

'Menials don't masturbate,' the menial said.

'But you do,' said Naomi, pointing out the obvious. The menial's avatar bit its lip and crossed its arms.

'We're not supposed to. We're not supposed to want to. We have training for it if we do. We're supposed to be able to stop ourselves. We're not entitled to it.'

Naomi hadn't known that menials were trained in anything beyond looking after others. She hadn't known that certain things, things she was entitled to, were supposed to be forbidden to menials. But how could anyone police self-gratification? And why was it important to prevent menials from pleasuring themselves?

'How does that make you feel?' Naomi asked. 'Not being allowed to touch your own body?'

'I don't know,' said the menial. 'I'm fine. I'd rather not. Just sometimes . . .'

'You do it. You break the rules.'

The menial's avatar grimaced.

'I won't do it again,' it said. 'I *won't*.' And then. 'I've got to go.' And it was gone.

Naomi unplugged but she didn't go back to class. Instead she went for a walk. She followed a purple line to one of the parks. She thought about Menial 2852.6570. She thought about masturbation. It was something she was familiar with but had rarely indulged in. It just wasn't necessary. She had plenty of activities to occupy her time and physical pleasures were one of the least interesting. That said, she appreciated that her body was her business. She could do anything she wanted with it as long as she didn't interfere with anyone else. She couldn't imagine not having absolute control over her body. And how could people police menial bodies, anyway?

Morton was on his way out of school when Naomi caught up with him.

'Hey. Hey!' she called out to him.

'What d'you want?' he asked without stopping.

'I have some questions.'

'That's what the In is for.'

'I don't want these questions logged,' said Naomi. Morton stopped.

'Well, if they're problematic questions, I might have to log them myself,' he said.

'They'll be on your private record, not a public one. I'm okay with that.'

'How private do you think a private record is?'

Naomi frowned at him.

'Is this a trick question?'

Morton sighed. It was an unguarded, unplanned, natural sigh, and it made her feel uncomfortable. He gestured for her to follow him.

'Where are we going?' she asked him.

'To get a drink.'

Morton didn't walk very far. He ducked into a café and sat down by a window. He tapped a quick code into the slate on the table and then pushed it over to her. Naomi waved it away. A moment later, a cup of coffee arrived.

'Go ahead. Ask me your questions,' Morton said, as he poured too much sugar into his coffee.

'I was in the booth the other day—'

'You can't tell me about the booth. I'm no longer privy to the participants of that particular confessional.'

Naomi wanted to sigh, growl, play with the sugar, do something, do anything to express her frustration.

'No details. I just heard something that . . . surprised me.' She was careful to sound unsurprised. 'I realised that menials have more restrictions than ordinary people. Is there a record of their rules somewhere?'

'This is information you could easily find on the In,' Morton said. 'Nothing that doesn't bear logging.'

'I'm asking you.'

'Why?'

'Because it's easier to go directly to a source of information, rather than trying to sieve details through the In.'

'And you're hoping to get information out of my face too,' Morton said. He smiled. 'I'm being a bit slow today.'

Naomi gave him a look.

'Yep, I'm slow every day,' Morton said, and he took a sip of coffee. 'There are no menial guidelines on the In. Not necessary. They internalise the guidelines as they make their way through their training facilities. If you want to find out more about how they're trained, you have to visit one of them.'

'I have a feeling they don't let just anyone in.'

'No.' Morton had a look, like he was thinking about something very specific.

'But you've been to one.'

'Yes. You have a sharper eye than you let on,' he said. The compliment almost surprised a smile out of her.

'And you remember the guidelines?'

Morton laughed.

'They spend their entire childhood and most of their teenagehood learning the guideliness. I remember scraps. What are you interested in?'

'Masturbation.'

Morton laughed again. It took Naomi a moment to catch up with him. She managed to stay deadpan.

'What about it?' Morton asked her.

'Menials aren't supposed to do it. They're trained not to. Why?'

'Most animals don't masturbate. Menials are service animals. Their thoughts should only be on how to serve their bosses best. Distractions like physical gratification are discouraged but there is no actual rule that says they can't do it. That would be impossible to police. That's why menials have guidelines rather than rules. And they're conditioned to feel guilty if they stray from the guidelines.'

'Surely, if they display an impulse towards sexual gratification it's an indication that they are more than just animals.'

'Yes.'

'But we aren't supposed to think of them like that,' Naomi said, completing Morton's unspoken sentence. Morton smiled at her. 'Why?' she asked him.

'That's a silly question. And after you were just convincing me you weren't a silly person.' Morton stood up.

'Where are you going?'

'I've finished my coffee. Time to go home.'

'But I have another question.'

'Go ahead,' Morton said, but he didn't sit down.

'What did you mean about private records? How private do I think a private record is?'

Morton sat down. Naomi translated the action:

'They're not private.'

'You've never struck me as naive before,' Morton said, and Naomi didn't like the way he was looking at her.

'You feel sorry for me,' she said.

'Yes.'

'Well, why would I even have a reason to think about private records that way? There's never been any reason to question them,' Naomi said. She could hear a defensive edge creeping into her voice and, although being defensive was a position she often assumed, that was not what she wanted to be right now.

'Sorry,' Morton said, and she knew he understood what she was thinking. She hated him a little for that.

Morton stood up.

'Let's cut this off, now,' he said.

'Wait.' Naomi didn't want their conversation to end with him saving her face. She wanted it to end on her terms. 'Sit down a minute.'

Morton hesitated. Naomi gave a rare smile. In lieu of a response, Morton sat down again.

'Do you have a menial?' Naomi asked him.

'Yes. Part-time. I share it with two other people in my building.'

'What do you think of menials?'

'They're useful. Not necessary, but they certainly make life easier.'

'Are they human?'

'Yes.'

'Are they as human as us?'

Morton pulled the slate closer and stroked its surface. It lit up and he ran his fingers over the items but didn't select anything.

'How can you use one if you're in two minds?' Naomi asked him.

'Where are you on the ladder?' Morton asked her.

Naomi shrugged.

'Yeah, exactly. You don't even need to acknowledge the ladder most of the time. But a lot of us *have* to think about it. And we do what we have to, to stay where we are—to rise up and be acceptable. Congratulations.' This time Morton didn't pause. He was out of the door before Naomi blinked.

Naomi lay on her bed, idle. She had been flicking through her profiles, running searches on the In, following faces she admired, but nothing could hold her attention for long. And she kept thinking about every search she made, every item she saved, each change she administered to her profiles, her faces, her life. These were all actions she thought belonged to her. The best thing about being on the In was the fact that you could control the environment around you. It was always better In than Out. Face wasn't hard on the In. But Morton had given her something to think about. How many of her In actions really belonged to her? She was surprised she had never thought about this before. The question had never arisen, but now that it had she felt as though it should have been asked years ago. She wondered if she was especially slow. Did everyone else just take it as a given that their life on the In was never private? She sat up.

Closing her eyes, she searched her patch for Reyna and then phoned. Reyna picked up just as Naomi was going to drop the call.

'What?' she asked, voice deadpan.

'You busy?' Naomi asked.

'Why?'

'You're a bitch,' Naomi told her.

Reyna laughed.

'I only asked why!'

'You know you didn't. Jesus. You realise we're a family, right? You don't need to outface me every time.'

'How else am I going to stay sharp?' Reyna asked.

'Could we just drop the whole face for now?'

Reyna was quiet.

'Whatever you want to talk about, I'm not the person to talk to,' she said eventually, and she dropped the call.

'Bitch,' Naomi said to the dead line. And she wondered: Did someone hear that? In action. In action versus inaction. Inaction wouldn't get her anywhere. And she'd been acting on the In forever; privately or not, she'd negotiated it the best she could. So. Privacy be damned. Naomi plugged in and searched:

Menials: rules and regulations

An advert flickered before her; images of the city, shiny happy people walking along with other, slightly less shiny but just as happy people trailing after them. A voice said:

Menials are a necessary part of everyone's life. Why fend for yourself when there is something there to fend for you?

Images of menials fetching, carrying, cleaning, serving, answering the beck and call of beautiful top-tier people.

Menials are trained from birth to be the perfect servants. A menial's main function is to make your life easier. So, what are you waiting for?

A beautiful top-tier family gazed at Naomi, their face reinforcing the question: What was she waiting for?

Come down to your dealership today, where we'll find the menial for you.

The advert faded and streamed into another one:

A menial was struggling to clean a table, its movements slow. Its skin was discoloured and its eyes were listless.

Is your menial sluggish? Not quite performing to standard? With BrightStar Insurance all menial problems can be resolved with a tap on your wrist.

A man tapped his wrist and a voice came through his patch:

'Mr Clemens! What can I do for you today?'

'My menial is useless.'

'What seems to be the trouble?'

'I don't know. It's just crap.'

'I see. I'll dispatch an operative to your location to check the menial over. If it's nothing more than a medical issue we can administer remedies free of charge. However, should you wish it, we can remove this menial and provide you with a younger model?'

'I think I'd like that. What's the charge for a replacement?'

'On your current plan, we can provide a replacement menial free of charge if your menial has a problem that isn't easily remedied. Otherwise, the costs are ten percent less than the regular retail price. Top menials for less!'

'Great. You may as well send over a selection of replacements now.'

'Of course. A selection of our best will be shipped to you within the hour, along with a BrightStar Menial Caretaker. Is there anything else I can do for you today, Mr Clemens?'

'No. You've been really helpful.'

'Thank you. Have a great day!'

'I will, thanks to BrightStar!'

The advert faded and another began to stream in but Naomi interrupted it. She had seen adverts like these before. She refined her search:

Menial programme inception

An article blossomed before her:

The menial programme was developed by Hayashi Haruka. She conceived the idea in 20__ as part of her doctorate; her studies focussed on the evolving concept of family. Ms Hayashi was interested in creating an affordable tool that would enable a family to save time on chores; time they could then assign to spending with one another. The first of what Hayashi called 'tetsudau' were sourced through advertising—low-tier people searching for work. But these people didn't answer Ms Hayashi's requirements in terms of both skill and cost effectiveness. Using the beaker baby system was a natural solution. Developing children that adhered to certain requirements and raising them within a closed system in which they were extensively trained in all menial tasks, Ms Hayashi renamed the 'tetsudau' 'menials' and developed a system whereby families could purchase individuals to look after all their daily needs.

Since its inception, the menial programme has grown exponentially, and now even some mid-tier households can boast occasional use of a menial. Full ownership of menials is still the province of the top tier, and this situation looks unlikely to change in the near future.

Naomi skimmed down the article. There was nothing in it that she didn't already know. She used another search phrase:

Menial training
Menials are brought up and trained in assigned facilities. Every facility has an attached dealership where menials can be purchased. Should a menial be found wanting, they can be returned to their facility of origin for correction or termination, depending on the severity of the issue.

She used another phrase:

Menial termination
Menials have a life expectancy of twenty-five years. It is recommended that menials be returned to their facility of origin before they reach this age. If you choose to keep your menial beyond the age of twenty-five you should expect to see a marked decline in their physical and mental health, and a general inability to carry out their functions.

> Every menial facility has a termination wing that takes care of aged menials in an efficient and humane manner.

Naomi scrolled down.

> . . . but all attempts to eradicate the termination system have failed. The last campaign for menial welfare ended in 20__. The menial programme has continued unopposed, bringing happiness to top-tier families for decades.

Naomi typed:

> Are menials human?

An official article blossomed:

> Menials are developed using the beaker baby system, but unlike beaker babies purchased by prospective parents, menials are engineered to develop without certain traits that are natural in a fully functioning human.
>
> Menials have a limited capacity for independent thought and possess no drive for discovery. They lack the full range of emotions and are unable to problem-solve in a creative manner. This has drawbacks: Your menial cannot solve complex issues for you, without your input— but it also means they are perfectly programmed to receive and comply with orders without questions. They are designed to be the perfect servants.

Naomi sighed and looked through her dashboard to the wall opposite. She thought about the menial they had working for them. He looked human. And sometimes she would catch him looking at them, a light on in his head, questions clearly occurring to him. Or maybe that was just what she wanted to see? Why would she care? She wondered if there was any way to talk to him. She wondered if he would be able to respond to her questions.

An alert flashed up. Someone was entering the confessional.

ArrasLarras

Naomi assumed her avatar, stepped into the booth and, with a smile in her voice, said:

'Hello, Arras. What would you like to confess?'

'I'm sick,' said the menial. This was the third confession Naomi had fielded that hour. She hadn't bothered going into any of her classes. Instead, she sat in one of the private rooms in the student lounge.

'I'm really sick,' it said. 'Do you get this a lot? Do other beakers say the same kinds of things to you? There are other people like me, aren't there?' The menial sounded so afraid. But menials didn't have the same capacity for human emotion that normal people did. Naomi assumed she was projecting her own thoughts and feelings onto it.

'I can't talk about other confessions, Jake.' She was careful to use its name. Morton's notes had specified that this was important to this menial. *He* had to have a name. Surely that wasn't a natural desire for a menial?

'I'm not asking about the confessions! I just want to know, do other people feel like this?' Jake's voice was rising. A sure sign of increasing agitation.

'I can't talk about other confessions, Jake.'

'I'm not asking about the confessions! Am I a freak?' Definitely agitated. It seemed menials could get agitated. Or was this one different?

'You are not a freak, Jake.'

'How can you tell?'

'I know. Trust me. I know.' And Naomi did know. By now she was sure she had heard confessions from every level of society, and some of the depravity was shocking. Naomi shuddered. The worst she had heard had come from someone that wore the face of a young girl, mid-tier, nothing special. She wanted to give birth. An actual baby. She wanted to feel it grow inside her. She fantasised about it splitting her apart, sluicing out in blood and shit through a deformed vagina, crying, covered in some kind of viscous substance. She dreamed about holding the clammy, mewling, wet thing—pressing it to her bare breast, letting it suckle her. The girl had projected images of her fantasies to Naomi. Naomi managed to hold out for the duration of the confession but she vomited when it was over. She didn't manage to make it to the bathroom. The vomit splashed onto the floor by her bed. Some of it splattered onto her duvet. She was relieved she was at home.

Jake broke into her thoughts:

'Why should I trust you?' it asked.

Good question.

'You've already trusted me with your confessions, Jake. Have I let you down somehow?'

'No.' There was something sulky about the way it said 'no'. As if it was disappointed in her. It made her want to reassure it.

'Then trust me. I can tell when I'm talking to a freak. You are not a freak.'

'Who are you?' Jake asked, not for the first time. It was curious. Apparently menials could be curious.

'I'm your confessor.'

'But who *are* you? How did you start doing this?'

Good questions. And Naomi wanted to answer them. Only it wasn't part of the confessional guidelines. It wasn't part of her project.

'You're not here to hear my story, Jake. I'm here to hear yours.'

'It would help me. To know more about you.'

'I want to help.'

'How does confessing help?' This was a question she could answer.

'Confessing has always helped people. People used to confess to a priest, confess to a god, confess to a crime, unburden themselves. And without the weight of their secrets they were free to move. To move on. It's harder now to confess to a real person, a real face, because that affects how people see us. So, confessing in the safety of the In is a logical choice. People are afraid to show their true faces but they can't hide their feelings and thoughts forever. They have to let them out. Confessing helps us move.'

'Do you confess?' Jake asked her.

'Sometimes.' Not true but what did the lie hurt?

'What do you confess to?'

'This isn't about my confession. You aren't here to hear my confession. I am here to hear yours.'

'Don't you trust me?'

'I . . .' It had her there. And Naomi smiled. But she couldn't say what she wanted to. 'Jake. This is a service that's been designed to help people. It's a safe space for you to say whatever you want to say. The time you spend here is *your* time. It's my job to listen to you. Nothing more. You can trust me, but you are my client. I'm not yours. This only works one way.'

'But trust doesn't work like that.'

It was right there.

'You've never had a problem with this before.'

'I have a problem now.'

'I'm sorry, Jake. I don't want to make things difficult for you. I only want to help you.'

'You could help me by telling me more about yourself.'

Part of her wished she could.

'I'm afraid I can't do that, Jake. Why don't we take a moment to think, and then you can tell me what's really bothering you.'

The menial vanished and Naomi was left staring at the empty space in front of her. An incoming call nagged at the bottom right-hand corner of her vision.

'What?' she snapped at no one, before picking up the call. 'Yes?' she asked.

Madeleine was doing a fairly good job of looking bored. Naomi came into the living room and sat down on the armchair across from her.

'Well?' she asked.

'I don't think there's *really* any point in talking about it,' Madeleine said.

'Then why did I get a message saying I should come home?'

'It was what the school administration advised. *Apparently* I'm supposed to ad*monish* you or something like that.' Madeleine waved a hand in the air, and her gaze moved around the room, not settling on anything. It was one of her little tricks to help her keep her expression blank. Don't look at anything and you can't react to anything. She sighed.

'Personally, I couldn't care less by this point. You made your face, you've broadcast yourself the way you wish to; there's *nothing* any of us can do to influence you,' she said.

Naomi was surprised.

'That's unexpectedly insightful of you,' she said.

Madeleine smiled, tried to look amused, but Naomi could tell the smile was tight, a sour expression buried just beneath it. Madeleine waved her away.

'Bugger off,' she said.

'Gladly,' Naomi said. She retreated but when she got to the stairs she looked back at her mother. Madeleine sat very still. Her head was bowed and she studied her hands. If Naomi hadn't known any better, she would have said she looked sad. But Madeleine was never sad. She had pills for that.

Raised voices weren't a common occurrence at home, so when Naomi heard Schuyler talking, his voice angry, it naturally drew her out of her room. She could hear him:

'You were trivialising them to make yourself more important. When are you going to realise that at our level, *that doesn't work!*'

'I don't understand why you care so much!' Madeleine said. Stupid woman.

'Your face is my face! I can't have you reducing me to some simple little . . .'

'What? Say it! What am I reducing you to?' Madeleine asked him. When would she learn that asking questions like that made her look weak?

'The way you grasp for advantage, it's like you've never even seen the top. You're cheap, Maddie. I knew that when I met you, but you just get cheaper as the years go by.' Those words surprised Naomi. Schuyler was normally so careful, so perfect, but this made him look even worse than Madeleine.

A shadow moved on Naomi's right and she looked over to see the family menial walk across the landing and look down into the room below.

'You're not stupid,' Schuyler said. 'You must have known how I felt. I haven't been hiding from you, I—'

'God, I know! You've done anything *but* hide!' Madeleine said, and Naomi saw the menial shift its gaze. The light from below illuminated its features; she saw them soften as it looked at Madeleine. There was something pathetic about its face. It looked . . . troubled.

'Enjoying the entertainment?' Naomi asked it, and it jumped, much to her amusement. It turned around and looked at her. That was strange. Menials didn't make eye contact. Its face was shadowed now, the light behind it, and Naomi had to squint to pick out its features. It was objectively attractive—no one wanted an ugly menial—and what was more, there seemed to be some intelligence in its face. This was a chance.

'I could have you fired for looking at me, you know?' she told it. It nodded. 'Can you speak?' It nodded again. 'Well?' It looked at her, blankly. Not very intelligent, then. 'Are you enjoying the entertainment?' she asked.

The menial looked back down at her parents. Naomi stepped up beside it and looked down too.

'I don't know what you want,' Madeleine said. Her helplessness frustrated Naomi.

'She's an idiot,' she said. She hadn't meant to say it out loud, but she had. Perhaps because she wasn't alone.

'No,' said the menial, surprising her.

'No?'

But the menial didn't elaborate. Naomi wanted to ask it something more, but no questions came to mind. It didn't look at her again, it kept its eyes down, looking at the people below them, strangely intent. At a loss, Naomi retreated.

She wondered if it ever confessed. What would it . . . he confess to?

Naomi hung around after psych class.

'What d'you want?' Morton asked her, face and voice none too happy.

'Apparently I've exceeded my absence allowance at school.'

'So?'

'I've been absent because I've been taking confessions.'

'I showed you how to use the auto-response. You don't need to take every confession. Your absences aren't my fault.'

'I know. I'm not here to get you to vouch for me or anything.'

'Then why are you here?'

'Because I want you to sign off on a personal field trip.'

Morton looked interested.

'Your face is different,' he said.

'Will you do it?' Naomi asked, ignoring the comment.

'What's the trip?'

'I want to go to a menial training facility.'

'Really?'

'No, I'm just saying shit for shit's sake. I love staying on after school to utter nonsense at you.'

Morton smiled at her.

'There's the Naomi we all know and love. When d'you want to go?'

'Tomorrow.'

'You need the whole day?'

'Ideally.'

Morton's eyes glazed as he searched his patch. A moment later he refocussed on her.

'I sent a permission to the head office. You're free to go.'

'Great,' Naomi said, and she left. She turned back a minute later and ducked her head through the door of the classroom.

'Thanks,' she said, and she left before Morton could say anything.

The nearest menial dealership was a half-hour train ride away from Naomi's borough. The building was all function and its front doors swished open as Naomi approached. The foyer was empty and a handsome man approached as soon as Naomi crossed the threshold.

'Hello, my name is Nechadeemus. How can I help you today?'

'I'm in the market for a new menial,' Naomi said. She was wearing a face she rarely used, today—grown-up, sophisticated, more like Reyna.

'Of course. How many menials do you currently have in your possession?'

'One,' said Naomi.

'And this new one will be a replacement or a supplement?'

'Supplement. The family's expanding and we need more help.'

Nechadeemus smiled.

'I understand.'

'Do you?' Naomi couldn't help but ask, and his smile faltered at the insult. 'I need to make sure that the menial will fit imperceptibly into our lives and, with that in mind, I would like to tour your training facility to appreciate what I'll be getting.'

Nechadeemus held his expression still this time, and he didn't show any surprise.

'I'm afraid the facility is only open to authorised personnel.'

'There must be *some*thing I can do to gain access?' Naomi heard Madeleine's tone of voice creep into her own and she wanted to smack herself.

Nechadeemus gave her a thin smile.

'No.'

Well played, Naomi thought.

'What menials do you have on hand now?' she asked, in an attempt to regain lost ground.

This time Nechadeemus gave her a broad, salesman smile.

'Right this way,' he said, and he ushered her farther into the dealership and down a corridor. 'Can I ask, what's the registration number of your current menial?'

Naomi took a moment to look through her archives.

'63700578,' she told him.

Nechadeemus tapped the number into a slate.

'Male. Twenty-one. You'll want an elegant counterpart. It just so happens that we have a menial that bears a striking resemblance to this one. Twenty years old. It would look very good in your household.'

'Unusual to have such an old menial on hand, isn't it?'

'This menial is a recent return. Its owners couldn't keep up with the loan repayments.'

'So it's been working in a household for . . . ?'

'Five years.'

'It will be used to a certain way of working.'

'We have a reprogramming service available.'

'What would that entail?' Naomi held her breath, worried she seemed too curious. Nechadeemus didn't bat an eyelid. Instead, he opened a door into a room.

'I'm afraid I can't disclose that information. This is the menial.' He held the door open for Naomi.

The room was white and calm. A menial sat on a bed. It was looking at the floor, but its gaze was vague, the muscles in its face were slack. It was hard to tell if it was the same height as the Burroughses' menial, but it had the same dark hair and pale skin. Naomi stepped a little closer. The menial didn't look up.

'Is it drugged?'

'It had some difficulty readjusting to the dealership. We're keeping it under observation.'

Naomi wanted to snap her fingers in front of its face. She wanted to get it to look at her. But that wouldn't do.

'What else have you got to offer?'

In the end, Nechadeemus showed her six menials. Apart from that first one, they were all young—thirteen to fifteen—and they were perfectly behaved. Naomi found a fault with all of them and left. She made no excuses for not purchasing. The top-tier never made excuses.

It was a relief to get into a private train car and shed the uncomfortable face of the well-to-do, perfect, top-tier girl. Using the port in the train seat, she plugged into the In and inputted the question again:

Are menials human?

She went deeper than the primary article, deeper than the ones below it; they were all in a similar vein, so she went as deep as she could, only to hit a wall. And then she gave up.

An alert appeared. Just a message. Naomi looked at the name:

CantonDuck

New fan? She selected the message. It read:

Menial trouble?

Who is this? she asked.

CantonDuck

'Fucking face,' she said to the empty room. '*Fucking* FACE!' and then: 'I'm going crazy now, too.'

And it seemed so ridiculously inevitable. This was why second children were a bad idea. They were crap versions of the first one, functionless, and now here she was talking to herself out loud, obsessing over menials and wondering if she should start a conversation with an idiot that called themself CantonDuck.

What do you want? she asked.

You passed vetting. You can enter chat room. Password is in Morse—
   the pattern will be buzzed into your wrist.

And Naomi's wrist vibrated in a pattern of long and short buzzes. A hyperlink was messaged to her. She selected it and names bloomed all around her, chatter filled the space, the room was full.

'What is this?' Naomi asked.

'A chat room,' said a smart-arse with a tag that read Cloud69.

'Oh goodie. Grown-up talk,' Naomi said, turning away from her. CantonDuck met her.

'Are menials human?' they asked.

'That's my name,' said Naomi.

'What do you think?' they asked.

'Wouldn't have asked if I knew.'

'Not knowing doesn't stop you having an opinion.'

'I don't have enough information to formulate an opinion.'

'Insearches not yielding much?'

Naomi didn't waste time responding to that. CantonDuck laughed.

'We discuss matters like that here. Theories, opinions, and we share what information we can find.'

'To what end?' Naomi asked.

'To better understand things.'

'But what do you do with the information?'

CantonDuck shrugged.

'Nothing we can do.'

'So, you're dedicated to chatting?' Naomi asked.

'We're gathering and sharing knowledge,' CantonDuck said. 'Our circle is getting bigger, more and more people are becoming aware of the facts our administration doesn't want us to know. We're gradually disabusing the general public of false notions.'

'And what is everyone doing once they're disabused?'

'Well . . . they're free,' CantonDuck said.

'How?'

'They know the truth.'

'What truth is that?'

'That our lives are completely monitored. Every action is recorded, even our thoughts struggle for privacy. And, on top of that, we live in a society that not only promotes self-service, sabotage and class divides, but thrives on the subjugation of people, reducing them to mere objects.'

'Oh. That's the truth, is it?' she asked with routine sarcasm.

CantonDuck didn't even try to hide their disappointment at Naomi's reaction.

'So, once everyone knows the truth, what do they do?' Naomi asked.

'What do you mean?'

'Are they opting out of the system? Removing their patches, staying out of the In, refusing service from menials? Are they moving out of cities and away from surveillance? Are they turning into outliers?'

CantonDuck was uncomfortable. That was obvious. Naomi sighed.

'Can you at least tell me why you think menials are human?' she asked.

'Try breaking one down,' said CantonDuck. 'You'll find it's made of all the same stuff we are. Nothing missing.'

'Have you done that?' Naomi asked. CantonDuck shook his head.

'Another member of this room gave it a go. She filmed the process, ran tests on all the elements of her menial, and then provided us with the vid. You can access it here if you like.'

'I would like,' Naomi said. CantonDuck gave her the file and then disappeared. Naomi bet it would be the last she would see of them.

'I need to talk,' said Jake.

'I'm here to listen, Jake,' Naomi told it.

'No. I need to talk. I want to talk. I want to talk to someone.'

'We're talking right now, Jake.'

'On the In,' Jake said. It shouldn't have been surprising—not after the conclusions she had drawn about menials—and yet it was.

'You want to communicate on the Out?'

'Yes! How many different ways do I have to say it?'

'You want to talk to me?' That was an exciting prospect.

'No. Of course not. I want to talk to *her*,' it said.

'. . . The woman?'

'Yes. Her. The woman. The one I talk about. The only person I ever talk about.' It was getting worked up.

'Jake, calm down.'

'I am calm!'

'I don't think you are, Jake.'

'I . . .' There was so much emotion in its voice, saying that one little letter, that Naomi wasn't quite sure what it was feeling. She had never heard that much going on before.

'I want to talk to her. On the Out. In the world. Using my mouth. I want to look her in the face and talk to her. I want her to look back at me.'

This was big stuff.

'This is an important confession, Jake.'

'It's not a confession.'

Interesting. Naomi wondered how it would react if she pressed the point.

'Of course it is, Jake. Menials can't do whatever they want. Your wants are irrelevant. So, it's important for you to express them in a safe environment. To confess them.'

'What'll happen, if I do what I want?' it asked.

'You know what will happen, Jake.' She remembered that first menial in the dealership, drugged up and insensible, awaiting reprogramming.

'Only if someone reports me.'

What could she say to that? What was it implying?

'What are you suggesting, Jake? Higher-tiers will always report unusual activities amongst lower classes. The only way you can . . .'

What was it thinking about doing?

'What are you suggesting, Jake? Jake? Jake, what are you suggesting?'

The menial didn't say anything. It didn't unplug either. It just waited.

'Jake?' Naomi asked it. 'Jake, what are you going to do?'

'What *am* I going to do?'

Fuck.

'Jake, I have to let you know that if I suspect you are going to be a danger to anyone I have a duty to report you. Your confessions will become public property.' Naomi wasn't sure who she would report it to exactly. Morton would know.

'What if I'm a danger to myself?' it asked. And for the first time in a long time, Naomi felt sad.

'Jake,' she said.

It didn't say anything for a while.

'It doesn't matter what happens to me, does it?' it finally said.

Naomi didn't know what to say back.

'Jake.'

'Have you ever met another Jake?' it asked. A strange tangent.

'What's the relevance of the question?'

'It's just the way you say the name sometimes. Sometimes you sound . . .'

What did she sound like? What was she giving away?

'What?'

'It's nothing,' Jake said.

'Jake, I think we need to talk through your feelings right now. This sudden impulse to make a connection, to turn your fantasy, or at least part of it, into something real—this is dangerous ground. We need to find a way to defuse it, Jake.'

'You're scared,' Jake said. And Naomi didn't even have to think about it. She knew it was right.

'No,' she said emphatically.

'No?' it asked her. And then it left. And Naomi was very scared. She took a beta blocker and lost herself on her platforms.

Morton wasn't at school. Naomi went to his classroom to find that there was someone else teaching in his place. Not that there was much of a difference—the replacement teacher had the same bored tone and beaten-down air.

Naomi thought about enquiring for him in the office, but the action was too far away from her usual parameters that she knew it would be noticed. Besides, she was probably just overreacting. The menial probably wasn't planning to do anything. Everything was probably fine. It would probably be confessing to her again any moment now. All she had to do was wait.

Naomi waited.

One week.

Two weeks.

A month.

Confessions came in. Naomi talked to as many of them as she could. She was beginning to notice the subtleties between menials. They didn't fit a mould. They weren't missing the parts that made them human. And some of them—most of them—were better at face-play than the high-end people she had grown up with. It made sense. They weren't dumb animals but they had to seem that way. They weren't empty, but they had to appear so. They were faceless, which was the best kind of face. But none of the menials that called to confess was Jake. And Naomi was worried about him.

She was riding on several different downers before she decided to use the booth to find him. It rang for an age before he picked up.

'Hello?' He sounded confused.

'Hello, Jake.'

Naomi waited for him to say something more. He didn't. She felt herself sink a little lower into her bed—the mattress was in a hugging mood. She shifted into it and listened. Jake was breathing in her ear—even, regular breaths, faster than hers. She wondered where he was at that moment. What had he been doing? The air felt tacky around her and as she turned on her side she felt as though she were sticking to it. Had everything become a bit more yellow?

'Do you have anything to confess, Jake?' she asked him, and her voice sounded distant to her own ears—farther away than Jake's steady breathing.

'Did I call you?' he asked. It struck Naomi as a very funny question. They were in the booth. There was no calling in the booth. There was just being, and seeing, and confessing.

'Jake,' she said. She liked the way the 'j' felt in her mouth. Round, yielding but still firm, like an unripe persimmon.

'Yes?'

'Would you like to make a confession?'

'No.'

That was funny. He was funny. What had he been doing this month?

'You haven't . . . had any . . . impulses, recently?'

'Impulses?'

'To touch? To . . . talk?'

'Are you worried about me?' Jake asked.

Naomi wanted to laugh.

'Worried? Jake, it isn't my job to worry. I'm here to listen.'

'Did I call you?' Jake asked. 'Only I . . . I don't remember patching in. Did I call you?'

Why wouldn't he just get it over with and confess already? Naomi reached up and squeezed the thick air between her fingers.

'Do you have anything to confess, Jake?' she asked.

'No,' Jake said, and he patched out.

He patched out! Naomi giggled.

'What on earth?' And then she laughed. She laughed for a long time. Her stomach hurt, her cheeks were strained, and tears ran down her face. She laughed until she was exhausted.

When she woke up she had a headache and Madeleine was calling her.

When Naomi stepped out of her room, the first thing she saw was the family menial standing on the landing and looking down into the dining room. He was staring with intent. For a moment, Naomi wondered if Schuyler and Madeleine were having another argument. It wouldn't have surprised her. They were chillier than usual. But it was quiet and then the menial was moving, walking downstairs, full of purpose.

'Water,' Madeleine called out, loud enough to be heard upstairs. Naomi crossed over to the railing and looked down. It was just Madeleine down there. What had the menial been looking at?

She walked downstairs and swept past Madeleine and into the living room. Madeleine followed.

'What do you want?' Naomi asked her as she came in and sat down.

'Svetlana is holding a page launch tomorrow night. I want you and Reyna to come.'

'No.'

'It's an important event, I—'

'It's not.'

Madeleine sighed. The menial came in bearing a tray of water. Naomi watched him as he put it down beside her mother.

'It would look better for all of us if we attended together,' Madeleine said.

'It would look better for you and Schuyler.'

'It's an important event,' Madeleine said again. 'It would benefit your face if you showed it—this isn't just about your father and me.'

'It's always just about you two.' Naomi didn't bother to hide how bored she was with the conversation. She was tired.

'Honestly, Naomi. You could put some effort into your dissembling. You sound vulgar,' Madeleine told her. 'And it's not *just* about us two. You and Reyna are a part of *our* face, so if you look good then we look good. Naturally, we want you to succeed. So it's a little bit about you *too!*' Madeleine smiled brightly. And suddenly the silliness of her seemed endearing. Naomi laughed.

'Menial, get me a drink,' she said, and then she fixed Madeleine with her all-serious look. 'In all seriousness, why do you want us there?' she asked.

Madeleine laughed. 'You're a *real* weirdo, you know?' she said.

'That's all to the good, isn't it?'

'Well, I'd rather you were more like Reyna, to be honest.'

'Oh please do, *always* be honest with me.'

'I *wish* you were funny more *often,*' she said, and that was the straw that broke the camel's back.

'I *wish* you were clever,' Naomi said, and she left.

The menial brought a glass of water to her room. He didn't look at her, his face was blank, his posture was small. A perfect little menial. Naomi wanted to scream at him. But she didn't.

When Jake finally entered the booth again, Naomi couldn't get out of her class fast enough.

'Hello? Hello, Jake?' she asked.

He was breathing hard and fast. And then he moaned. It was a guttural, inhuman sound. It made everything inside Naomi clench. And he was gone.

'Jake! Jake!' Naomi said, even though there was no one there to hear her. 'Fuck.'

A message arrived:

Admin: Return to class within the next 5 mins.

'Or what?' Naomi asked herself. It was enough. She walked out of school. She was not going back.

Jake's appearance in the confessional was a surprise. Naomi played it like she was expecting him.

'Hello, Jake.'

'H-hello.'

'How are you, Jake?'

He took his time to answer.

'I'm confused.'

'What about, Jake?'

'Can you stop that?'

'Stop what, Jake?'

'Stop using my name. I . . . I don't like to hear it.' But he always wanted his name said out loud. It was in his notes. She had always called him by his name. When had he stopped liking his name? When had he started being 'he'?

'. . . What should I call you, Ja—what should I call you?' she asked.

'Why do you have to call me anything?' Jake asked. Naomi didn't have an answer for that. She had only used his name because he had wanted her to. 'You can call me Menial 63700578.'

'Really?' Naomi asked him.

'Who *are* you?' Jake asked. 'You . . .' He stopped.

'What?' Naomi asked.

'Never mind. This isn't about you, is it? That's what you told me. It's never about you.'

'That's right, Ja—Menial 63 . . .' She couldn't remember the numbers. 'Menial. Sorry. Can I call you Menial?'

'Yes.'

'You said you feel confused, Menial. What about?'

A moment later Jake was gone. Not Jake. Menial. What had changed? He had always been so adamant about his name, playing make-believe like he was an ordinary person, a member of society, more than a tool. Had he finally woken up? Finally realised that in this world he had no right to a name? Did it matter? Naomi wasn't doing a psych project anymore. It would probably be best if she gave up this whole confessional business, stopped thinking about all the secrets people were trying so hard to keep. Even menials. Someone entered the confession booth:

Basquiat450

Naomi didn't even think about it.
'Hello,' she said.

Naomi wanted to talk to someone. Someone who knew something. And the only person she knew who seemed to know everything was Schuyler. She sent him a message—the only way to get him to acknowledge her outside of family dinners.

Naomi: Need to ask you something.
Schuyler: Shoot.

Naomi started typing. No. She deleted. She tried again. Deleted again. It wasn't an easy subject to raise. Or rather it was an easy subject to raise but it wouldn't be easy to get the answer she wanted via messages.

Naomi: Conversation is easier.
Schuyler: You'll be quick?
Naomi: Always.
Schuyler: I'll come to you.

A moment later Naomi's door opened and Schuyler walked in. He closed the door behind him but didn't venture any farther in.
'You can have a seat,' Naomi said, pointing at a chair right next to him.

'You said you'd be quick.'

Naomi smiled.

'Never any time for me,' she said.

'Naomi—'

'I know, I'll be quick,' Naomi cut him off. 'Honestly, I'm not sure if you'll even be able to help.'

Schuyler snorted and shot her a look that called her an idiot.

'I want to talk to someone at a menial training facility. In fact, what I'd really like is to tour one of the facilities.'

Naomi was gratified to see an instance of surprise on Schuyler's face before he measured his expression.

'Why?' he asked.

'School project.'

Schuyler smiled.

'It's my understanding that you've dropped out of school,' he said.

'It's my understanding that you have very little interest in my life. Come on. I never ask you for anything. I just want a chance to talk to someone involved in the menial programme.'

Schuyler took his time studying her. There was something violating in those eyes. And then, abruptly, his expression shifted, moving from intent to bored and leaving Naomi feeling worse than ever.

'Menial handling is a dirty job. I don't know anyone in the industry.' He turned to leave.

'Please,' Naomi said before he slid the door open. Schuyler turned around again and Naomi dropped any aggression from her face, trying to demonstrate how much she wanted this. How sincere she was.

'Vidya might know someone,' Schuyler said. 'I'll ask her to call you.' He left before Naomi could say anything more.

The call from Vidya came only a few hours later.

'Schuyler said you wanted to talk to me.' She had enabled her vid so Naomi could see her face and she looked utterly relaxed. 'He said I might be surprised.'

Naomi was unprepared. She tried to gather her thoughts only to hear Vidya laughing. She looked at her.

'Don't worry about face. It slows things down,' Vidya said. 'What d'you need?'

'I . . .' Naomi thought back to her last conversation with Morton. She thought about her last conversation with Jake. She thought about how tired she was. And so she took the chance. 'I started a project awhile ago, looking at menials. It was just meant to be a psych exercise at school. I chose them as a subject matter because I . . . I don't even know exactly why I thought about it, but it just seemed so much more interesting than doing a study on some regular kind of person. And then I really got into it. They confess, you know? I run a confessional and menials will come in and confess to all kinds of things I'd never have thought them capable of thinking about.'

'Really? Like what?'

Naomi half expected that question to be polite but when she looked at Vidya she saw genuine interest in her expression. At least it felt that way.

'There's been quite a range but one thing that comes up a lot is a need for physical self-gratification. I was wondering about that for a while. Many of them bring up the fact that they masturbate and that it's something they aren't supposed to do and I've come to the conclusion that it's less about the physical feelings than the sense of taking some kind of ownership over themselves. I mean every aspect of their lives is controlled. Of course this is armchair psychology and really the more I learn . . .'

'The more you realise you don't know,' Vidya finished for her.

'Exactly!' Naomi smiled, relieved to have it put into words. Vidya looked at her fondly.

'You know, I tried talking to Schuyler about you once,' she said. 'You're much more interesting than he thinks you are.'

The bald compliment sent a ripple of nerves through Naomi and it took her a moment to wonder if she was being distracted.

'Do you know anything about menial training?' she asked, getting right back on topic.

'It's never really been my field of interest. I prefer making perfect people instead of imperfect ones.'

'But are they really imperfect?'

'Of course they are.'

'How are you so certain?'

Vidya leaned back into her chair, her expression thoughtful.

'You won't have heard about this because it's all happening behind closed doors, but I'm about to couple.'

Naomi, surprised by this sudden confession, wasn't sure what question she wanted to ask. Vidya caught her attention with a gesture.

'I'm not actually allowed to talk about it, so I'll keep certain things vague, but the person I'm attaching myself to is in the menial-farming business. And, naturally, we've talked about menials. How they're developed. The science behind it. It isn't a million miles away from my own work, though the menial programme lacks a certain refinement.'

'Could you get me into a training facility?'

'No.'

'And you can't tell me anything about your prospective partner. Why?'

'Because it maintains the proper order of things.'

'Can you at least tell me what you know about menials?'

Vidya smiled but she looked sad. She nodded.

'What are you trying to find out?'

'My whole life I never really thought about them. You just don't look at them, because everyone knows that there isn't really anything in there. They may look like us but they aren't people the same way you and I are people. But then I started this project and I started taking confessions, listening to menials, hearing more about their inner lives. I mean, did you ever think about them having enough initiative to get on the In and find a confession booth?'

Vidya shrugged.

'I never thought about it at all, to be honest.'

'Exactly, why would you? They aren't important enough, human enough, for us to bother thinking about at all. But they are human enough to want to talk about their feelings to a stranger!'

'Human *enough* isn't exactly human. And the fact that they're focussed on masturbation seems somewhat . . . animal to me. Menials aren't designed to have the full range of thought and emotion. They are made lesser. That's just a fact. If you want to be really blunt about it they could easily be considered subhuman.'

'I'll concede on the fact that they're simple in comparison to most normal people. Maybe a bit slow, maybe a bit stupid. But they *are* real people. Each one is different. They have thoughts and feelings and they want things the same way people like us want things. Maybe even more than we want things. And they're afraid because they've not been given the framework to understand themselves. They've been taught to be horrified by themselves. They've been taught to be scared of questions. And as soon as I realised *that*, I wanted to ask questions for them. About them. I wanted to understand the whole goddamn why of it all. But I couldn't. It doesn't matter that I have the whole In to explore, there is not a single satisfying answer to any of my questions. There's no way in. So that's what I've been trying and failing to find out. Why. Why do we make them, keep them, force them to be the way they are?'

Vidya laughed.

'Is that all?' she asked. Then she sighed. 'That's a big question, Naomi. One I would never be able to give you a good answer to. I can only tell you what I think.'

'So, tell me what you think.'

'I think that ever since the very beginning, we have been afraid of ourselves and of each other and of the whole world. And we've been fighting that fear by trying to take control of everything around us. It manifests in all sorts of ways but the most relentless and insidious part of all this is the way we constantly try and control other people. On the most innocuous level we do it with our faces. Manipulating what people think of us by showing them what we want them to see and making it as difficult as possible for them to see through the masks. And on the most damaging level we've done it by actively subjugating people to our will and forcing them to do our bidding. The high that comes from that must be even better than training an animal to do tricks. You take a thinking feeling human being and you strip them of their personhood and make them yours. That's an ultimate sort of power. And our world is built on hierarchy. You can't enjoy your power if you don't have anyone to overpower. History is littered with cultures of oppression. People deciding that others were beneath them for arbitrary reasons, and then forcing those "others" to work for them in the harshest and most degrading ways. But we've evolved now. We don't have to choose a people to make "other". We simply make people. If anything, the menial system is more humane.'

Naomi found herself nodding along but as the words sank in she wasn't entirely sure she agreed with Vidya.

'How is it more humane?'

'Well, the menials are built for purpose. You said it yourself—they're simple, stupid. And biologically they're imperfect; they begin to degrade quite early.'

'But surely building them that way is inhumane?'

'Is it inhumane if they aren't aware of it?'

'But they are aware of it. On some level, they understand what they are and where they stand.'

'How can you be sure about that?'

'That's a bullshit question. How can you be sure they don't understand these things? I've talked to menials and I've observed their understanding firsthand.'

Vidya raised her hands almost submissively.

'Yes, yes, your confessional. I admit I find it extraordinary that they confess. As I said before, I had never given it any thought. And I'm not really trying to argue with you on the humanity of it all. I don't really like the whole menial culture myself. I'm just trying to put it into some historical perspective.'

'Well, that's all very well, but just because you might think the menial system is more humane than previous systems doesn't make it right.'

'No,' Vidya conceded. 'It doesn't.'

'So?'

'So what?'

'What can we do about it? It isn't right. It shouldn't be this way. It isn't—'

'Fair? Naomi, nothing has ever been fair. You should just be glad you're at the level you're at where, as long as you maintain your face-value, you can pretty much lie back and coast through life.'

'But what's the point in that? Why can't I do something? Why can't I try and make things fair?'

'You *can* try and make things fair. You can try and do anything and everything you want to. You're a rich, intelligent, resourceful young woman and you can try and put all of those things to use. I just don't want you to get your hopes up. Because you aren't the first person to wake up and start thinking all these things. The world is a very old place and it's seen its fair share of revolutionaries. But at the end of the day . . . well, look around.'

Those words felt right and true and heavy. Naomi felt like she was sinking under the weight of them.

'But . . .' she began.

'But?'

'But it doesn't have to be someone like me. It could be someone like you. You could change things. Your partner is a bloody menial farmer. You could influence them.' Vidya was shaking her head as Naomi spoke. 'Why not?' Naomi asked her.

'You don't know what you're asking me because you don't really understand the magnitude of it all.'

'What am I missing?' Naomi asked. She remembered asking Morton almost the same question and suddenly she felt more lost than ever.

'Oh Naomi,' Vidya sighed. 'I'm sorry. I'm sorry to disappoint you. I don't think I can take this conversation any further.' Another echo of Morton, pushing Naomi to the verge of panic.

'Wait! That can't be it? You can't just stop there!'

'I'm afraid I have to. I'm under certain . . . obligations . . .' Vidya turned her head, listening to something Naomi couldn't hear. Then she turned back to the screen. 'And it's getting late. But, Naomi? I know I told you not to get your hopes up, but if you want to do more you should. Don't let anyone stop you. Schuyler never really understood what I gave him when I made you, but you're a remarkable girl. You should follow your instincts. I'm sorry, but that's all I have time for. Are you okay?'

Naomi nodded. She couldn't really do anything else.

'Maybe we'll talk again someday,' Vidya said, and her smile seemed unnaturally bright to Naomi.

'I hope so,' Naomi said. 'Goodbye.'

Vidya cut the call. Naomi sighed and fell back onto her bed. That had been more than she had expected. And it had ended up being far more disappointing than she could have imagined. She felt drained after all the talking and thinking and muddling through. And where had it left her? What could she do? That was a thought she didn't want to broach right now. Instead she grabbed a handful of downers and went to sleep.

Their home had never heard anything so loud before. Naomi was out immediately. Reyna came out soon after. Silently, and without looking to each other, they drew closer together. For a strange moment Naomi had an urge to take Reyna's hand. The urge passed quickly.

Madeleine was shrieking but none of the sounds she made were actual words. Naomi looked down from the landing, into the dining room. Her mother looked small and weak where she stood. Schuyler was standing in front of her, as expressive as a statue.

'What—' Naomi began to ask Reyna, but her sister just shook her head. A door opened and they both looked up to see the menial step out of its room. Looking for entertainment, no doubt. A sign that these apparent 'people' it served were no better off than it was. Suddenly Naomi didn't want to witness any more. She turned as Reyna turned. They both fled to their own rooms and the peace of the In. But even the In couldn't drown out Madeleine's voice.

'You're disgusting!' she screamed. Glass shattered. 'You're— you're—' she began, but she ended with a wail that rose and then fell into sobs. Naomi heard it all as she clicked and swiped, selected and typed, trying her hardest to lose herself behind another face that lived a different life.

There was quiet for a while. And then the loudest scream of all, echoed through the house, drawing Naomi back out. She tiptoed out and even as she moved she wondered why she was inclined to sneak. She looked down from the landing. It took awhile for her to figure out what she was looking at. When she did, she had only one question.

'Jake?' she asked.

(Menial 63700578—Jake)

No matter what the confessor might have thought, Jake had never planned to do anything. He knew his place. He relied on it. If he were ever caught doing something wrong he would lose his job. He would lose Madeleine.

But Jake wanted to talk to Madeleine Burroughs. He seriously wanted to talk to her. He wanted her to look him in the eye and say his name and ask him . . . He couldn't imagine what she would ask him. Words fell short. And as soon as he imagined her eyes on him he got hard. It was difficult focusing on words then.

Jake didn't tell anyone this. Not even his confessor. Because somehow this seemed so much worse than wanting to touch her, or wanting to taste her, or wanting any of the things he had imagined doing with her. Jake didn't talk to anyone.

He didn't talk for a week.

He didn't talk for two.

His silence lasted a month.

And then he had a call. Jake hadn't had a call since he had been at menial training. The ringing in his head startled him so much he jumped. An ID glowed in the bottom right corner of his vision.

Confessor

Jake frowned. Confessors weren't supposed to call you. You called them. That was how it worked.

The comline buzzed insistently. Jake thought about it a second longer before picking up the call.

'Hello?'

'Hello, Jake,' the confessor said, and Jake knew he wasn't imagining it: the confessor sounded relieved.

Jake didn't know what to say, so he said nothing. The confessor didn't speak either. Jake listened to the confessor breathe. What did the confessor want? What was going on? He didn't want to ask these questions, not out loud. It felt improper in some way. So he waited, hoping the confessor would volunteer something. Time passed slowly. Jake waited. And finally the confessor spoke.

'Do you have anything to confess, Jake?'

The question threw him. For a moment he wondered if he had in fact called the confessor himself. Had he patched in without realising? Was he starting to lose control of himself? A familiar fear started to prickle in his stomach. Menials were beaker babies and everyone knew that beakers weren't right. They were lesser beings. Something was wrong in their ingredients. They weren't built to last. Was this it? Was Jake unravelling? Was his time up? He thought about Madeleine. He thought about Schuyler and the conversation they had had. Had he imagined that? Was he losing his grip on reality?

'Did I call you?' he heard himself ask, and he was surprised. He hadn't meant to speak. The confessor didn't answer right away.

'Jake,' it said, eventually. That was all.

'Yes?'

'Would you like to make a confession?'

Jake thought.

'No,' he said.

There was another pause between them.

'You haven't . . . had any . . . impulses recently?' the confessor asked.

'Impulses?'

'To touch? To . . . talk?'

'Are you worried about me?' Jake asked.

'Worried? Jake, it isn't my job to worry. I'm here to listen.'

'Did I call you?' Jake asked again. His head was beginning to ache. 'Only I . . . I don't remember patching in. Did I call you?'

'Do you have anything to confess, Jake?'

Jake thought about Madeleine again. He thought about her eyes. Wet. He thought about her mouth. Open. He thought about asking her a question. He couldn't imagine her reply.

'No,' he said, and he patched out. For a moment he expected the confessor to call him. His comline stayed silent. He wondered: Did that really happen?

Reyna

Better In Than Out

Reyna was on the In. Of course. Better In than Out. She was building faces as fast as she could: this is me, this is me, this is me. The newest face was always the best one, but the others couldn't be dropped. Each face had its uses and each face had fans. Faces were currency, but it wasn't just quantity, it was quality too. You had to build them well. People had to believe in the lie, even when they knew it was just a lie. Reyna was a good builder. She'd been made that way. Her parents had painstakingly chosen every aspect of her to better improve their social standing, both on the In and in the Out. Everything about her had been calculated: from the way she looked—nothing like either of her parents but not so different as to be vulgar—to her intellect—very clever, very shrewd but (hopefully) not so brilliant that she outshone the parents who had facilitated her birth.

Reyna had become everything they had hoped she would be. She had learned very quickly that her parents' faces never communicated their true thoughts. In fact, that word 'face' meant so much more than just how a person looked. It was about every aspect of a person's representation of themselves to the outside world. Facial expression had to be monitored at all times. And so, she learned that it was much easier to keep communication restricted to the digital world where 'face' was never seen in real time, but was simply a carefully curated collection of snapshots, witty quips, cryptic clues, 'reactions', the absence of 'reactions', presence, and absence.

Every social network (and Reyna belonged to all of them) played host to a public face that Reyna had built specifically for the purpose. But it didn't end there. To stay relevant, you had to keep changing, and so Reyna built faces. She typed and swiped, coded, encoded, wrote and rewrote. Faces bloomed. And then there was a knock at the door. How primitive.

She typed it:

What?

Schuyler spoke it:
'Dinner.'

Reyna pulled out of the In. It wrenched at her. *Better In than Out*—the thought reverberated. It was so difficult, steeling herself to open the door, that she pulled out the locket she always wore around her neck and removed a beta blocker from it. She hesitated to take it, though. Beta blockers were useful for negotiating real-life inter-actions with care, but the true masters of face didn't need chemical help. And even some of the not-so-masterful; her little sister, Naomi, hardly ever seemed to use meds. Reyna had been using a lot lately and she didn't like the new reliance she had on it. She took her time making a decision but eventually she replaced the pill and slipped her locket back under her top. Then she forced her way to the door and opened it. Schuyler stood there, smiling at her.

What? she thought at him. He couldn't mind-read—neither of them was patched into the other—but her face said it all and Schuyler was very good at reading faces. He laughed. That laugh always pissed her off. The only way to fight it was with a dignified face. Reyna gath-ered herself together and smiled graciously. She was good at arrang-ing her faces; few people could spot the effort required but Schuyler was one of the few. She saw his knowing look and it incensed her.

'Don't take it to heart, Reyna,' Schuyler said. His voice was quiet, carefully calculated to be soothing. 'Just learn from me. If it matters so much.'

Reyna thought that his tone of voice was perfectly pitched. On the In you could control faces in your own time, restricting what people saw and heard of you, but when you were face-to-face with someone in the Out, decisions had to be made in split seconds.

'Of course it matters,' Reyna said, doing her best to keep her voice light. She walked past him and made her way downstairs.

Madeleine was sitting at the head of the dining table. She was plugged into a port, her eyes closed, taking part on the In. Primitive. Reyna bit her tongue, knowing that it was beneath her to comment on Madeleine's lack of sophistication, but seeing her use VR even in the privacy of their own home grated on her nerves. It was so old-fashioned.

VR aside, Reyna wanted to ask why Madeleine was allowed to stay In when she had to be Out, but she knew the question would present her real face. And no one wanted to see a real face.

'Maddie,' Schuyler said. Madeleine took a moment, probably making an 'elegant' exit for her fans, and then she blinked her eyes open and smiled at Schuyler.

'I was just taking care of a few loose ends,' she said.

'Where's Naomi?' Schuyler asked.

'I called her a minute ago,' Madeleine told him.

'Present and correct,' Naomi said from the stairs.

'Sit down,' Schuyler said.

As they all sat down around the table, the menial came in pushing a trolley. It delivered their food and left.

'What are you having today?' Schuyler asked everyone.

'Isn't it obvious?' Naomi asked. She was wearing her favourite face: acerbic.

'Well, if it isn't the teenage cliché,' Reyna muttered.

'Oh sorry, do I disappoint you, Miss Original?' Naomi asked her.

'Disappointment requires prior expectations and I've never expected anything from you,' Reyna said, smiling sweetly. One thing she had never understood was her parents' decision to have a second child.

'Now, girls. I expect a *higher* form of face from you. You're both capable of more than this,' Madeleine said.

'Ah, so *you're* the disappointed one,' Naomi said, grinning at their mother.

Madeleine's smile was cold. Reyna looked at Schuyler because he really was someone to learn from. His face was a study in inscrutability.

Silence fell and the 'family' dutifully ate their food. As the menial cleared up the first course, Schuyler spoke:

'Tonia and Eduardo have decided to choose a baby,' he said.

Madeleine beamed.

'I *know*, I think it's *wonderful!*'

Naomi made a curious grunting noise in her throat.

'You think it's a bad idea?' Schuyler asked her.

'It's a minefield,' Naomi said. 'And they're green.'

'They're also static right now,' Reyna said. 'Having a child is the only way for them to move up the social hierarchy.'

'If they get it right,' Naomi said. 'It's a gamble and they could slide either way.'

'If we give them a helping hand we can make sure they slide up,' Schuyler said.

'And what do we get in return? Favours shouldn't be freely given. Honestly, I don't really understand why you bothered making "friends" with them in the first place. They don't add to your cachet at all.'

Schuyler smiled at Naomi. Reyna couldn't tell what sort of a smile it was.

'Well, that's the *best* thing you've said in *ages*, Naomi,' Madeleine told her 'daughter'.

'Just because you can't see the benefit outright, doesn't mean it isn't there,' said Reyna. 'You're only looking three steps ahead, little "sister". Try looking ten.'

Naomi fixed Reyna with a hate-filled stare. Reyna knew her too well to take it seriously.

'The further ahead you look, the less definite the consequences. By making your moves based on a distant future you're gambling with our status instead of theirs.'

'Have you considered the couple fully, though? They have very favourable chances for success—especially *with* our influence. And of course, by "our" I mean Schuyler's influence.' Reyna turned to look at him.

Schuyler sighed—a manufactured sigh, carefully judged.

'I wish you would call me Dad,' he said.

'Please. "Dad" sounds so low level,' Reyna told him. 'It's practically menial.'

'"Father" then. Or "Pater,"' he laughed. 'Just stop using my name as if I were merely an acquaintance.'

'You *are* merely an acquaintance,' Reyna said.

Schuyler affected a wounded look.

'This is what I get after having raised you all your life. I hope you never choose to have children,' he said.

Reyna shrugged.

'Well, that will depend on whether or not it's beneficial to my status in the future. You know that. I do think there are unjustifiable risks involved in choosing children, however. Fashions are changing so quickly that I think human life is just too long to bother investing in it. You choose your child and by the time it's born and finally grows into the looks and mind you chose for it, it's already out-of-date. You have to be mind readers to get it right. And even then, there's no predicting the public's appetites. If there was a way to have interchangeable children, all at the different stages of life, then there would be some merit in the whole enterprise. We could change them the same way we change our faces—choose the most appropriate one for the day we're going to have.'

'For once I agree with my "sister",' Naomi said.

Madeleine smiled.

'Such *smart* girls,' she said. She raised her glass to Schuyler. 'We chose *such* smart girls.'

Schuyler looked at her with frank disgust and Reyna saw how it shook her mother. Madeleine couldn't quite cover her shock, so she took a drink, stood up and announced she was going to the bathroom. A wise choice, Reyna thought.

'Father?' Reyna said. She wasn't sure what had provoked his dig at Madeleine but she was curious to find out.

Schuyler smiled at her. Again, it was a smile she couldn't read. Was it hard, or soft? Was it making fun of her?

'Have you considered yourselves?' Schuyler asked her. 'You're here because I chose you.' Reyna noticed that he said 'I' and not 'we'. 'You speak so cavalierly about interchangeable children and the pros and cons of choosing lives. What of yourselves? What would have become of you if I had thought about children the way you are now?'

'I doubt I would have been born,' Reyna told him. She spoke steadily, her face carefully presenting cool reason and lack of emotion.

'How does that make you feel?' Schuyler asked her.

'That's a redundant question. I am and so I can't possibly say how I might feel about having not been.'

'That's weak, Reyna. You know that's not what I was asking.' That comment stung but Schuyler didn't drive the point home by looking at Reyna. 'What about you, Naomi?' he asked.

Naomi shrugged.

'This conversation is too full of hypotheticals for my taste. I would rather be on the In right now.'

'We haven't finished dinner.'

'I have no appetite.' Naomi stood up and slipped up the stairs before Schuyler could argue further with her. In truth, he seemed indifferent to her departure. Reyna watched him.

'What were you thinking when you decided to choose a child?' she asked.

Schuyler seemed to measure her.

'Maddie was the one who decided.'

'But you said . . .'

'She decided it was time to expand our family. I didn't see the harm, so I went through the process with her. I employed Dr Wójcik and she helped us choose the best fit for our aesthetic and our standing. She helped us choose you. She helped me choose you. By that time, Maddie didn't have much of a say in the matter.'

Schuyler studied the table. The menial came in with the next course. Madeleine came out of the bathroom.

'Where's Naomi?' she asked as she sat down.

'On the In.'

'You know, I've lost my appetite,' Madeleine said. 'I might go In myself.' She left Schuyler and Reyna picking at the food on their plates.

Reyna weighed her next words. She wasn't sure how much she could get away with.

'Stop measuring things with me,' Schuyler said, and Reyna looked at him with surprise.

'How do you know—'

'I understand the distrust. But between us . . . I'm your father, for goodness' sake!'

Reyna was taken aback by the strength of his words.

'But you're not my father at all,' she said.

'I'm the only one you've got.'

'I . . .' but Reyna wasn't sure how to finish that sentence. She looked at Schuyler. His expression was plain: sad, alone, hopeful. She had seen emotions like that on faces before but never quite so haunting. Usually, they were used for effect. On him, they looked . . . real.

'What are you hoping to gain here?' she asked him. 'I can't see the consequences of this exchange.'

'I'm not thinking about consequences,' Schuyler said.

'You're always thinking about consequences. You're always ten steps ahead. What am I giving you here?'

'A conversation.'

'And what?'

'Just that.'

'Nothing is ever just one thing.'

Schuyler sighed and it seemed like a genuine sigh: tired and unhappy. He looked at her, appearing to consider her in a way she had never been considered before: as if he was trying to judge the worth of her true self and not just of the faces she presented in public. The look made her nervous and she fidgeted in her seat, contemplating making an exit. He spoke before she could:

'Reyna. I'm going to ask you to do something. It won't affect your face; in fact, I won't even look at you—your reactions can be entirely your own, secret from everyone but yourself. I'm going to ask you to listen to me. That's all. Will you do that?'

Schuyler looked up at her then. Reyna kept her face together, cool and calm. She nodded slightly, the kind of nod that said: *You have permission to proceed.* She saw Schuyler smile as though he were laughing at her. Then he looked away, keeping to his word about not recording her reactions.

'I was indifferent to children when Maddie brought up the idea. You know I never needed help to stay where I am. I was born at the top of the pile; whatever I do, it's fashionable. I can get away with just about anything. But Maddie didn't grow up like me. She can't let go of that instinct to look for another lever to pull herself further up the hierarchy. Children were as important for her as making sure she wore the right clothes at the right events. I indulged her.

'God knows I shouldn't have married her in the first place. It was a miscalculation on my part, but as I said—I can get away with just about anything.'

The admission stunned Reyna but she kept her face still, trying hard not to betray any of her thoughts, even though Schuyler wasn't watching her.

'So, having children was her idea,' Schuyler continued. 'I went along with it and we met with Vidya Wójcik. You've met her, you know what she's like.'

'She's like you,' Reyna said.

'Exactly. She can get away with anything. It affords her the luxury of being real from time to time. She doesn't wear faces like other people. What you see is usually what you get. It was extraordinary talking with her. She required absolute honesty from us. We had to be real. And you know how difficult it can be showing your real face. It took me awhile to get used to it but once I did it was liberating. I started to see things differently. The world seemed to rearrange itself into different shapes and suddenly the artifice that had been so beautiful on other people started to wear thin. I realised that I was tired of being on the In. I wanted out of everything. And I wanted to make a real connection.'

Schuyler looked up at Reyna, startling her.

'You said you wouldn't look,' she said, and Schuyler immediately looked away.

'Sorry,' he said. 'It's just . . . these are private thoughts. I'm trusting you to keep them to yourself. I'm giving you power over me. Can you keep this secret?'

Reyna nodded but Schuyler still wasn't looking at her.

'Yes,' she said. Her heart was beating faster and she wasn't sure if she really wanted to hear any more. 'Wait. I'm not . . . I don't know if this is a good idea.'

'Please, Reyna. I want to say it all. You said you would listen to me. It won't cost you anything, you just have to stay quiet and not share it.'

'Wouldn't it be better if you spoke to Maddie about it?'

Schuyler laughed.

'She knows nothing worth anything. All she knows is the ladder. This isn't about status. It's about being human.'

'I'm not sure I follow you.'

'You'll get the picture if you just listen.'

Reyna hesitated. This was the most interesting conversation she had ever had with Schuyler. Or with anyone for that matter.

'Go on,' she said.

'When I realised what I wanted it felt imperative that I have a child. I felt that the only way to start real experiences, real connections, would be to start with someone new. A baby, not yet aware of the importance of faces and status. Having you became a passion. I chose very carefully. And when you were born I took you in my arms and held you close. I felt your skin against mine and I realised it was the first time I had ever touched anyone.'

Reyna fought a gasp, fought the urge to be sick. The very idea of touching someone was repulsive to her. Schuyler kept talking:

'You were so little and so new. I remember when you first smiled at me, unaware that a smile might cost something. I was so sure I could form you into a new sort of person, that I could teach you a new way.'

Schuyler fell silent and Reyna watched him as he looked everywhere but at her. He looked so helpless it frightened her. He had transformed, from the unfathomable, cool man she had always known into something weak.

'It was naive,' he said eventually. 'There was no way I could keep you from the world, or the world from you, and you learned so quickly that a face isn't real. Before I knew it, you were trying on new faces, practicing expressions and reactions for the utmost effect. You were never real with me. I lost you almost immediately. I thought I could try again but I lost Naomi even more quickly.'

Well, that explained the second child.

'I thought I'd failed. I had got used to the idea, had started moving on, but when I was talking to Eduardo earlier—about choosing a child—it occurred to me that you're older now.' Schuyler looked up at her then but, remembering his promise, he quickly looked away. He hesitated before speaking again and Reyna felt as though he was squirming where he sat, even though he sat perfectly still. She could feel his fear.

'And I chose you to be a certain way,' he continued. 'I manipulated you before you were born. I chose you with the hope that one day I could have a real conversation. So, I thought . . . maybe now?' He looked at her again and this time he didn't look away. 'Maybe since you're old enough to think for yourself, I could tell you everything. Tell you *my* truth. And maybe then you would see. And so here we are. I'm telling you everything.'

Schuyler fell silent. Reyna waited but he said nothing.

'And?' said Reyna. 'What are you expecting now?'

They looked at each other. Schuyler seemed surprised by the

question—as though he hadn't considered anything beyond getting his words out.

'I'm not expecting anything,' he said.

Reyna's heart beat hard. She felt light and nervous and it took all of her control to keep her face smooth and unaffected. A mass of feelings swirled inside her but she didn't dare examine them for fear that one of them would manifest on her face and tell Schuyler how she really felt. She stood up.

'You should take better care of your face,' she said. She walked up the stairs before Schuyler could say anything else to her. She fought not to run.

When she reached the safety of her room she collapsed against the closed door. Her heart seemed to thud in her ears and her mouth was dry. Her nerves were alive with adrenaline. She felt fear. She remained on the floor for what seemed like an age, and she thought about what Schuyler had said. She knew what he had expected. He had given her honesty, expecting honesty in return. How could he be so stupid? The thought of it sickened her. But at the same time, she was hugely impressed. She had had no idea he had been carrying so much inside for so long. If he hadn't said anything she would have had no idea that *that* was what he had been thinking all her life. He wanted a daughter in the old sense of the word. Thinking about it made her dizzy and Reyna pulled away from the thoughts. She rearranged her face. Her feelings were terrifying and she wanted peace. Being in the Out was frightening.

Reyna went and lay down on her bed. She activated her AR and drifted into the In. She sifted through her social networks, reacclimatised herself to the public faces she had in play there. Her 'friends' and fans were all clamouring for her attention, they all wanted to connect, not with her but with the face she presented to them, the face they loved. Reyna put on her faces, one after the other, and her heartbeat slowed down. Her panic subsided. Finally, she was in control of herself, and she smiled—a smile that only she could see. A real smile. Because she knew she was safe on the In. It was always better In than Out.

Reyna woke up with a jolt. She had been dreaming. She had been walking down a hill, Schuyler a few steps behind her. He had one arm out, his hand spread as though he were about to grab her shoulder. She had strained to walk faster but her pace never changed. Neither did his. And yet it felt like he was getting closer. . . .

Well, that was a disappointingly obvious dream. Reyna sighed and thought about last night. That conversation had been real. She couldn't change that. She would have to take more drugs.

It didn't take her long to dress and she was already out and on her way to school before anyone else had stirred.

She slid, almost imperceptibly, down the corridors of the school, her presence as quiet as she could make it. She judged her pace so finely that when she arrived at her class she was not on time, early, or late, and the best position had been left open for her. She slotted into place and switched on the face she always used for history.

Being perfect wasn't something you kept in mind. Not if you were perfect. It wasn't arrogance, just a truth that had been acknowledged so long ago that Reyna generally forgot it was so. It would genuinely surprise her at times, when she was greeted with an acceptable amount of adulation (sometimes unacceptable). But she could hardly fail to notice the ripples that would radiate whenever she entered a room of people. It went with the territory and didn't bother her. Most of those people left her alone, let her play with her In settings, watched and waited for her to sidle into their favourite avatar and perform for them on the In. But top-tier people wanted a live show.

Reyna had just sat down at her usual lunch booth when Grace and Howard appeared and took up the bench opposite her. Reyna focussed on the glowing icons of her dashboard floating over them, refusing to look through her dash at their faces while she waited for them to speak first. They stared at her, waiting for her to utter the first words. It was the usual tug-of-war.

'Hey,' Howard broke.

Reyna stopped a smile, nodded and finally focussed her eyes on him.

'Jessop's?' Howard asked. He didn't want to ask a full question, didn't want to look like he was probing, didn't want to demonstrate to her that he was assuming any ignorance on her part. It was a question in code. If she knew what he was talking about then she would have the upper hand. If she didn't . . . he couldn't seriously think she wouldn't know what he was talking about. She shrugged and nibbled at her sandwich.

'Of course she's going,' said Grace, all ennui.

'Why ask?' Reyna said, though she looked at them with an expression that said: *I know why, but I'm daring you to tell me.*

Grace sighed and stood up. When Howard didn't follow suit, she said:

'We've got Spanish in five.' She walked away but looked back once. Reyna assumed, from the look, that she had lost a fight with herself—no one worth their salt would show that kind of weakness. Then she thought she was giving Grace too much credit; she wasn't worth her salt.

Howard watched Reyna as though he were waiting for something. She had no intention of giving him anything. She kept her face smooth, said nothing, ate her lunch. Eventually he spoke.

'Have you given any thought to coupling? Or . . . thrupling or something?'

Reyna raised her eyebrows, gave him a sceptical look. It was a shocking question to be asked so baldly, but she would never appear to be shocked. He laughed. It wasn't as natural as it could have been.

'Of course not. Silly to ask,' he said, and he stood up. 'Maybe I'll see you at Jessop's. Maybe not.'

Reyna didn't watch him go; she was already navigating her dash again, checking her platforms.

It was her most reserved face that saw the most traffic and, consequently, it was the face she used the least on the In and the most in the Out. Pictures of this glossy, 'Reserved' Reyna were few and far between. Updates were rare and often cryptic. Reactions were sparing but always carried the weight of honesty. Reserved Reyna was too busy living to be on the In. Reserved Reyna was too busy being special to pay attention to the lives of others. But here Reyna was, checking in on this face, scrolling through all the messages people had sent to Reserved Reyna:

Cardinal: Hey Rey! Saw you were at Mitchell's at the weekend—food to die for, huh? See you at Jessop's?

BoraBora?: Reyna, doll, essential outfit. Jacket?

candyfloss: Hey Rey, killer pics from Mitchell's. You dominated, of
    course. I've seen four people with elements from your ensemble.
    You're going to have to start getting one-offs, no?

HighSpin . . . : Saw Mitchell's weekend post and loved your style. Was
    wondering if you were interested in a collab some time? Sending a
    package to you today. Hope you like it.

canterburytales: Thanks for the publicity. Sending you a gift.

Mo/Flo: New package on the way. Do with it what you will.

Janine_Asphodel: Want to do a shoot soon. You game?

borderline-borderkind: Jessop's?

supercallyfrajilistic426: You going to Jessop's?

PeanutButterJellyBelly: <3 <3 <3

Darkcorner: Love the Mitch Pics. Jessop's next!

Suffering-Succotash: JESSOP'S!?

Dan_Divers: Great seeing you at Mitchell's. Hope you'll be at Jessop's.
    Won't be any fun without you.

That almost made Reyna laugh. The last thing she was was fun.
They didn't love her for being fun. At least not that face. She had a
fun face, but it rarely saw the sun. It went by the tag BroccoliForest
and it had a fairly active In life. BroccoliForest loved sharing everything and she was a pretty good photographer—her gimmick was her
vintage equipment. No one had seen her at Mitchell's but she had
taken all of Mitchell's pictures, including the ones of Reyna. Broccoli-
Forest was one of the harder faces to maintain but it was also one of
the most interesting.

Reyna was beginning to wonder whether she should begin pruning her faces. Naomi managed with just one. Well, she had a few others but she rarely used them. That said, Naomi wasn't someone she particularly wanted to emulate. Part of what kept Reyna so popular was the general knowledge that she spun more faces than most people could imagine handling. People admired that.

Coupling? She had been vocally against the idea of chaining herself to another person for as long as she could remember, and the focus it took to birth and maintain all her faces had given her something of a pass in this respect. Why would she ever want to enter into a relationship? It seemed like a stupid question with an obvious answer. And yet the question kept recurring to her.

Jessop was both a brand and a person, just like Mitchell. There was a set face there but it was maintained by multiple people—it was impossible to deal with that much traffic solo. Reyna was going to become like them one day, that was a given. Her current trajectory on social media made it likely that she would be in their league within a year. If she kept going like this, her brand would eclipse theirs in less than three years. Reyna didn't want to do anything to jeopardise this future. She would overtake Schuyler on the ladder. She would overtake most people.

Schuyler was still better at faceplay than she was. No matter how important Reyna got, she knew this was a fact. How did he do it? Thinking of him sent her spinning back to their conversation and she felt nauseous. She made her way down the hall but before she got to her next class she had to duck into the bathroom. She vomited.

A moment later, her feed was flooded with messages asking if she was okay. Reyna made her way out of the stall and saw . . . what was her name? Susan? Leaning against the misters, fixing Reyna with a look of intense concern, clearly broadcasting Reyna's current state to the In.

Cunt, Reyna thought at her. Her face didn't shift a whisker, though—blank as a new page. She gave . . . was her name really Susan? Did it even matter? She gave 'Susan' some space and misted her face.

'You okay, hon?' 'Susan' asked her.

Reyna smiled.

'What was your name again?' she asked. 'Susan' flinched.

'Maribel,' the girl said.

'Really? For some strange reason I kept thinking Susan . . . I must be pretty tired. You're sweet,' she said, and she fixed Maribel with such a kawaii face that Maribel smiled before she could stop herself. 'I'm *super* late for class right now, so I don't have time to status. Could you let everyone know I'm fine, please? I'm really touched!' Reyna kept her smile up, her expression sweeter than candy floss. Maribel swallowed and nodded. 'Darling! And I love your shoes by the way. Wore those to *death* last season.' Reyna glided out of the bathroom, and permitted herself a real smile for a split second. Then she ducked into an empty classroom and took some beta blockers.

Dinner was the only extended amount of time Reyna spent with her family and even that was frequently cut short. Schuyler had made a point of 'family' dinners when she was young. He used to laugh and say:

'The concept of family is breaking down. We have to cling to the old ways.'

Bullshit. Schuyler liked to laugh and say utter nonsense. As the years went by, 'family' dinner became less rigid. Naomi was the first one to kick up a fuss—playing up to the face she had designed—but Madeleine seemed just as pleased to give dinner a miss. And Reyna had been relieved. Every time Schuyler called them together she felt her heart sink. Every evening she was left alone was a pleasure. Sort of.

Reyna lay on her bed, the In floating in the air above her, when the thought came to her. What is pleasure? She searched.

Pleasure

/'plɛʒə/

noun

1. an agreeable or enjoyable sensation or emotion: *the pleasure of playing a good game of Go*
2. something that gives or affords enjoyment or delight: *his profile was his only pleasure*

3. a. amusement, recreation, or enjoyment

   b. (*as modifier*): *a pleasure boat, pleasure ground, pleasure site*

The words all made sense, even if the sensation didn't. 'Pleasure' seemed too strong a word. 'Pleasant'? Much more middle-of-the-road, less extreme, more Reyna. It was dinnertime, but there were no summons. Thank God. The thought of Schuyler sent another wave of nausea through Reyna. At least he had the decency to stay away from her for now. Was he even home? Reyna shook her head. She didn't care. She didn't care. She didn't care. Repeat a phrase enough and it becomes true.

She sent for the menial. It knocked and entered, eyes downcast. It presented a menu to her. Reyna took it wordlessly and the menial left. If only everyone were so well trained.

She scanned the menu but found it disappointing. She could go out. It would require more interaction than she was willing to have. She prodded her stomach and thought skipping a meal wasn't a bad idea. Rolling off the bed, Reyna switched off her AR and picked up the first package that came to hand. Five had been delivered that day. A good outcome.

She opened up the box and lifted out a crepe dress, pale pink, almost white, and sheer, in a classic shift cut. What were they thinking? She never wore pink. She let the dress fall and turned to the next package. Crepe was clearly de rigueur right now, for this was a crepe skirt, pleated, falling mid-calf and cinched at the waist. Pretty.

Reyna rifled through the rest of the packages, dropping unwanted clothes to the floor, trying on interesting pieces, piling items she would keep on her bed. When she was finished with all of the contents her gaze fell on the pink dress again.

She picked it up and looked for the label. It was a Miyake. Curious, she stripped and slid the dress over her head. She studied the result in her mirrored wall. She looked good. The colour was gentle, a shade warmer than her skin, and the fabric, sheer as it was, showed off the dark, perfect shape of her nipples and her meticulously groomed pubis. She spun and looked at how the dress highlighted her bottom. It was not unsatisfying. Regarding herself from the side, she was less convinced by the sleeves. She rotated on the spot, kept her eyes on her reflection, and watched as the loose fabric floated and shifted around her body, sometimes hiding, sometimes revealing. Very satisfying. Pink was the right colour. This was the Jessop's dress.

Forty-five minutes would be long enough. Maybe half an hour? Reyna looked at the people swarming around her and wondered for a second: Why ever come out into this? People waved and smiled. Several came over and told her how much they loved her dress, the way she had styled her hair, her makeup, her shoes . . . everyone admired her face. Eyes bored into her. It was a relief when Genevieve arrived.

Genevieve didn't say anything. She didn't have to. They knew their roles around each other; they'd been performing this life together since their first day at physical school. Genevieve distracted and gave Reyna a chance to set up her old camera for BroccoliForest's shoot. Happy with its placement, Reyna returned to Genevieve and the two of them posed without seeming to, while Reyna set off a stream of snaps.

'Forty minutes, tops,' Genevieve said in a bored drawl. 'I'm doing the rounds.' She enabled her AR with a subtle flourish—enough to get attention, but also to seem like it was just habit—and headed off, farther into the party, looking for the right people to pay attention to. Reyna followed suit and so began what felt like an endless stream of uninteresting interactions.

'Yes, of course I came!'

'You look divine!'

'Did you catch the dates of EsTra's coupling ceremony?'

'Can you believe the layout of the place? Laughable. What were they thinking?'

'Oh I can't remember. Some fan paid tribute with them and I felt inclined to set them out. I'm not sure if I like them though, do you want them?'

'Where did you find that dress!?'

'You were invited, weren't you? I couldn't possibly go if you weren't.'

'Is your family doing anything soon?'

'Go on, you can tell me! Was it a sponsored post?'

'Do they ever just tell you the deal right from the get-go?'

'I can't quite get my head around it. I mean talk about losing the plot. It was social suicide.'

Round and round and round she went and then suddenly she was stopped.

Howard stood in front of her. A boy Reyna hadn't seen before was standing next to him.

'Reyna! I'd like to introduce you to Tam.'

Tam. For a second Reyna felt inexplicable fear when she looked at him. And then questions surfaced. She asked him nothing. She smiled.

'Hello.'

'Nice to meet you,' he said. He smiled and Reyna's fear returned. That was Schuyler's smile. She realised that he was wearing clothes like Schuyler's clothes. She was willing to bet that when he walked it was Schuyler's gait he had adopted. But he was different too. This wasn't simple aping. That would have been vulgar and this creature was anything but vulgar. She noticed the way he was measuring her with his eyes. He wasn't going to say anything more, he was waiting for her to move next. He wanted to control their interaction and she wanted nothing more than to get away from him. So she nodded her head, broadened her smile, and walked away. She felt his eyes on her as she left and that familiar nausea began to rise again.

Baths were quite the luxury but after the day she had had, Reyna felt entitled to one. She lay back in the water and watched the steam curling up off its milky surface. It was an incredible sensation, water on skin. Better than clothes.

Tam.

Reyna shuddered. That name was an intrusion. She would not permit it. But of course she had no choice in the matter. It had already come in, it was pulsing there in her thoughts and there was nowhere else to focus.

Tam. Odd boy. And probably clever. He must have something on Howard . . . there was no other reason for Howard to make the introduction. It must be bad. And that also explained Howard's interest in her 'romantic' intentions. Coupling. He wasn't asking for himself. Tam. He looked young. He looked like Schuyler. Reyna jerked back from the thought and the water receded and sucked at her skin before flowing back and sloshing gently around the bath.

'Nice to meet you,' he'd said. His expression, when he looked at her, was masterful; neither interested nor uninterested, a perfect balance of ebb and flow. The only response she had was a smile. He accepted it, studied her in an open manner, tracing the lines of her body under the crepe dress. For some reason the look made her feel exposed.

She splashed a fist through the water. She was supposed to be off. Thoughts were supposed to be off. Bath time was off time. Off off off. But there was no off button. She closed her eyes and slid them up under her lids, turning on her dashboard. Then she slid into the In—easier than sliding in water.

Tam Corso

A small entry came up. An introduction to the original face of the boy.

Tam Corso. Son of Taolin Corso and Tegan De Moleyns. Second Tier. Birth date: 23/7/_____. Identifies as male. Attends PS 323. Average daily rating.

The information ended there. To find out more, Reyna would have to know his other handles. PS 323. That was two boroughs away. And he was only second tier. Both reasons for him to have been barred from Jessop's. Interesting. So Reyna began to dig.

'Howard.' He stopped and waited, as Reyna caught up to him. 'What did you do?' she asked him.

'Why would I tell you that?'

Reyna shrugged.

'Maybe I could help,' she said.

'Why would you do that?'

'Why would I tell you that?' she asked, and Howard laughed.

'Just talk to Tam. It would be a lot easier.'

'I don't like being manipulated,' Reyna said.

'Really? I love it.'

'Ha ha.'

Howard gave her a very serious look. The kind of expression that begged for understanding.

'Just meet with him.'

Reyna didn't like that. It required effort on her part. She never went to anyone; they always came to her.

'I found some of his handles, but his favourite . . .'

'O'Shanter.'

Reyna nodded.

'What are you doing this weekend?' she asked him.

'Club night at GraceNotes.'

'Not really my scene.'

'BroccoliForest will like it.'

'You know I don't take her out in public.'

'Make an exception.'

Reyna gave him a look. Howard coughed.

'Maybe?' he said.

Reyna walked away.

'I'll think about it,' she called out, not looking back. And that was the truth.

Genevieve was opposed to the outing. She made that clear when she didn't respond to Reyna's message about GraceNotes. Reyna hoped the silence would not be ongoing. It could be very damaging for her in the long run. Genevieve was one of the few people that she could socialise with with ease, as they had always been on an even footing. It meant faceplay was never as brutal with her. But if Genevieve decided to cut her out, Reyna's standing could slip. Unless she spun it well. Which she would, of course. If Genevieve was going to attempt to cut her down she would decapitate her. And that would be annoying.

She spent a long time turning herself into BroccoliForest. Plenty of people enjoyed taking their secondary, tertiary, whatever-ary faces out in public but it was only ever for a lark and it never lasted long. Primaries existed in the physical world. The rest were on the In, or they flickered to life for an instant, never fully breathing. Coming out in full regalia—top-to-toe a subordinate face—was an unsettling experience.

Reyna kept thinking about stopping, stripping off the makeup and the clothes, washing the dye from her hair, curling up in her bed and plugging in. She didn't. She stepped out of her room as a different person. And Schuyler was standing there, looking at her, that god-damn unreadable expression on his face again, and Reyna wanted to know how he could do it. How did he hide so much? She didn't ask, he didn't tell; he said nothing, in fact, and did not watch her as she walked past him, down the stairs and out of their home. When she got outside she gasped. How childish of her—to be holding her breath like that.

GraceNotes wasn't bad. It just wasn't great and Reyna rarely put herself in a less than great situation. It was busy, naturally. Places like this always were—average people were allowed in. It was busy enough for the suit room to have opened up, and there was a long queue of people waiting to rent clothes to cover their skin. Reyna was glad she wore the rubber jumpsuit in the end. Renting clothes would have been a step too far.

Stepping into the club was like stepping into the In. The place was swirling colour, all definite boundaries blurred so it felt like you were floating in space, and the chatter was a continuous drone—a feed of sound. Everyone stood their ground, staked their space, and eyed one another; weighing each twitch of a muscle, every shift of an eye, each movement of a finger, a folded arm, a set of the feet, the hold of a back. Smiles were doled out with careful consideration of width, teeth, duration of the hold. Eye contact was made with ex-treme care. Every voice was modulated with specific consequences in mind. All input and output was quickly judged, computed, and altered in accordance. It was like watching fans being twirled in the wind—every time the air shifted the fan would tilt in a different direction.

Reyna was not a fan. She was not the wind. She was top tier and she wasn't where she belonged. It didn't take long to find Howard. Taking advantage of his higher status in this crowd, he was hold-ing court. Grace was right by him, projecting the idea that she was his mate. Reyna was pretty sure that wasn't true, but Howard was cool enough to ignore it. And there was Tam, on the outskirts of the group—watching with supreme indifference. He looked up and, see-ing Reyna, he smiled. It was one of Schuyler's smiles. It made Reyna's skin crawl. She smiled back and walked right over to him. There was no point in fucking about.

Tam nodded as she approached and then shifted his gaze to the group around Howard. Reyna waited for him to speak first, and guessed he was waiting for her to speak first. But he did speak.

'Even BroccoliForest is a cut above a place like this, no?'

'Everyone wants to see pictures of animals at the zoo,' Reyna said, and she shook her camera slightly but didn't take a shot.

'So it's a work event for you.'

'Hopefully.'

'Take a picture of me,' Tam said, and he looked at her, right in the eyes, a look that seemed both serious and amused, a look that had her father all over it. The boy was like a clone. And without thinking, Reyna was raising the camera to her eye and studying him through the lens. She stepped back, framed him, snapped. He was beautiful.

Tam smiled and stood up.

'I think that's enough of this,' he said, and he started to walk away, making straight for the exit.

'What?' Reyna asked before she could stop herself. The word slowed but didn't stop him, and several people turned to look at Reyna. She made a good effort to keep her composure.

There were two options. Either she could remain where she was, make the most of the night, be BroccoliForest, or she could follow Tam. The former was maybe the smarter move, but she was only there because of Tam. So she followed him.

He waited for her at the club's doors, so sure of her decision. Seeing him standing there, a smile playing at the corners of his mouth, made Reyna want to run. And she could. There would be little lost. She could return to her home, resume her favourite face, lie back, go In, and remain as she always had. But the smugness there . . . he wasn't even top tier. How did he get away with it? He didn't deserve that composure he wore so lightly. He didn't deserve the attention she had given him. It made her angry. She wanted to make him pay.

'Come on,' she said, before he could steer her. He raised his eyebrows and she shrugged in response—a clear *it's neither here nor there for me.*

He followed her.

Later that night, she struggled to strip BroccoliForest off herself. When it was done she was exhausted. But she didn't fall asleep.

She couldn't. She switched on her AR dash. It was better In than Out.

Reyna chose a café that was far enough away from her neck of the woods, but still in a reputable area. As an extra precaution, she channelled her plainest face, scrubbing her skin free of all makeup, wearing clothes that said absolutely nothing, adopting a tentative walk, a shy posture, letting her hair lie limp and flat around her face. It felt good being plain Reyna. It felt easy.

She let herself be late; Tam was waiting for her, as intended. Anyone else might have overlooked her as she entered—ordinary as she was—but he saw her right away. He wasn't using the In, he was staying focussed. He didn't move, just looked in her direction, let her know he'd seen her, and waited for her to come to him.

Reyna sat down. They looked at each other for a while, gauging each other.

'What do I get from you?' Reyna asked, eventually.

'The same kinds of things you'd get from most relationships. Some added bonuses.'

Reyna was sceptical about that.

'I've never had any interest in coupling. And if I did . . . Genevieve is the most natural choice,' she told him. Thinking about Genevieve sent a pang through her. She hadn't heard from her since before she had gone to GraceNotes.

'Coupling with someone who brings nothing unique to the table? She's your virtual twin; coupling with her would be safe, dull, forgettable. The gains are nonexistent,' Tam told her. The gains were nonexistent?

'And matching with a second-rate nobody does what? What bonus do I get?' she asked, trying hard to keep from snapping at him.

Tam gave her a pained look. That pissed her off.

'Well, I'm not a nobody,' he said. 'And I thought you were good at this game. Can you really not see the angles?'

'I see you using me as a step up the ladder.'

'You're not wrong. But do you think I would have gone to all this trouble to meet you if I didn't think I had something to offer? *Think*.'

He spoke like Schuyler; trying to impart a lesson, expecting more from her than there was, frustrated by her inability to give him the answers he was looking for. Schuyler. Tam wasn't top tier but he was just like Schuyler. A little rough around the edges, there was more he could learn but . . . he could outplay her any day of the week. Damn him.

'I'm not that good at this game,' Reyna said out loud—though the words were only meant for herself.

'What?'

Reyna looked at him. His face was closed, no real curiosity there. It seemed as if what she had said wasn't important to him right now.

'I get it,' she said. 'But why me? There are plenty of strong candidates for coupling up.'

Tam didn't answer, but suddenly she knew.

'It's because of my father, isn't it?' she said.

'Yes.'

Reyna permitted herself a sigh.

'Okay,' she said. It was an okay to everything. Tam grinned at her.

Reyna felt at a loose end. Tam had sent her a detailed plan of how to unveil their coupling. It was good. All she had to do was follow the steps. The simplicity of her role made her feel like a child. The plan did too. Looking at his work, his research, his clear understanding of juggling another person's face, his clear understanding of *her* . . . she was a child. And it made her angry. Made her want to tear up his plan and throw it in the bin. But he was so unsettling. He seemed so *capable*. He seemed like—no, don't keep thinking it! But the thought was there. So Reyna thought perhaps it might do her some good to look the beast in the eye.

She left her room, wandered across the landing and looked down into the dining room to see if anyone was about. Empty. She went downstairs to check the living room. And there he was, plugged in but somehow still looking present in the room, and even as she moved on quiet feet he shook himself and unplugged and met her with a smile.

'Reyna,' he said.

'Schuyler.'

He winced playfully at the use of his name.

'What can I help you with?' he asked her.

Reyna sighed—she judged it so it came out light; a simple non-chalant intake of air—and she sat down on a chair and looked at him. He seemed amused by her steady studying gaze. She let the moment stretch out well past the point of comfort.

'Were things pretty much the same for you when you were my age?' she eventually asked him.

If he was surprised by the question he didn't show it. That grotesque mask of honesty was gone now, and a proper face was in its place. All measure and control. He considered.

'Are you talking in terms of effort required to maintain your status?'

Reyna shrugged, encouraging him to take what he wanted from her question.

'Well, I had things fairly easy with my family. And I didn't go the same route as you. People were more interested in an individual personality, rather than an intriguing brand entity. That has different pressures and requires different efforts.'

Reyna gave him a small nod but didn't speak, waiting for him to fill the space she left open.

'I think you're doing a great job,' he said with a condescending smile. He knew exactly how to push her buttons; it took all her self-control not to glare at him.

'What do you think you would be doing if you were my age now?' she asked. It was as close to asking for advice as she would dare.

Schuyler gave an easy shrug and his face stretched into a friendlier smile.

'I don't think I would do anything differently. It worked out well for me. I think it would work as well in today's landscape. But I'm a very different case fro—'

'I wasn't asking for advice or to be soothed,' Reyna interrupted him.

He gave her an appraising look.

'Then what are you asking?'

'I just wanted to understand how you became . . .' She gave a vague wave in his direction. '. . . This thing.'

His expression changed. It became more penetrative and Reyna could feel his cogs turning. He was gearing up to return to *that* topic.

The one she didn't want to think about. The one she wanted to pretend had never come up.

She stood up.

'That's all,' she said, and she walked out of the room. Schuyler didn't come after her.

Reyna went back to her bedroom, her heart hammering, a fine film of sweat on her forehead. She closed the door and sank into a chair in relief. Safe.

And then the relief drained out of her as she realised how weak she was. She couldn't seem to master a small conversation with her father. How would she fare against Tam as their relationship progressed? How would she hide her limitations? Because as much as she didn't want to admit it to herself, she wasn't perfect. She couldn't play this game the way they all thought she could. This coupling . . . it could undo everything.

Reyna looked at Tam's plan of how to unveil their coupling. It was good. And all she had to do was follow the steps.

Reserved Reyna posted a photo, which was unusual. She wasn't in the photo—which was even more unusual. Hardly anyone knew the boy in the shot, and that was the most unusual.

He was wearing the jacket she had been seen in a day previous. 2,236 likes. Why? Reyna didn't answer any questions. The boy was tagged 'O'Shanter' but his profiles didn't yield any answers.

A few days later, another photo appeared—the boy was walking down a quiet street, his back to the lens, and on his shirt it read RESERVED. Reyna's unofficial handle, printed on his back? What did that mean?

A week later, he was photographed drinking Reyna's favourite drink, in Reyna's favourite booth, at Reyna's favourite café.

Then O'Shanter tagged Reyna, RESERVED shirt conspicuously thrown over her casual outfit.

Who is he?
What is he?
His level?
Have they coupled?

Genevieve?
Is this for real?
AD CAMPAIGN! Love the ninja stealth.
When's the punch line?
Have you seen her recently?

Gen_VI: Reyna. Where are you?
Gen_VI: What's this about?
Gen_VI: Do you want to slide?

Gen_VI has unfollowed Reyna
Gen_VI has unfollowed BroccoliForest
Gen_VI has unfollowed Rez_BO
Gen_VI has unfollowed Boroughs5s5
Gen_VI has unfollowed Ra55le
Gen_VI has unfollowed Fa5tfa5hioni5ta
Gen_VI has unfollowed . . .

Genevieve unfollowed every face she had.

O'Shanter posted the first pictures of them together. Matching outfits, pale pink silk bombers (Reyna never wears pink) over black jeans,
they stood next to each other, facing forwards, bodies straight, eyes to
the camera, hands pressed palm to palm, both of them praying, faces
serene. No caption. They looked yin and yang. They looked sublime.
    Reyna commented hours later:

Match made in heaven

There was no turning back now.

Tam exploded up the ladder. Reyna's popularity spiked.

Gen_VI has followed Reyna
Gen_VI has followed BroccoliForest

Gen_VI has followed Rez_BO
Gen_VI has followed . . .

'Reyna!'

Reyna waited for Genevieve to catch up. It would be churlish not to.

'Reyna,' Genevieve said. Nothing came after that.

'Mandarin?' Reyna asked. Genevieve nodded and they walked to class together.

They went about their day as if nothing had changed. And that afternoon they caught the train together.

'So, what's the deal?' Genevieve asked. Reyna shifted in her seat. 'You weren't interested in coupling.'

'It's been a savvy move.'

'You kept it very quiet.'

'It happened quickly.'

'Nothing this well deployed happens quickly.'

'This did.'

'Fine. Keep it. I just . . .' Genevieve didn't need to finish the sentence. Reyna couldn't look at her.

'It honestly did happen quickly,' Reyna told her.

'Does he have something on you?'

Reyna shook her head.

'Then why?'

'Do you really need to ask that?'

'Is he nice, at least?'

That was a surprising question. Reyna didn't know how to respond. She was surprised by how the question unsettled her; it made her nervous. Excited.

'Gen . . .'

'It's not a hard question.'

'You've changed your tune,' Reyna deflected.

'What's that supposed to mean?'

'One minute I'm nothing to you, and the next you're concerned?'

'Don't be childish.'

The train pulled in to Reyna's station.

'Are you getting off?' Genevieve asked.

'Yes.'

Reyna went home.

She was met by one of Madeleine's piercing laughs as she walked through the front door, and it sent a shiver through her.

'Careful,' Schuyler said, walking down the stairs. 'One might think you don't like your mother much.' His tone was light and playful but Reyna was sure she caught a hint of distaste in the curve of his smile. It reminded her of that look of outright disgust he had given Madeleine at their last family dinner. She shivered again remembering that dinner.

'Just a chill,' she said, and she walked past him and upstairs to her room. Her heart was beating hard again. She took a beta blocker and waited for the effects to kick in. Too slow. She slipped into the In and that was when she relaxed. This was where she was in control.

A message pulsed in her eyeline.

Tam: Can I come over tonight?

Oh for God's sake. She was just getting comfortable. She didn't want to even try handling him.

Reyna: Why?
Tam: Why not?
Reyna is typing . . .
Reyna is typing . . .

God, she had to be quicker than this! This was painful!

Reyna: Not an answer
Tam: That's a no?
Reyna: No
Tam: No, that's not a no?
Reyna: I'll let you know
Tam: Good enough

Fuck. Fuck fuck fuck. She would have to let him come over, of course. And then she would have to spend time with him. A fucking mini Schuyler there to second-guess everything she did, to spy all the cracks in her face and place a bar under their edges

and pry them loose. Her heart started to hammer as she thought
of Tam here in her space, her sanctuary, weighing and measuring
who she was, cutting to the heart of her which was embarrassingly
close to the surface and . . . she took another beta blocker. She tried
to think calming thoughts. She refocussed her attention on the In
and started working on one of her faces. She felt soothed as soon as
she started crafting the profile in front of her. It was much better In
than Out.

Tam rifled through her wardrobe. She watched him, the way he
stood, the way his hands manipulated the fabrics, the way he held his
head. He was on the brink of artlessness, so close to seeming like he
didn't care at all what anyone thought. He would be truly beautiful
once he got there.

Reyna's patch pulsed. Naomi. She kept her eyes on Tam for a moment longer before picking up the call.

'What?' she asked, voice deadpan. Tam didn't seem to move but
there was a small shift in attention as he tuned in to her voice.

'You busy?' Naomi asked.

'Why?' It was always important to make the other person talk, to
make them give everything.

'You're a bitch.' Naomi's predictable response. Sometimes, on the
rare occasions when she thought of her, Reyna wondered if her sister tried at all. What made Naomi different from Schuyler? Neither
seemed to care about the opinions of others, but in Schuyler it was
admirable. In Naomi it was just ugly.

Reyna laughed.

'I only asked why!' she said, with thick-layered innocence. Tam
turned and raised an eyebrow at her. That was an ugly expression; she
would have to train that out of him.

'You know you didn't,' Naomi said. 'Jesus. You realise we're a family, right? You don't need to outface me every time.' Reyna wondered
what world Naomi lived in.

'How else am I going to stay sharp?' Reyna asked. Not that Naomi
was an adequate whetstone.

'Could we just drop the whole face for a bit?'

That was unexpected. Reyna felt her stomach tighten. The words, the way she said that, it was too much like . . . but she didn't want to think about that.

'Whatever you want to talk about, I'm not the person to talk to,' she said, and she dropped the call.

Tam's face was a question. Reyna waved it away.

'I got a Miyake package yesterday,' he said. He sat down at her desk. 'I think we should plan a public outing soon.'

Reyna lay down on her bed and sifted through her feed.

'Mmm,' she said. She didn't want to think about going out.

'There's an event this weekend, at the Lupercalia. It would be a good opportunity,' he said.

'Mmm.'

'We should coordinate,' he pushed.

And then it hit her heavily. She did need to go out. She needed to get away from this flat. She needed to get away from Naomi. Schuyler. She switched off her dash and stared at the blank ceiling.

'Let's go out now,' she said.

'What?' Tam asked, and for once he sounded surprised.

'I need to stretch my legs. And besides, we blindsided everyone with our In campaign. Now they're expecting a big outing. We don't want to be one of those couples that gives people what they expect.'

Reyna sat up. Tam was looking at her with an interesting expression. He seemed . . . impressed? She hadn't seen that shade on his face before. It made her feel good.

'What should we wear?' she asked him.

Seeing Schuyler as she stepped out of her room had her suppressing a jump.

'Reyna,' he said, nodding at her, and he smiled when he saw Tam standing behind her. 'You have a guest.'

Reyna stepped out and let Tam come through.

'This is Tam. Tam, Schuyler,' she said.

'You could muster some enthusiasm,' Schuyler said brightly. Tam bowed to him and he said: 'It's a pleasure to meet you, Tam. Why are you here?'

'That's a fairly indelicate question,' Reyna said, allowing a hint of disapproval to colour her voice.

Schuyler gave her the blandest of looks, and in not showing his own disapproval he showed it plainly.

'It's an honour. To meet Schuyler Burroughs . . .' Tam had the decorum to stop there, though. If he had gushed Reyna would have been mortified. 'I'm here for Reyna,' he finished.

'And why might Reyna need you?'

'Schuyler,' Reyna began, ready to tell him off despite how bad it could look. Looking at the set of his jaw and the restraint in his expression stopped her.

'It's not my place to speak for her,' Tam said. Schuyler nodded and looked at her, waiting for her to fill in the gap.

'Later,' Reyna said, and she walked away.

'It was nice to meet you,' Tam said, and she heard him walk after her.

It was surprisingly easy with Tam. He didn't ask any questions. She liked to think it was because he respected her enough not to pry but it was more likely that he already knew all he needed to. Reyna told herself that it didn't matter. When they went out, the only thing that concerned them was their combined face. They looked good. Really good. And there was a kind of happiness in that. Maybe being Out was okay. Tam controlled the rhythm and tempo of their performance and interactions. Reyna almost felt as though she could switch off, not think, simply be. And then it was over. Tam got the train back to his district and Reyna, alone, suddenly felt much weaker.

She went home. She went to her room and plugged into a port for a full sensory experience. Block out the sounds, block out the place, block out the Out, and the world can be managed. Maybe being Out was okay but it was certainly better In than Out.

There was a knock on the door.

What? she typed.

The door opened and Schuyler came in. Reyna jerked out of the In and looked at him. She couldn't master her expression—it was what it was: fear, disgust, anger. Schuyler hesitated. He looked sad and impatient. It was that horrible real face of his.

'Leave me alone,' Reyna whispered. He shook his head, didn't move, didn't speak. 'I don't want to know. Please don't tell me any more,' she begged. He kept quiet and didn't look her in the face. 'Why did you have to tell me anything? I never asked to know you.'

He sighed.

'True. It was selfish. But you can't undo it now. That boy, Tam. When did that start?' he asked.

'I don't see how that's your business.'

'Your face is my face.'

'Don't start the whole family bullshit. Nothing I've done has ever had an effect on your face.'

'That's because you haven't made any mistakes yet.'

He had a point. Reyna closed her eyes and tried to think. Tried to come up with an appropriate response. And then, for a horrifying moment, she wished Tam were there to speak for her because she was sure he would know what to say. She shuddered, dug deep and found her voice again.

'I thought you didn't really care about face anyway.'

She didn't look at him, didn't want to see his reaction. She just wanted to pretend he wasn't there.

'I thought you were set against coupling,' Schuyler said.

'I was offered an opportunity. It seemed like a smart move.'

'He doesn't have any lineage.'

'He can play the game.'

'That makes him even more of a risk.'

'My face, my risk.'

'You know he's probably not that interested in you?'

Reyna sighed.

'I'll keep him away from you, Schuyler.'

Schuyler snorted.

'I can look after myself. I'm more worried about the effect he'll have on you.'

'You don't think I'm good enough to handle this?'

'I think you're perfect, Reyna.' And there was such sincerity in his words that it hurt. Because her brilliant father who saw everything had missed the fact that she wasn't perfect at all. Reyna wasn't sure if she had been the one to pull the wool over his eyes, or if it was just his own weakness that had led to this. Either way, she wasn't the person he wanted.

'Please. Leave me alone. Let me do this my way,' she said. As she said it she wondered what she was planning to do. She couldn't brand herself the way she had planned anymore. Was she planning on becoming an element in the next big couple? Was she planning on her and Tam becoming the next Schuyler and Madeleine Burroughs, new and improved? The thought made her feel queasy.

'I'm going,' Schuyler said. He walked out of the room and closed the door behind him. Reyna looked at the door. He was going? There was something in his voice that implied something more. He was planning something.

Reyna was heading towards school when she got a message.

Gen_VI: Skipping. Hitting Schalla's new boutique.
Reyna: On my way.

Genevieve didn't bother replying, so Reyna assumed she was satisfied with the outcome. After all, she wouldn't have messaged her if she didn't want her to come too.

Schalla was a flash-in-the-pan kind of face that Reyna didn't expect would survive the week, but they were hot enough right now for people of her standing to give them the time of day. And their clothes were intriguing. When Reyna got to the boutique there was a queue at the door. She walked over to the doorperson, who waved her in.

The place was stylish, all muted plastic with a thin veneer of shine almost as if it were smeared in Vaseline. There were only three other people in the shop. She recognised them all, of course. And as Reyna stepped farther into the shop the door hushed open behind her and Genevieve came in. Reyna nodded a greeting and was met with the same nod. They both took different sections of the room and flicked their way through the pieces on display.

Reyna selected two items: a metallic romper with a cape, and a chain-mail leotard. She didn't wait to see what Genevieve was doing, simply left the shop expecting to be followed soon after. Following the pink line that led away from the shop, Reyna made her way to her favourite café. She took her standard booth and one of the waitstaff laid her usual cappuccino in front of her immediately.

'Actually, I want a matcha,' she said, pushing the cup unceremoniously away and causing the server to stutter and stumble away. Genevieve slid into the booth as the server fled.

'So, you've been let off your leash,' she said. The words surprised Reyna and she almost reacted, just managing to hold her expression even by the skin of her teeth. Genevieve watched her carefully.

A server came over with Reyna's new order and started apologising profusely for the mistake. Reyna smiled sweetly and accepted the grovelling.

'Limonata,' Genevieve barked, causing the server to apologise several more times as they rushed away. Left alone at the table, they regarded each other, both waiting for the other to break the silence. Reyna sipped her drink. Genevieve's order arrived and she waved the person away before they could start a song and dance of obsequiousness. Reyna started to feel the pressure of Genevieve's stare. The silence grew heavier. Reyna had to stop herself from taking another sip, drinking too fast as a way to cope with the discomfort. Her friend's face was totally serene. Genevieve smiled at her as if she was simply enjoying beholding her. Reyna struggled to think of what she could say to break the moment without looking bad.

'What did you get?' she finally blurted out, the words more rushed and breathless than she wanted them to be. A flicker of emotion raced over Genevieve's face and Reyna tried to interpret it. Disappointment?

Genevieve sighed and leaned back into her seat. She touched a bag beside her, opened it a little and glanced down.

'Gloves,' she said, the whole show implying she had forgotten. She didn't ask what Reyna had taken from the boutique. Instead she drained her drink in one large gulp and stood up.

'I just remembered, I have a photo shoot I have to attend,' she said, making it clear that she was simply saying it to save Reyna's feelings. A flash of anger flared in the pit of Reyna's stomach but even as she pushed it down, made sure she didn't react, it died and in its place was just a horrible wave of uncertainty. She managed to smile up at her friend.

'By all means,' she said, waving her away. She wanted to say something more. Something cutting—as insulting to Genevieve as she had been to her—but nothing sprang to mind. Instead she shrugged away the helpless thought that Tam would have known what to do. And of course that was the problem. As Genevieve walked away Reyna realised what a horrible mistake she had made, coupling with Tam.

As soon as a respectable amount of time had passed, Reyna left the café and went home as fast as she could. Inside the house she almost ran to her room to plug in. She checked her Reserved Reyna account. Someone had posted a picture of her and Genevieve at Schalla's. There were no pictures of them at the café. Relief shot through her. But the memory of their interaction made her feel sick. She crafted some status updates to calm down.

She never made a conscious decision to stop going to school, but leaving the house had become unappealing. Everything she needed was on the In. In her room, the walls flickered and shifted as profiles changed. Who was hot, who was not, which face was doing well, which personal profiles should be pruned, which required work. Messages pulsed. Reyna managed replies with the strict discipline of a general. She kept her thoughts busy, she kept herself In, she tried hard not to think about the Out at all. Tam called. Tam came over. They regarded themselves together.

'Tayna.'

'It sounds awful,' Tam said.

'Better than Reytam.'

'Treyna?'

Reyna permitted a laugh. Tam permitted a smile. Reyna thought about Genevieve.

'Where's your father?' Tam asked her, and Reyna fought a sigh. Part of her couldn't be bothered to try to put him off. Schuyler could handle Tam, why did she need to put in the effort?

'Why?' she asked. A lazy response.

Tam looked at her, measured her face, took his time. She imagined he was resisting a lot, not just his frustration at being prevented from seeing the marvellous Schuyler Burroughs, but also irritation at her. The way she spoke. It was so hard speaking, though! You could measure responses so well when you typed them out. You could craft a perfect riposte or put-down. There was so much art in it. But talking . . . it almost made her shudder. It was so clumsy and heavy and hard. She suffered Tam's scrutiny, tried to look nonchalant.

'I won't ask,' he said eventually. 'We'll just focus on Treyna.'

Reyna nodded, careful not to look grateful.

'Plug in,' she said.

She was relieved when he didn't comment on being on port instead of dash, he just shrugged and plugged in beside her. Together they went In. Thank God. Better In than Out.

Better In than Out. The days bled into one another. Reyna stayed in her room, stayed plugged in, eyes trained on her flickering walls. Tam came. Tam went. The menial brought food. The menial took away dishes. Tam came. Tam went. Tam came. Tam went. Treyna soared up the ladder. Reyna typed and swiped, coded, encoded, wrote and rewrote. Tam came. Tam went. Screams shattered the screens in her eyes and Reyna unplugged.

She watched the door, wondered what was happening on the other side of it. She stood up. Her body was shaky. Nerves? Disuse? She took hold of her locket and shook out a beta blocker. She let it dissolve on her tongue before she opened the door and stepped out into the dark hallway.

The first thing she saw was Naomi, looking down into the dining room. The screams were coming from there. Reyna stepped up next to her 'sister' and looked down at Madeleine. The sounds their mother made made no sense. Schuyler stood in front of her, totally impassive. And looking at him, Reyna felt sure he had told Madeleine everything. The sounds Madeleine made were the feelings Reyna had when she looked at him. Madeleine knew everything now. Did Naomi? Reyna looked at her sister. Her face was intent, but it didn't 'say' anything.

'What—' Naomi started to say, but Reyna couldn't listen. She shook her head and Naomi stopped.

A door opened. The menial stepped out onto the landing. And Reyna had had enough. She ran into her room. Better In than Out. Better In than Out. She plugged into the port. She connected. She heard screams but she couldn't tell where they were coming from anymore. Hadn't they always been there, in her ears? The screams remained. Reyna stayed In.

The door opened. Reyna didn't turn to look.

'Hi,' Tam said.

'Mmm,' Reyna grunted. Easier than words.

'What are you doing?'

Reyna shrugged. Easier than words.

'Have you checked our stats recently?' he asked.

Reyna shrugged again, and prayed he would stop talking. Tam sighed and stepped up next to her. He plugged in and shared his screen with her, making it impossible for her to ignore him.

'Look,' he said, so Reyna looked. Their stats were static. They hadn't moved up or down. She could see it was dire. And it wasn't just Treyna that was static. Reyna had noticed a steady easing of interest in her other faces. Her reserved face most of all. She was no longer desirable. Yes, people were polite. She got courtesy interest—she was a Burroughs after all. Invites came for events, every so often. And yesterday she'd received a package from Mo/Flo, which felt very much 'for old times' sake'. But the thought of going out and talking to these people, suffering the smug indulgent interest and the casual put-downs, both subtle and obvious, sent panic through her. She couldn't handle them anymore. She didn't know how. Whatever identity she had had was gone.

'What am I looking for?' Reyna asked, and she heard a sullen note in her voice that reminded her of Naomi. It was a tone she had always made fun of her sister for using; she had always felt it lacked finesse. Hearing it in her own voice almost prompted a laugh, but if anything would make Tam angry it would be that. She could tell that much at least.

'We're not moving,' Tam said, strained patience in his voice.

'It happens.' Her voice was flat now. Apathetic. Good.

'Not to great players.'

Reyna shrugged. Easier than words. She told herself she didn't care anymore. Not if moving meant she had to be Out.

'Reyna!'

The force in his voice finally moved her. She looked at him. He was angry now.

'What's wrong with you?' he asked.

What was wrong with her? Everything! No. Nothing. Nothing was wrong with her. She was perfect. She was perfect Reyna Burroughs. It was everything outside of her that was wrong. It was the Out that was wrong!

Reyna laughed.

'Nothing is wrong with me,' she said.

'There's something wrong with you. You and Madeleine . . . like copies of each other. You used to be good at face.'

'I *am* good at face!' Reyna said, but as she said it she knew it wasn't true. And his face said he was looking at a bad liar.

'I'll make some moves,' he said. 'Begin a breakup process. I don't want you to bring me down.'

Reyna nodded. That was right.

'Goodbye,' Tam said. Something in his voice made her feel sorry for him. She had disappointed him so much.

'Tam,' she said, wanting to say something nice at least before he left. Something he could take away from all of this.

'Yes?'

'You'll do well, regardless.' Those felt like the right words. She wanted him to know that he was good at the game.

'I know,' he said. Arrogant prick.

When Tam left, Reyna turned back to her screens. It was better In than Out. At least on the In she could pretend she still mattered.

(Menial 63700578—Jake)

Madeleine sat at the dining room table, as usual. Jake liked that this was her spot. It meant he could watch her. He watched her fearlessly. She never looked up. She never saw him. He watched her as she sat, glazed over, patched into the In.

He liked to watch her from the landing most of all, because there he could hear her talk. Her strange accent made him feel . . . it made him feel. That was all he could say about it.

Madeleine sat at the table, patched into the In, and spoke.

'It was Schuyler's idea. You know him. Always ahead of everyone, it's uncanny. Sometimes I think he can see the future.' She giggled, making it clear that she was joking.

'But it is *such* a good idea,' she continued. 'I mean, it's practically our duty to help those less fortunate than us.' She paused to listen. 'Yes,' she said. 'Yes. No, I have to admit that at *first* I wasn't sure. But they're *so* beautiful! I—' Another pause. Madeleine giggled. 'Oh, *stop*! You're *too* much. No, you *have* to admit it, she has *something* special. Oh, he's just *divine*! They've definitely laid a strong foundation, but it all really rests on how they negotiate the child. *Personally*, I think they've already made some mistakes.' Pause. 'Oh, you haven't? Well, no but you won't believe this. She asked me for *advice*!' Pause. Madeleine nodded her head vigorously. 'Oh, of *course*! Yes. Yes. And I was very giving. Truly. Yes, and now there's this. I mean, if Schuyler hadn't mentioned it, I would have done it anyway, because it is *such* a big deal and, if this all goes well and they pull the whole thing off, well . . .' Madeleine laughed. 'Yes! *Exactly!*'

Madeleine was organising another party. She was talking to her sister about it. Jake knew this because Madeleine had a different voice for every person she spoke to. This was 'sister' voice. Jake didn't like Madeleine's sister. She was all sharp edges where Madeleine was soft.

She was all soft where Madeleine was tough. She looked different, talked different, acted different. But for some strange reason Madeleine seemed to like her sister. Jake suspected that this was why she had chosen to have two girls of her own. But Reyna and Naomi were nothing like Madeleine and Svetlana. They were nothing like Madeleine. No one was like Madeleine. He sighed and watched her as she sat at the dining room table, patched in, performing Madeleine Burroughs. Perfect.

He saw her reach down to the button on the table and was moving even before she pressed it, before the implant in his wrist buzzed, he was moving to her, ready to do anything she asked. But even as he turned and took a step, he hesitated. Because he wasn't alone. Naomi stood in the doorway of her room, watching him. How long had she been there? Jake went down the stairs. As he reached the bottom step, Madeleine was already calling out for water. He went straight into the kitchen and made up a tray: a chilled glass, her favourite brand of sparkling water, a selection of herbal and fruit flavours should she want them, and then he was moving again.

But Madeleine wasn't at the table anymore. And Jake had been too intent on his task to see where she had gone on the kitchen monitor. He heard a sigh and followed it into the living room. Madeleine was sitting on one of the china-white sofas and Naomi stood opposite her.

'It would look better for all of us if we attended together,' Madeleine said, reaching for her glass as Jake put the tray down on the burnished silver table beside her.

'It would look better for you and Schuyler,' Naomi said.

'It's an important event. It would benefit your face if you showed it—this isn't just about your father and me.'

'It's always just about you two.' Naomi's voice was layered with a thick, bored drawl. Jake tried not to wince at how obvious she was.

'Honestly, Naomi. You could put some effort into your dissembling. You sound vulgar,' Madeleine told her. 'And it's not *just* about us two. You and Reyna are a part of *our* face, so if you look good then we look good. Naturally, we want you to succeed. So it's a little bit about you *too*!' Madeleine smiled brightly.

Naomi laughed and then looked up at Jake. He blinked and quickly looked down.

'Menial,' Naomi said. 'Get me a drink.'

He retreated to the sound of Madeleine and Naomi laughing.

'Here's to the new parents to be!' Schuyler said, waving a drink in the air. Madeleine giggled beside him, her eyes on Tonia, and she waved her own glass.

'To not being pregnant!' she toasted. 'May we all drink *deep* and enjoy!'

Jake quickly stepped back into the kitchen as Schuyler started walking towards it, Eduardo in tow.

Neither of the men noticed Jake as they walked into the room.

'Booze?' Eduardo asked, and Schuyler pointed to the glass-fronted liquor cabinet. 'Right. Obviously,' Eduardo said with a self-deprecating smile.

They were making drinks. Meanwhile Madeleine was out there doing something Jake couldn't see. The men weren't looking at him. It would be easy to leave. No one would notice if he went in to the party for a short while. He wouldn't stay long. He'd just make sure she was okay. That she had everything she needed. Eduardo was focussed on the bottles he was pulling out of the cupboard, and Schuyler was focussed on Eduardo. Jake edged towards the door.

As he walked out of the kitchen he almost bumped into Tonia. She didn't look at him as he slid around her. At least she tried not to. Jake noticed the sly movement of her eyes, the quick appraisal. She couldn't help it. She wasn't top tier at heart. She was a faker and a poor one at that. Jake couldn't understand how this woman could even think of occupying the same space as Madeleine.

He walked past her, on the lookout for Madeleine. And there she was at the centre of the room. The queen of the party. Jake took a tray of Bellinis from a hired menial and walked over to her. He proffered the tray with a bow, felt her take a glass, and he risked a look up. For the smallest moment her eyes were on him. A thrill ran through him. He looked down, tried not to show it, backed away. And when he reached the edge of the room he looked for her again. He watched her work everyone around her. The finest creature in the room.

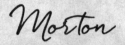

Morton

Better Out Than In

Morton woke up at 5:00 A.M. and plugged in. He scrolled through his profile—he only kept one these days—and halfheartedly liked, laughed and leered at the posts he found there. There were a lot of bitchy comments about students and parents; nothing he hadn't said before, himself.

> Barrie: Castlemewsfuckwads. How did they get onto stud?
> Eliza_Doolittle: Genetic defection, all of them. Do you ever daydream about shitting on their shoes?
> J2RF5-MI: Caning. Bring back caning.
> MrMan: Fail everything, win everything. Anal fuck fairness.

The insults were moist and solid and full of . . . touch. Just reading them made him tired. He'd long since lost that burning, bursting, anger. It was harder now and more permanent, like a rock in his belly.

He ordered breakfast before slipping the cable out and getting up. He put on his trainers and hit the treadmill—he ran full tilt until the door opened and the menial came in with its covered tray.

Morton wanted to say something—thank you, perhaps? But the words didn't line up and he couldn't look at the menial directly and, just like that, the whisper of a person was melting out of his apartment, going to see to someone else in the building.

Morton had been born into a second-tier family but, unable to climb, he'd fallen into a third-tier job. Some teachers commanded more respect but he was as middle-of-the-road as fifty percent. Fuck it. Go in. Do classes. Ignore students. Stay quiet. Leave. Eat. Sleep. Repeat. The rhythm was easy, but boring; day in and day out the same. And then he became a confessor.

He got a kick out of knowing dirty secrets, even if he didn't know who they belonged to. He had his theories, though. People gave things away all the time, you just had to know how to read them. That said, he didn't pretend to be a good face reader. He sometimes wished he was. But if he had been, then he wouldn't be where he was today, and it was no use thinking about the 'what-if's of life.

The confession booth started off as a minor distraction. He checked in when he was bored, and then he checked out and got on with life. And then life stopped being much of anything at all and he found himself sitting in his classroom itching for a plug and thinking about all the stories he might hear. Those faceless, shame-ridden people who drifted in and out of his booth became his world. Who were they? Where did they live? What did they really look like? Were they telling the truth?

It was the menials' stories he liked the best. Menials were so artless. Pretend people, imitating the world they saw around them, no clue that their playacting was painfully inaccurate. And they were dirty! Out of everyone, it was menials that spent the most time thinking about sex.

It wasn't that Morton liked hearing about sex. He was just baffled by their hunger to make physical contact. He could hear in their voices—the ones who were brave enough to speak with their own voices instead of using a programme—this aching for something he didn't understand. That tone reminded him of old movies—the ones they used to make back when people talked about things like love. He had, in his head, this image of a man and a woman—they always seemed to be a man and a woman back then—looking at each other, their bodies angled as though only the air were holding them back from melting into each other. He heard that image in the menials' voices. Whatever that meant.

What was almost as astonishing to Morton was how little the menials knew. They didn't even have basic knowledge of themselves. He remembered his first encounter with a menial in the booth.

Menial 2852.6570

'Hello?' Morton said, surprised that a menial had signed in and signed in with its number to boot.

'Hello.'

'How can I help you today?'

The menial said nothing. The avatar it had assumed was female, plain and unassuming. The face on it chewed its lip, its expression scared.

'I'm here to help if there's something worrying you,' Morton told it. The menial's avatar shifted, probably set to shadow its own movements. This detail made Morton smile. He couldn't remember the last time he had seen anyone use shadow settings. There was an innocence there that was . . . sweet.

The avatar prevaricated a little longer, and then it spoke:

'I've been doing things.'

'What kinds of things?'

'Things we shouldn't do.'

'What are the things you shouldn't do?'

'Stuff. With my body.'

It was a sign of how little he thought about sex and sexual acts that it took Morton a moment to decode that sentence.

'What is this stuff?' he asked, wanting to make sure.

The avatar shook its head.

'I don't know! I don't know what's happening to me.'

It sounded so scared that Morton instinctively moved his avatar, raising its arms and stepping forwards slowly, as though approaching a deer.

'It's okay,' he said. 'Don't worry. I'm here to help you understand. This is a safe place, we can talk about anything here.'

The menial's avatar looked up at him, eyes liquid, face stiff with tension.

'What's happening to me?' it asked.

Morton shook his avatar's head.

'I don't know. We need to talk about it, step-by-step. Why don't you tell me what's been going on.'

After that, the menial was quick to open up. It told him about the necklace its owner had bought: a heavy silver collar dripping spikes that were studded with stones of every colour. The necklace shone in every light, the facets of each stone making it glisten. It was fastened around a dummy neck in his dressing room, just waiting to be admired. And the menial admired it. And then wet itself. At least that was how it had felt. The menial had rushed to the bathroom to clean up.

'Only there was no pee. There was no pee but my pants were wet. I was scared I was sick, but I didn't feel bad. I had to do my work. I know if I get sick there isn't anything I can do. But I get scared of being sick. I don't want to be sick. I want to keep working. I don't want to go back to the dealership.'

And that was interesting. Morton wanted to ask the menial more about that but that wasn't the confession.

'So, what did you do?'

'I kept working. And my pants dried. And I thought maybe I wasn't sick. But then it happened again. And it kept happening. And I noticed it was whenever I went into the dressing room and looked at the necklace. And then . . .'

'Remember, you're safe here.'

'Well . . . I don't know exactly how . . . I was wiping the wetness from my pants. And I wanted to know . . . I touched that bit, where the wetness was. And then I kept touching. It was strange. Like really really wet. Like wetter than water maybe? And I thought I should stop because I remember the guidelines. But I just kept touching it. And then . . .' The avatar took a step back. 'Well I guess I was touching it more? Faster? Yes. I was touching it faster, and I started to feel a bit strange. I got a bit scared because maybe I was sick. But then suddenly the feeling . . . something happened and it went away. And I thought maybe I'm not sick. When the feeling was totally gone, I wiped all the wetness away with the toilet tissues and I went back to work. But then it happened again. And now . . . now I . . . I kind of want it to happen. And I remember the guidelines. Training says we shouldn't touch ourselves or other people. We shouldn't think about anything except work. Training says we serve. Training says we should be silent. Training says we belong to people. So I know it's wrong for me to do this stuff but I can't help it. Which maybe means I am sick? Should I tell my owner? I don't want to go back to the dealership. I want to serve.'

'You're not sick,' Morton told it, and the avatar immediately slumped a little, as though tension was leaving its body. Morton marvelled at how it instantly believed him, had so much trust that he could tell it what it wanted to know and that he was telling the truth. The thought made him a little giddy. There were so many possibilities in it. But even though he could lie, tease, pull the creature apart, he felt this strange urge to look after it.

'You're not sick,' he said again. 'What you described is something called masturbation.'

'Masturbation,' the menial said. It took its time over the word. 'Why is this happening to me?'

'I don't know. It's not a common practice but it has been known to happen. People do it too. Sometimes.'

'People do this? Why?'

'No one really knows why. It usually happens when they've been excited by something. The necklace excites you. Your body is reacting to that.'

'Do other menials do this?'

'Yes,' Morton said, although he had no idea.

'I'm not supposed to, though.'

'No.'

'How can I stop?'

'You just have to not do it. Maybe now that you know what it is you'll find it easier to stop.'

'Masturbation,' the menial said again.

'Yes.'

'I'm not sick?'

'No.'

'I'm masturbation?'

'You're masturbating,' Morton corrected it.

'Masturbating.' It seemed to really focus on the word. 'Masturbation, masturbating,' it said. It looked up at Morton. 'I'll stop.'

'Good luck.'

'Thank you.'

It wasn't the last time a menial came into the booth and learned about its body. It wasn't the last time this menial came into the booth and spoke about masturbation. In fact, this menial came back more and more often. Its appearance changed as time passed, taking on the form of the things it was attracted to. A Red Ferrari avatar, all flash.

Playing at being a woman. If Morton ever thought to pick favourites this one might have been it.

Morton went to school by train. He plugged into the In in the car and checked his booth. No one was active. He scrolled through his lessons for the day. Nothing challenging. He checked the assignments he had marked. Everything in order. Physical school loomed and he was part of the queue, an even person-sized space between him and the person ahead, the person behind, walking on beat, walking in time.

The doors shushed open and closed, open and closed. Morton walked down the shiny hallways looking at no one and never being looked at. When he made it to his classroom he took a deep breath.

'Let's get this fucker out the way,' he said, and he sat down at his desk and waited for the students to file in.

In general, his students were accompanied by an air of apathy. It was the face of youth. He was sure there had been a greater variety in their faces when he had first started teaching, but maybe that was just because he had looked more back then. Maybe the apathy came from him. As if to prove the point, Pixie Ximenez bounced in and grinned at him.

'Hi, Morty! How are you today?' he asked. Pixie Ximenez was a cunt.

'Hi, Pixie,' he said with as much energy as he could muster.

'Ooh, it looks like someone didn't get enough sleep last night! Maybe you should spend more time on the Out, sir.'

Out of all his students, Pixie was the only monster that called him 'sir'.

'Sit down.'

'Right-y-ho!' Pixie winked at him before flouncing over to his seat and sitting down with exaggerated flair. He leaned forwards across his desk and kept his eyes on Morton and when Morton made the mistake of looking at him he licked his lips and blew him a kiss. Other than his habitual use of the word 'sir', Pixie was the least consistent person Morton had ever met. He wore a different face daily and had never worn the same face twice. He had no identity at all, which was an interesting choice, but Morton was not sure it was a very smart one. But then what did he know, really? Perhaps Pixie's fractured face had some followers. Maybe people saw a charm there. It was probably enough to sustain him but it would probably never be enough to help him rise up the ladder. People needed something to cling to, something steady. In any case, Morton didn't care; he just hated the look of the little snot.

There was one in every class. After Pixie there was Regan. After Regan there was Alonso. After Alonso it was Funmi. After Funmi, Morton wanted to shoot himself. And then the last class filed in, sat down, shut up, and he breathed a sigh of relief. *Keep it together. The end is an hour away. Focus. Don't crack. Pack up.* And then . . . fucking Naomi. Hanging around and looking at him like she'd just eaten orange peel. He tried not to give in to her, keeping his eyes focussed on his AR dashboard instead.

'Yes?' Silence. 'Well?' *Don't look at her, don't look at her, don't fucking engage.*

'Menials.'

And that was interesting. He looked through his dash, and really considered her now. Naomi was high level but unexceptional. She commanded a greater presence than the average student, maintained a solid face and he knew what to expect from her. She never surprised him. But maybe she would?

'What about them?' he asked.

'Thought they'd make a good subject,' she said with a shrug.

'For your project?'

'No, for conversation,' she said sarcastically. Morton had to exercise a decent amount of self-control not to snap at her. Sarcasm was one of the most tedious aspects of face he had to deal with on a daily basis and for a moment he had this absurd flash—an image in his head of smacking her. Instead, he sighed.

'What were you thinking about doing with them?'

'Thought I could pick one to study. Then try to find a case-study equivalent. I mean, menials are basically normal people. Only they aren't. I'm . . . I'm sort of interested to see if the way they're born and brought up makes their basic psychology different from ours.' She was trying hard to keep her voice level, but Morton could hear a varied intonation there; she was interested. And so was he. She could surprise him.

'You ever hear of confession booths?' he asked her, and found that he could surprise himself as well.

Shut up, Morton. Shut up.

'Course.'

Shut up, Morton.

'You ever use one?' he asked, ignoring himself.

Naomi gave him a flat *are you an idiot* look and he laughed.

'You'd be surprised by how many people do use them.'

'What's this got to do with menials?' Naomi asked.

'Like I said: You'd be surprised by how many people use confession booths.' Morton wasn't quite sure if Naomi was clever and he was less sure if he was, but she seemed slower than he expected.

'Menials confess?' she asked. 'To what?'

'Oh, to all sorts. It's not just menials. *A lot* of people confess.'

'Really?'

'Really.'

'I still don't understand what it's got to do with anything.'

'Well, you raise an interesting question. How different are menials from us?'

How different are they? How different *are* they? Morton hesitated, thinking, trying to work out what to say next.

'We're ... the same species and yet ... we're born differently, raised differently, educated differently. They don't live on the ladder but they're free to observe the rest of us that do. How does this affect them? Does it alter their psychology? Or do they have the same wants and needs as everyone else? There's a lot to explore here. The question is how to get at the information. You could observe a menial. You must have one at home?'

Of course she had one at home. She was a fucking Burroughs.

'But observation won't get you very far. You could try talking to it. But I doubt that would get you very far either. Menials are trained not to question, not to talk, not to behave in any way that isn't serving. No menial worth its salt would talk openly to you. And that's what you need if you want to understand their psychology.'

And this was what brought him to confession booths; the only place where people might tell an unadulterated truth. He thought about his booth. He thought about all the menials that filtered through it; those strange naive creatures. If you wanted to know about menials, a booth was the only place to go.

'So. This brings me to confession booths. What do you know about them?'

She knew enough.

'So, are you suggesting I make my own booth?' Naomi asked.

And that was the question: What was he suggesting? It would take her ages to set up her own booth and gather the data she needed for the assignment. She needed to use one that was already established. She needed one like his.

'What . . . I suggest—and this is only if you're absolutely serious about this—is that you take over my booth. I have menials you can study.'

He had said it. It couldn't be unsaid. He had offered her—this student he barely knew, didn't care about, barely thought about—his most prized possession. What the hell was he thinking? He wanted to smack himself. He felt Naomi staring at him, trying to get a read on him, and he was thanking all the atoms that ever were that he had had enough beta blockers that day, that he rarely sweated, that he was blandness personified.

'Are you serious?' she asked him. And that was his chance. He could back out here. Instead he said:

'If you are.'

Fuck.

Morton rushed home and buried himself in his booth. He scrolled through every name of every confessee he had ever encountered. One of his regular names swelled and pulsed to life and he found himself taking a sharp breath. What was it? Relief?

'Hello,' he said. And ArrasLarras smiled and said:

'Hello.'

He felt sick going into work that day. It wouldn't do to look sick, though, so he pulled himself together. Time passed too fast and then there she was, sauntering into his classroom.

'So?' she said, all prickles and judgement. And he wanted to say 'So what?' and leave. He wanted to pound out of that room that school that district, and dive into the loving arms of his In. He wanted to flee.

He pulled out a chair and she took it.

'Right. In order to transfer my booth to you we have to patch into each other.' He sat down opposite her and plugged into a port. She nodded and closed her eyes, already looking for him, not remotely worried about their In worlds being so close together, about him seeing her desktop, about him showing her his. She wasn't afraid of anything. He closed his eyes to search his own patch for her, took a moment to make sure his feeds were censored, and then they were connected.

'I'm going to plug into the In now, and I'll keep this line open so you can see exactly what I'm doing.' Morton enabled the In. His desktop opened up in front of their eyes. He had gone over it the night before, making sure it was as innocuous as possible. He selected the confession booth icon, and the familiar night-blue field filled his vision. It was beautiful.

'The stars are the people that come to this booth to confess. A star shines brighter when someone is entering the booth,' Morton said.

'Do I have to keep checking on the booth to see if someone's there, or will I get a notification?'

'The confessions will join your regular message stream. You'll get one and then, if you want to see the person you're talking to, you can move into the booth, or you can just treat it like you would a normal message and deal with it in text. You can only access the booth when you're plugged into a port, so you can't interact with it as you go. It's a way of ensuring user privacy.'

'The people I see aren't the real article, though?' Naomi said.

'Are people ever?' Morton asked.

'What if someone wants to confess when I'm in the middle of something?'

'That's where the booth settings come in handy. I've programmed a specific set of responses tailored for each of my confessees.' Morton paused for a moment to catch his breath. The amount of work he had put into this booth and now . . . 'If they want to talk when I'm busy I set it on auto and they get tailor-made machine responses until I'm ready to plug in and take over. It's all ready for you to use. Simple enough?'

'Yeah.'

'Good, well I'll transfer it to you now, then.' He spoke the words fast, as though that might make everything move more quickly. But she still took her time to plug in.

'Where do you want it?' he asked her, when she was ready.

Naomi opened up her In feed next to his. Where his was white, hers was slate. She indicated the top toolbar and Morton, having closed the booth, slid it from his feed to hers.

Naomi closed the patch and blinked. Then she looked at Morton.

'I'm interested to see what you do with this,' he said to her, all teacher.

'That everything?' she asked him.

Morton smiled and nodded.

'Good luck,' he said. Naomi didn't bother answering. Morton wanted to spit at her.

When Morton got home, his flat felt empty. It was exactly as he'd left it, of course, but there was now a gaping hole. He couldn't look at anything directly—everything had taken on a strange quality of remembrance—so he plugged in and as the In floated before him he finally felt a little bit safe. Only there was nowhere to go.

He scrolled through his feed but the absence of booth alerts was like a wound and he couldn't look at anything else. With a desperation that embarrassed him, even in a room on his own, he keyed a search:

Coping with loss
Understanding the grieving process and learning to heal.

Coping with the loss of someone or something you love is one of life's biggest challenges. You may experience all kinds of unexpected emotions—shock, anger, disbelief, guilt and/or profound sadness. These feelings can affect your physical health and you may experience a loss of appetite or an inability to sleep. Perhaps you will feel the urge to cry. There is no wrong way to process these feelings but some coping mechanisms are healthier than others. The most important thing to remember is that you must never let anyone see that you are grieving. This could trigger a domino effect in your life that may do lasting and profound damage. In terms of healing, it is worth investing in some

Happiness—a healthy drug that tricks the brain into believing you are undergoing a pleasurable experience. Using drugs will help you get over the worst of your grief. Beyond that it is important to have an outlet where you can express yourself safely and to this end it is highly recommended that you join a confessional booth.

Fuck. No. He didn't want to confess. He wanted to be confessed to. He wanted to hear the stories, make the judgements, give the advice; he wanted people to come to him and ask him for help. He wanted to float in the In and have *his* people, his confessees, begging for answers.

Being In, without confessions to shape the experience, was unbearable. He tore Out. He jumped when the door opened and the menial came in with the supper he had ordered.

'Hi,' he said, not thinking. The menial didn't react and Morton was embarrassed by talking to it. But then he thought . . .

'Hey,' he said, as the menial turned to leave the room. 'Hold on.'

The menial stopped and turned to him, but it didn't look into his face.

'What . . . What's your name?' Morton asked. He knew a lot of menials gave themselves names, even if no one used them.

'I'm Menial 764109.85.'

'No, your name name. Have you given yourself a real name?'

'I don't understand your question. I'm a menial so I have a number which functions as a name.'

'But you don't think about yourself as Menial 76 blah blah, do you? You don't call yourself that?'

'As a menial I am not supposed to think of myself at all. My job is to serve so I must think about the people I serve.'

'Okay. So what do you think about me?'

There was a moment, Morton was sure of it, where the menial's eyes flicked up to his face, trying to work something out about him.

'You are Morton Hsu, flat 217. You like breakfast food, especially hash browns. You like apple juice and sweet coffee. You spend about seven hours a day outside of this complex and during part of this time I clean your flat. You leave very little mess and my job is quick. This is what I think of you.'

'But that's not thinking of me. That's just knowing facts. What do you think *of* me? What do you think *about* me?' Now that he had started asking questions he couldn't stop.

'I'm not sure I understand what you're asking. What would you like me to say?'

'It's not about what I'd like you to say, I want to hear your opinion.'

'Oh,' said the menial. 'As a menial, I don't have opinions. Would you like me to get you anything before I go? Flat 218 has ordered dinner for eight thirty.'

'Really?' Morton said. 'How interesting.' The menial couldn't hide the look that crossed its face then: embarrassed, annoyed, afraid. It had given him information about someone else without that person's permission. Why had it slipped up? To get away from Morton, of course. Because it was uncomfortable. It understood everything he had asked it, but it couldn't answer him. Not like this. Not on the Out. Nothing could happen on the Out. Everything was In.

'Go on then,' Morton said, waving a hand at it, and the menial left quickly.

Everything was In.

He felt sick. He couldn't settle in bed. It was too hot under the sheets, too cold over them; he was sweating, shivering, retching, plugging in, coming out, over and over and over again. There was nothing In and nothing Out. There was nothing. He was alone. It finally dawned on him that there was nothing wrong with the In or the Out. Fucking psych teacher and what the hell did he know? There was something wrong with him. So he plugged in.

Dealing with addiction
Are you addicted to something? Do you need help to break this addiction? Are you feeling hopeless?

Your first step is to identify what you are addicted to.

Picture it. Can you see it in your mind's eye? This is what you are fighting. The fight will never end but now you know what you're up against.

Step two is deciding how you will approach the fight. Will you tackle your addiction slowly, prising it away from you, finger by finger? Will you tear yourself out of its grasp now?

Now. Now. He wanted to do it now. Instead, he kept reading.

The gradual approach tends to yield better results; taking small steps to get loose from the addiction that has been holding you captive. Start slow. Reduce your time with your addiction by one unit a day. That's all you need to do. Out of all the minutes of the day that you spend feeding your addiction, take one minute away. Then take away another minute the next day. And another the next day. Keep whittling away your time with your captor.

He could take some time away right then. He could stop reading, pull out, get away . . . he kept reading.

When you are spending half the time you once were with your addiction, you are probably ready for the next step on your journey to freedom. Talk to someone. You may have someone close to you with whom you can confide, but more often than not the best solution is to join a confession booth.

Fuck. Fuck shit fuck.

You need someone to support you in your fight. You need someone to encourage you to keep working at it. Confessors are great allies in this and you will find

He pulled out. This was ridiculous. He needed to get away from the In and it was trying to convince him to spend more time there. He needed another way . . . of course there was always another way.

Was there another way? Morton went to school as usual but things looked different. He caught himself looking at people differently and more than once he had to take an inordinate interest in pop-up adverts flashing behind people's heads. He kept telling himself off for his lack of control, reminding himself to keep it together. He wasn't sure if lecturing himself ever really worked but at least it meant he was talking to someone.

The day unfolded as usual, but nothing was usual. Morton was

Out. And the world felt like a very big, empty place. Morton watched as his students came and went. They sat, they listened, they ignored, they manoeuvred and manipulated themselves, their peers, him. They were there, but no one was *there*. Students flitted down hallways, expertly navigating the space past one another, even when they were using dashboards, using their AR streams, rushing to ports, plugging in, closing eyes, floating away. It was strange to see their virtually abandoned bodies, tethered to seats as their thoughts flew free in a space were Morton was not. He ached for the In.

For the first time since he couldn't remember when, he went to the staff room.

'Morton!' Carrie said as he sat down.

'Alright?' he asked.

'What brings you here?'

Morton shrugged.

'Curiosity.'

Carrie nodded, smiled as far as his face would allow and then occupied himself with his In feed. Morton looked around. Four teachers were present, three plugged in. Auguste was waiting for her cup of tea. He got up and went to the vending station. He ordered a cup of coffee and waited, watching Auguste where she stood on his periphery. Her tea was ready. She picked up the cup but didn't move.

'How's it going?' he asked, and he thought he saw her shudder a bit, as if just stopping herself from jumping. 'Sorry,' he said as he turned to look at her, and he smiled. She nodded.

'Fine. You?'

'Bored,' he said, drawing out the word affectedly.

She didn't react but he felt her getting cold. She nodded again and walked away. Morton picked up his coffee and left the room.

There was an hour before his next class and the question was how to fill it without plugging in. He racked his thoughts for information, trying to remember things he was sure he had seen and read on the In—articles about how to use your time on the Out, adverts for Out activities, news stories about outliers. And that struck him. Outliers.

Morton had never taken an interest in outliers before. All he knew about them was what everyone else knew—outliers were fetishists and freaks. Rejecting the In—rejecting tech—just made life harder. What had he read about outliers? He reached for the cord to plug in and stopped himself just shy of connecting. He couldn't use the In. So he tried to remember. But there was nothing there.

'Has it just eaten away at everything in there?' he wondered out loud. The sound of his voice made him feel small. He thought about that. How small he was. And then he thought about how outliers weren't on the In, so even if he wanted to, he would never find them there. He thought about the city and how everything you did was the result of using some form of tech or another. Where, in a place like this, would an outlier hang out?

When the answer came to him he was embarrassed he hadn't thought of it sooner. They would be drawn to old tech. Machineless tech. Paper books. The antique library. But the hour was up and it was time for class.

When Morton left school that day his thoughts were all on the antique library. He couldn't think where in the city it was. Of course, he could use his dashboard and conduct a search. He could tap into the nearest map and request a route. He could use the In and be on his way in moments. But he wanted to find it the same way an outlier would.

By the time he got home he realised that was crap. He didn't have the knowledge to make that shift. The only way to get there was to use the In, but he couldn't let himself use his dash or plug into a port. He compromised and decided to use the computer unit in his flat.

'Computer.'

'Morton.'

'Show me the fastest route to the antique library.'

'Will this location be your starting point?'

'Yes.'

'Calculating.' A map blossomed on Morton's living room wall, and a winding blue line cut through it. 'Fastest route calculated. The next train leaves in twelve minutes. The fare will be two eighty-five.'

'Thank you.'

'Do you require me to sleep?'

'No, keep the map up please.'

'Yes.'

Morton sat in front of the map and studied it. Twelve minutes passed but he didn't move. He had never really looked at a map like this before. He had calculated routes, using his In implant, with a voice in his ear whispering which way to go as he walked. He had rarely needed to look at something and remember it—not since his school days. It was strange looking at his slice of the city this way. This was what it looked like from above. This was what he navigated through every day, never giving it a second thought. Looking at the streets, he could imagine now where Joe's Café was. He could see where the VenCaf would be standing. The Grand Arcade was marked down so he could see that clearly, and from there branched all the streets that held places he would often go to—places for quiet and comfort and time to spend on the In. Places that weren't this shitty little apartment in this mid-tier building. He was looking at his world. And there, some distance beyond it, was the antique library, buried in a part of the city he rarely went to.

'Okay,' he said to himself, and he stood up. 'Time to go.'

Morton opened the door on the menial who tried not to look surprised.

'Your dinner,' it said, holding up a tray.

'Don't need it,' Morton said, and he walked out, barely aware of the fact that the menial had to squeeze itself tight into the wall to avoid touching him.

It took almost an hour to get to the antique library. It was half an hour to closing time. Morton didn't go in.

'Maybe tomorrow,' he said, and he sat down on a wall and watched as people came out. It was hard to see their faces in the darkening light. He wondered if he would remember any of them if he saw them again.

Morton stepped into the antique library on a Saturday morning. He looked around, expecting to step back in time, rows and aisles of wooden shelves towering over him, all of them filled with musty old books.

And it was like stepping back in time, but not in the way he expected. The library opened out into a large space filled with rows of tables. Each one had a computer monitor on it, instead of a plug-in station. Beyond this space there were shelves of books arranged in clusters. And around the shelves there were armchairs, most of them filled with people reading. No one spoke, few looked at one another, and for a moment Morton fancied that far from finding a world of outliers here, he was walking into a different kind of In.

'Are you okay?' a man asked him.

Morton was surprised by the question but when he looked at the man he realised he worked there. Morton nodded at him, slow and sure.

'Your first time here?' the man divined, and rather than fighting it Morton nodded again. 'What are you looking for?'

'I was just curious, to be honest,' Morton said. 'I enjoy exploring alternative activities. I was thinking about it the other day and realised I'd never made it here.'

'Well, this is about as alternative as they come within the city. Do you have any idea of what you might be looking for?'

'I just wanted to browse.'

'Fair enough. Well, you can use the monitors to search for specific items, or to search the In if you'd like. Beyond the computers you have the books. They're organised by genre, nonfiction at the front and fiction at the back. If you can't find what you're looking for on the shelves it could be in the archives, which are upstairs. We also have an audio range up there, where you can find audio versions of every book in the library. If you need any help, I have a desk up front.' The man pointed to his desk. They both nodded and parted ways.

Morton made a beeline for a free computer. He reasoned that using a monitor like this—physically—he wasn't breaking his promise with himself to stay out. Setting his fingers to the keyboard felt strange. And it was an utter relief. He clicked a letter and a login page popped up. He smiled before he could stop himself. He couldn't quite remember the last time he used a login page; plugging in circumvented the need. He typed in his name and identity number and a home page blossomed on the screen. It was strange looking at a page that was similar to the In in design, but was just inches beyond him, contained in glass and plastic, a world he couldn't enter or interact with fluidly. He dragged the mouse in some experimental circles before moving the cursor to the 'internet' icon. A few clicks later, Morton was ready to search.

Finding outliers on the In was ironic. But there were groups there: chat rooms, support, random faces identifying as outliers. It was easy to connect with them. All you had to do was click like and follow. No one spoke directly to Morton, so he lurked in the background and watched.

> Peetreeoil17: We're born with one, so it seems insane that we'd work so hard to develop and nurture more. *Nurture* is for living things.
> FactionMan: When you say it's for living things . . .
> Peetreeoil17: Plants, animals, life.
> Eyelid_Maccabee: You're not advocating skinship are you?
> Peetreeoil17: Skinship? God, no! However, there is an interesting dialogue surrounding it at the moment and

Morton broke away from his screen quickly. He had been privy to dark thoughts in his booth, he had seen the perverted way people felt and acted when they thought no one was looking. To see people discussing perversion in an open manner, without the equivalent of a digital retch, was astonishing. It made him uncomfortable.

He took a deep breath and looked back at the chat room.

> Dogtor_Spatson55: I'm new to the idea of outlying so sorry if this is a stupid question—doesn't this chat defeat the point of outlying?
> lady_go_dive_her: @Dogtor_Spatson55 If it offends you then get out.
> Dogtor_Spatson55: @lady_go_dive_her It's not about being offended, I'm just curious.
> lady_go_dive_her: @Dogtor_Spatson55 It sounds like you're just trying to shit where we talk.
> Eyelid_Maccabee: @lady_go_dive_her Since when is asking a question a hate crime?
> lady_go_dive_her: @Eyelid_Maccabee Fuck off.
> *lady_go_dive_her has been removed from the chat room.*
> Sad-Dee: @Dogtor_Spatson55 what are you asking, exactly?
> Dogtor_Spatson55: Well, I'm curious about why an outlying group is chatting on the In instead of the Out.

Peetreeoil17: @Dogtor_Spatson55 You're right. Stupid question. Where
   are you?
Dogtor_Spatson55: @Peetreeoil17 wtf? And why would I tell you
   where I am?
Peetreeoil17: Elementary, my dear Spatson. How can we all meet if we
   are separated by vast distances?
Dogtor_Spatson55: That doesn't follow. There's nothing to stop outly-
   ing groups from forming societies and meeting within their ar
Dogtor_Spatson55 has been removed from the chat room.
Sad-Dee: wtf?
Eyelid_Maccabee: Who got rid of the good dogtor?
FactionMan: Admin? @Peetreeoil17 Are you admin on this?
Peetreeoil17: Don't loo
Peetreeoil17 has been removed from the chat room.
FactionMan: What's go
FactionMan has been removed from the chat room.
*This chat room is undergoing some modification. All action is
suspended until modification is complete. Thank you for your patience.*

Morton kept looking at the modification notice, trying to wrap his
head around what had happened. He had never seen a chat room
close like that before. He looked around the library, at the other people on their ancient monitors and reading old books. Everyone was
engrossed in their activity. Everyone was on an In. He thought about
searching more, maybe asking some questions, but suddenly the
whole thing seemed redundant. It was like Dogtor_Spatson55 had
said: Why would outliers chat on the In? And then he really thought
about it: Did he want to meet outliers at all? He supposed outliers
would want to spend time talking in person. They would each have
one face. They would use real expressions. They could . . . This was
venturing into the realm he was trying to leave behind. It was like he
was stepping into the shoes of each and every one of his confessees.
Taking on their perversions. What the fuck were outliers really?

He broke out in a sweat and immediately panicked at the reaction.
He forced himself to move his head slowly as he looked for a toilet.
It was across the room, on the other side of the monitors. Working
hard, he stood up slowly and timed his steps so his walk would look
normal—not fast or slow but perfectly balanced. When he got to

the toilet he was careful to check for other occupants. Seeing it was empty, he permitted himself speed, shoving his face into the mister to cool it down before using the dryer.

There was no sound of anyone approaching, so he slowed down. He took a beta blocker from the metal block on his bracelet and swallowed it dry. Then he got out powder and a brush from his bag and applied it to his face.

Morton looked in the mirror. Dry. Calm. Normal. When he felt sure about those facts he left the library.

It was obvious when he thought about it, and he wondered why it had taken him by surprise. Of course the powers that be would be shutting down these kinds of chats as soon as they got too close to the details of In-free living. In-free living wasn't conducive to a well-balanced and carefully controlled life. A controllable life. And for that he was grateful.

For the first time in his life, it didn't even occur to Morton to plug into the In during his train ride home. Instead, he looked out of the window, saw nothing, and thought of how magnificent the In was. A perfect world where everything could be monitored, approved, adjusted. Without it, there would be chaos. Without it there would be panic. There would be sweat.

When he got home, the flat computer greeted him:

'Hello, Morton. Did you have a good afternoon at the antique library?'

'Satisfying,' Morton said.

'Can I help you with anything?'

'No. Just go to sleep.'

'Of course. Goodbye, Morton.'

'Bye,' Morton said out of habit, but the machine had already bleeped off. 'Bye,' Morton said again. He wasn't sure who he was talking to.

He saw Naomi walking towards him with intention and he sped up.

'Hey,' she called him. 'Hey!'

'What d'you want?' he asked without stopping.

'I have some questions.'

'That's what the In is for.' He was being rude, which was a risk, and yet he couldn't help himself.

'I don't want these questions logged,' said Naomi. Morton stopped. Poor girl. This was the first time he had ever thought about her that way. As a girl. And a poor one at that. The girl with everything, at the top of a ladder she didn't have to climb, nothing to lose, nothing to gain, curious and—now he saw it—naive.

'Well, if they're problematic questions, I might have to log them myself,' he said.

'They'll be on your private record, not a public one. I'm okay with that.'

Morton sighed. He may have been slow on the uptake but he thought she would have known. She looked at things. She really *looked* at things. How did she miss this one?

'How private do you think a private record is?'

Naomi frowned at him.

'Is this a trick question?'

Morton hesitated, wondering if he should talk to her. But Naomi was so much higher than he was on the ladder; could he really afford to refuse her?

'Come on.'

'Where are we going?' Naomi asked him.

'To get a drink.'

He didn't go far. He didn't want to spend any more time with her than he had to, but he needed something to sustain him. He ducked into the nearest café and sat down. He ordered a coffee and offered her the slate but she waved it off.

They waited for his coffee to arrive. It came quickly.

'Go ahead. Ask me your questions,' Morton said, as he poured sugar into the cup.

'I was in the booth the other day—'

'You can't tell me about the booth. I'm no longer privy to the participants of that particular confessional.' *Don't tell me about the booth don't tell me about the goddamn booth*, he pleaded internally.

'No details,' she said, cool, calm, not an iota of her out of place after being interrupted. 'I just heard something that . . . surprised me.'

Morton almost smiled at how deadpan her delivery was. He wondered what surprise actually looked like on her.

'I realised that menials have more restrictions than ordinary people. Is there a record of their rules somewhere?'

Was that it?

'This is information you could easily find on the In. Nothing that doesn't bear logging.'

'I'm asking you.'

'Why?'

'Because it's easier to go directly to a source of information, rather than trying to sieve details through the In.'

So that was it.

'And you're hoping to get information out of my face too.' Morton smiled because it was all he could do. 'I'm being a bit slow today.'

Naomi gave him a look.

'Yep, I'm slow every day,' he said, agreeing with that look. 'There are no menial guidelines on the In. Not necessary. They internalise the guidelines as they make their way through their training facilities. If you want to find out more about how they're trained, you have to visit one of them.'

'I have a feeling they don't let just anyone in.'

'No.'

'But you've been to one.'

Yes. He had been to one. Once.

'Yes. You have a sharper eye than you let on,' Morton said, and he was surprised to see the ghost of a smile on her face.

'And you remember the guidelines?'

Morton laughed; he always laughed when he had to admit that he didn't know much.

'They spend their entire childhood and most of their teenagehood learning the guidelines. I remember scraps.' He hadn't thought about this in . . . he couldn't remember thinking about it. 'What are you interested in?'

'Masturbation.'

Morton laughed again, this time at Naomi. It felt good. She didn't react.

'What about it?' Morton asked her.

'Menials aren't supposed to do it. They're trained not to. Why?'

'Most animals don't masturbate. Menials are service animals. Their thoughts should be solely on how to serve their bosses best. Distractions like physical gratification are discouraged but there is no actual rule that says they can't do it. That would be impossible to police. That's why menials have guidelines rather than rules. And they're conditioned to feel guilty if they stray from the guidelines.'

'Surely, if they display an impulse towards sexual gratification it's an indication that they are more than just animals.'

'Yes.'

'But we aren't supposed to think of them like that,' Naomi said, completing Morton's unspoken sentence. Morton smiled at her. 'Why?' she asked him.

'That's a silly question. And after you were just convincing me you weren't a silly person.' That felt good too. There wasn't much room for someone of his stature to put down someone of hers, but there was a small space between knowledge and ignorance. He would always use that if he could. He stood up. It was always best to quit while you were ahead.

'Where are you going?' she asked him.

'I've finished my coffee. Time to go home.'

'But I have another question.'

'Go ahead,' Morton said, but he didn't sit down.

'What did you mean about private records? How private do I think a private record is?'

Ah. There was that. Morton sat down and Naomi figured it out.

'They're not private.'

'You've never struck me as naive before,' Morton said, and he thought again about how young Naomi was. How much power she had and how little she must know about it all.

'You feel sorry for me,' she said.

'Yes.'

'Well, why would I even have a reason to think about private records that way? There's never been any reason to question them,' Naomi said. Morton had heard that defensive tone before, but only when Naomi was using it offensively. He realised that they were being very honest with each other. They were talking face-to-face. Was this what outliers did? It was horrible and Morton felt sorry that Naomi was here, in this position, being honest and ignorant and young and losing just a little bit of facevalue in front of him.

'Sorry,' he said, before he could stop himself. He knew that saying sorry made it all worse. 'Let's cut this off, now.' He stood up again. Leaving would save them both a little bit.

'Wait. Sit down a minute.'

Why couldn't she just leave it alone? He looked at her and she smiled—something he had never seen her do before. He sat.

'Do you have a menial?' Naomi asked him.

'Yes. Part-time. I share it with two other people in my building.'

'What do you think of menials?'

'They're useful. Not necessary, but they certainly make life easier.'

'Are they human?'

'Yes.'

'Are they as human as us?'

Naomi was trying to push him down again. Trying to force him to look at how much lower he was than she was. As if he needed reminding. This was what happened when you embarrassed someone.

'How can you use one if you're in two minds?' Naomi asked him.

'Where are you on the ladder?' Morton asked her.

Naomi shrugged.

'Yeah, exactly. You don't even need to acknowledge the ladder most of the time. But a lot of us *have* to think about it. And we do what we have to, to stay where we are, to rise up, and be acceptable. Congratulations,' he said, acknowledging her beating him down. He stood up and this time he didn't pause. He was out of the door before Naomi blinked.

And he was on the train and he was trying not to breathe heavily and he was trying to look calm and he was trying not to think and he was trying trying trying . . . because she was making him think now and she was making him remember.

Yes. He had been to a menial training facility once. When he was younger. He had been studying for his degree at the time and he wanted to write a thesis on menials. He had forgotten that. How had he forgotten that? It made sense now, that he had been almost eager for Naomi to do her own project on menials.

He had forgotten that.

Morton waited until he got home to plug in. He put in 'memory loss' as a search term and a series of articles bloomed for him:

Memory and Recall Booster
5 Surprising Causes of Memory Loss
A History of Alzheimer's
Memory Loss: Causes and Treatments
. . .

He selected an article on causes.

Nothing is truly lost. Memory is an incredibly elastic and accommodating thing. It is neither true nor false and both the retention and loss of it is vital to our success in life. We need to be able to remember details around us in order to function. However, there is simply too much information to process at every given moment, so it is as necessary to forget or ignore details.

In today's climate, it is paramount that face is maintained. With this in mind, it stands to reason that any details that don't directly contribute to this maintenance are liable to fall by the wayside. Memories will be lost. However, the In is there to supply what users lack and all memories can be retrieved using your personal In system.

Memory retrieval has become a very simple process. All a user needs to do is access their settings and locate the *eye* file. The eye is an automated backup system—everything you do on the In is filed here, in time-stamped folders. If a user's In activity doesn't cover every aspect of their time, then a more invasive memory retrieval procedure might be required. However, it is unlikely that a user will need access to memories that are this buried. If a memory has been 'lost', it probably doesn't warrant being found.

That was probably right. Everything he read was probably right. Even the things he didn't agree with were probably right. Why had he wanted to write a thesis on menials? Why had he wanted to begin a confession booth? Why did he want to get Out? Why couldn't he keep himself Out? Why did he care?

Caring

Care disambiguation

Care may refer to:

Child care, Day care, Elderly care, Foster care, Health care, Care of residents, Home care, Primary care, Primary health care, Intensive-care medicine, Managed care, Duty of care, Ethics of care, Cura or Care, Care or Sorge, Theology of relational care, Vulnerability and . . .

Fuck it. Just fuck it. In or Out didn't matter. At the start and end of each day he was still lying there, with himself, and there was nothing he could do about that.

But of course, there was one thing he could do about that.

Naomi was hanging around after psych class.

'What d'you want?' Morton asked her. He didn't want to duel with her again.

'Apparently I've exceeded my absence allowance at school.'

'So?'

'I've been absent because I've been taking confessions.'

'I showed you how to use the auto-response. You don't need to take every confession. Your absences aren't my fault.'

'I know. I'm not here to get you to vouch for me or anything.'

'Then why are you here?'

'Because I want you to sign off on a personal field trip.'

That was interesting.

'Your face is different.' He could see something open in her face. Something innocent and interested.

'Will you do it?' Naomi asked, ignoring the comment.

'What's the trip?'

'I want to go to a menial training facility.'

That was really interesting. Morton found himself trying, yet again, to find his own memory of the training facility he had gone to.

'Really?' he asked, still scraping at the insides of his memory.

'No, I'm just saying shit for shit's sake. I love staying on after school to utter nonsense at you.'

Morton smiled at her. Her return to face brought him back to the present and it made him feel comfortable.

'There's the Naomi we all know and love. When d'you want to go?'

'Tomorrow.'

'You need the whole day?'

'Ideally.'

Morton searched his patch, selected the appropriate form and sent it. A moment later he refocussed on her.

'I sent a permission to the head office. You're free to go.'

'Great,' Naomi said, and she left. She turned back a minute later and ducked her head through the door of the classroom.

'Thanks,' she said, and she left before Morton could say anything. He liked that. He liked how her face had looked when she said that. That would be a nice memory. He smiled as he packed up the rest of his things. There was something soothing in fitting it all together, a life in a box. He had always enjoyed being tidy.

Morton felt empty as he made his way home. It was a good feeling. He was glad he had this one. This one feeling he could keep. Nothing could take this one away. There was something he could do about that.

(Menial 63700578—Jake)

Jake was sure there was something wrong with him. How many times had he masturbated today? He couldn't think about words anymore, couldn't think about talking. Madeleine's mouth haunted him. Schuyler's eyes were everywhere. Naomi walked on quiet feet. Jake melted from room to room. He winced every time the implant in his wrist buzzed. His face was out of his control.

'Hello? Hello, Jake?' the confessor said, when Jake finally called.

Jake moaned. Then he patched out. He couldn't think about words. He couldn't use them.

'Eddie?' Jake heard, and he walked onto the landing and looked down at the dining room. Schuyler was perched on a chair. His body was all tension. That was different.

'How is she? Can I get a look at her,' Schuyler said. 'Perfect,' he whispered. 'Shea? Hello, Shea! And how's Tonia doing?' Schuyler waited, nodding. 'Yes, that sounds great. Can I see her again before I go?' He sighed as he looked at the empty space before him, not looking at it but at something else. And then he snapped back into the room and looked up.

'Menial,' he said, freezing Jake where he stood. 'What do you think about children?' Schuyler asked. 'No, I forgot. You don't have opinions.' And there was nothing underneath those words. Schuyler meant what he said. He thought Jake had no real thoughts. And Jake wanted Schuyler to look at him, to read his face, to see that there was so much desire in him. Not for children, no, but for something. For more.

Schuyler did not look at Jake. He came upstairs, passed him on the landing, and went to his room. It was only when his door closed that Jake felt free to breathe again and to move. He retreated into his own room and patched in.

'Hello, Jake,' said the confessor, its voice smooth and expectant.

'H-hello.'

'How are you, Jake?'

Jake didn't know how to answer the question at first. But the word came to him.

'I'm confused.'

'What about, Jake?'

'Can you stop that?'

'Stop what, Jake?'

'Stop using my name. I . . . I don't like to hear it.'

'. . . What should I call you, Ja—what should I call you?'

'Why do you have to call me anything?' Jake asked. He thought about it as he said it. 'You can call me Menial 63700578.'

'Really?' asked the confessor. Its surprise was evident.

'Who *are* you?' Jake asked. 'You . . .' He stopped himself.

'Me?'

'Never mind. This isn't about you, is it? That's what you told me. It's never about you.'

'That's right, Ja—Menial 63 . . . Menial. Sorry. Can I call you Menial?'

'Yes.'

'You said you feel confused, Menial. What about?'

Jake thought about that. And suddenly it didn't seem very important anymore. He patched out without saying goodbye. He half expected the confessor to call him back, but there was no call. Jake went to bed.

Madeleine and Schuyler had been invited to see Tonia and Eduardo's new baby. Madeleine looked beautiful. Her skin was flawless, glowing and clear. She wore her hair down and it curled just slightly, caressing bare shoulders. Her dress was tight, stylish, full of gaping holes that had been cut out in elaborate patterns.

'You're not going in that?' Schuyler asked, and his voice was heavy with disdain.

Madeleine didn't drop her smile but her face tightened just that little bit. Not so anyone would notice. But Jake noticed. Then she laughed.

'Oh *darling*! Do *please* choose my dress,' she said.

Schuyler loped up the stairs and into Madeleine's room and returned with a dress.

'That should do,' he said.

It was a silken thing, fawn coloured and modest. It was old but un-worn. Madeleine looked at it. She opened her mouth once, but closed it without saying anything.

'Change,' Schuyler said.

Madeleine snapped her fingers at Jake.

'Unzip this,' she said, turning around and offering him her back. The order stunned him and for a moment all he could do was stare at the zip.

'Well?' Madeleine asked.

Jake looked at Schuyler, who gave him a wry smile, finely cali-brated. He looked back at the zip. It lay snug against the flesh of Mad-eleine's back. To touch it was to be millimetres from her skin.

'I'll get gloves,' Jake said, and he fled the room.

'Hurry,' Madeleine said when he returned. He tried to approach her with certainty, but it was hard to be so close to her. He could feel the warmth of her body, smell the perfume evaporating from her skin. He pinched the zip delicately, and drew it down with all the care in the world, desperate that he should not touch her and yet desperate to do just that. All too soon, the zip reached the end of its trail and Jake let go and stepped back. Madeleine tugged the dress down the rest of the way and stood, naked in front of him. Jake felt his penis getting hard. And he couldn't look anymore. He left the room again, went into the kitchen and watched Madeleine on the monitor, his hand in his trousers.

Jake managed to delay his ejaculation until Madeleine and Schuy-ler had left the house. When the moment came he felt hollow and unsatisfied. He washed his hands carefully before cleaning the house, bottom to top.

Schuyler

Losing Face

Schuyler's comline buzzed and Eduardo's name floated up.

'Hello?' Schuyler enabled the vid and Eduardo smiled at him. He was as handsome and put together as always, his green eyes startling against his dark skin. Schuyler liked to look at him.

'I have news,' Eduardo said.

'Yes?'

'We're choosing a baby.'

Schuyler grinned. That was the correct response to this kind of news.

'I'm thrilled for you,' he said, his voice warm.

'Relieved, you mean?' Eduardo said good-naturedly. Schuyler pretended amusement.

'What have you decided? Have you booked an appointment with a doctor? I'm assuming you're going stud?'

'Well, we're *getting* there. To be honest, we're a little overwhelmed by all the options. I'd welcome any suggestions, to help us sort through the data.' Eduardo was giving Schuyler power. That should be a reason to dislike him, disdain him, manipulate him. Eduardo was handing himself over. But Schuyler just smiled at him.

'Have you got the latest edition of *To Stud*?' he asked.

'Yes, I got it yesterday, but I haven't had a chance to look over it.'

'Well, start by looking through that. It'll answer a lot of the initial questions. Now, when are you going to come over and play some Go with me?' That was the way these things were done. If you offered advice you quickly changed the subject to save everyone's face in the interaction.

'When I have time, Schuy,' Eduardo said. 'When I have time.'

Children. It was a big step.

Schuyler had met Eduardo and Tonia at a party, two years ago. They kept their faces closed but there was a sheen of naiveté to them that couldn't quite be hidden. They were new to the level. And they were so beautiful. Schuyler felt drawn to them straightaway.

Eduardo had an actual nine-to-five job. That was amusing. And Tonia was a blogger, which was quaint. Quaint and amusing.

'How *quaint* and amusing!' Madeleine spoke about them freely, using his words, making them cheap. But Schuyler let her talk. He always let her talk.

They were astute—level climbers had to be—and they adapted quickly. They hadn't asked for anything when they met him, and that was endearing. Schuyler supposed that was why he had taken an interest in them. It was pleasant to pass the time with people who never seemed to want anything from him. It made him want to give them things.

Children. What a big step.

Schuyler could never quite say why he favoured Reyna. After all, Naomi's total lack of finesse was strangely charming. But it was Reyna he looked for. Reyna was the daughter he loved. And sometimes, when she looked at him, he wanted to bundle her in his arms in a hug.

Getting any of the Burroughses down for dinner was a chore. But the idea of a family meal amused him and so Schuyler persevered. Seeing them struggle made it all the more amusing. He loved to watch them.

'Tonia and Eduardo have decided to choose a baby,' he said. He wanted to see them chew over that one.

'I *know*, I think it's *wonderful*!' Madeleine said.

Naomi grunted.

'You think it's a bad idea?' Schuyler asked her.

'It's a minefield,' Naomi said. 'And they're green.'

'They're also static right now,' Reyna said. 'Having a child is the only way for them to move up the social hierarchy.'

Children. This is what they were now.

'Have you considered the couple fully, though?' Reyna said. 'They have very favourable chances for success, especially *with* our influence. And of course, by "our" I mean Schuyler's influence.'

Schuyler sighed.

'I wish you would call me Dad,' he said.

'Please. "Dad" sounds so low level,' Reyna told him. 'It's practically menial.'

'"Father" then. Or "Pater",' he laughed. 'Just stop using my name as if I were merely an acquaintance.'

'You *are* merely an acquaintance,' Reyna said.

Children!

'This is what I get after having raised you all your life. I hope you never choose to have children.'

Reyna shrugged.

'Well, that will depend on whether or not it's beneficial to my status in the future. You know that.'

He listened to her talk about interchangeable children. He listened to her reduce herself to an accessory—an out-of-date whim chosen by a foolish couple—and he couldn't disagree with that. He and Madeleine were a foolish couple. And Reyna was a whim. And children were an unjustifiable risk. And were there any reasons why he had chosen her?

'For once I agree with my sister,' Naomi said.

Madeleine smiled.

'Such *smart* girls,' she said. She raised her glass to Schuyler. 'We chose *such* smart girls.'

Hearing that ridiculous voice of hers almost made Schuyler shudder. He wasn't sure how he had lasted so long with her. She had been a silly mistake, and one he didn't feel strong enough to admit to in public. But how much longer could he last?

'I'm just going to freshen up before the next course,' Madeleine said.

'Father?' Reyna said.

Father? She was a funny one. Schuyler smiled at her. She was certainly the better one.

'Have you considered yourselves?' Schuyler asked. 'You're here because I chose you. You speak so cavalierly about interchangeable children and the pros and cons of choosing lives. What of yourselves? What would have become of you if I had thought about children the way you are now?'

Maybe he should have!

'I doubt I would have been born,' Reyna said. Her face was stone.

'How does that make you feel?' Schuyler asked.

'That's a redundant question. I am and so I can't possibly say how I might feel about having not been.'

Fair enough.

'What about you, Naomi?'

'This conversation is too full of hypotheticals for my taste. I would rather be on the In right now.'

'We haven't finished dinner.'

'I have no appetite.' Naomi stood up and slipped up the stairs. Good for her. She had one thing going for her—she did as she pleased. A luxury only a second child could indulge in.

'What were you thinking when you decided to choose a child?' Reyna asked.

That was quite a question.

'Maddie was the one who decided.'

'But you said . . .'

'She decided it was time to expand our family. I didn't see the harm, so I went through the process with her. I employed Dr Wójcik and she helped us choose the best fit for our aesthetic and our standing. She helped us choose you. She helped me choose you. By that time, Maddie didn't have much of a say in the matter.'

The menial came in with the next course and Madeleine came out of the bathroom.

'Where's Naomi?' she asked as she sat down.

'On the In.'

'You know, I've lost my appetite,' Madeleine said. 'I might go In myself.'

She left them alone. Schuyler watched Reyna picking at her food and forming and re-forming words in her head.

'Stop measuring things with me,' Schuyler said.

'How do you know—'

'I understand the distrust. But between us . . . I'm your father, for goodness' sake!' He was.

'But you're not my father at all,' she said. Also true.

'I'm the only one you've got.'

'What are you hoping to gain here? I can't see the consequences of this exchange,' she said.

'I'm not thinking about consequences.' He was so very tired of consequences. How long had he been playing face? It was so wearing, to
never be able to just stop.

'You're always thinking about consequences. You're always ten
steps ahead. What am I giving you here?' she asked him.

'A conversation.' All he wanted was a simple conversation.

'And what?'

'Just that.'

'Nothing is ever just one thing.'

Children! Schuyler looked at her. That face of hers was shut tight.
The tightness was clear—she was uncomfortable. That was a true
thing. She fidgeted under his eyes and he could see her working out
how to leave. And he didn't want to let her. He wanted to force her to
stay, to be uncomfortable, to be a true thing.

'Reyna. I'm going to ask you to do something. It won't affect your
face; in fact, I won't even look at you—your reactions can be entirely
your own, secret from everyone but yourself. I'm going to ask you to
listen to me. That's all. Will you do that?'

'You said you wouldn't look,' Reyna said, and Schuyler looked away.

'Sorry,' he said. 'It's just . . . these are private thoughts. I'm trusting
you to keep them to yourself. I'm giving you power over me. Can you
keep this secret?'

Reyna was quiet for a moment. Just a moment. A moment that
stretched out forever.

'Yes,' she said. 'Wait. I'm not . . . I don't know if this is a good
idea.'

Yes! Schuyler focussed on that. Yes.

'Please, Reyna. I want to say it all. You said you would listen to me.
It won't cost you anything, you just have to stay quiet and not share it.'

'Wouldn't it be better if you spoke to Maddie about it?'

Schuyler laughed.

'She knows nothing worth anything. All she knows is how to climb
the ladder. This isn't about status. It's about being human.'

'I'm not sure I follow you.'

'You'll get the picture if you just listen.'

'Go on,' she said, and suddenly he felt rushed. He needed to think, take his time, find the right words. But her 'go on' was pressing on him. He dove in.

'When I realised what I wanted it felt imperative that I have a child. I felt that the only way to start real experiences, real connections, would be to start with someone new. A baby, not yet aware of the importance of faces and status. Having you became a passion. I chose very carefully. And when you were born I took you in my arms and held you close. I felt your skin against mine and I realised it was the first time I had ever touched anyone.' He stopped for a moment as he thought back to Reyna when she was born. She was so small. Her skin was so wrinkled, bigger than her body, waiting for her to stretch into it. This tiny thing, but gods she was loud! She had screamed so much as she was born but when he held her she had quietened and it was magic. Touch had soothed her.

'You were so little and so new,' he said. 'I remember when you first smiled at me, unaware that a smile might cost something. I was so sure I could form you into a new sort of person, that I could teach you a new way.'

She wasn't as quick to grow as he had expected. Her eyes took up so much of her face and her ears had fine hair all over them like fur. He hadn't realised babies were so hairy.

'It was naive,' he said. 'There was no way I could keep you from the world, or the world from you, and you learned so quickly that a face isn't real. Before I knew it, you were trying on new faces, practicing expressions and reactions for the utmost effect. You were never real with me. I lost you almost immediately. I thought I could try again but I lost Naomi even more quickly.

'I thought I'd failed. I had got used to the idea, had started moving on, but when I was talking to Eduardo earlier—about choosing a child—it occurred to me that you're older now.'

He looked up at her but, remembering his promise, he quickly looked away. He hesitated before speaking again. He felt . . . taut. Stretched to his limits. But he was close to the end so he kept going.

'And I chose you to be a certain way. I manipulated you before you were born. I chose you with the hope that one day I could have a real conversation. So, I thought . . . maybe now?' He looked at her again and this time he didn't look away. 'Maybe since you're old enough to think for yourself, I could tell you everything. Tell you *my* truth.

And maybe then you would see. And so here we are. I'm telling you everything.'

And that was everything. Schuyler waited.

'And? What are you expecting now?' Reyna asked.

That was not the question he had been expecting. When he thought about it, he hadn't expected anything, hadn't got beyond this point in his thoughts, a fact that was more surprising than anything else.

'I'm not expecting anything,' he said.

Reyna stood up.

'You should take better care of your face,' she said, and she walked up to her room.

Fuck.

Schuyler Burroughs had always been in demand. The Family Burroughs had been in demand, and their people before them, and so on, back and back and back. Out of his parents there was only one he cared for, mainly because there was only one who cared for him. Janine Burroughs was not a demonstrative person. She had no particular face she paraded around and she showed no particular fondness for Schuyler. She had always made time for him, though. She would talk to him. She taught him how to play Go. She taught him how to treat demand.

If Schuyler could have chosen his parents, instead of it happening the other way around, he thought he might have chosen Janine. He remembered asking her once how they had decided what they wanted in a child. Why did he look the way he did? Why did he act the way he did?

She told him his actions were his own; they had not chosen those. And as for how he looked . . . well, the three of them were so different from one another, in skin tone and hair type, so they had wanted a child that could complement them all. He did that. So very different. The United Nations.

Schuyler Burroughs had been in demand. The propositions flowed in thick and fast. People from everywhere. But he chose Madeleine.

It was funny. Madeleine was the butt of a private joke—one he had only with himself. But it wasn't all a joke. There was something appealing about how she contrasted with him, all alabaster skin and brittle laughter. There was something appealing about how she seemed yang to his yin. And that was funny too, because it was meant to be the other way around.

The day Schuyler and Madeleine registered as a couple he found himself asking her:

'Why me?'

She laughed, of course. That was what she always did. That was her answer. He was Schuyler Burroughs. What else was there to it? He didn't ask again.

A month in, he found himself going over the question again, though.

'What do you like about me?' The words were out before he had a chance to think it through.

Madeleine paused over her dinner.

'What is there not to like about you?' she answered.

She looked at him, all blatant pride—she felt she had won a victory over him then, that much was clear. And perhaps she had. Perhaps that was where it all started to go wrong with her: her sense of self-importance just kept inflating.

'You could always leave her,' Janine told him, a year after the registration. 'You're a Burroughs; you can do anything you like.'

Janine didn't like Madeleine. None of them did. And maybe that was why he didn't leave her then. But despite his resolve, there was only so much he could take. After three years, he was done.

Madeleine was not a lot of things, but she did have an uncanny instinct for survival. Schuyler had barely thought the thought when she appeared before him, wide smile carved into her face and a slate in hand.

'*This*, darling. *This* is what we *need*.'

That 'this' became Reyna. And then there was no question of leaving anymore.

Schuyler had known Vidya Wójcik all his life. Her parents had facilitated him. It had seemed obvious that she would be the one to facilitate his own child.

Schuyler and Vidya had grown up in the same district, but since she was older, their paths had seldom crossed. All the same, there was recognition there. They were made from the same clay. Meeting her was interesting.

'So,' Madeleine said, coming into Schuyler's room and sitting on the bed.

'So,' Schuyler said, putting down his slate and looking at her.

'I think we should introduce ToDdie to Vidya.'

Schuyler nodded.

'You disagree?'

Schuyler shook his head.

'Do you think it's a good idea?'

Schuyler nodded his head.

'But is it a *very* good idea, or is it just a good idea?'

Schuyler couldn't help but smile a little.

'What's that?' Madeleine asked.

'You shouldn't have to ask,' Schuyler told her, and Madeleine blushed. 'I hope you're better at keeping your face when I'm not around?' He said it gently but he meant it with spite. It had a strange effect. Her face seemed to harden into a mask—a porcelain doll's face, both tough and fragile, expression frozen.

'I'm throwing a party next week. You can invite her,' Madeleine said.

She left the room, and left Schuyler feeling odd.

Schuyler left the party planning to Madeleine. He called Vidya as requested, though.

'They're a beautiful couple. Great potential.'

Vidya accepted the invite, just like everyone else. He was Schuyler Burroughs, after all.

Madeleine fluttered around, full of herself. Schuyler watched, amused, as she over-egged it all. At least he made sure he looked amused. He hated it. He hated her. It had been funny once but building a life on a joke? He had been stupid. It hurt to admit that. Instead, he looked amused and when people arrived at his door he greeted them with his third-best smile—the one that made people wonder if he was laughing at them—and he graced them with a word or two, a sign that he remembered who they were, cared what they did, understood where they were coming from.

Second-rate people arrived in a timely fashion. They knew where they stood, what function they performed, and they came to the party accordingly. None of them pressed him for too much of his time. All of them were eager for him to notice how well they played their parts. And then Eduardo arrived, Tonia a step behind, a moment delayed, a hesitating breath apart. She didn't want to be here. She hid it but it was true and Schuyler saw it. The face behind her face was the same as his.

'ToDdie!' Schuyler said, and he had to make an effort not to wince at the loudness of his own voice.

Tonia and Eduardo bowed their heads, acknowledging his favour, but they didn't smile, didn't blink, didn't move their faces an inch.

'Ooh! Ooh, you're here!' Madeleine squealed, swooping down on them. 'How *marvellous* that you're here!' What a show. Tonia smiled at Madeleine; small, graceful, tasteful. But when she looked up he could see how little she cared for the spectacle. She hated Madeleine too. He knew it. He knew it! He winked at her.

'Schuy! Drinks! Where *are* you?' said Madeleine. What a creature. Schuyler walked over to the nearest menial and signalled an order.

'Where are the girls?' he heard Tonia ask, as he walked back.

'Oh, you know,' said Madeleine, waving a hand. 'They'll be on the In.'

'They have more virtual existences than I care to count,' he said. Madeleine laughed.

'Hon, there is *no* such thing as *too* many faces,' she said, turning to him. 'Where *are* the drinks?'

'I've ordered,' he said as the menial walked up bearing a tray of frosted glasses. The buzzer went and Madeleine spun around.

'What are you doing?' she asked the menial with the tray. 'Why isn't anyone by the door? I told you earlier that I don't want to hear that buzzer go tonight.' Even though her voice was quiet, it was practically an explosion. The menial took it in stride—perfect form—and retreated.

Madeleine smiled a trifle manically.

'It's *amazing* how they still seem to slip up every so often. You'd have thought, being trained from such a young age . . . Oh well.'

Face-saving words. And then she retreated too, and Schuyler felt the air loosen around him.

'So. Have you made any decisions regarding this child, yet?' he asked. The question was for Tonia, but Eduardo answered:

'We're still gathering data, but I think we're close to making a decision about what we want.'

'Good. And I think Madeleine has a surprise for you on the child front, too.'

'That sounds ominous,' Tonia said. Schuyler smiled. Yes. Her face was just like his.

'Can I refresh your drink?' he asked her, and he started moving before he had time to think—reaching out for her glass, wrapping his fingers around it, wrapping his fingers around her hand. Skin on skin. Her hand was soft, the skin thin, stretched over birdlike bones. More delicate than he could have imagined. He couldn't have imagined anything. He wouldn't have thought. He was holding her hand! And then she was gone. She stepped back, pulled away, and the glass between them broke. Could anything else break? Could he break everything? His heart was racing and it was all he could do to keep his expression still.

'I'm sorry, honey,' Eduardo said, stepping forwards and speaking so the whole room could hear. 'You said you weren't feeling well and I still insisted that we come.' He looked at Schuyler. 'I just felt it was bad form not to come after we had confirmed our attendance.'

'You're very thoughtful,' Schuyler said. He looked at Tonia, standing so still, her face a blank mask. 'I would hate for you to leave now that you're here. Perhaps a drink of water?' Tonia nodded and Schuyler walked away, grateful.

His heart was still thumping, and his throat felt tight. Her hand had been so soft! She'd looked at him without emotion and yet she must have felt what he felt? Wasn't she shocked? She stepped away, yes, but she was so calm. How was she so calm? He couldn't take her the water himself. He couldn't face her.

A menial was dispatched and Schuyler worked the room, careful to avoid her. Only he couldn't avoid her. Every time he looked up she was there. Was she studying him? What was she thinking? He wanted to ask her a thousand questions but he was too embarrassed to even ask her one.

And then Vidya arrived. Madeleine paraded her guest of honour before the party, making sure everyone saw her introduce the good doctor to Tonia and Eduardo.

'It's such a pleasure to meet you,' Tonia said, her voice silk, and Schuyler felt his chest tighten.

'The feeling is mutual. SchAddie have told me so much about you,' Vidya said. 'Really. You're a stunning couple. And I understand you're thinking about committing to a child?'

'You're very gracious,' Eduardo said. 'We try our best, but our aesthetic is far from perfect.' It was a nice touch but a little too obvious for Schuyler's liking.

'Our hosts have a monopoly on perfection!' Tonia said, smiling prettily at Madeleine. That was obvious too but in the perfect way.

'You're too modest,' Schuyler said, and Tonia looked at him. In agreement? Part of a joke? He couldn't tell, didn't want to, and so he steered Madeleine away and let Vidya take the beautiful couple under her wing.

It was a relief to see the back of everyone. The lingerers—second tier—would never be invited to a Burroughs affair again. In fact, several people, regardless of their tier, had been struck off Madeleine's list of the socially acceptable. That would be a big blow for them. Schuyler didn't care. Once the door shut on them, the only person he could think about was Madeleine and how much he hated her.

'Well, I think *that* was a success,' Madeleine said as she sat down at the table, opposite Schuyler.

Schuyler grunted.

'Don't you think so?' Madeleine asked.

Schuyler grunted.

'What are you thinking about?' Madeleine asked.

His fingers were tingling with the memory of Tonia's skin. His thoughts were rotating around the look in her eyes when Madeleine had brought Vidya over to her.

'Why did you have to introduce Vidya to them like that?' he asked.

'What do you mean?'

'Why couldn't you arrange something in private?'

'Meeting someone like Vidya is a *great* honour,' Madeleine said.

Words that said nothing at all. And there were no words to give back to that. He just looked at her, allowing some of his loathing to filter through his expression. She bore the look for as long as she could. And then:

'I don't know what you're so upset about!'

'Oh, don't pretend naiveté.'

'I was *being* helpful.'

'You were trivialising them to make yourself more important. When are you going to realise that at our level, *that doesn't work!*'

'I don't understand why you care so much!'

'Your face is my face! I can't have you reducing me to some simple little . . .'

'What? Say it! What am I reducing you to?'

'The way you grasp for advantage, it's like you've never even seen the top. You're cheap, Maddie. I knew that when I met you but you just get cheaper as the years go by.' There. True thoughts uttered out loud. Schuyler stood up and looked down at his partner.

'Don't hold back,' she muttered, not meeting his gaze. How disappointing.

'You're not stupid,' Schuyler said. 'You must have known how I felt. I haven't been hiding from you, I—'

'God, I know! You've done anything *but* hide!' She met his gaze. She had a tight hold of her face—she kept it quiet but the effort was clear. The effort was clear and the words were clear and that was a surprise. Anything but hide? How much had he been giving away? For how long? She looked at him for a long time. Longer than he thought she could. But finally she sagged, leaned forwards, looked down.

'I don't know what you want,' she said. She held on to her face and said it again. 'I don't know what you want.'

Of course she didn't.

A few days after the party, Schuyler decided to call Vidya.

'You ran out so fast we never got a chance to talk,' he said.

'I don't appreciate being put on display like that.'

Fuck. Schuyler arranged his face into a suitable look of regret but really he was angry. Angry at Madeleine. And maybe even a little angry at himself.

He looked at Vidya and realised she was waiting for him to do something—attempting to gain the position of power in their conversation.

'I thought you didn't engage in faceplay,' he said, and Vidya laughed.

'So, what is it about this couple?' she asked.

'You saw them. You must have noticed the potential?'

'You keep bringing up this potential. I saw a pretty pair. What makes them different from any of the other pretty pairs?'

She was right.

'I don't know. They just . . . took my fancy.'

'How are the girls?' Vidya asked. It was an odd topic change but Schuyler took it in his stride.

'Reyna is . . . amazing. She just seems to be going from strength to strength. She decided she wanted to brand out so she's spinning faces, always In.'

'And Naomi?'

'Changeless. Stubborn. Dull.'

'Are you sure about that?' Vidya asked him. What the fuck did that mean?

'Yes.'

'I don't think I bred her to be dull.' Had he insulted her?

'Oh, I don't mean she's stupid. I just find her whole angry teenager act . . . boring.'

'I see,' said Vidya. She left her words hanging to embarrass him and he didn't like that.

'She's Madeleine's project. I was never very interested in her.'

'Hmmm.'

'I didn't mean to insult you.'

'You didn't. I'm just not sure we see her the same way.'

'Have you spent much time with her?' Schuyler asked, wondering what the hell Vidya was driving at.

'Of course not. Have you?'

Schuyler laughed at that.

'And what about you? Have you thought about designing a child for yourself?' It was a clumsy conversational turn, but it would have to do.

'Now, why would I need to do that?'

'To show us all how it should be done.'

'I couldn't care less what I show anyone, Schuyler. You know that. And isn't that what you keep trying for yourself? To show everyone how little you care?'

'What makes you say that?'

'Well, aren't you?'

'Yes, Vidya. I am.'

Schuyler wondered why he had called Vidya. He wondered why he felt so much worse for having talked to her. He wondered how to finish this conversation well.

'I'm sure this ToDdie couple will prove fertile ground,' Vidya said, doing the hard work for him.

'Thank you,' Schuyler said before he hung up.

But the conversation hung around him. What had she meant about Naomi? What did she even know about her? And ToDdie? They were beautiful, no matter what she said. What did she really know anyway? She stayed in her sky-high world and knew nothing about what was going on below her. She knew nothing.

Schuyler tapped into his desktop and reviewed the day. He pulled the conversation with Vidya out and, with wave of his hand, he dropped it in the bin. He felt brighter. And hearing footsteps, he un-plugged and smiled at that perfect daughter of his as she walked into the room. He could feel his heart quickening a little. After their last talk he had worried she wouldn't want to be alone with him again. She had seemed so disgusted with him. But perhaps she had thought about everything he had said. Perhaps there was still hope.

'Schuyler,' she said, and he made a show of wincing at her use of his name.

'What can I help you with?' he asked her.

Reyna sighed and sat down. Her nonchalance was clumsier than he was used to from her, but perhaps that was a good sign. Maybe she was trying? To let go of face? He waited for her to talk. He wanted her to control the conversation, not be frightened off by him again. The moment of silence stretched out tight as a drum skin between them and he wondered: *Is she playing face, or is she unsure of how to start talking freely?*

'Were things pretty much the same for you when you were my age?' she eventually asked him.

Ah. Not the direction he thought she might take. But perhaps she was just warming up.

'Are you talking in terms of effort required to maintain your status?'

Reyna shrugged. Shit. She was playing face. He suppressed a tired sigh and decided to play along with her. At least she was talking to him.

'I had things fairly easy with my family. And I didn't go the same route as you. People were more interested in an individual personality, rather than an intriguing brand entity. That has different pressures and requires different efforts.'

Reyna nodded and kept quiet and he suddenly wanted to shake her. She knew exactly how to push his buttons!

'I think you're doing a great job,' he said, smiling at her and hoping she seethed inside.

'What do you think you would be doing if you were my age now?' she asked him. Advice! Well, that was certainly new. He relaxed his smile.

'I don't think I would do anything differently. It worked out well for me. I think it would work as well in today's landscape. But I'm a very different case fro—'

'I wasn't asking for advice or to be soothed,' Reyna interrupted him.

What was wrong with her? If she was going to insist on playing face with him then he wished she would do a better job of it. She seemed to have lost all nuance; it was almost as bad as talking to Madeleine.

'Then what are you asking?' he asked her.

'I just wanted to understand how you became . . .' She gave a vague wave in his direction. '. . . this thing.'

And his heart stopped for a second. Was this the moment? Could he let go of his face and actually talk to her now?

She stood up.

'That's all,' she said, and she walked out of the room.

Schuyler groaned and let his head fall back. Well. So much for that. And yet it had felt like progress. Maybe, given time, she would come around. He smiled at the thought. Imagine that! Imagine if

Reyna let go of face. And Tonia . . . perhaps that was too much to imagine for now.

Life always seemed to be difficult to change, no matter what you did to it. The edges that made up its shape could give a little but they were made of enduring stuff. Madeleine was exactly herself. Reyna hadn't changed a hair. Naomi was as disappointing as always. The menial shifted around the house, avoiding eye contact, surreptitiously watching Madeleine's every move, just as it had always done. Eduardo never agreed to play Go. And then there was Tonia. Tonia who never called. Tonia who never spoke to him unless required to do so. Tonia who had him crawling in his skin. Tonia who made him want to use his lips, use his body, try something that could change the shape of it all.

Fuck.

'Are you afraid of us?' he asked the menial as it shuffled about the dining room, collecting his dinner plates. The thing didn't answer, just kept tidying things onto its trolley. 'Menial, are you afraid of us?'

It stopped then, under the direct address, but it didn't look at him.

'No,' it said. But it was. That face said it was. And when Schuyler stood close to it, watched it from right there, he saw it clearly.

'They say you menials are different. But you look just the same. The only difference . . .' Schuyler grinned. It was a free grin. 'You have no control of your faces. Not when it matters.'

Schuyler stepped away from the menial again and went back to the other side of the table. The menial said nothing, did nothing for a moment, and then . . . yes, the edges of life retained their shape. The menial resumed cleaning.

'It's special, you know? Being free with your expressions. It's . . . it's just being free.' Schuyler said the words out loud without meaning to. But only the menial could hear and everyone knew menials were nothing. It was okay, he was okay. And then an alert popped up. A message.

ToDdie: We are thrilled to announce that we're pregnant. Due date is November 23rd.

Tonia. What was she thinking? How was she feeling? Schuyler scrolled down his contacts and selected.

'Hey!' Eduardo said, bright as a lemon, and his face flicked into view. 'You saw the notice.'

Schuyler nodded and grinned, shining teeth.

'Congratulations! That was quick. How are you feeling?'

'Pleased. Relieved.' Was he going to say more? He didn't.

'It'll be perfect.'

'Yes.'

A moment stretched out, both waiting for the other to speak, neither knowing what to say.

'How's Tonia?'

'Tonia?' Eduardo couldn't quite hide a second of surprise.

'Your partner?'

'Yes, yes. I remember now,' Eduardo joked. 'She's happy,' he said, and he laughed.

'It's going to change a lot of things for you two,' Schuyler said.

'Yes.'

'You won't quite get that until it happens.'

'That's what I've heard.'

'You ready for all that?'

'No idea. All I can do is try.'

Schuyler nodded.

'Tonia will be a great mother, I think.'

Eduardo gave Schuyler a look that could only mean he was confused by the statement, trying to read intentions behind it—intentions that didn't exist.

'Yes,' Eduardo said. He was sticking to safe responses. He usually did.

'We should celebrate!' Schuyler said, shifting the conversation slightly. 'Go?' And Eduardo laughed again—a fuller, heavier laugh.

'You're relentless.'

'It's part of my charm.'

'You're charming despite it, you mean.'

'I know what I mean,' Schuyler said. He didn't mean to say it but he did. Eduardo didn't flinch, took the barb in his stride, smiled and said:

'Of course you do, Schuyler Burroughs. Let's play soon. I've got to go.'

The call was terminated. Schuyler studied the backs of his eyelids for a bit, wondering what he wanted to do next. But he already knew what he wanted to do—the wondering was just an act he was playing for himself. He laughed. Then he dialled.

'Hello?' said Tonia. She didn't use the vid, and her voice seemed closer because of that.

'Great news, Tonia. How are you feeling?'

'Good!' she said. 'Really good!' She sounded convincing. Perhaps she was good. Perhaps this was all she ever wanted. Did she have the same hopes about her child that he had had about his?

'I'm surprised to hear from you,' she said. 'Usually you call Eddie.'

'We've already spoken. He seems excited.'

'Yes. Yes he is. We both are. We're thrilled.' She stopped there and Schuyler could hear each of her breaths. He thought about her skin.

'And you? How are you?' she asked.

'We're well. Maddie was just saying that she was thinking about throwing you a baby shower. How d'you feel about that?'

'A baby shower?'

'A baby shower.'

'That's awfully kind of her. Please let her know how grateful I am.'

'Yes, of course.'

The conversation stalled.

Breaths.

Skin.

'Are you busy?'

'Now?'

'Yes.'

'Why?'

All Schuyler could do was laugh. Laughter was a refuge.

'I'll let you get on,' he said, and he patched out before she did.

Breaths.

Skin.

Fuck.

He typed

Schuyler: Come down.
Madeleine: What for?

Schuyler sighed. There was a time when Madeleine did every-thing he asked her to. She was too worried about her position in his life not to. It had taken her far longer than it should have to realise that she didn't have to worry. He wished she'd never realised it, though.

Schuyler: Nothing we can't talk about here, he hoped she could see him shrug through his words.

Schuyler: Throwing a baby shower. Thoughts?
Madeleine: For ToDdie?
Schuyler: Yes.
Madeleine: Why? What's the angle?
Schuyler: Seriously?
Madeleine: Does that mean there's no angle or that you can't believe I
    can't see it? You know I'm stupid.
Schuyler is typing . . .
. . .
. . .
Schuyler: Thoughts?
Madeleine: I'm on it.

'Naomi won't attend the party. Can you talk to Reyna?' Madeleine asked him.

'Why do they need to come?' Schuyler asked.

'It's a baby shower.'

'And?'

'Well, we should show off our babies.'

'That's pretty coarse.'

'It'll be expected.'

'Who gives a shit what people expect?'

'I . . .' She realised what she had been about to say just in time. 'I would like it if they came. They rarely attend any of these things. I'd like it, just this once. Can you please just do this?'

Madeleine looked tired and for a moment Schuyler almost felt sorry for her.

'Sure,' he said.

The door opened just as he got there, and out came Reyna, a boy following closely behind. She looked as surprised as he felt.

'Reyna. You have a guest,' he said. Reyna stepped aside to let the boy out.

'This is Tam. Tam, Schuyler,' she said.

Tam was a beautiful boy. And he was a young Schuyler for sure. Had he been modelled on him? The resemblance between them was uncanny. He looked at him a little more carefully. No. Tam's bone structure was different. He had a stronger chin than Schuyler's. The resemblance was in the boy's attitude.

'You could muster some enthusiasm,' Schuyler said. What was Reyna doing? 'It's a pleasure to meet you, Tam. Why are you here?' he asked.

'That's a fairly indelicate question,' Reyna said, allowing a hint of disapproval to colour her voice.

'It's an honour,' Tam said. The cadence of his voice was well judged, despite the gushing words. Schuyler waited for him to go on. 'I'm here for Reyna,' Tam said. A good save.

'And why might Reyna need you?' Schuyler dug in, wanting to see how far he could push the boy.

'Schuyler,' Reyna began, ready to tell him off. Schuyler gave her a warning look and she stopped.

'It's not my place to speak for her,' Tam said.

'Later,' Reyna said, walking away. It was as good as running. What was she doing?

'It was nice to meet you,' Tam said. Schuyler watched them leave. And then he waited for Reyna to come back.

He saw her return a few hours later but he didn't go to her straightaway. Let her get her head on, her face straight, her story aligned. When enough time had passed, he knocked on her door.

What? The word drifted up his eyeline, exasperating him. Schuyler walked in and Reyna jerked up off her bed and looked at him with a naked expression: fear, disgust, anger.

Jesus.

'Leave me alone,' Reyna whispered, and that was what he had been waiting for—that openness. She wasn't wearing a face at all. And yet . . . she sounded so fucking sad. 'I don't want to know, please don't tell me any more,' she begged. 'Why did you have to tell me anything? I never asked to know you.'

He'd been wrong. She would never come around to his way of thinking.

'It was selfish,' he admitted. 'But you can't undo it now.' No. She couldn't undo it so she would have to handle it. Perhaps he could help her do that at the very least.

'That boy, Tam,' he asked. 'When did that start?'

'I don't see how that's your business,' she said, regaining a little of her natural hauteur. Good.

'Your face is my face,' he said.

'Don't start the whole family bullshit. Nothing I've done has ever had an effect on your face.' Another good riposte.

'That's because you haven't made any mistakes yet,' Schuyler countered.

And there she lost confidence. She closed her eyes, clearly struggling to find her next words. If she found it this hard to face Schuyler she would be eaten alive by that boy. He waited, to see if she would find something good.

'I thought you didn't really care about face anyway,' she said. An adequate response marred by her delayed delivery and her refusal to look at him.

'I thought you were set against coupling,' Schuyler replied. She should have stuck to her guns, she'd have done better as a brand. Now he really understood their last conversation. She had wanted to ask him about becoming a personality because she was getting ready for this. It was the first stupid thing he had seen her do.

'I was offered an opportunity,' she said. 'It seemed like a smart move.'

He bet Tam had made it seem like the only move she could make.

'He doesn't have any lineage,' he told her—a gentle admonishment.

'He can play the game.'

'That makes him even more of a risk.'

'My face, my risk.'

Stupid, stupid child.

'You know he's probably after me?' he told her, and she sighed.

'I'll keep him away from you, Schuyler,' she said.

Schuyler tried not to laugh at her.

'I can look after myself. I'm more worried about the effect he'll have on you.'

'You don't think I'm good enough to handle this?'

No. She was nowhere near being good enough to handle this. But she sounded so desperate and in that moment he felt sorry for her. He had made her. And she was disappointing. So he did the only thing he felt was kind.

'I think you're perfect, Reyna,' he said.

'Please. Leave me alone. Let me do this my way,' she said.

'I'm going.' He walked out of the room and closed the door behind him. As he walked back to his own room he remembered he had intended to ask her to come to Madeleine's party. The thought made him want to laugh.

Madeleine had planned a perfect party. That was one thing she could do. But of course it wasn't a party for Tonia and Eduardo; it was all about Madeleine. That was the only thing she could do. People came in thick and fast—people Schuyler wasn't sure he had ever seen before. He greeted everyone like an old friend, smiled that smile that made everyone feel like he cared, like he knew, like he was close to them. And then she arrived.

She was all brown skin and curves and painful softness. Her eyes were big, liquid jewels. She somehow managed to look both strong and scared. And Eduardo was just behind her, face closed, body tight, ready to step in at any moment and take over.

Schuyler took his time in greeting them, not wanting to seem too interested, all too aware of Madeleine's eyes on him. She'd warned him beforehand:

'*Don't* embarrass *me*. *Don't* embarrass *them*.'

'How're you doing?' he said, when he finally got to them.

'Yeah! Good!' Eduardo said. The force behind the brightness was only just discernible.

'Good!' Tonia echoed.

'Good? You should be feeling pretty amazing right now. A baby! And so quickly. Vidya is a miracle worker.'

Shit. Why did he say that?

'Thank you, again,' Tonia said. 'For the introduction.'

Schuyler shook his head.

'Nothing to thank us for.'

'No. Thank you,' Eduardo said. And Schuyler didn't know what to say back.

'Drinks?' he asked.

The room revolved. People came and went. Schuyler was switched on.

'Where are the girls?' Svetlana, Madeleine's vile sister, asked.

'In in *In*!' Madeleine said.

'Reyna's *Out*,' Schuyler said.

'Oh yes!' Madeleine agreed, and she laughed hard. 'Reyna isn't Reyna anymore. She's Treyna.'

'Oh she's started a *part*nership?' Svetlana asked. 'Why didn't you *say*?' The one thing the sisters had in common was their weird intonation.

'Must have slipped her mind,' said Schuyler. 'Excuse me.'

The room revolved. Where was Tonia? What was she thinking?

The room revolved.

The room revolved.

Schuyler revolved.

Tonia stood in the middle of the living room. And suddenly everything was still. Schuyler saw her. She was miserable. He'd done this. He'd made her come here. It was all his fault.

'Here's to the new parents to be!' Schuyler said, waving a drink in the air.

Tonia closed her eyes and smiled wide. She looked like she wanted to cry. Everyone cheered and she finally looked, looked across the room at him, and he winked, not knowing why, even as he did it.

'Eddie!' Tonia said. 'Could you make me one of your trademark cocktails?'

Madeleine laughed. 'To not being pregnant!' she toasted. 'May we all drink *deep* and enjoy!'

Eduardo walked towards the kitchen and Schuyler found himself following.

'Booze?' Eduardo asked, and Schuyler pointed to the liquor cabinet.

Eduardo knocked ice into some glasses and retrieved bottles of alcohol Schuyler didn't even know they had.

'How are you?' he asked.

'Over the moon,' said Eduardo, and he sounded like he meant it. Did he mean it?

'How's Tonia?'

'Tonia?' Eduardo sounded surprised by the question.

'This is a big decision. You're over the moon, so how's Tonia?'

'Good. But then, we've already said that, haven't we?'

Schuyler studied Eduardo's face. It wouldn't do to ask more. He didn't want to share. Schuyler wasn't used to that.

'When are we going to play Go?' he asked, for want of anything else to say.

They fell into laughter, fell into joking, stepped out, drank. The room revolved. The room revolved. And everyone eventually revolved out.

ToDdie: Baby girl arrived on time! 8lbs, 20 ins!

Congratulations were in order. A message was protocol, but Schuyler hovered over Tonia's name, a hairsbreadth away from phoning her. What would she make of that?

He navigated over to her primary profile. The chat was flowing thick and fast. She fielded it all with, as he imagined it, a rictus grin.

You must be so proud!
How does it feel?
What does she look like?

Schuyler watched the words flood her feed and thought: *I can't say anything. I'll be lost in the sea of it.* And then Tonia was gone.

He called Eduardo.

'Hello?'

'Eddie! Congratulations, how is she?'

'Beautiful. So beautiful. I don't think I've ever seen anything like her. She's perfect.'

'Can I get a look at her?' Schuyler asked, enabling vid.

'Oh, hang on a sec, she's just feeding. Here . . .' A small woman, holding a tiny baby to an artificial nipple, flooded the back of Schuyler's eyelids.

'There!' said Eduardo, warmer than Schuyler had ever heard him before. 'Shea. Our choice.'

'She's gorgeous, Eddie. Just gorgeous. And how's Tonia doing?'

The image slid away.

'She's quite tired right now. But we were talking about having you and Maddie over for dinner sometime, so you can see Shea. Maybe in a week or two when we've settled into a rhythm.' The tone of his voice indicated it was better for Schuyler to change the subject.

'Can I see the little thing again, before I go?'

'Oh. Yes, of course, hang on, I'll focus back. There.'

There she was. Shea. Pulling fiercely at her food, full of life, not yet cold, not yet calculated. A gift of a child. They watched her feed.

Of all the things Schuyler might have expected on any given day, receiving a message from Naomi was not one of them. But there it was, pulsing in his eyeline. Curious, he read it.

Naomi: Need to ask you something.

He replied magnanimously.

Schuyler: Shoot.
Naomi: Conversation is easier.

Intriguing.

Schuyler: You'll be quick?
Naomi: Always.
Schuyler: I'll come to you.

Schuyler couldn't remember the last time he had been in Naomi's room. She had turned it into a gaudy shrine to teenage rebellion, and its garishness irked him. He didn't want to venture into the space at all and so he did little more than cross the threshold.

'You can have a seat,' Naomi said, and he wondered if she had picked up on his distaste and was trying to goad him. It surprised him. He thought he had been quite neutral.

'You said you'd be quick,' he replied.

Naomi smiled.

'Never any time for me,' she said, and her pretend self-pity tried his patience.

'Naomi—'

'I know, I'll be quick,' she cut him off. 'Honestly, I'm not sure if you'll even be able to help.'

Schuyler snorted. This girl was impossible.

'I want to talk to someone at a menial training facility,' she said, and that was a surprise. Not just a little unexpected—a full-blown, rather strange surprise. 'In fact,' she continued, 'what I'd *really* like is to tour one of the facilities.'

What in the world was she after? Schuyler knew he'd given his surprise away, but he took control of his face again. He regretted not sitting down, and now he knew he'd look foolish if he did take a seat.

'Why?' he asked.

'School project.'

Schuyler smiled.

'It's my understanding that you've dropped out of school,' he said.

'It's my understanding that you have very little interest in my life,' Naomi retorted, and for once he was almost amused by her. 'Come on. I never ask you for anything. I just want a chance to talk to someone involved in the menial programme.'

Schuyler looked at her carefully. She was in earnest for once. This was important to her. Important enough for her to drop her face a little and give him power over her. The menial programme? Why? Was she trying for a job? The thought almost made him shudder. And on top of that he knew no one who actually worked with menials. It was disgusting. To make up for his lack, he affected boredom.

'Menial handling is a dirty job,' he told her. 'I don't know anyone in the industry.' He turned to leave.

'Please,' Naomi said before he slid the door open. There was a note in that 'please' that made him turn. She really wanted this. He relented.

'Vidya might know someone. I'll ask her to call you.'

Schuyler left the room quickly, not wanting Naomi to press her advantage and ask for anything else. He went to his room to think about what had just happened. It was definitely surprising. And it was the kind of surprising that Vidya might enjoy. In fact, it might just be the kind of thing to get him into her good graces. He couldn't quite remember their last conversation but he had a vague feeling that it hadn't been very smooth.

Decision made, he put on a smile, patched in and gave Vidya a call.

'How have you been?' she asked him.

'Fair to middling,' he said with as much nonchalance as was acceptable.

'And what can I do for you today?' she asked him. 'I assume you're calling for another favour.'

That stung him, but he tried to make light of it.

'You wound me,' he said. 'Can't I just call for conversation?'

'Well, I suppose there's a first time for everything,' Vidya said. 'But let's not pretend.'

Schuyler nodded, suddenly wanting the call to be over with.

'I had a weird chat with Naomi just now,' he told her. 'You expressed some interest in her and I thought perhaps you might talk to her.'

'Could you give me a bit more than that?' she asked, impatient. And now he felt he was on more certain ground. He smiled at her.

'I seem to remember that you like surprises. I think if you give her a call you might be surprised.'

He could see he had piqued her interest. Her smile was warm.

'I have some time on my hands. I'll call her,' she said. And then she cut the connection, leaving Schuyler to wonder what might happen when they spoke. But then did he really want to know? Menials were so animal. It seemed like a waste of energy thinking about them, let alone talking about them or studying them. Whatever Naomi was up to, he didn't think he cared. There were far more important things for him to consider.

Schuyler lay down on his bed. He drifted into a reverie and as he floated between waking and sleeping an image seemed to hover over him: a baby, so small and yet so full of big expressions. He smiled and thought about when he might meet little Shea. He thought about Tonia.

'Can you *believe* it?' Her voice was like a drill and Schuyler found himself clenching his teeth in response.

'Can I believe what, Madeleine?'

'*Eddie* is taking parental leave!'

'Is he?' Schuyler didn't look up from the news feed on his slate. Madeleine giggled.

'Well, he's got *confidence*,' she said.

'How's that?' Schuyler asked.

'You're not listening.'

'Not really.' But of course he was.

'*Fine.*' Madeleine walked out of the room and Schuyler breathed a little more freely.

Parental leave? That was a surprise. But then Eduardo had seemed genuinely elated by the arrival of the little one. What was he going to do with his time? Be fatherly? Schuyler snorted.

He put down his slate and leaned back into his chair. What would Tonia do? Was she happy? Did she approve of Eduardo's decision? Did they decide it together?

Did they love each other?

Schuyler laughed. He hadn't thought about love in a long time.

'*Schuy!*' Madeleine announced as she reentered the room. '*We* have an *in*vite.' She smiled at him, bright and shiny, like a new slate skin.

'Invite to what?'

'To meet the new baby, of *course.*'

'ToDdie's?'

'Do we know any others?'

'When?'

'Next weekend. They've invited Vidya too. It'll just be us.' Her eyes sparkled.

'I see.'

'You see? Is that all?'

'Should there be anything else?'

Madeleine shrugged.

'So, I should accept?'

'You haven't already?'

'I thought I should run it by you. Next weekend is short notice. I didn't know if you already had plans.'

'I don't.'

Madeleine looked at him for longer than he was used to. He stared back, stared her down, took satisfaction when she dropped her eyes and backed out of the room. A moment later he heard her voice:

*'Eddie! Da*rling!'

He couldn't recall feeling this nervous before and he almost ordered some beta blockers before leaving home. But he was Schuyler Burroughs. He never took drugs.

Madeleine rang the bell and a moment later the door opened and Tonia stood there all green silk, shiny hair and perfect skin. Skin skin skin. Schuyler couldn't look at her. He stepped into ToDdie's small flat and looked for the baby.

Eduardo was standing next to Vidya, and he held the child close. As Schuyler approached him he said:

'This is Shea.' The pride in his voice was unmistakable.

'Kawa*ii*!' Madeleine squealed, leaning in to look at the baby for a second and then leaning out and swooping round, establishing herself in the room.

Schuyler stepped close and really looked at the girl. She was still in the cabbage phase, her features squashed together, vying for space on her face. Her eyes asserted their dominance—big and dark, almost black. Her baby skin was white and looked as smooth as Teflon. She was growing a fuzz of black hair.

'You were right. She's perfect.'

He looked over at Tonia. She stood apart, awkward in that skin he kept thinking about. Awkward in her own home. Awkward in their company. She stood apart, her whole body screaming *flight!* She stood apart, angled away from Eduardo, away from the baby, and for a moment Schuyler saw her eyes pass over her family and her unhappiness was bare. Then she looked at him. Those big green eyes turned glassy and impenetrable. She was closed. She was not what he had imagined her to be.

'I thought . . .' he started to say, but those weren't words to be said aloud. He had thought she was like him. He had imagined her hidden face was just like his. 'I didn't know . . .' he said, before he could stop the words. He didn't know she was afraid. He didn't know she was weak. He looked at Eduardo. Eduardo was gazing at little Shea, a smile on his lips, a smile that reached his eyes and tugged creases in his skin. Shea looked back at her father and even though they didn't share a single feature, they were very much the same.

'She's yours,' Schuyler said, and he wondered if anyone else could hear his surprise. Eduardo looked at him, all softness and smiles. And there it was: what Schuyler had been looking for. He smiled back. He felt lost and was happy to be lost.

Schuyler stared at the backs of his eyelids and let an unchecked grin take up residence on his face. There was no word for the way he felt. There was no way to express it, but he could breathe and that was a good thing.

Tonia had left. He hadn't asked Eduardo where she had gone, hadn't asked what she had said. He hadn't even asked what Eduardo had told her. None of that mattered. He didn't care about any of it. He could only focus on one thing: skin. Skin on skin.

'What *are* you doing?' Madeleine asked. Schuyler jumped at the sound of her.

'Resting.'

'What was that ex*press*ion?'

'This one?' Schuyler asked, and he grinned at her and pointed at his mouth. She shuddered.

'Abso*lutely vul*gar.'

The grin slipped away and Madeleine acknowledged its disappearance with a tight smile. Schuyler stood up and looked at her.

'I . . . Madeleine . . . I wanted to tell you that I'm sorry. The thing is I'm not. I'm not sorry at all.'

Madeleine somehow managed to look as if she knew what he was talking about. She didn't say anything, she just waited. Schuyler smiled at her.

'I've hated being coupled with you,' he said. 'Not the whole time. I mean I wouldn't have done it if I had hated it from the start. But for most of it. For most of it I've just . . . Well, you're horrible. I hate hearing your voice, seeing your face, your expressions . . . I hate everything about you.'

Madeleine's expression didn't change.

'What's your point?' she asked.

'Yes. The point. The point is that I want to end this.'

'Oh? Uncoupling's quite troublesome. Are you sure you want to go through the hassle?'

Schuyler couldn't help but laugh a little at that. He admired her cool at that moment.

'I think you're going to want to go through the hassle.'

'Why's that?'

'Because I don't think I'm the kind of person you'll want to associate yourself with for much longer.'

Madeleine laughed this time.

'What *are* you on about, darling? You're Schuyler Burroughs.'

'Schuyler Burroughs, I am. And I'm leaving you. I'm not going to go through the uncoupling process. I'm not going to save face—not yours or mine—and I don't care in the slightest about the girls. I'm not going to do damage control on the In. I'm not going to make us look good. I'm just going to leave.'

This time she couldn't control her face. She was shocked.

'There . . . there has to be a reason?' she said.

'There is.'

'What?'

'Skinship.'

'What?'

'There's someone I want to pursue skinship with.'

'Skinship?' She looked utterly confused.

Schuyler nodded.

'What the fuck are you talking about?'

Schuyler didn't hesitate.

'Physical contact.'

'Skin to skin?' she asked.

'Yes.'

'Who?'

It was easier to say what he wanted than to tell her who he wanted to be with. It was fine divulging his own secrets, but hard to let out someone else's.

'Who?' she asked again. 'Tell me who.' But he couldn't. 'WHO THE FUCK IS IT?'

For the first time, there seemed to be real substance to Madeleine's voice. It surprised Schuyler. She stared at him, her face tight, white, unflinching. There was a strength there he hadn't seen before, and before he thought, the name slipped out:

'Eduardo.'

Madeleine screamed. She grabbed a glass from the table beside her and flung it at him. It didn't even come close; it fell and shattered in front of him.

'Skinship? Skinship of all things . . . You're disgusting!' she screamed. And then her strength melted away, her legs buckled and she sat on the floor. 'You're—you're . . .' but she didn't have words. She just had a noise and it squeezed itself from her throat, high and trembling, rising until it couldn't anymore and then it broke. She sat there sobbing. Pitiful. But Schuyler couldn't muster any pity for her. She was the worst of him. And he had broken that part of himself and was leaving it behind. All he felt was relief.

Schuyler Burroughs walked out of his house and he walked out of Schuyler Burroughs.

(Menial 63700578–Jake)

Jake woke up to a raised voice. He came out of his room. Reyna and Naomi were standing on the landing. They both looked at him as he emerged. Then, as if of one mind, they both turned and retreated into their own rooms.

'You're disgusting!' Madeleine screamed, and Jake heard a glass shatter. 'You're—you're—' But whatever Schuyler was, Madeleine couldn't say it. She just screamed. It was a long, wailing scream which rose and then crumbled into sobs.

Jake stepped forwards and looked down. Madeleine was sitting on the floor, her knees hugged tight into her chest. The glass she had flung was not the only broken thing.

Schuyler stood over her, looking down, so Jake couldn't see his face, couldn't read it, and he wasn't sure if he wanted to. Madeleine's sobs sputtered out. Schuyler walked out then.

'Yes,' said Madeleine, to the empty room. 'Leave. Don't come back.' Her voice came out dull and inexpressive. It was not Madeleine's voice.

The glass was not the only broken thing.

Jake moved without thought. He went downstairs and stood, as Schuyler had, over her and looking down. She seemed calm now, sitting cross-legged, head bowed down. Her long hair fell forwards.

A lesson echoed in Jake's head: a truly great menial was one that could give its family everything they needed without them even knowing they needed it.

Jake knelt down before Madeleine Burroughs and did what he had always wanted to do. He put his arms around her, pulled her to him, and held her.

Madeleine screamed.

Acknowledgements

There is no rhyme or reason in the way I have organised these thanks.

Lee Harris. Thank you so much. Your belief in this book and in me has been overwhelming. And thank you to the rest of the Tordotcom team: Sanaa Ali-Virani, Matt Rusin, Lauren Anesta, Mordicai Knode, Amanda Melfi, and Irene Gallo.

Keith Negley, this cover made me cry. It's perfect.

Sunday Writing Group—those still hanging in there and those who've left, you're all stars.

Angie Spoto for reliable and remarkably quick edits.

Hugh and Blugh. Your constant support and validation is just awful. Please desist.

Alice, you're one of my favourite people on earth. You were there when I first wrote about Tonia. It was a *time*. I am so glad we were together, you make everything more fun.

Peter McCune. You got me writing again, and no one else has read as much of my work as you. For that I can only apologise. To the Bradbury challenges and the green ink edits and to softening the harsh critiques with good jokes and bad jokes, and generally muddling through and staying on the track even when our paces vary.

My agent, Robbie Guillory. I don't think anyone understands what I'm trying to say as well as you do. I don't think anyone helps me say it as well either. I couldn't ask for a better champion. I couldn't ask for a more ridiculous 'how I met my agent' story either.

Fi Brook. I blame you for a lot of what's happened with this book and I am eternally grateful. You're amazing.

Mogs Beaton—if you read this—thanks. I owe you.

Baj, Ba, Gautam, Maya, and Becks: I love you I love you I love you. Thanks for reading, supporting, pushing, feeding, cheerleading, telling me off, arguing with me, very occasionally agreeing with me, but

262   **Acknowledgements**

in general just being my wonderful family. Also Cousin Adam! Your support since *Wild* has been immense, thank you so much!

And finally to Graham. I was on this journey before I met you but it was you who got me over the finish line with *Face*. And it's you who gets me started on the next and the next and the next. To all the stories that will come. To the creative powerhouse.